KT-440-228

Eden
GARDENS

LOUISE BROWN

headline
review

Copyright © 2015 Louise Brown

The right of Louise Brown to be identified as the Author of
the Work has been asserted by her in accordance with the
Copyright, Designs and Patents Act 1988.

First published in Great Britain in 2015 by Headline Review
An imprint of HEADLINE PUBLISHING GROUP

First published in paperback in 2016 by Headline Review
An imprint of HEADLINE PUBLISHING GROUP

1

Apart from any use permitted under UK copyright law, this publication may
only be reproduced, stored, or transmitted, in any form, or by any means,
with prior permission in writing of the publishers or, in the case of reprographic
production, in accordance with the terms of licences issued by the Copyright
Licensing Agency.

All characters in this publication are fictitious and any resemblance
to real persons, living or dead, is purely coincidental.

Cataloguing in Publication Data is available from the British Library

ISBN 978 1 4722 2610 5

Typeset in Bembo by Palimpsest Book Production Limited, Falkirk, Stirlingshire
Printed and bound in Great Britain by Clays Ltd, St Ives plc

Headline's policy is to use papers that are natural, renewable and recyclable
products and made from wood grown in sustainable forests. The logging and
manufacturing processes are expected to conform to the environmental
regulations of the country of origin.

HEADLINE PUBLISHING GROUP
An Hachette UK Company
Carmelite House
50 Victoria Embankment
London EC4Y 0DZ

www.headline.co.uk
www.hachette.co.uk

Louise Brown has lived in Nepal and travelled extensively in India, sparking her enduring love of South Asia. She was a Senior Lecturer in Sociology and Asian Studies at the University of Birmingham, where she worked for nearly twenty years. In research for her critically acclaimed non-fiction books she's witnessed revolutions and even stayed in a Lahore brothel with a family of traditional courtesans. *Eden Gardens* is her debut novel.

Louise has three grown-up children and lives in Birmingham.

Praise for *Eden Gardens* from Lovereading.com:

'A truly brilliant novel, one I found difficult to put down and can thoroughly recommend'

'Beautifully written, you can smell the spices, feel the heat, and your heart will break. You will laugh, cry and you will want a sequel'

'Enthralling novel set in the colourful landscape of Calcutta in the 1940s... Louise Brown brings the smells and colours of India alive and shows a different side to British colonialism'

'India in the 1940s is really brought to life in this engrossing novel... what stays in mind are the evocative descriptions of the tastes, smells and colours of India and the moving stories of headstrong Maisy and loyal Pushpa'

'This is not a love story, a fictional account of another side to living in India in the 1920s-40s nor a family saga. It is all of the above and I loved it'

For my father, Peter John Brown

MORAY COUNCIL LIBRARIES & INFO.SERVICES	
20 41 06 80	
Askews & Holts	
F	

Chapter One
Maisy

IN 1934 AN earthquake tore an eight-foot-long gash in the wall of our flat, and a lump of masonry landed on Pushpa's head during the final tremors. Mam said the injury made our ayah simpler and slower. I doubt Mam was right about Pushpa, but I do know India's great disaster marked a divide in my life just as surely as it ripped a hole in the wall and put an end to the policeman's shouting. Pushpa leaned round the door to the living room in the moments before the quake began, watching a gangly British inspector speak to Mam. I peeped from behind Pushpa, mesmerised by the way the man's neatly clipped ginger moustache bristled with annoyance and excitement.

He coughed and cleared his throat. 'Mrs Brooks, you are well aware that it's unacceptable for British women to engage in immoral trade in India.'

Two young European constables flanked him. One smirked, the other stood rigidly to attention, his mouth wide open.

Mam threw back her head and laughed. 'What's wrong with having a few *chota pegs* with old friends? Everyone likes a little drink.'

1

The red beaded curtains dividing the living room from the veranda swayed, and I glanced away from the inspector as they began to dance and jump.

'Mrs Brooks,' the man continued, unaware of the rattling curtains, 'we've good reason to believe you are a prostitute and that you carry out your activities in this flat. Brothels may be legal in Calcutta, but only Indians and a few women from other nations work in them. We cannot tolerate British women in the same business. As I told you some weeks ago, our women must be beyond reproach.'

'Where's this gossip from?' Mam said, hands on her hips.

'Your neighbours.'

'You mean that toffee-nosed cow downstairs.'

The slack-jawed constable snapped his mouth shut and gazed past Mam, transfixed by the empty tea cups chattering on their saucers.

'We've heard a similar story from a number of residents in this mansion block,' the inspector said.

His loud, cold voice overlay a distant rumble, like a deep, angry growl, and as the two sounds merged together I thought I'd wet myself in fright. I crossed my legs and clung to the back of Pushpa's sari, panicking because I was certain no one should wee themselves when they were eight years old, even if the floor was vibrating under their feet.

'They claim a stream of men visit you,' he went on, loving the sound of his own arrogant voice and oblivious to the shouts of alarm in the street. 'Your daughter no longer attends school and is known to run wild in the city. And, we're told, you are permanently inebriated.'

If he meant she was drunk, he was right. Mam had gimlets

with lunch, several 'special tiffins' in the afternoon, and we lost count of the number of large whiskies, called *burra pegs*, in the evening. She slept so heavily through the mornings that I couldn't shake her awake.

'You can't prove it.'

'Madam, you are a disgrace. It's outrageous that you conduct yourself in this manner in the heart of white town. Having said that, we are mindful of the embarrassment a scandal would cause, and so you and your daughter will be deported home along with the other undesirable characters who wash up on these shores.'

I didn't know what he meant by 'home'. Maybe he meant the Kalimpong home for abandoned European children where Mam warned I would be imprisoned by the Salvation Army's child-catchers if I strayed too far from the flat. Or perhaps he meant the home Father used to talk about: England, the wonderful place where King George lived and where the streets were always clean. I didn't want to go there, king or no king, because Queen Alexandra Mansions was my home and I'd never been outside Calcutta.

Although I wanted to stay, the flat seemed to be doing its best to get rid of us. The pedestal fan swayed and crashed on to the rug; Mam's bottles slid left and right on the sideboard before toppling to the floor with a crash. The whole mansion block shifted up and down and, with a groan followed by a crunch, a gap opened in the wall and then closed, leaving a crack that I could have pushed my arm through if I'd dared to try.

'Evacuate the building!' the inspector thundered.

Pushed and jostled by other frantic residents, we scrambled down the stairwell, a fine powder falling on us from the ceilings. In the street we pressed ourselves against the building,

Mam glaring at the woman who'd snitched on us and who was panting in terror, her eyes shut so tight it turned the lines around them into deep folds. Mam muttered that she was a bitch and she hoped a brick would land on her head.

No bricks fell, only a bit of masonry that glanced off Pushpa, grazing her temple and the top of her ear. A thin line of blood trickled along her jawline.

'It's an omen,' she cried. 'What tragedies lie ahead of us?'

'Shut up, Pushpa,' Mam shouted. 'I have this in hand.'

The earth steadied itself, my knickers were surprisingly still dry, and Mam, covered in a thick layer of white dust, smiled at the policeman.

Next afternoon, Mam went to the police headquarters on Lal Bazar Street in her bias-cut, turquoise satin dress and came back two hours later looking surprisingly cheery. She winked at us, and Pushpa's stricken expression vanished in an instant. The policeman with the bristly, orange moustache called round that evening and spent a jolly time with Mam without once speaking in his stern voice. He enjoyed himself so much he was like a different man, and after all his hard work dealing with the effects of the earthquake he had to have a long lie-down in Mam's room. When he left shortly before midnight, Mam poured herself an especially large *burra peg*.

'Another job done well,' she said. Wrapping herself in a silk négligé that was starting to fray around the hem, she stretched out her legs on the chintz sofa and lit a cigarette.

We left Queen Alexandra Mansions three days later. Our new address wasn't on the other side of the world; it was on the edge of Dharmatala, a different part of the city. The furniture was piled on to a couple of carts, known as *garries*, and I spent the morning feeding the horses with bits of carrot while they stood placidly in the road, their wee creating a frothy yellow pond. Father's teak writing desk, the beds, sofa, table and chairs, and most of the supplies from the storeroom, including all the tins of corned beef, were tied up with rope, Mam's cheval mirror balancing precariously on top and draped with the Christmas decorations. I was sad to leave, but Mam insisted the flat was likely to be demolished and that we needed to make a fresh start in a place where nosy neighbours wouldn't report us to the police.

The new home was part of an old house in an overcrowded street filled with other crumbling houses, bad smells and too many people. The wheels of the *garry* splashed through big puddles of brown water, the lane was strewn with empty coconut shells and the walls of the buildings were marked with dark red *paan* stains where natives had chewed and spat out betel nut. A toddy shop was tucked into an alley near the corner, and Mam said that was convenient; there'd be no more need to send the sweeper on long journeys to buy supplies.

'What a perfect place,' Mam said. 'We'll be set up nicely here.'

Our neighbours, most of whom were Eurasians, or what Mam called 'half-halfs' – half white, half brown – gathered to watch our belongings being unloaded. A little group of ragged Indian children looked on, too. A girl who was about the same age as me stared at my hair, golden-blonde like Mam's and cut so it brushed my shoulders. Hers was shiny and black and reached all the way down her back in a tight plait. Even poor Indian girls had the most beautiful hair.

Mam said Father married her because of her hair; because she looked like a memsahib even if she didn't talk like one.

'He called me his English rose,' she declared. 'He said I was the loveliest girl to step off the boat.' That part of the story was absolutely true; in the days before the drink crept up and stole her looks, no one was as pretty as Mam. I imagined her stepping daintily on to Outram Ghat in her best violet dress and jaunty little hat, a parasol in her hand. Only hours after disembarking, her beauty had stunned all Calcutta and she was swept into a heart-stopping romance with my adoring father.

Of course, that's not the way it really happened. I pieced together the story from the rambling tales, sprinkled with odd words, which Mam told in a strange accent whenever she drowned her memories right the way through to the bottom of a bottle.

Mam arrived in the steam bath of Bengal in a third-class railway carriage surrounded by natives, bundles of clothes, a belligerent nanny goat, and several hens that roosted in the overhead luggage racks, their droppings sticking in the passengers' hair. She journeyed across the whole of India on a hard, unforgiving bench in the cauldron of May, the sun threatening to buckle the tracks while inside the train the passengers baked, the upcountry men perspiring so profusely that Mam kept a handkerchief soaked in cologne over her nose. The ceiling fan had long ceased turning and the block of ice placed in a zinc bath in the middle of the carriage provided no relief. The ice melted quickly, the water slopping from side to side and spilling out of the bath with every turn and brake of the train. It ran over the floor, soaking Mam's only decent pair of shoes, while the goat chewed a hole in her handbag.

Mam had worked in a rough pub near the docks in Bombay and her rail fare to Calcutta was paid by the owner of a disreputable hotel off Park Street. He promised her a position as a barmaid on a much better salary, for which she was obliged to pour *burra pegs* of whisky while fighting off the advances of the patrons. Being a white barmaid in India was a rotten job, she said, but it was better than being a skivvy at home; domestic service in England was no different from slavery.

Mam never did any cleaning in Calcutta; she said she'd cleared up enough shit, including her own. She grew up in Leeds and became a reluctant housemaid shortly after her twelfth birthday. When the Great War broke out she joined the Barnbow munitions factory, doing all the risky jobs and getting a big bonus in her pay packet for volunteering to handle the explosives and pack them into shells.

'I worked day and night in nothing but my drawers and vest,' she said. 'The cordite turned my skin yellow, and thirty-five lasses were blown to kingdom come in an explosion in the room next to mine, but I swore, even when I was picking the bits of mashed flesh out of my hair, that I'd never go back to earning a ruddy pittance as a rich cow's servant.'

At this point in her story she'd lift up the bottle, look surprised to see it was empty and say, 'Who's been golloping me drink?' Then she'd weave her way to the sofa and search behind it for a fresh supply.

After the war, Mam tried working in a factory with her

sister, Dolly, sewing ready-made clothes, and she did a spell in Schofields department store before she was sacked for being rude to a crotchety but esteemed patron. The job didn't pay enough, Mam said, to put up with all the bleeding rubbish you had to face, day after day, from customers who acted like they'd got sticks up their arses.

Britain in 1918 presented Mam with another, even more pressing problem: a frustrating lack of men. There weren't enough troops returning from the trenches to marry all the girls impatient for husbands and Mam had no intention of being a spinster; it wasn't in her nature.

'Only half the lads in our street came back,' she said. 'My brother Freddie had his head ripped open by a blinkin' shell, and they never found Jack. He vanished into the mud somewhere near Ypres.'

Mam kept a picture of Jack in a jewellery box on her dressing table, and she'd get it out now and then, usually at the point when the whisky slurred her speech so much it would have been hard for me to understand what she was saying if I hadn't heard it so many times before.

'He was the most handsome man I ever set my eyes on.' She'd gaze at the photograph of big, dark-haired Jack, a perfect young man in shades of sepia. I put my fingers in my ears to silence her next words because they embarrassed me and made me feel queasy. 'We were courting for months and you wouldn't believe what we did on his mam's sofa before he went to war. He had the most beautiful body; strong and pure white. He might have been only twenty but he was all man.'

I don't know how long she grieved for Jack and her brother, but Mam was nothing if not a fighter and so soon after the war she filled a trunk, used the money she'd saved from packing shells, and boarded a cargo boat to India, telling everyone at home that she was on her way to a better place, somewhere far away from chilly Britain, somewhere she could be in the sun for a while, where she wouldn't have to slave all day for a stuck-up bitch. She was going to be a memsahib and have servants of her own. They laughed at her and said she was soft in the head and that she'd better tidy up her manners if she wanted to be posh.

Dolly scoffed. 'Don't be daft. Girls like us can't pass ourselves off as ladies.'

'You'll get yerself into trouble, mark my words,' her mam said. 'You've got ideas above your station, young lady, and nowt good will come of it.'

'She'll be back here with her tail between her legs before the year's out,' her brother Bert said.

'But I didn't listen to them,' Mam told me with glee. 'I said, "Just you watch me. I'll catch myself a rich husband, I'll have servants to wait on me and I'll never come back to a lousy dump like this."'

Mam's predictions were rarely correct: unlike her brother Freddie and the eternally young Jack, she did return to that street in Leeds. But for once she also proved her doubters wrong: after many false starts, she found a husband, and a servant, and her own place in the Indian sun.

I never had any contact with my family in England, not even a solitary birthday card, but I had a large family of sorts in India: I had lots of uncles, dozens of them, who visited in the evenings, each one on a different night. I rarely saw them when

Louise Brown

I was small because Pushpa dragged me out of the bedroom while Mam, dressed only in her underwear, was getting ready to meet them, deftly applying powder and scarlet lipstick, her Apple Blossom perfume filling the room with fragrance. During the hot weather, Pushpa settled me in my bed on the veranda and I lay listening to the clatter of carts and the tinkle of rickshaw bells. A cooling evening breeze sprang up and I grew drowsy watching the gentle sway of the tatties. The mosquitoes droned, flying cockroaches whirred past, and on good nights Mam's muffled laughter lulled me to sleep. Sometimes, I'd hear other less comforting noises, perhaps a strange cry from one of the uncles or an animal-like grunting that I felt, deep in the pit of my stomach, was something bad and dangerous. On those nights I buried my head under the pillow and screwed up my eyes as if it would help muffle the sound. When an uncle left early, Mam would come to wish me good night, stroking my hair and kissing me with the smell of whisky and cigarettes on her breath. The vivid lipstick had been wiped from her mouth but its pigment always stained her lips a pretty shade of red.

It was harder to keep me hidden as I got older, and I began to see a lot more of the uncles. I met Uncle Jim several times and was appalled by the state of his furred teeth. He dressed with the attention to detail required of a sergeant major, his teeth being the only things neglected by the carbolic soap, starch, and polish. The reek from his mouth was disgusting. I didn't know how Mam could bear to be near him, and I knew, beyond any doubt, that I could never do what she did.

'Thank God, he doesn't expect me to kiss him,' she said. 'And to think he goes on about Indians staining their mouths with *paan*. He's got a ruddy cheek.'

10

Most of my other uncles had far better teeth. They were British men in trade or in the army, or they were Scottish supervisors and mechanics in the jute mills. A few became regulars but all left eventually, returning home or moving on to the next posting, usually without saying a word of goodbye.

Some of the uncles complimented me when I passed the living room and they were resting on the sofa, holding their drinks. 'Aren't you pretty?' they said. Or they said things like, 'You're going to be as gorgeous as your mother.' At that point Mam ordered me to spend time with Pushpa or to read one of the books suggested by my tutor, Mr Banerjee, about people in England during the olden days – a place and time I struggled to imagine.

Bill was my favourite uncle until the day he put his hand up my skirt. He brought us expensive presents and Mam was sure he was going to ask her to marry him. He wasn't like the others, who visited for an hour or two; he wanted to stay with us, eat beef stew and steamed plum duff, and to talk to Mam about home, reminiscing about the frosty mornings and the way things were so well ordered. Mam said he was mad.

'What part of England did you live in, Bill? I remember frosty mornings when we'd scrape the ice off the inside of our windows, and the order of things was that I cleaned grates and laid fires while the ladies of the house slept until midday and went to afternoon teas and parties.'

Bill's eyes followed me closely and I wondered whether I reminded him of someone: perhaps I looked like his daughter or his niece. When he gave me presents he asked me to stand close while I opened them, the gift balancing in his lap. One day when Mam went out to speak to another of the uncles who had stopped his car at the end of the lane, Uncle Bill asked me to sit on his legs and he tickled me until Pushpa came in and fixed him with a look. I was glad to go to my room because I didn't like the way Bill breathed or the roughness of the way he bounced me up and down on his knee.

About a year later, he visited when Mam was shopping at Whiteaway's. Cook was at the market and Pushpa had gone to see her friend.

Bill leaned on the doorjamb and grinned. 'Aren't you going to invite me in, Maisy? Why don't you put the kettle on? I'm parched and could do with a cup of tea. I've been checking accounts at the docks all morning.'

He watched me making tea the way Pushpa taught me: the tea leaves, water, milk and sugar all mixed up in the pan and boiling gently to a rich brown syrup.

'You'd better watch it, making tea like that,' Bill teased. 'Next thing, you'll be drinking it out of a saucer. You'll be turning native before you know it.'

I never worried about that. Although I spoke Bengali and some Hindustani, I couldn't be any whiter.

He stood so close to me I could feel the heat of his body and smell his armpits, his shirt damp with acrid sweat. It was a stink I knew from Mam's room after she'd been entertaining an uncle during the monsoon.

'When are you going into the business? You're old enough, surely? There's plenty of money in it for the right girl.'

He's joking, I thought. I was only twelve, though Mam often told people I was nine to make herself seem younger. Besides, Mam wanted me to marry an officer: she'd never allow me to join her trade. And then, a second later, the man Mam thought would be my stepfather was behind me, kissing my shoulder and neck, breathing deeply, tobacco and tea combined in his hot saliva. He pulled up my skirt and yanked at my knickers.

I twisted round to escape, begging him, half in terror, half in revulsion, to stop.

'Come on, Maisy. You know you want it,' he said a moment before his wet tongue filled my ear. He grunted and pressed himself against me, his finger jabbing between my legs. 'Like mother, like daughter,' he groaned.

'Get off her, you filthy bastard,' Mam yelled, cracking a frying pan across his head. She'd dropped her bags of shopping by the door and was waving the pan at him.

Bill rubbed his head and laughed. 'You don't want me to get Maisy into the business too soon, eh? Worried about the competition?'

'No one messes with my daughter. I'll have the law on you.'

'You think the police will help you? They don't help prostitutes. You may be white but you're a cheap white whore. And there's nothing worse than that. The police prefer the black tarts because at least they're supposed to be cheap.'

'Clear off and die, Bill.'

'I'm on my way,' he said. 'You might think you're better than all these greasy niggers around you, but you're no different from them. I can buy them and I've bought you. You do as I say: undress, lie down, kneel and suck my cock. In ten years you'll be selling yourself to wogs. You'll be living in a filthy hut, sitting on the floor, eating with your fingers and stinking of garlic, and that daughter of yours will be whoring in Sonagachi along with all the other tarts.'

Louise Brown

I untangled my knickers, smoothed down my skirt, and followed Mam into the street.

'Fuck you, Bill,' she screeched, and spat in his face as he turned.

A Eurasian woman living opposite glanced in horror at Mam and ushered her children inside.

Bill wiped the spit from his face. 'Like I said, Babs, you're only an inch away from them. Degenerate, that's what we call people like you.' He surveyed the street, which was silent for the first time I could remember. The half-halfs watched the fight from their windows and doors, and a group of Indian children rushed out of the little *bustee* – the slum – at the end of the road to witness the excitement. 'No, I was wrong,' he said. 'You're not an inch away. You're right here with them in black town. You and that girl of yours have got bad blood.'

Mam marched back into the house. 'That showed him,' she laughed, and grabbed a bottle of arrack. 'I bloody showed him.'

She put her arms around me and I could feel her shake. She'd certainly shown Uncle Bill and the rest of the street something special, although I wasn't sure exactly what it was, except that she could spit with precision and swear with breath-taking coarseness.

Bill was wrong; we didn't live in black town. Dharmatala, though, wasn't white town either. It was somewhere in between. We were a stone's throw from the wide avenue of Chowringhee, and within sight of the British city, but still not quite part of it. Our lane was a busy place that got busier every morning as servants from the north of Calcutta travelled south

14

to their jobs in the homes of the cleaner, wider streets of the European city. In the early evening they'd return on foot or on bikes, moving fast, an army of Indian workers on the move.

Bill wasn't right either about us being like natives. We looked completely different, and all the uncles were white men. Mam didn't mix with Indians, and she'd have been livid if she knew I played with local children in the street while she slept deeply, numbed by drink and the night's work. Pushpa would call me in to dust down my clothes in the hot weather or to help me wipe the mud off my legs in the rainy season.

'Stay inside,' she'd scold, in a mix of English and Bengali. 'Don't go so far from home. We'll go out together later. It's safer when you're with me. The city is full of *goondas* – thugs – and there's too much disease.'

The *bustee* at the end of our road harboured many diseases, that's for certain. A dozen tiny shacks had been erected on the site of a small building, which had collapsed in on itself, and all were visited by chronic sickness that left its mark on the residents. The grown-ups had dark shadows under their eyes and the children had scrawny limbs and bulging bellies.

Madan lived in the first of the rooms with his elderly mother, and his wife, who, every week or two, collapsed, foaming at the mouth, and lay immovable on the floor for days on end, folded into a tight, angular parcel, her mind and body cripple/ by some terrible affliction that not even constant prayers / gods and goddesses could relieve.

'Hello, Missy Sahiba,' Madan called as he rushed back forth between shaving men on the pavements and his caring for the two feeble women.

Pushpa and I watched Madan shaving a client, who

a low stool by the roadside. He scraped the man's grey bristles with a sharp razor and turned to me.

'Want to try?' he said, offering me the blade. The customer gave a start and Pushpa pulled me away, and I saw Madan catch her eye, a softness in the glance. He knows Pushpa well, I thought. So those nights when I spotted a figure sliding into the passageway that led to her room at the back of our house I knew Madan's mother and his wife would have to share him for a little while.

Lali lived opposite Madan. Her parents and five brothers and sisters were squeezed into one windowless, spotless room, its mud floor compressed, beaten and swept until it looked and felt like stone. Lali gave me two bangles exactly the same as her own. They were red and made of glass and they would have looked so pretty on her dark brown wrists if Lali hadn't been so thin.

I was ten, perhaps eleven, and Lali was the girl who'd stared at me when I first arrived in Dharmatala. Lali looked after her little brothers and sisters, carrying the smallest boy on her back in a sling she'd made from an old sari. Sometimes she'd strap him to my back too but he'd bellow and wriggle and I couldn't wait for Lali to untie him. We'd run in a bedraggled gang through the lanes of the neighbourhood and far beyond, past the people asleep on their string beds, past the men, half naked, taking baths at the standpipes; almost their whole lives lived on the streets.

I hoped Father wasn't watching me from heaven as we charged among the poor white men in Wellington Square, who were having a smoke and a drink while philosophising about India and complaining to each other about their bad luck. I knew how disappointed Father would be to see the dirt on my bare feet, but I put the disturbing thought right out of my mind and we headed for Chandni Chowk, where we paused to take a leisurely look at the stalls and all the things we couldn't buy.

Outside the New York Soda Fountain on Dharmatala Street, Lali smacked her lips and I put my grubby fingers on the windows, gazing at the ice cream and cool drinks people were enjoying just a few feet away. One or two of the smaller children pressed their noses against the glass, leaving smears of snot. And then, holding hands and steeling ourselves for the highlight of the day, we peered into the taxidermist's shop, shivering in horror and delight at the sight of the stuffed animals, at the open, roaring mouths of the tigers with their long, pointed teeth. Gathering all our courage and cheering each other on, we'd race in, stand stock-still surrounded by the terrifying, bone-dry creatures, and scream as loudly and for as long as we could before the taxidermist's assistant chased us out with a long stick.

In the *bustee*, Lali prepared a cooking fire. 'Here, stir this,' she said in Hindustani as the baby wailed in my ear.

A mush of rice and water simmered in a pan. When it had cooled the children sat in a circle and dipped their fingers into the mess. Lali and I helped the two tiniest by pushing it into their open mouths, collecting the bits that oozed over their chins. We didn't waste a bit.

Lali was a little mother to those children. Their real mother went to work at dawn and rarely came home before nightfall. I saw her a few times, a bowed sliver of a woman who seemed as if she should be Lali's grandmother.

Lali's father was a rickshaw puller, an upcountry man who'd

come to Calcutta for a better life. He wore a vest and a *lungi,* which looked like a long skirt, and he sucked on sugarcane to give him the energy to work. It had corroded his teeth, turning them into brown and green stumps.

'Where is your father?' Lali asked one day.

'He's dead.'

'Why did he die?'

'He had a fever.'

She took me by the hand to a little shrine in the corner of the yard where a statue of a goddess sat on a donkey, a broom in her hand. She was garlanded with pink flowers and surrounded by tiny mounds of rice, sticks of incense and bright yellow turmeric on a big green leaf.

'You must do *puja,*' Lali said.

I didn't want to. Mam told me it was what the heathens did, though as I'd seen Pushpa do *puja* every day of my life and, as it didn't seem to involve scary magic, I said a prayer, partly to please Lali and partly to help Father, who I wasn't sure would be in heaven without some holy words being said on his behalf.

'This is Sitala,' Lali said, rearranging the garland as if she owned the little idol. 'She takes care of us and makes sure the cholera doesn't come to our homes.' The statue stared back at me. I hoped she was good at her job because I'd heard about cholera. I knew it was when people died because they had shit themselves until there was nothing left inside – they were hollow and dried up.

If only Sitala had listened to Lali's prayers. Cholera did come to the city in the rainy season, spreading from the worst of the slums to the fancy parts of town where people got water out of taps and had flush toilets in their own homes. Mam stopped seeing the uncles for a while and drank some extra arrack.

'It's for medicinal purposes,' she explained. 'It's got to be healthier than the filthy water we're obliged to drink.'

I was kept indoors for weeks and when I was let out Lali and her family had gone. A new group of people was living in their room; a different set of pots was stacked in the corner, and another idol stood in the shrine. Ganesh, the elephant-headed god, had replaced Sitala.

'Where's Lali?' I asked a neighbour.

'The family went back to their village.'

'And Lali? Did she leave me a message?'

The woman didn't reply. She turned her face to the pan she was cleaning and began to scour it with a handful of ash.

Whenever I smell fresh green coriander, whenever it's chopped or even bruised and I catch a trace of it, I'm taken back to my childhood and I'm with Pushpa, walking the streets of Calcutta, visiting her friends and stopping at our favourite *jhal muri* cart. The man would spoon puffed rice into a tin. He topped it with onion and chilli, peanuts, *chana dal*, slivers of fresh coconut, a big pinch of cumin, and then he added coriander, roughly chopped so that some of the leaves were still whole. He sprinkled the mix with salt and lemon and shook the tin, and, with a smile to Pushpa, he tipped the *jhal muri* into cones rolled from newspaper. It was the most delicious snack I've ever tasted, and we'd wander down the road, not speaking, concentrating only on eating, on finding the very last grain of rice before it lost its crunch.

Mam and Father didn't want me to eat food in the bazaar. Mam forbade me, but that just made it all the more tempting.

'You can't trust street food. The Indian talent for uncleanliness is astounding,' Father lectured.

'And the spices they use are enough to kill a grown man,' Mam added, never having acquired a taste for Indian food, and only recently developing a tolerance for Cook's mild Anglo-Indian curries.

It was the spice I liked, the tamarind, coriander and chilli; far nicer than the brain cutlets and mutton chops we had at home.

'I am like an Indian girl,' I said to Pushpa one day as I drank a cup of hot *masala cha* – spiced tea. I blew on it and a cloud of steam enveloped my face.

Pushpa was taken aback. 'Miss Maisy, you are a British girl. You are a little sahiba.'

She was wrong: I didn't feel that way. I was in between: not Indian but not fully British, a little sahiba with a taste for bazaar food, for the sound of Bengali, for the chaos of the streets in black town, for the wonderful, vibrant colour of it, the deep azure of the sky, the flowers, the brightness of the light at midday. The smell of coriander reminds me of that place I loved – at once alien and familiar – the magical, intoxicating space I enjoyed in the gap between two worlds.

Pushpa said I was a little sahiba but she treated me like an Indian girl, almost as if I were her own daughter. When I was very tiny, she took me to bathe in the Hooghly. I sat on the steps of Zenana Ghat in my knickers and vest, dipping my toes in the water as she immersed herself, fully clothed, in the river. She emerged with a broad smile, her drenched sari stuck to her plump body.

'Don't tell Memsahib and Sahib we've been here,' she said. 'Your father won't let you come again. He'll say there are crocodiles.'

I looked into the muddy brown flow speckled with tiny, iridescent flakes of mica and was rigid with fear, expecting a monstrous mouth to suddenly snap me up.

'*Chhee, chhee,* child. Don't worry; the Ganga is a holy river. It will bring you blessings,' she laughed, splashing water over me and then wrapping me in her warm, wet arms.

We kept other visits secret from my parents, too; that meant just about anywhere we went north of Dalhousie Square. The narrow, winding alleys of Burrabazar, the places of the Armenians, Chinese and the Jews, and the roads round the Nakhoda Mosque were off limits to girls like me. In fact, they seemed to be off limits to women of any type, except Pushpa, who walked through Calcutta as if she were a seasoned explorer and owned some important part of it. Sometimes we'd take the tram far up the Chitpur Road to visit her friends; unusual women who wore a lot of make-up and laughed far more loudly than other Indian ladies without ever trying to cover their mouths with their hands. These ladies liked to sing and dance, and they made a fuss of me, pinching my cheeks and feeding me so many sweets that Mam and Father used to fret about my poor appetite in the evenings and worry I was sickening for some deadly tropical disease.

Pushpa's favourite pastime was eating. She knew the cook on every food stall and in every cheap Indian restaurant in the city, but she refused to buy from anyone except the very best. We'd sit on a bench by the road and eat off leaf plates, me sitting close to her, bewitched by the aromatic foods and the familiar, comforting smell of coconut oil in her hair.

'There was a time, Miss Maisy, when I never had enough to eat. I was always hungry and had no flesh on my bones,' Pushpa said. She repeated it often, usually as she put the last piece of sweet, milky *sandesh* into her mouth, bits of it sticking to her lips.

She certainly wasn't hungry any longer and though she was still beautiful, the Bengali sweetmeats were building a soft layer around her middle. It made her lovely to cuddle but meant a slowly expanding roll of fat spilled between her blouse and sari.

Pushpa didn't care about the effect of the food on her figure, and neither, I guess, did Madan. I saw the way he watched her every morning as she went out of the house in the soft light that comes just after dawn. It was her job to check the *dudh wallah* was milking his cow into a clean pail and wasn't diluting the milk with contaminated water. After Father died, Mam had become obsessed with the purity of our milk, refusing to buy it from Keventer's Dairy and making Cook boil the *dudh wallah*'s supply until it was thick and barely drinkable. Madan stood in the road, leaning against a wall, holding a *bidi* – a hand-rolled cigarette – to his mouth, his eyes never straying from Pushpa. She paid the milkman and saw him off with a friendly wave as he pulled his slow, placid cow along to the next customer, and as she turned to come back through the door into the house, she'd hesitate for a second and, glancing up the road at Madan, she'd smile.

'I don't want you wasting your time with the locals,' Mam insisted after the worst of the cholera had gone and we had only typhoid and the usual dysentery to keep from our door.

'I don't spend money getting you educated by Mr Banerjee for you to pick up a disgusting chee-chee accent. Who's going to be interested in you if you sound like a bloody Eurasian? I'd send you back home so you could learn proper English in a boarding school but it costs too much. Besides, imagine the bleeding toffs you'd have to meet.'

I didn't go to boarding school in England or one of the posh schools in Darjeeling. I didn't even go to a local private school. They didn't want to take me: Mam, the schools thought, was not quite pukka. Instead, Mr Banerjee came to the house twice a week, armed with the great works of English literature and full of hope – always dashed – that I would prove to be a scholar.

'Shakespeare is essential reading for anyone with the slightest interest in English language and literature,' Mr Banerjee said. 'It is a central part of the curriculum taught at any decent school here or in England.' He sighed and pressed his palm against his forehead as if coping with a terrible headache.

'Miss Maisy, you have been given the gift of intelligence and you have English as your mother tongue, and yet you squander these great advantages on cheap novellas and magazines filled with the most frivolous tittle-tattle.'

Mr Banerjee squinted at me. His sight was so poor that he wore thick glasses, his eyes appearing like two black dots in his round face.

'That's what comes of too much reading,' Mam said. 'There's a lot of them like that round here. He's a *babu*, like educated gentry, and they're far too clever for their own good, especially when they're as poor as the Banerjees. He's got a son who's just the same, college educated and working as a clerk in a shipping company. Fancy being that clever and still having to scrape together a living from clerking and private teaching.'

Mam's work paid far more and she didn't have any problems with her eyes.

Margaret had a brilliant mind. All her family told me. I was glad in that case that she had a big nose. It made her brilliant mind and long black hair more bearable.

She lived in part of a house immediately behind ours. Long ago the buildings in the neighbourhood had been subdivided into separate flats. We had the better part of our house; our rooms were at the front, facing the street, and we could climb the three storeys to the flat roof and look over the cluttered, haphazard rooftops of the city, northwards to the disorder of black town, south and west to the grand palaces and buildings of British Calcutta. We had a miniature garden with a straggly mango tree and a few bushes right in the centre of the building for our own use, but Mam didn't like sitting there. She said it was overlooked by the snooping half-halfs and they gave her no privacy or peace.

We'd catch sight of Margaret's family from our roof. They'd walk on to their little balcony or we'd see them pass the window, the shutters open and the blinds lifted. They dressed in English clothes; the men wore trousers and shirts and the father and eldest boy went to work in suits. We saw them stride down the road every weekday carrying briefcases. The girls had dresses, some remarkably similar to my own.

'It's pointless when they ape their betters like that,' Mam said. 'They can't see it'll never work. They can't pass themselves off as British when they're the colour of dirt.'

24

Margaret wasn't a dirty colour. She was almost as fair-skinned as me and if it wasn't for her black hair and brown eyes, you'd never guess she was Eurasian; she could pass for white.

I met Margaret a few months after they moved in. She was carrying a pile of books and about to disappear up the narrow alley that led to their flat.

'Hello. I'm Margaret,' she said with a smile. 'I've seen you lots of times on your roof.'

I glanced at the titles of her books and she made me promise to visit her flat so I could take a better look at them.

Margaret's home was very neat but it was spoiled because too many ill-assorted pieces of furniture and knick-knacks were crammed into a tiny space. Her mother bustled around, shouting at the servant.

'Margaret is going to be doctor, aren't you, darling?' she said pouring the tea. 'She's a very clever girl; top of her class at school.'

'Yes, it's true,' John, her older brother, added. 'She has a brilliant mind.'

Margaret showed me her clothes, which didn't take long as she had very few, and her books, which took much longer as she had quite a collection.

'You should come to my house and see my things,' I said.

The next day she examined my clothes, which didn't take long either, but she lingered over the gifts brought for me by the uncles. I had more teddy bears and Shirley Temple dolls than I would need in several lifetimes, and a vast selection of hair accessories, handbags and embroidered handkerchiefs.

'You're lucky to have so many generous relations,' Margaret said.

25

'Both my parents are British, so we'll be related to a lot of rich and important people.'

Margaret looked inside the bags and examined the hairclips. 'I envy you,' she sighed. 'I wish I could have such pretty things.'

Margaret visited often, sometimes with her books. She had schoolwork to finish and there wasn't space at home because she had to share a room with her two sisters.

I liked it when she spread her books over my bed. She was the first friend I'd had for years – the first since Lali had left – and, to be honest, I was bored being by myself. I was bored with Mam, who either slept or drank, and bored with Pushpa, who was growing old and had stopped taking me on adventures in the city. There was no one else, only Mr Banerjee with his bad eyes and constant sighs. Margaret was a fresh breeze sweeping through my dreary life. On Fridays she'd buy plum cake from Hogg's Market on her way back from school and she'd stop to give me a slice. And on Saturday mornings we'd go to Eden Gardens and then visit the big department stores on Chowringhee. We'd try on hats and annoy the sales assistants, enjoying ourselves so much that we forgot the time until we noticed the clock on the Whiteaway Laidlaw building.

'We're late again,' Margaret would call, and we'd rush to get seats for the matinée at The Globe. Margaret loved the cinema, swooning whenever Clark Gable appeared. She had a scrapbook filled with newspaper cuttings and pictures of him that she kept hidden between her copies of *Intermediate Algebra* and *The Student's Companion to Nineteenth-Century English Poetry*. We saw every film he'd been in, sometimes several times, and our favourite ones were those he starred in with the fabulous, extraordinarily glamorous Jean Harlow with her cloud of platinum-blonde hair.

'I'm going to marry a man like Clark,' Margaret sighed, linking arms with me as we sauntered home, stopping now and again to buy treats from the food stalls.

'You will,' I said. 'You're bound to meet lots of people when you're a doctor.'

'And you're so pretty you could marry a prince. My brother says you look like a princess.'

'Really?' I was thrilled. 'Did John actually say that?'

'No. It was Philip.'

The thrill died: Philip was five.

We practised for the day we'd meet Clark. We put on lipstick and painted our nails bright red with Mam's special polishes. Margaret did up my hair like Jean Harlow's.

'It's not the same platinum blonde,' she said, 'but it's not far off.'

Margaret laughed at herself and pulled faces in my bedroom mirror. I stared at her in amazement, the crimson of Mam's lipstick beautiful on her full mouth, her hair black and glistening against her luminous skin. Thank God, she still has the nose, I thought. Without it she'd be utterly perfect.

Mam wasn't so happy about Margaret's visits.

'How many times have I told you? It's important to watch who you mix with. That family are riff-raff; I've seen them blowing their noses with their fingers like full-blooded Indians. I'm telling you, you can't see her again.'

'No, Mam,' I cried. 'She's my only friend.'

Even Mam could see the point.

'All right. But don't see her often, and never invite her here at night.'

Sometimes Mam must have taken me for a fool.

At Christmas, Margaret's family had a tree exactly like ours. I saw her father struggling up the alley with it and heard the shouts of the children when they opened the door. On Christmas morning Mam and I watched the whole family leaving for church dressed in their best, the youngest girl with new pink ribbons in her hair and Philip's face made red by vigorous scrubbing. I waited for them to return, excited because I was going to give Margaret a gift – some of my hair ornaments she liked best. I wrapped them in layers of green tissue paper and finished off the parcel with gold thread.

I heard the family clattering up the alley and rushed after them down the dark passageway between the buildings. I could hear them going into their living room, Margaret's mother shouting angrily about the smell of singed Christmas dinner.

Margaret opened the door and I jumped forward to hug her. She didn't return the embrace.

'Merry Christmas,' I said, and pushed the present into her hands.

She frowned.

'Margaret,' her mother shouted from the kitchen.

'Thank you,' she said quietly and tried to give the gift back. 'I can't take it.'

'Yes, you can. They're the diamanté butterfly hair clips you love so much.'

'I've nothing to give you in return.'

'It doesn't matter.'

'It does.'

Margaret's mother shrieked her name again.

'I'm sorry. I have to go.'

'Will you visit us later today? We've a big Christmas cake and a sherry trifle and no one to eat them. And I've got some news: Clark and Jean's film *Saratoga* is going to be on again at The Globe.'

'I can't. My mother says I shouldn't see you any more.'

My heart skipped a beat. 'Why?'

'She says your mother isn't . . .' She searched for the words. 'She isn't, you know . . .'

I knew very well what she meant. I'd heard it before from the police officer and from Uncle Bill. I'd seen it in the faces of the assistants at the Army & Navy Stores and in the dismissive glances and cold shoulders of the British ladies in Eden Gardens, and in that moment I wished Mam wasn't Mam. I wished I had a mother who didn't make me cringe.

'Will you hurry up, girl?' Margaret's mam shoved her aside, gave me a sharp look and closed the door in my face.

Margaret didn't do her homework on my bed any longer, and the family avoided me in the street. I watched her through the blinds as she returned from school each day, her shoulder weighed down with a bag of books, and I tried to calculate how long it would be before she became a doctor.

I went to see *Saratoga* without her. Mam came with me instead and slept through most of the film so she didn't realise that I cried. It was too sad seeing Jean on the screen when she'd died in real life; she hadn't been much more than a girl herself. I did my hair like Jean's, in her honour, the way Margaret used to do it for me, and I wondered if she also cried when she saw the film. I don't know if she did but I do know how pleased she was with the magazine cuttings of Clark I posted under her door a few weeks later. She went on to the balcony that same afternoon, squeezing between the railing and a rack of wet washing, and even from that distance I could see her smile at me. She waved and as she turned her head the sunlight danced on the diamanté clips in her hair.

On some winter mornings the Maidan was covered with dew that looked like a dusting of fine snow, each blade of grass weighed with tiny droplets of water that sparkled in the early light until the sun rose high enough to burn them away. By ten o'clock the ground was bone dry and the mists lingering in the dips and hollows at dawn had vanished. Father took me to the Maidan shortly after daybreak and we'd walk along the paths, and then for what seemed to be miles over the grass, making trails through the dew and soaking my shoes as thoroughly as if I had dropped them in the Hooghly.

I loved the Maidan's wide, uncluttered spaces. Father told me that before Britain brought civilisation to India it had been a thick, steamy jungle filled with man-eating tigers. I held his hand tightly and scanned the trees in case their descendants were stalking us, but in those days the only animals we saw were goats and horses, and chattering monkeys swinging among the branches.

We shared the park with lots of other people: pedlars setting up carts and rickety tables to sell snacks to the visitors; destitute villagers looking for places to rest; drunken sailors sleeping off their hangovers; jobless white men who couldn't find hostel beds. People hurried to work and youths hung around smoking and chatting, or slouching against one of the statues of famous Englishmen I'd never heard of. Rich white people rode their horses at a trot through the busier parts of the park and then in its quieter heart they broke into a gallop, sweeping by us with thrilling speed.

On Saturday afternoons, Father took me for tiffin on the veranda of the restaurant overlooking Outram Ghat. When the air was clear we could gaze over to Howrah, the city on the other side of the giant, pale brown river, although often the shipping on the Hooghly was so busy I couldn't see the far bank. We watched the passengers arriving by boat from Britain, and those coming ashore from steamers sailing to and from Rangoon, Singapore and every part of the East. I'd count the ocean liners, the tugboats, and the small, Indian flat boats with their bowed roofs, or the larger ones whose oarsmen worked in unison against the powerful flow of the river to the sea.

'Is Calcutta the centre of the world?' I asked on our last visit to the restaurant, only a few days before Father died. I was looking at the jam-packed jetties, the crowds crossing the pontoon bridge and the big ships moored along the embankment, and I remember thinking there couldn't possibly be anywhere busier than Outram Ghat.

Father chuckled. 'No. Good God, Maisy. London is the centre of the world. That's where history is made.' He leaned back in his chair and lit another cigarette. 'When you grow up, you'll marry an important British man, a *burra sahib,* and you'll probably go home for a while. I should imagine you'll live in London.'

'But I like living in Calcutta with you and Mam.'

'You'll like London far more.'

'How do you know?'

He didn't answer; he took another sip of tea, smiled, and continued fashioning a life for me. 'You're going to be a fine lady and when you come back to Calcutta you'll live in a mansion in Ballygunge or Alipore. Mark my words, you're going to be a splendid memsahib, a true *burra mem,* and in the mornings I'll watch you riding over the Maidan.'

I swirled the strawberry sauce into my ice cream and watched my father dream.

Eden Gardens is in a corner of the Maidan next to a cricket ground that has the same name, and we'd go there because Mam said the cream of Calcutta took a walk around the park in the early evenings. Mam liked to marvel at the seven-tiered Burmese pagoda and even Father was impressed.

'The oriental mind sometimes does have the capacity to understand beauty,' he remarked. 'Though the structure is nothing compared with the Victoria Memorial.'

Mam didn't agree, teasing that the Memorial, only recently added to the greater glory of the city, was like a giant unappetising wedding cake, a white monstrosity, depressing and austere – much like the deceased Empress herself. Father took offence and went for a purposeful stroll around the lake, his hands locked behind his back, while Mam and I played hide-and-seek near the pagoda. The musicians in the bandstand struck up a tune and Mam whirled me round as if we were on a dance floor. Father flinched when he saw us and did another circuit of the lake.

After Father died, I stopped walking on the Maidan in the mornings. Mam rarely woke before midday and it was hard getting her out of the house before the late afternoon. By five o'clock she had usually bathed and dressed and was raring to go, and so our afternoon and evening visits to Eden Gardens continued uninterrupted.

'It's a good place to meet people,' Mam insisted. 'We always see Uncle Stan there, and didn't we run into Harry the other week?'

We bumped into some of the uncles with surprising regularity, and there were a lot of handsome young men in the Gardens who made me blush when they spoke to me. But what was even more remarkable was how their greetings changed with the seasons and with the company they kept.

In the hot weather and the monsoon they were usually unaccompanied, and sauntered over to share a few words with us, but in the cool season they ignored us in favour of new companions – girls straight off the boat from England.

'They've come to India to catch a husband,' Mam sniffed, glaring at the posh girls. 'It's a bloody marry-go-round.'

Men who a few weeks before had laughed with Mam now pretended they didn't know her.

'They've got bigger fish to fry,' Mam snorted. 'But they'll make do with the local produce once the husband-hunters go home.'

Mam had gone fishing for a husband but she'd only landed Father. Perhaps that's why there was more than a trace of bitterness in her expression as she looked at those polished young ladies, with their up-to-date London fashions and their accents so refined they sounded as if they were speaking another language, which they might as well have been for all the conversation we had with them.

On my fifteenth birthday, Mam and I were walking near the pagoda, accompanied by Pushpa. I was wearing my best dress because we'd been to Flurys to celebrate with a special tea. A group of upper-class girls were visiting too, and I caught their glances. They were sniggering, not bothering to hide their amusement.

'Look at that beastly dress.'

'Stitched together by a *darzi wallah*, a local tailor, I should imagine.'

'Mother insists all our clothes are sent from home. It's the only way to keep up with fashion.'

I pretended not to hear.

The girls linked arms and walked past us into the shade of the pagoda.

'Did you hear her speak? What a frightful singsong voice. She sounds Welsh.'

'She must be one of those poor whites. Mother says they are like the natives – almost like another race.'

Pushpa pulled me to her side and gave a little shake of her head. 'They are jealous, Miss Maisy.'

'Yes,' Mam added loud enough for them to hear. 'Let's hope for their sakes that their fathers have plenty of money because they'll need it. It's no good being poor if you're a bitch with a face like a bleeding slab.'

British people like those snooty girls didn't want to know us, and in a kind of misplaced revenge, Mam didn't want to know the Eurasians. She was adamant they were unsuitable company because, unlike us Anglo-Indians, they were 'of the country'.

'I know they make a big palaver about having British blood

in their veins, but they're not right,' she said, wagging her finger at me. 'They're not *pukka*-born, not true-born. They're too Indian. They are like mongrels, not pedigrees. It's a blessing you're not friends any longer with that girl with the big nose. You can't trust them, Maisy. You can't place them. They're in-between. They're neither one thing nor the other and you don't know whose side they're on. And believe me,' she insisted, 'those half-half women are loose. They'll give it on a plate to any white man who they think will marry them.' It was a curious thing for Mam to say, but I suppose she had her reasons, the most important being the fact that she wanted me to marry a respectable man, a man of standing and the embodiment of a superior race: a British man – just the same type as the loose half-half women were after.

'Men like that are hard to come by,' Mam stated. As there weren't many to go around, we had to watch out for the competition.

Mam's enthusiasm for finding me a husband was odd when she'd never been that keen on her own.

'A husband gives a woman a place in the world, and a rich husband gives her a better place.' Besides, she said, it hadn't always been bad to be with Father.

'He had his good points,' she said. 'He made a very gentle-manly and courteous suitor.' It must have made quite a change for Mam.

'He gave me flowers, even sent me a poem.' She looked around for it but gave up the search in frustration, reasoning she must have thrown it out in one of her bouts of drinking and cursing the day she met him.

I could imagine Father writing poems. He enjoyed writing and spent a lot of time, when he was at home, sitting at his desk, drinking Bovril and eating anchovy toast while composing letters to the papers, many of which made it into print, on diverse topics such as the impossibility of Indians governing themselves successfully, the disgraceful state of public sanitation in the native areas of the city, and the immense benefit of the works undertaken by the Calcutta Improvement Trust.

He might have written Mam a poem but I'm not sure he loved her, not even a fraction of the way he loved me. Mam said he doted on me so much because I was truly a marvel; neither of them could believe I'd been born. But I was his daughter, that's for certain. I've got his green eyes and a mouth that's just a bit too big for my face. I was born nine months after the wedding, and I didn't have – couldn't have – any brothers and sisters. Father developed a medical problem shortly after the marriage. It was diagnosed by a specialist and confirmed by common sense: it was his age. He'd waited until his late forties to marry Mam, the woman of his dreams, and the marriage equipment simply hadn't had the lifespan of the rest of his body. Mam had a different diagnosis: Father had a Hindu mistress, one who sucked all the life out of his body and left nothing but shrivelled-up balls for his legal wife.

'I won't have you making shameful allegations like that,' Father said in horror. 'I swear, as God is my witness, I have never touched another woman.' As he was a God-fearing man, Mam believed him, and instead set about bringing all the shame on herself.

Mam had always had a taste for gimlets and a peg of whisky. She said it was the Irish in her. The cook bought the spirits for her until it proved too expensive to fund out of the house-keeping and she switched to arrack, which was cheaper, harder, and more likely to rot her gut. The sweeper had a reliable supply from a shop that served it under the counter, and he brought it to the flat in discreet parcels because although English ladies are inclined to drink, they do so with style: gin and tonics, and Pimm's, and they don't get drunk, at least not in public, unlike Mam who arrived at the Railway Institute Christmas Ball stinking of rough spirit and humiliating Father so badly he thought he'd never be able to hold his head up again in the offices of the East India Railway.

'It's not the conduct expected of a wife of someone in my position,' he complained when Mam was sober. 'You're letting the side down and you'll have to pull yourself together. Get rid of those bottles in the storeroom, finish with the *burra pegs*, and let's make a clean start. You need to find some ladylike hobbies and put an end to this dreadful sloth. We have to think about our reputation.'

'Reputation?' Mam yelled. 'That's all that matters to you. We go to church, we do the right things, we seem to be happy, but it's all a sham. You're a sham.'

'All I have ever asked is for you to behave in a manner appropriate to the wife of someone of consequence.'

Father stood a little more erect. 'You know how important it is for us Anglo-Indians to set an example. I don't want any bad behaviour on your part dragging us down; I don't want anyone confusing us with Eurasians. Some of them are fine people, I don't deny it, and we've a lot of them at the railway but, for heaven's sake, Barbara, we're a cut above them.'

Mam didn't disagree with that point.

'We've a new fellow from home starting soon. His name is Harold Percy. He'll be the next assistant, third class, to the Controller of Stores, and we need to create the right impression.'

Mam gave a start. 'I thought you were in line for that job?'

'Well, yes, but Percy got it. He's a grand chap, so I'm told.'

'You mean he's some useless toff who can't get a job back home but whose father knows someone here on the board of the railway.' Mam may have pitied the natives and despised the Eurasians but she saved her most virulent, unforgiving hatred for the English toffs.

'No doubt Percy comes with all the right qualifications: a top school and a good family,' Father said.

'That's right; it's all about the breeding,' Mam shrieked. 'He's from good stock, is Harold Percy – like a prize pig.'

'Barbara, you will be civil to him. I insist.'

Mam swore under her breath.

Father tried very hard to be someone of consequence and we did things the way they did back home. Although Father had never been home, he knew the way English gentlemen behaved and the clothes they wore. He'd be sure to wear his *sola topi,* his pith helmet, even in the winter, and to put on his suit for every formal occasion, and many informal ones too. Cook prepared Anglo-Indian fries and curries, the like of which Mam said she'd never tasted in England but her ignorance of which she put down to her own humble origins in a northern town.

'We have our own little bit of England,' Father would say often and with satisfaction. 'There's nothing Indian about our flat.'

'Except that your gran was a Hindu. You hid that fact away, didn't you?' Mam joked one evening shortly after we'd begun tucking into chicken curry. It was the only time I saw Father truly angry.

'Never repeat that.' He thumped the table, catching the edge of my plate and making it somersault across the room and crash into a photograph on the sideboard of King George at his coronation, Queen Mary smiling graciously by his side. I wasn't sure what upset Father most, Mam's jest or the thick blob of curry that splattered across King George's face, dyeing it the colour of saffron.

Arrack was Mam's deceitful lover, courting her at night, wrapping her in reckless embraces and then, after nights of the headiest passion, dumping her alone and broken-hearted the next morning, a lump under the sheet trying to slip back into sleep between bouts of retching into a pail.

Father was rarely there to see her like that. Each morning he'd check his watch and prepare to leave, counting out his supply of Woodbines, tapping and straightening them to remove the wrinkles, and then slipping them into his beautiful silver cigarette case that he polished and buffed to such a sheen I could see my face in it. He left at exactly nine thirty, not a second sooner or later, for the short walk and taxi ride to Clive Street and East India Railway House.

I went to his office once, and was pleased never to go again. It was in a big, dark, damp building and was almost certainly the dullest place on earth. Father sat at a desk covered with ledgers. Dozens of slips of papers were skewered on two metal spikes and they fluttered in the draught from a ceiling fan whirring and rattling above his head. Occasionally he'd write a chit and give it to one of the peons who carried messages from Father's office to other offices up and down the building. Father was so engrossed in his ledgers and chits that he forgot all about me and it was only when I began to cry because I wanted to go to the toilet that he stopped totting up the railway's coal stores and accounting for the number of railway sleepers in the depot.

'I'm sorry, Maisy,' he said, rushing me out of the musty railway building. 'Forgive me.'

Our visit to Howrah Station was better, even though it ended badly. We went to meet one of Father's colleagues, who arrived from Delhi on a train pulled by a giant engine. It came to a halt with an enormous hiss and an eruption of steam that caused a disturbance among the pigeons in the arches high above us. I recoiled at the noise but it seemed only the pigeons and I were bothered by the commotion. The men wrapped in blankets on the platform didn't stir from their sleep and the hawkers continued shouting, '*Paan, bidi, cha*' – pan, cigarettes, tea. I relaxed and let go of Father's hand. The smell wafting from the first- and second-class refreshment rooms had reminded me I was hungry.

'Can we go there?' I asked Father, pointing to the exit at the far end of the third-class hall. When we'd arrived I'd seen one of Pushpa's favourite snack wallahs selling *chanachur* by the buses, and hunger pangs made me think it would be a good idea to go straight away and buy a big portion for us all to share. And then I looked at Father's intent expression as he spoke, and I remembered, with a gnawing in my stomach, his firm strictures on street food.

Father and his friend met another railway man and they all ignored me while they laughed and talked about lengths of track and a new extension to the railway. Growing frustrated and bored, I edged away and, once I was free of them, I skipped up and down the platforms, looking through the open doors of the trains. I ran across the first- and second-class hall, peeped into the hairdressers, pulled a face at a surprised Indian man in the Enquiry Office, and then belted across the whole of the station and out on to the street.

The snack wallah's pushcart was parked by the buses and he was haggling with a family. The man grinned when he saw me.

'Where's Pushpa?' he asked.

'She's gone to see her friends.'

'Want something to eat?'

'Yes, please.'

I hopped and jumped back into the station with my bag of *chanachur* and whirled into the *zenana* rest room – the ladies' waiting room – where I ran among the women, stuffing the spiced crispy dal, noodles and peanuts into my mouth and spilling some over their feet. Two fat matrons in burqas made a fuss of me, touching my hair and saying how pretty I was. I liked those ladies, especially when they started feeding me gooey sweets from a tin. I played with their grandchildren and was having such a good time rolling marbles under the seats that I forgot about Father until the attendant came in and led me to him. He was standing by the war memorial, ashen-faced.

'I thought you'd been abducted,' he said, gripping my hand so tightly it hurt. 'Never wander away again. You have no idea of the danger you were in.'

'I was having a nice time with some ladies,' I protested.

He wiped bits of *chanachur* and sticky sweets from around my mouth. 'Sometimes, I can see your mother in you,' he said.

I looked at him in surprise. Father was such a clever man who told the truth most of the time, and yet I knew for a fact that I was nothing like Mam.

Although Father left for work at half-past nine every day he didn't always return at the same time. I waited for him, standing on a footstool on the veranda of the flat and leaning out over the street. I'd spot him marching down the road, his *sola topi* bobbing along above the heads of the Indians around him.

'Don't worry, love,' Mam explained when he was late. 'There's been some thieving at the Jamalpur depot and your father's counting how many brooms and packs of tissue they've got left.' She'd settle comfortably on a basket chair with her sundowner drink and stretch out her legs on the footrest.

Her words didn't reassure me. I wanted him to be at home and I was terrified he'd leave like he did when Mam picked a fight with him. She'd shout the same bad things while he stood with his back straight, his head bowed and his face totally expressionless apart from a faint twitch in the corner of his mouth. Although he returned a day or two later I was sure one day he'd leave and never come back.

Mam believed Father when he said he didn't have a Hindu mistress, but she didn't trust his promise for long. I heard her confiding to Pushpa.

'There's another woman. I know it.'

Pushpa smiled in embarrassment and shook her head. 'The sahib is a good man, Mem.'

Mam was unconvinced. 'I'm going to find out, once and for all.'

That's why, a few days later, Mam and I were standing in a dismal alley.

'Mind the puddle,' Mam hissed, and pulled me to her side so that only one of my feet sank into the mud. I clung tighter to her dress. It was too dark for me to see where I was stepping and I was petrified I was going to fall into one of the open drains filled with a sludge of old food and lumps of shit. I couldn't spot Father among the crowd but Mam said she still had him in her sights.

'There he is. See? There's no mistaking him; he's a foot taller than the Indians and the bloody idiot's still wearing his *topi*.'

Kebabs sizzled on a barbecue stall, the face of the fat stall-holder cooked almost as well as the meat. He wrapped a kebab in a flatbread and handed it to a customer, and suddenly I felt hungry and missed Pushpa. Light from the shops and the stalls shed a soft glow over the street, the alleys leading off fading into blackness. Above us, people went about their business on their verandas, sometimes coming into sharp focus in a shaft of light. A couple of old women squatted on their veranda, peering into the street, and making loud and very rude jokes about the pedestrians. A young woman hung wet saris over her railings, water from them dripping on to the man selling fried snacks below. He cursed her and dragged his stall a few feet along the road so his patties and fries didn't turn soggy.

'He's gone into that building.' Mam pulled me sharply across the road, not noticing the horse that nearly trampled me, or the stares of the men who looked open-mouthed at a white woman hauling a small girl through the streets.

We stopped at the foot of a narrow staircase. Mam breathed fast, and I recognised the smell of arrack.

'Stay here,' she ordered, but then hesitated. 'No, it's not safe. Come on.' She leaped up the steps two at a time, with me scrambling behind her.

No one answered when she knocked on the door, so she banged again, louder and harder. I squeezed next to her.

A beautiful woman in a red sari opened the door, her lips painted the same colour as her sari, her black hair loose and her eyes rimmed with thick kohl. She smiled and bent down to look at me, her gold filigree earrings falling forwards and swinging in front of my eyes. She was mesmerising.

Behind the woman, Father was standing with his back to us. He took off his jacket and threw it on to a pile of cushions. He turned to look at my mother, and his face froze. The woman frowned, slid back into the room and snapped the door shut. Mam howled and began to kick the door. 'Ernest, you fucking bastard. Get out here.' She would have cried if she hadn't been so angry. 'You promised. You swore. You lying bastard.'

An audience assembled rapidly at the bottom of the stairs and when Mam gave up shouting and her curses had turned to tears it parted, silent and astonished, to watch us walk back home. She stopped a short way along the street and looked back at the rooms on the first floor of the building, all of them in darkness, their blinds pulled down.

Mam squeezed my hand. 'It'll be all right, Maisy. We'll be all right.' She wiped the tears from her cheeks.

I stared back at the closed blinds, too, filled with despair and sure the woman had bewitched Father so she could steal him from us. Her magic was holding him captive in that horrible flat in the dirty alley. I wanted to scream into the night air, to shout to him and tell him to leave her and come home straight away. I wanted him to play ludo and cards with me, to sit at his desk and write his stupid letters. It didn't matter if he hardly spoke to Mam as long as he was there with me. I thought he loved me most in the whole world, but he didn't: he loved the Hindu woman more than he loved me, and in that moment I realised I wasn't the centre of his world in the way he was the centre of mine.

Father did come home. He was there when I woke the next day, my eyes puffy and with a heavy weight like a stone in my tummy. Things, though, were very different in Queen Alexandra Mansions after the nightmare of that night and I never forgot the terror of thinking I'd lost him. Mam and Father rarely spoke and they lived separate lives in the same small flat. Mam stopped drinking for a while – I suppose it must have been the shock – and Father spent more time at his desk and at work, or perhaps, I seethed, with the Indian witch.

I saw the woman again a few weeks later. I was with Pushpa in New Market and we were searching for dress material among the hundreds of rolls of fabric stacked around the stallholders. They unrolled one, then another, until a mountain of material was spread before us, fine cottons, silks and satins, none of which, Pushpa insisted, matched the shade her memsahib required.

And then out of the corner of my eye I glimpsed a startlingly beautiful woman gliding along the aisle a few yards ahead of us. She stopped for a moment and reached up into a stall to brush

her hand over a length of transparent emerald chiffon, her gold
bracelets falling down her forearm with a musical clink.

'Do you think she's a pretty lady?' I asked Pushpa noncha-
lantly, trying to disguise my hatred of Father's dazzling mistress.

Pushpa looked quizzically at me and then laughed. 'Miss
Maisy,' she exclaimed, 'she isn't a lady.'

Chapter Two
Pushpa

THE FEVER KILLED Sahib in two days, shrinking his big body into a little yellow corpse. Life drained out of him so fast that the water poured into his mouth leaked from his backside a few minutes later or was puked on to the floor in a torrent. The doctor said contaminated milk was the source of his troubles.

'And I know where he drank it,' Memsahib added, though she kept her lips sealed and didn't tell anyone where the place was; the shame would have been too much.

I prayed to Sitala and did *puja* in Kalighat. Ma Kali's three red eyes glowed redder than usual in her black face and I was sure she'd heard my pleas. No illness, I thought, could resist the might of Ma Kali. I must have left the *puja* too late because by the time the blacksmith severed the head of the petrified goat, silencing its terrified bleating and the scraping of its hoofs, the sahib was almost as dead as the animal I sacrificed to save him. The blood gushed over the temple's courtyard, spreading around our feet in a shiny pool, while back in Mem's room the pool of sweat in which Sahib lay grew bigger and darker.

'Ernest, for God's sake, drink something,' Mem pleaded, wiping him down with a sponge. Her hands, which never cleaned the house, cooked, or washed the clothes, were sore because she'd scrubbed them so often with a stiff brush, and her long nails were cut short, their polish peeling off. Mem didn't ask anyone else to wipe up the shit and wash the floor. She strode around with a bottle of disinfectant in one hand and a cloth in the other. It was shocking to see a white woman like that. If it wasn't for her golden hair, her well-covered frame and the way she carried her head, you'd have thought she was a sweeper. When they carried the sahib on a stretcher into the ambulance, she climbed in with him and held his hand. At the very end of her husband's life, the memsahib was a good and dutiful wife.

'Shall I leave?' I asked Mem a few days after the sahib died. 'Will you and Missy Baba go to your father's house?'

Mem sat at the sahib's desk in her best dress – the one that looked like an undergarment – and didn't seem like a widow. Surely, she'll return to her family, I thought. British women could marry again and she was young enough to have plenty of children. Her face was as lovely as a girl's and she had the kind of body that pleases a man.

'I think I'll try to make a go of it here,' she said, and pushed Miss Maisy towards me. 'Please stay with us.'

She drummed her fingers on the table and settled her nerves by lighting another cigarette.

What she meant was that her old home could wait because Percy Sahib couldn't. Percy was the sahib's so-called friend from the railway, the new man fresh from England who took the job the sahib thought was his own and who was given an even better job within weeks of arriving. Although Sahib thought Percy was his friend, I knew from the instant I saw him that Percy wouldn't be anyone's true friend.

Percy couldn't wait to lay claim to the sahib's wife. The old mattress was heaved out of the flat by two sweepers, who gagged at the smell even though they were used to dealing with filth. It was replaced by a new mattress and fresh sheets so the room smelled of lavender and the memsahib's perfume.

Although I'm ashamed to admit it, I was glad Percy was there. I was even glad that he disrespected the memory of the sahib by dishonouring his widow because, in all truth, I was desperate for her and Miss Maisy to stay. I'd worked in the sahib's flat for so many years I couldn't imagine starting again with another family.

Working for Sahib had been good. He was one of those Englishmen you could rely on to do things the proper way and life was easy once we learned the rules. We followed the rituals found in the great palaces of England. Even though Sahib had been born in the railway colony at Jamalpur, his mother said he'd acted like a *burra sahib* from the moment of his birth. His funeral showed how honourable he'd been because some Englishmen and their wives from the railway attended, and afterwards there was a party at which the memsahib showed great courage, fortified by her usual bottle of spirits.

I thought I heard someone say that Sahib was buried in the cemetery in South Park Street, so I went later with Miss Maisy to see where they'd put him in his shiny, wooden box. No one should have to spend time in that place full of ghosts, either in life or death. The British built stone tombs for their dead as big as houses, though I don't know what use they are to ghosts. They are like shrines at which no one does *puja*. Tombs of white people who'd died of malaria or cholera, or the torture of child-birth, were squashed together in a grey, cursed village of the dead. We walked back and forwards in the lanes between the tombs but we couldn't find one carved with his name.

Miss Maisy gripped my hand tightly, frightened by a pye-dog that stalked us, growling menacingly behind tree trunks, creeping along to reappear between the graves a few feet in front of us. Her other hand held a bunch of flowers, drooping in the heat. I'd promised we were going to say prayers for her father and when we couldn't find him she cried into her posy.

'Has Father gone to hell?' she sobbed.

'No, Missy Baba. He's gone to a new, good life.'

'But he's not here, and Mam says he wasn't here for us either when he was alive.' She laid the flowers one by one on top of a lichen-covered grave.

I discovered much later that the sahib was buried in a cemetery without big tombs or mausoleums, one that had only small headstones for the *chota sahibs*, the little white people. It took a long time to find because I had to match the name written on a piece of paper. It said 'Ernest Brooks 1873–1932'. The monsoon rains had turned the grave into a puddle and I placed a few flowers in the mud at the edge nearest the headstone, lit an oil lamp and did *puja* for the sahib.

I've said that prayer every day for Sahib, year after year, because I owe him a lot. He never shouted at me or beat me. He didn't make me work until I dropped and he never touched me, even when I worked for his mother and father and was still young enough to turn a man's head in the bazaar. Every night I expected him to come to my room. I expected him to slide into my bed in the dark, or to use me when his parents went out. He never did, not even when they both died and he was left alone, a middle-aged man without a wife. So, even though I liked Sahib, and even though he was kind, I knew for certain that he was not like other men.

Sahib told everyone, including us servants, that his ancestors were pukka sahibs and pukka mems – genuine sahibs and memsahibs.

'It's not as the sahib claims,' Cook said quietly to me when I first started working in the flat. He picked fish bones out of the kedgeree and whispered as if we were conspirators. 'His grandfather wasn't an important British officer. Sahib is lying.'

Cook had worked for the sahib's parents since the time they lived in the Jamalpur railway colony. He'd listened to gossip in the colony and he liked to repeat it, adding his own spice to the stories and shaping a fuller history of the Brooks family than the sahib knew himself.

'He says his grandfather was a *burra sahib*, but he was nothing of the kind; he was a Tommy in the Fort William barracks. His name was Edward Brooks, and he liked women, and fighting, and he drank more than any man in the regiment.'

This didn't surprise me because I knew for a fact that many of the British couldn't live a single day without alcohol.

Cook took a loud slurp of his tea and continued the tale. 'This Edward Sahib had a keep, a girl of fifteen he found in the bazaar. Even though she was as black as polished ebony she was so beautiful they said men were love-struck when they saw her.'

'How did he find this beauty?' I asked.

'I don't know. Maybe he bought her from her parents; maybe

she came from her village during a famine. Don't worry about little details like that, Pushpa, what's important is that he put her in a *kutcha* house – a little makeshift house – on the edge of Bowbazar, and she treated him like a god, kissing his feet, and giving him sons. She wasn't just any black whore, and when the regiment went home to England, Edward Sahib stayed in Calcutta and married the girl. He couldn't bear to leave her.'

'What was she called?'

Cook shrugged. 'How should I know? No one does. Anyway, he took her and the children across the river to Howrah, and set up a piggery to cure bacon for the troops in the Chinsurah depot.'

He must have become a rich man, I thought, because as well as loving alcohol the British are also addicted to bacon.

'But the story has a sad end,' Cook went on, his speech garbled as he crammed a handful of kedgeree into his mouth. 'The bacon wallah died soon after he set up his piggery and only one of the sons grew to be a man. The rest were killed by cholera and fever. Only our sahib, Alfred, survived.'

It was lucky, I thought, that Alfred took after the bacon wallah and not his black-faced wife. He was so fair you could hardly tell his mother was Indian.

'You know the rest of the story, don't you?' Cook said. 'He got a job on the railways and married an English girl. And now I'm here cooking their kedgeree and you are about to call the sweeper to empty their thunderbox.'

I met the English girl when she was an old woman. She was called Emily, and was our Brooks Sahib's frail mother. I heard the story from her own lips as I cleaned their little flat and sorted her clothes, bringing her tiffin when she rang a tiny brass bell.

'I was the prettiest girl in Calcutta,' she said. The memory animated her face and brought a flush to her paper-thin, white skin, so I could see she was telling the truth about her beauty. 'I was invited to every party in the cold season, and all the finest young men wanted to marry me. I could have had my pick.'

Something must have gone badly wrong, I thought, looking at her aged husband, son of the bacon wallah, who sat in the shade of the flat, rarely venturing on to the veranda in case the sun glanced against his skin and turned him golden brown.

'Papa was terribly rich and we had a grand mansion near Chowringhee,' she sighed, lost in her memories, hardly aware I was there. She didn't expect me to respond to her ramblings, and sometimes I thought she might have been talking to the parrot, who sat, mute and mangy, in a cage on the veranda.

'That was in the days before he was cheated out of every penny he owned,' she said, indignantly.

I heard a different version of the story from Cook, who said her father was a swindler who had countless debts, and even more enemies, and was chased from one end of Bengal to another by angry creditors. One drunken evening he put an end to his troubles and blew his head off with a hunting rifle on a steamer making its way to Assam. He murdered his wife too, so that they found her a few days later floating in a mangrove swamp. She was bloated and had a cord tied around her neck.

'My poor, darling Papa and Mama were killed by *dacoits* – brutal outlaws,' she said, her voice shaky. 'And I was saved from madness and grief by my dear Alfred.'

What she meant was that she was orphaned, impoverished and stained by so much scandal that the only person who'd marry her was a Eurasian railway clerk. I felt sorry for Emily Brooks. She often talked nonsense about her youth and she expected me to listen to the same story over and over again, but I was fond of her and so I listened and smiled. She was unusually polite and kind for a memsahib and I learned a lot of good English from her, not just the jungly words and dirty phrases I learned in the beds of British men.

'What happened to the woman?' I asked Cook later, having almost forgotten her because I was thinking too much about all the other people in the story.

'Which woman?'

'The bacon wallah's wife: the dark woman without a name.'

'She stayed in Howrah, or that's what they say. Alfred Sahib forgot about her when he got a job on the railway. A peon in the bank told me he sent her a bit of money now and again. Perhaps he did. I only know I saw him squeeze tears from his eyes and tell everyone his mother died years ago on the ship taking her back home to England.'

I sometimes wonder if Sahib knew more about his dead relatives than he admitted. During Dipaboli, on the night of Kali Puja, we filled our homes with lights for our departed ancestors and the whole city was lit by hundreds of thousands of tiny candles and oil lamps. Even the British joined in, and Calcutta sparkled. Brooks Sahib was the only man I knew to forbid lights on Kali Puja. Missy Baba cried and whined and tugged at his sleeve, and still he refused. He said it was a heathen practice and the flat might burn down, but I knew better: he banned the lights because he feared the black face of his deserted grandmother returning to haunt him.

'*Koi hai?* Is anyone there? Some more tea, Pushpa,' Mem ordered sharply the first time she came to the flat. She rattled her cup on its saucer. She didn't know how to behave and if she wasn't white I'd have sworn she was low-born. She was Miss O'Neill then – half the age of the sahib – pretty and loud, with her dress cut so low that her breasts spilled up and out into a pillow of white flesh.

He married her soon after and the men who came to drink with Sahib on the eve of the wedding laughed and talked about the lucky bridegroom.

'Ernest, you dog, you had us all fooled. We thought you were a bachelor for life.'

Another, unsteady with the whisky, elbowed him. 'You lucky bastard. You've still got a decent supply of lead in the old pencil, eh? She's gorgeous. She's a fresh young thing.'

'Young but not so fresh, I'll wager,' a drunk man said, and belched into his glass.

It was true; the memsahib wasn't fresh. A blind man could have seen that. Mem wasn't a real British lady, not like the handful who came – only once – with their husbands for drinks in the evening. They smiled at each other when she wasn't looking and laughed at secrets they didn't share with her. But she had a kind of revenge because their own husbands were glancing at Mem behind the backs of those polite British ladies, fascinated by her lively, flushed face, and her body in those immodest English dresses. They must have wondered what a stout, middle-aged man like Brooks Sahib could give to a woman like her. I knew, and it was nothing but his name. And that, I was sure, wasn't enough.

On the wedding day I prayed with Cook and the sweeper for the marriage to be fruitful, for Sahib to be granted a son. The next morning the sweeper looked alarmed as I handed the sheets from the marriage bed to the *dhobi*, the washerman who came to the flat twice a week. The sweeper noted there were no signs of blood and exclaimed, 'Perhaps Mem is still untouched.' I stifled a laugh.

Despite this unpromising start, some of our prayers must have worked their magic. After the wedding, Mem puked every morning and sometimes every afternoon. She began to swell, the shameful English dresses no longer fitting around her middle, and nine months later, Miss Maisy made an auspicious entry into the world. Mem didn't have to writhe on a bed for days. She was counting the tins of peaches and fruit cocktail in the storeroom when a trickle of water, then a stream, spread over the floor. She gripped her belly, groaned and then her hands sank to her thighs, between which, a minute or two later, a tiny head appeared. Sahib laughed and said the speedy arrival was a sign of punctuality and good manners, but the cook was horrified to learn the birth happened in the storeroom. It took the sweeper two days to clean the room and several visits from a Brahmin to purify it sufficiently for Cook to work again on his coconut macaroons.

Sahib held his daughter, plump and very pink, in his own plump and pink hands. She had his mouth and her mother's blonde hair, and for several minutes I watched him staring at her and questioning, I should imagine, if this new life was really any part of him. Her mouth spread into a yawn, wide and fat lipped, and then he knew that she was his; she was unmistakably her father's daughter.

Cook and the sweeper hesitated by the door to Mem's room as she lay recovering.

'Congratulations,' they both said, not really meaning it. They knew Sahib must have wanted a son.

'Next time it will be a boy,' Cook said, adding that we would sacrifice a chicken to hurry the little sahib on his way.

It was as if the memsahib was reborn after Miss Maisy's birth. Many more people were invited to the flat, all of them by Mem. Cook grumbled about preparing extra food, and the sweeper, who usually only worked in the flat for an hour a day, was asked to undertake extra duties growing flowers in a large number of pots that cluttered the veranda. Sahib's friends visited occasionally to drink a peg of whisky with him, the smoke from their cigarettes drifting in lose spirals around the vegetation and through the new beaded curtains.

'Quite a jungle you're growing here, Ernest,' they said.

The sahib nodded wearily.

Mem flirted shamelessly with the men who visited but it was only after she'd seen the sahib with his mistress that she let one lie with her. The man who received the favour was Percy Sahib, and I knew he was going to bring us trouble. He had the evil eye, for sure, and it was looking with envy at Sahib, greedy for the pleasures of his pretty wife.

Percy was new to India but he was learning to be a *burra sahib* as if he'd been born to the role. He was Sahib's superior at the railway. Cook said this was because Percy was born in Britain, and had only just left there, and so was more British. He was a pukka sahib: he'd probably spoken to the King, whereas Brooks Sahib had lived in India all his life. The closest he'd got to Britain was when he went to stand outside Government House to celebrate the King's visit, and even then he never got to meet the King, he only watched him drive past in a carriage wearing a giant hat.

Percy was not going to be a little white man like Sahib. He wanted more, including the memsahib, sniffing round her like a dog at a bitch so that the other guests had their suspicions confirmed – Mem was not as mindful of her honour as she should have been.

'Barbara, darling, give me a light,' Percy said, smiling and waving a cigar at her while he leaned against the rail of the veranda in his white flannels. Other times he'd say, 'Fancy a trip to the races tomorrow?' Or, 'Is that husband of yours looking after you well?' and, 'How does a fine girl like you enjoy spending her afternoons?'

When there was only me with them and I was busy clearing up, collecting glasses and emptying ashtrays, he'd get close to her, whispering things that made her laugh, and then glance fleetingly at me as if she'd just remembered I was there. To save everyone embarrassment, I pretended to be deaf, or not to understand, and the time he placed his hands on her breasts I pretended to be blind too.

I didn't know then whether Mem really loved Percy or whether all she wanted was revenge, a way to repay the sahib for his indifference, for keeping a beautiful Indian mistress and for hiding his heart and desire in a place she could not reach. She was careless with her reputation and I dreaded the day the world would discover that she spent hours locked in her room with young Percy Sahib, because then all the shame would be hers. Although Mem and I were from different races, I understood more about her than she could ever imagine. Despite her crude, blunt ways she deserved to be loved, and, for all his kindness, the sahib wasn't a man who could love her.

It puzzled me when Mem didn't want to return to her family in England after Brooks Sahib died. Even when Percy Sahib began to treat her badly, she never spoke of her family or showed any sign of needing them. I thought this was strange because when my own husband died, I wanted nothing more than to go back to my father's house by the great river. Life had been hard in Baba's home, but I've never forgotten it or the *maya* – the ties of love and affection – that bound me to it and the people who lived there.

We were tenant farmers who grew rice, vegetables and jute. Baba and my brother, Hari, fished every morning for extra food and I'd watch them from the riverbank while I filled our pitchers, Hari framed against the rising sun as he stood in the boat and threw his nets on to the flat surface of the water. They always returned with a plump fish for my mother to fry. After we'd finished our chores and collected firewood and dung, I went with Ma and my little sister, Anjali, to the fields, Baba apologising frequently because he couldn't let us stay inside the house. Such luxuries were only for the rich, and so we ignored our shame, pulled the ends of our saris over our hair, and worked in the earth like low-caste women.

Ma taught me the things she thought a girl should know: all the things that would make me a good wife and mother. I made cheap food taste delicious; I learned to spin top-quality thread; I pounded paddy; I turned reeds into baskets. I knew the stories of the gods and goddesses; I painted pictures with clay and rice flour, and I memorised the words to every song sung by the women of the village. Ma had an enchanting voice, and she sang throughout our long working days.

'Baba and I will find you a fine husband,' she said, stopping the spinning wheel and taking the bunched-up thread from my fingers. Drawing out the fibres, she twisted the yarn, pulling to make it finer. 'He will be strong and kind. You have nothing to fear, Pushparani; he will be good to you.' She handed the thread back to me and, touching my forehead, she gave me a blessing.

I remember a beautiful Bengal, where warm rain brought life to our crops, and bright green fields and silver water shimmered under a brilliant sun. But I also remember another Bengal, where the world turned deadly for a few horrifying hours. Dark clouds massed over the distant sea and powerful winds began to buffet the house, sweeping baskets off the veranda and on to the black surface of an unrecognisable river. The sudden gale whipped white flowers from the khas grass, ripped up the bamboo grove and slammed a tree branch against the fence in front of the house. Ma's little brown goat bleated in terror and Ma hesitated by the door, wanting to bring her inside. From the window I saw her tether grow taut and snap. Her legs buckled and then an enormous gust picked her up and flung her against the smashed fence, a broken post skewering her soft belly.

The house groaned.

'Pushpa, Hari, quickly,' Baba said, pushing Ma and Anjali out into the storm. I followed them and was blown off my feet, landing crumpled against the outside wall. Hari was behind me but before he could walk through the door, half the thatched roof somersaulted up and away, and with a crack that was audible above the roar of the storm, a beam broke and crashed into the house. I looked in through the window and saw it pinning Hari to the floor.

Anjali screamed at the sight of the impaled goat twitching on the fence and began to run blindly towards the flattened bamboo grove by the water's edge. The wind knocked her over and, time after time, she scrambled to her feet, still heading towards the river that had become a monstrous, boiling sea. Uprooted trees and parts of houses were tossed in the torrent and a neighbour's cows struggled to swim, their eyes rolling and frantic in the seconds before they were sucked under the surface. The great river spilled its banks and spread over the fields. Anjali turned and headed back to us as the water rushed towards her but her young legs were slower than the surge and it caught her, sweeping her feet from under her and dragging her into the flood.

Baba staggered, bent against the wind and yelled her name: 'Anjali. Anjali.' I saw his mouth forming the words but I couldn't hear him above the howling of the storm. He stumbled into the water, struggling to keep his balance, but she was gone, swallowed by the river that had given us its bounty for so many years. It claimed its price – even fish are not free – and spat her out three villages downstream.

The storm took my sister and it smashed Hari's pelvis so he never walked properly again. It destroyed our house and crops, and when it was spent and we were almost completely destroyed, the moneylenders came to scavenge what we had left. Baba went to work in a Calcutta jute mill to pay off the creditors but the money he sent home was never enough and our debts kept increasing.

Baba returned in summer for the jute harvest, but the man who stepped off the boat was not the one who'd left us almost a year before. He sat on the veranda taking short, shallow breaths. The doctor said the air in the mill had aggravated his tuberculosis and that he couldn't do anything to help him. He was dead by Kali Puja and the start of the cool weather.

Something inside Ma died with Baba and she wasn't a widow for long. After a few weeks, a fever severed the last thread tying her to earth. A day later, the moneylenders took our last possessions and the landlord rented the farm to another family. Hari and I were orphaned and homeless, and as the boat taking us to a new life pulled away from the riverbank, we looked back at our ruined house. Hari put his arm around my shoulder. It was one of those exquisite days I remember from my childhood when the sun is bright and the land is lush. Colours dazzle, a gentle wind carries the fragrance of flowers and light plays on the surface of the water. Caught by the current, the boat moved downstream quickly, and the house became blurred in a heat haze. I looked again and my heart jumped: Ma was spinning yarn on the veranda and Anjali was running towards the bamboo grove.

'See,' I gasped.

'What?' Hari asked.

In delight I glanced at his face, and then back at the house. No one was there; the only thing that moved was the ragged tarpaulin roof billowing in the breeze.

Mem made a bad choice when she picked Brooks Sahib as a husband, but at least the sahib was kind. She chose him from among the customers of the sleazy club where she worked, just off Park Street. Perhaps I'm being unfair to say she picked him because her options must have been very limited. No respectable British man would have made her an offer of marriage, and the sahib was probably the best of a very bad lot. She could have refused him, though, and stayed a barmaid all her life. That was the difference between Mem and me: I had no choice. I was forced to marry and, unlike Brooks Sahib, my husband certainly wasn't kind.

After Ma died, a boatman took us upstream to live with an uncle we'd never met. It was Uncle who arranged my marriage, and of course it had to be to a high-caste man because we were Brahmins, even if our part of the family was poor. Uncle said he'd heard the need for speed from the women of his household.

He looked at me and frowned. 'It seems the blossom has already ripened. You should have been married long before now. Your parents were lax about so many things. No wonder they ended as paupers. We can't have an unmarried girl in our house; we've got a reputation to consider and I have two daughters of my own to marry off. If we are quick, though, we might avert a disaster.'

It was indeed a disaster and not only because I was getting older in a place where brides were required to be young. The real catastrophe was that the small dowry my parents had collected for me had been washed away with Anjali and the rest of our lives. No man of our caste wanted a girl – even a young and pretty one – without a dowry.

Three prospective bridegrooms inspected me before I was chosen by my husband. The other suitors didn't like me; they said I was too skinny, or too short, or my hair wasn't long enough. When my husband sent his nephews to check me, they rubbed my face with a towel.

'You wouldn't believe the tricks some of these girls and their parents play,' one of the nephews complained to the matchmaker. 'They stand in a weak light, looking as pale as the moon, and when you rub away the make-up you find they're the colour of mahogany.' The nephews scowled at the idea of inferior, dark-skinned brides being palmed off on their family.

Nothing but my skin came off on the towel and I was judged acceptable despite my skinny arms.

'She's got decent teeth,' the older nephew said as they left.

The younger one agreed. 'She's very pretty, really. Both her eyes look in the same direction and there's no trace of a squint.'

Everyone enjoyed the wedding, except me and Hari, who lay in the corner of the courtyard, silent and angry. I hated it when the women bathed me and anointed me with oil and turmeric, and I was sure I'd faint when they brought me out of the house on a wooden seat and carried me seven times around my husband. None of it, though, was as terrible as the moment he looked at me for the first time under my veil. He was a withered old man with a sly glint in his eye. They made me garland him with flowers, guiding my hands because they shook so much. The women ululated and blew conch shells. An iron bangle was placed on my wrist and vermilion was rubbed into the parting of my hair.

On the night of the third day, the 'auspicious night' when the marriage was to be completed, our bed was strewn with flowers and the girls and women of the family joked about what was going to happen to me and how I'd give the old man a son to add to the four he already had. Next day, there was blood on the sheets of my wedding bed and the family told the village they'd been given the gift of a virgin, no one knowing or caring that I was made a wife by the prod of a long, bony finger.

The gossips said my husband was killed so soon after the wedding by the sexual demands of a young bride and the strain it placed on his heart. They smashed my bangles while they were still on my wrists, they shaved my head, and my wedding dress was replaced by widows' clothes. I was forbidden to marry again and people feared me because they thought I'd bring them bad luck. My husband's foul breath no longer filled my mouth and part of me was glad the old man was gone, but the consequences of his death were to shatter my life for a second time; I'd become a star-crossed widow and celebrated my thirteenth birthday on the same day.

Mem didn't have to live in poverty, a burden in her in-laws' house, but like me, she lived half a life. She was married to the husk of a man and not to his heart, and certainly not to the part that rules his passion. Sahib wasn't as old as my own husband, although he might as well have been. It didn't matter how much Mem groomed herself, styling her hair, putting on make-up and wearing revealing clothes, the sahib failed to notice. Her beauty was seen by everyone except the man she married. I could have told her why, but I couldn't bring myself to explain that the sahib's desire wasn't stirred by the heavy breasts of the memsahib and her soft, milk-white thighs, but by the straight, sinewy, brown limbs and the small, hard buttocks of the youths lingering round the back of Howrah Station. Sahib didn't keep a Hindu woman, as Mem often claimed. Instead, he loved a boy called Amal who, when he grew to an adult, became half woman, half man, and took the name Amala. She was beautiful in women's clothes and she loved the sahib the way he wanted, far better in the sahib's mind than any complete woman could.

The night Mem followed Sahib to Amala's room, he returned home in the early morning and sat silently on the veranda, watching the dawn spread over the street. Mem had witnessed everything, but I guarantee she understood nothing. I took him tea as the sounds of the new day unfolded: the *dudh wallah* delivered milk; a rickshaw passed by, squeaking under the weight of a fat passenger; a group of beggars chatted loudly as they made their way into the centre of the city. The sahib didn't speak but took the cup from me and nodded his head. Poor Sahib; he should never have married Mem, and she shouldn't have married him. They each wanted something the other could give – honour and a good name – but they couldn't love each other. And for that reason, I pitied them both.

That snake, Percy Sahib, stayed close to Mem through the funeral and supported her through her grief. In the weeks after Brooks Sahib died, he spent far more time in Mem's bed than her real husband had managed in their entire marriage. They had no shame. On a late afternoon, when the rain stopped and the sun appeared, Percy lay on a rumpled sheet, the warm light turning his chest hair golden and glossy. I busied myself sorting Miss Maisy's clothes and as I walked silently back and forwards past the half-open door, I glanced in and listened to Mem.

'Why don't you make a decent woman of me?' she asked.

Percy took a drag on his cigarette. 'Come on, Babs, it wouldn't be right. Old Ernest's barely cold in his grave.'

'What about later? Christmas, perhaps?'

'I'm not sure I'll be here. I might be posted to Delhi.'

'We'll come with you.'

Percy paused. 'Look, you're a fantastic girl, the best I've ever had, but we're not right together. I mean, we're not right for marriage. It wouldn't work.'

'You mean I'm not good enough for you.'

'I didn't say that.'

'You did in as many words. Don't you think you owe me something after all this bloody time?'

'I'm not cut out for this, Babs,' Percy said, climbing off the bed. 'I've been meaning to tell you for a few weeks, and this wouldn't have been the time I'd have chosen, but as we're on the subject, I'm afraid there's someone else.'

Mem was silent.

'We met at the Tolly. Playing tennis. Doubles. You know how it is.'

Mem couldn't have known how it was because she didn't play tennis and she never went to any kind of club. She said it was because the people in them were boring – toffs, she called them – but Cook said it was because they wouldn't allow her in.

'Let me guess,' Mem cried. 'She rides, shoots and is a useful fourth at bridge.'

'How did you know?'

'And what am I supposed to do now you've found this nice girl?'

'Go back home?' Percy suggested.

'Home to what? To my mam's bleeding house and a job cleaning shit for some rich cow? You're fucking joking, aren't you?'

The buckle of Percy's belt snapped shut.

'Come on, darling,' Mem said invitingly. 'She can't give you what I can.'

'That's true. No one gives me what you do.'

I heard low voices and then the slap of her hand against his skin.

'You bastard,' she shrieked. 'Do you think I'm some cheap whore you can use and throw away?'

Percy left that day, not for the last time, but for the first in a long line of last times. Mem always had him back and they repeated the same arguments until the day, three months after his marriage, Percy announced his young bride was pregnant. He got up from Mem's bed, saying something about new responsibilities, promotions and a post in Delhi. And for the final time he eased into his clothes, kissed her goodbye and strolled out of the flat, dropping his condom in the bin as he left.

I didn't think badly of Mem and what she did after Percy Sahib abandoned her. We all have to earn a living and it's better to lose your honour than starve in the streets. I know all about this because I used to be in the same business as Mem. North of the Marble Palace, off the Upper Chitpur Road, there's a neighbourhood called Sonagachi, and it was my home for almost fifteen years. It's a place where women sell their bodies. Some call it selling our shame: I say it was the only way I could survive when I was a widowed child.

Women are supposed to return to their fathers or brothers when their husbands die. This wasn't possible for me because I was orphaned and my brother was a cripple. My husband's eldest son took me to Uncle but he refused to see me, and I sat weeping on the step of the veranda, watching Hari hobble around the courtyard doing odd jobs, the pain in his legs forcing him to rest often on a bamboo mat outside the servants' room.

'I'm sorry, Pushparani,' Hari said. 'You know I'd take care of you, but I can barely take care of myself.'

'Is Uncle good to you?' I asked, knowing the answer by his threadbare clothes.

Uncle sent me back to my husband's family and although they didn't want me, they grudgingly let me stay. My sons-in-law barely tolerated me, and my daughters-in-law hated me. Some of my dead husband's grandchildren were older than me and I would have joined in their games if widows had been allowed to play.

Instead, I was kept busy with chores. One of my jobs was to keep the courtyard tidy. The shortest blade of grass had to be uprooted and the yard swept. Every morning I also cleaned the floors of the house and applied a fresh coating of mud, smoothing it so it dried hard and perfectly flat. If I was alone, I decorated the floors before they set, drawing the patterns Ma taught me.

One morning a daughter-in-law walked into a room as I was finishing a design. I thought she must be admiring my skill and that everyone would marvel at the bird I'd created. I sat back on my heels to look at my work. The daughter-in-law stood over me, placed her foot on the design and rubbed it backwards and forwards, smearing the bird back into the mud. I let out a wail so loud the rest of the family came running.

They watched as I rocked to and fro, my arms locked around my knees and my widow's white sari caked in mud.

'Help me,' I sobbed. 'Please, help me.'

'She wants our help?' a daughter-in-law said in disbelief.

She was wrong: I wasn't asking them for help; I was calling to Ma.

'No more pictures,' my eldest son-in-law warned. 'It'll bring us bad luck. Stick to cleaning the courtyard.'

Sensible widows make an effort to be pious. You have to obey all the rules of widowhood: eat one meal a day, making sure it's frugal, and fast for a whole day and night during every full moon and every new moon. I'd always been skinny but on a widow's diet I became emaciated. My breasts, which had only recently started to grow, shrank into my chest and my skin stretched tight over my bones.

I prayed when I wasn't working and my new family said it was good. I pretended to pray for my departed husband, but really I was pleading for a thunderbolt to strike the whole lot of them, for a cyclone to rip their world apart. I hated them.

Everything that went wrong in the house was blamed on me.

'The harvest is terrible,' one of my sons-in-law said, looking at the sacks of rice on the back of the cart. 'Someone must have put a spell on us.' The fool had forgotten the rains had been late that year and everyone's harvest was poor.

My youngest daughter-in-law picked the yellow crusts from her son's eyelashes and glared at me. 'Poor little Bablu, why are his eyes always sticky?' she asked.

The prettiest daughter-in-law, Manali, ran around after her child, a scrawny, sallow girl who had only recently learned to walk, and who left a trail of diarrhoea wherever she went. Manali screeched constantly and scolded me for not helping to clean up. 'This is your fault. She's like this because of you,' she yelled.

My elder daughter-in-law was the worst, not only because she was the most powerful, the oldest and the mother of teenage sons, but because she had a vicious nature, pinching me whenever I did something that displeased her and laughing while she did it, always pretending she was playing as her fingers dug into me.

I heard them explaining to kin and the neighbours that I brought misfortune to the house.

'She's unlucky. Look what happened to our father-in-law: he died within two months of the wedding.'

They glanced sideways at me and one whispered, 'She's jealous of us. She has the evil eye.'

All the women nodded.

'She keeps looking at my son,' a neighbour added.

'I think she's possessed,' Manali declared. 'Notice how she shakes when we go near. I'm scared to be close to her.'

My son-in-law, the husband of the woman who took such pleasure in pinching me, wasn't worried about being near me. He took a different kind of pleasure from me whenever he could; in the cowshed, in the godown, in the orchard among the mango and guava trees. He was brutal and furious, and mercifully quick, and I began to understand why his wife looked at him from beneath her veil with such loathing.

Manali gave birth to her second child almost a year after I'd been widowed. Women were supposed to return to their parents' home for their deliveries but Manali's baby came early and she was hurried into the family's *athurghar*. In those times women in rich families in that part of Bengal gave birth in a special hut secluded from everyone else. The *athurghar* in my husband's house was a foul, windowless place, and even though I hated Manali, I felt sorry for her and imagined how agonising it must be to be shut in the hut with only the *dai* – the old midwife – to help her endure the pain.

The other daughters-in-law rushed around the *athurghar* looking for gaps in the walls and stuffing them with rags.

'We don't want any evil spirits getting inside,' they said, and turned in unison to look at me.

Manali thrashed and shrieked in the *athurghar* for two whole days and when the screams from the hut eventually stopped, I thought she must have died. After a long pause, a high-pitched wail pierced the silence of the compound.

'It must be another girl,' the eldest daughter-in-law said.

I saw Manali the next day when the door of the *athurghar* opened and the *dai* came out. She was lying on a mattress with her newborn daughter at her side. She stared at me, the exhaustion in her face transforming into venom.

'See what you've done,' she shrieked. 'I haven't had a son because you cursed me.'

I backed away.

'You will pay for this, Pushpa. I promise.'

Manali had to spend a month in the *athurghar* to fulfil the birthing rituals, and during this time I made a plan: I wouldn't let her torment me for a moment longer because I was going to escape from all of them. On the day she was to rejoin the family I woke as usual before dawn but I didn't start my chores.

I crept into the room where Manali usually slept, opened her trunk and pulled out her best sari. Putting it on, I threw my widow's clothes on the floor and then tiptoed out of the house, through the gate in the bamboo walls of the compound, and on to a path that joined the road. I ran and ran through the pale light, the mist swirling low over the fields. As the sun rose, I came to a crossroads and waved to a man driving a bullock cart.

'Are you going to Calcutta?' I asked. It was the only place I knew that was a long way from the village.

He shook his head. 'No, but I can take you to Jamtala. You can make your way from there.'

I dragged my sari over my cropped hair, climbed into the cart and sat behind him on big bales of golden jute.

'I can't pay you,' I said.

He looked back and smiled. 'I'm sure we can do a deal.'

Within a year I was living on Masjid Bari Street in Sonagachi, the place where widows, poor women and the daughters of prostitutes can make a living – a good one when you're young and fresh, and before you've had children. My hair grew long and I ate so much my body filled out: I developed breasts and hips that Aunty, who ran the brothel, said the customers would pay a fortune to enjoy. Aunty let me choose lac dye, kohl and nail varnish from the boxwallah – the pedlar – who visited the brothel, and Aunty definitely knew a lot about hips and make-up because every single man who came into the brothel liked me and spent a long time haggling with her.

'It's only her third time,' Aunty emphasised to the clients, squeezing my cheeks to show how plump and healthy I'd become. She meant third time that day. 'See how young and firm she is. I've saved her for the best customers.'

I was lucky to work in that brothel. I didn't stand in the streets with cheap women but was kept inside, where it was safer and the clients had more money. When I was new, Aunty told me that I was her special girl, and for the first time in my life I had a little room to myself. I had a picture of Lakshmi on the wall to bring me wealth and beauty, and I had a green blanket to sleep on and a blue one for the business. Although the room was my own, the partitions in the brothel were so thin I could hear the heaving and grunting of everyone else's customers. Kamala, Aunty's other special girl, worked and slept in the next cubicle and as well as listening to the familiar sounds made by her customers, I also heard the cries of her hungry baby. Kamala arrived in Sonagachi only a few weeks after me, and I saw Aunty checking her teeth, the same way she'd checked mine.

'You're clearly not a virgin,' Aunty said, looking at the week-old baby in Kamala's arms. 'That wasn't very clever, was it?'

Kamala shook her head. She'd worked in a jute mill in Howrah but the wages were low and she'd trusted a man who promised he would help her. He bought her a few meals from a roadside stall and then left her pregnant. I was glad she was older than me and not as pretty, but to everyone's surprise it didn't stop her having almost as many customers. Aunty said Kamala must have been good at the business otherwise the customers wouldn't keep asking for her, especially when she'd already had a baby and her woman's parts weren't fresh and tight. She had a *babu,* a rich, regular client whom she kept so happy he paid a handsome monthly stipend to Aunty, and big tips to Kamala. She was clever in other ways, too. She saved a lot of money and every year she added another gold bangle to her wrist.

'One day,' she said, 'I'll have a business of my own and I'll wear saris of Benares silk.'

I envied her and wanted a baby like her pretty little daughter. I looked after Samita while Kamala was with her customers, hiding her under my bed and playing games with her when she woke. Even though I was jealous of Kamala, and her good luck, she was so kind to me that I grew to love her like a sister.

'Why don't you buy gold?' she asked as she admired her jewellery collection, the bangles jangling on her wrist. 'You've plenty of clients; you can afford it.'

'I don't have as much money as you,' I said.

Kamala stared at me through narrow eyes. 'You can borrow this,' she said, handing me a heavily worked bangle made of real gold, not the rolled gold cheap women wore. 'I can't have my sister looking poor. You'd think none of the customers liked you.'

Sonagachi offers you a living, but it is a pitiless life, especially at the start, and a few of the women hated me almost as much as my daughters-in-law had done. Aunty scoffed and told me to ignore them.

'They're not so pretty and they're getting old. The customers prefer girls like you.'

There were other bad times, like dealing with the drunks who were either too rough or fell asleep on me, or the old men who took so long that Aunty had to bang on the wall.

'Haven't you finished? I'm running a business here.'

Despite these things, and despite the worry about getting pregnant and catching diseases, it was better than being with my daughters-in-law and suffering their constant complaints. Better than being raped by my son-in-law among the mango trees or clawed by my husband's hands with their thick, curving, yellow nails. In Sonagachi, I was paid.

You can only stay in that business for a short while. The fat creeps on to your stomach and the lines spread around your eyes. Your women's parts get tired; they're slack if you have children, and they weep from too many men and too many illnesses. You're old and spoiled after ten years, fifteen at most, though some of the girls I knew stayed on till they were middle-aged, working in smaller, darker rooms, earning enough for a plate of rice and dal from men who couldn't afford anyone younger. Then they'd move their trade to worse places, to Harkata Lane or to the alleys of Sinduriapatti, where they sold themselves for five paise a time. I swore I'd never sink that low and so when the customers picked me less often as they relaxed on the cushions, deciding who to buy, I refused to join the business in the Kidderpore Docks filled with its half-naked coolies and the stink of jute and sweat. Instead, I met a Tommy from Fort William who wouldn't buy girls in the 'rags', the regimental brothels, because he said they were riddled with 'the clap'. He rented me a room on the edge of Burrabazar and I rolled up my picture of Lakshmi, folded my blankets, and said goodbye to Aunty.

Kamala lifted my case on to a rickshaw. 'Don't forget us,' she said. For a moment I thought she was crying but as Kamala didn't like sentimentality I decided there must have been dust in her eyes.

'Here's your bangle.' I took it off for the first time in years and handed it to her.

'You keep it,' she said. 'I've enough of my own.' That was true; her bangles covered almost every inch of her forearms. 'Never take it off,' she said.

The girls waiting for customers waved to me as Kamala walked beside the rickshaw.

'I'll miss you, little sister,' she said. This time I was certain there were tears in her eyes.

'I'm not going far. I'll visit often.'

The rickshaw wallah's pace quickened. Kamala held up her hand and I caught her fingers.

'Goodbye, big sister,' I said.

I let go of her hand when the rickshaw came to the corner of Masjid Bari Street and turned on to the Chitpur Road. I didn't dare look back.

My new job was no easier than the one in Sonagachi. The soldier stayed in Calcutta for only a few months and, when he left, a new British man, a boxwallah – a businessman – with a wife in England, made me a servant in his home. I cleaned his flat and at night he'd take me to his bed for a short while. When he went back to England he passed me to another man, and he to another, until I ended up, by some good fortune, as the maid-servant of Emily Brooks, the old but still graceful wife of Alfred Brooks, son of Howrah's bacon wallah. It was an astonishing, unsettling experience to work in their flat and to live with them and their quiet son, Ernest, because, for the first time since I was a child, men who slept near me didn't sleep with me.

Despite the death of her father and the spoiling of her mother, Miss Maisy shone with a fresh and captivating beauty. She had the best of Mem's looks but hadn't inherited the coarse ways Mem had brought from that place in England where the King and Queen had clearly never been, nor been able to spread their example. By the time she was twelve, Miss Maisy had stopped befriending urchins from the *bustees* and I no longer had to scold her for running barefoot in the street, her legs caked in so much mud she could have been mistaken for an Indian. I was sure Miss Maisy was going to be a pukka British lady.

Madan wasn't so confident. 'She'll learn her mother's ways. How will she meet an honourable man when it's only Mem's customers who come to the door? Mem doesn't know any respectable men. I tell you, Pushpa, Memsahib's got bad blood, and the daughter's will be the same: she'll be a rich man's keep.'

I was unhappy at the thought. I wanted something better for Miss Maisy because she was a sweet and joyful child.

I'd have had a baby of my own when I lived in Sonagachi if only Aunty had let me. Every time my bleeding stopped and I began retching into a bucket, she ordered the *dai*, who doubled as midwife and abortionist, to get rid of the problem. Babies, she said, were bad for trade, and it didn't matter how much I wept, Aunty just shook her head and instructed the other girls to hold me down while the old *dai* got on with her business. She stewed herbs and roots and made me drink the foul broth, and then she massaged my abdomen, kneading it deeply. A day later, sometimes two, the baby was gone.

Eight times the *dai*'s fingers gripped my insides, prising out the growing life, and I think she must have scarred my body for ever because when I was a woman and had the freedom to have children, all my babies were born half-grown or they died in my arms after only a few hours, one or two every year until my body gave up and no babies came, either alive or dead. I wrapped each of them in red cloth, and put them on a little raft covered in flowers, and watched them float away, bobbing down the river, and my heart broke every time. I made plaits, mixing my hair with long threads and hung them from the champa tree – the barren tree – in the temple at Kalighat, but my prayers were never answered. None of my babies lived, and I kept on buying lengths of red cloth.

Miss Maisy was a gift for Mem – a miracle child – and she was a gift for me, too.

'She is a good girl,' I told Madan. 'Sometimes she's silly and has no sense, but she has a good heart. Did you know she sings Bengali songs? I taught her them when she was so little she could barely speak English, never mind Bengali.'

Madan wrapped his arms around me in the dark of the room. His breath, scented with the cloves he sucked to ease his tooth-ache, was warm on the back of my neck. It was December and so cold we needed thick blankets. As I drew the cover over us, Madan moved slightly, stretching his legs and groaning with the pain in his knees.

'We're getting old,' I said. Sitting up, I began to massage his legs, squeezing the muscles that had grown weaker in the years I'd known him.

He stroked my cheek. 'As I get thinner, you, my love, are getting fatter.' He patted my thigh. 'I like plump women.'

He stayed with me for an hour or two before leaving to care for his mother and his wife, the pitiful, broken woman, who

I resented for the simple reason that she wouldn't just give up and die.

'Stay longer,' I coaxed.

'I have to go. It's my duty.'

I hated it when he said that, and I admired him for it, too. Madan was from one of the lowest castes, only a shade above an untouchable. He was the kind of person my own caste despised because they thought them dirty and polluted. My uncle married me to an old Brahmin because he said it would bring the family respect and honour. I laughed at the thought. Uncle must have died years ago and yet I still wanted to tell him that Madan, a man he would have shunned, lay pressed against one of his own kin. He loved me even though he knew what I'd been and how I'd lived.

He got slowly to his feet and bent to kiss me goodbye. 'I'll see you tomorrow when the milkman comes.'

I watched him disappear into the night, the man I loved, who was growing old and hobbling awkwardly on his bad knees.

Chapter Three

Maisy

SUNIL BANERJEE HAD an unforgettable face. Mam said he was good-looking for a Bengali despite the little gap between his top front teeth. She said she didn't know how anyone as ugly as my tutor had fathered a son like Sunil; either his mother was a dazzling beauty or the boy was a changeling. Unlike Old Mr Banerjee, he didn't need to wear thick glasses, which was lucky because he had the most striking eyes. They were big and dark brown with long, black, glistening eyelashes that brushed against my cheeks when he kissed me. In 1942, my boring life in the ramshackle house in Dharmatala was transformed. The narrow shafts of sunlight streaming through the blinds of sweet-smelling grass no longer fell on my unread books. They shone on Sunil, who kneeled at my feet and promised me the earth, if only he had the power to give it.

Old Mr Banerjee had developed a heart problem after the previous Kali Puja and he wheezed his way through lessons during the cold weather, gripping his chest if I failed to do any homework or gave silly answers to his pedantic questions. When the doctor ordered him to avoid anxiety and take some bed rest, Sunil stepped in as my tutor. He was reluctant at first.

'I have a lot of other commitments,' he explained. 'And I do some managing in the export trade.'

I was puzzled; Mam told me he was a clerk in the Kidderpore Docks and he seemed far too young to be doing anything very important; he was only a year or two older than me.

'My life,' he declared, 'is devoted to politics and literature. My friend Charu and I are working on a new abridged Hindi and Bengali translation of the Communist Manifesto for activists in the jute mills.'

Charu must have been keen to continue the task because he waited in the lane for Sunil to finish our classes, chain-smoking and glancing at his watch every few minutes.

'I'm writing a novel too,' Sunil said.

'Can I read it?'

'It's in Bengali.'

'Why don't you write it in English?'

'Because it's the language of the colonisers.'

'Will you read it to me? I can't read Bengali but I can understand it.'

He softened. 'Would you like that?'

I nodded.

'I'll read Tagore to you too, but not in those terrible English translations. We'll use the originals.'

Our new lessons were spent on the chintz sofa, Sunil reciting poems by the great Bengali writer, or reading from his own handwritten manuscript that told the sad tale of an impoverished, orphaned country boy who arrives, friendless, in the teeming city. I listened, enthralled, and within days I became an attentive student.

It wasn't so much the content of the story that charmed me as the charisma of the narrator. I was dazzled by his brilliance, and I stared at him while he read, fascinated by his chocolate-brown skin and the blue-black hair that curled into the nape of his neck. Pushpa said it wasn't good to be so dark. She said it was a sign of low origins even though the Banerjees were from a high caste. I didn't worry about that because looking at Sunil made my heart beat even faster than poor old Mr Banerjee's. Sunil was forbidden; more prohibited than the spiciest bazaar food, further out of bounds than the alleys and by-lanes of Burrabazar. And that made him all the more desirable.

My unenthusiastic tutor soon developed a passion for teaching. He inched closer to me on the sofa and glanced at me often. Within a fortnight the glances became a gaze and, a few days later, he started to caress my hands. He ran his fingertips over my cheek, tracing the contours of my mouth. 'You are my very heart,' he promised, Tagore's *Gitanjali* abandoned and wedged deep between the cushions.

I didn't find out what happened to the orphan boy in Sunil's novel; the last chapter we read left him sleeping on the steps of Calcutta's High Court. The dog-eared manuscript was stuffed into Sunil's shabby briefcase and instead he recited new poems he'd written about a young man's undying love for a beautiful girl with golden hair. Our lessons grew longer, annoying Charu, whose whistles from the street grew shriller. Sunil couldn't have heard, and he no longer rushed to continue the translation of his boring political tracts. He spent his afternoons stroking my breasts through the fabric of my dress and later, caressing my thighs until the day he was brave enough to slip his fingers into my knickers.

Watching him from the veranda when he left, I brushed against the blinds, moving them slightly. Sunil looked up. I thought he'd seen me and was about to wave goodbye but Charu grabbed his elbow and hurried him along the lane.

Charu resented me; that was obvious. I was keeping Sunil from his friends and making him neglect his important work. So, the next time Charu waited, roasting in May's unrelenting heat, I resolved to make peace with him and went to the door as Sunil was leaving.

'Hello, Charu,' I said.

'Hurry, brother,' Charu said, thrusting a newspaper into Sunil's hands.

'Would you like a cold drink?' I asked.

Charu glanced at me and then hustled Sunil away, hectoring him about the time and the meeting they would probably miss. I paused in surprise, wondering why he wouldn't speak to me. Was it because of Mam? Did he think she was brazen and degenerate in the way Uncle Bill claimed? Did he think I was the same as her? For the first time I started to worry that Sunil might think I was shameless too. After all, I'd let him do things to me that nice girls should never allow. And then I remembered his poems and vows of everlasting devotion, and I regained my senses. Sunil and I had nothing in common with Mam and the uncles. Mam was in a dirty business: we were in love.

Sunil always wore a pristine white cotton *dhoti* and *kurta* – a long loincloth and shirt – in the Bengali style. In the spring he also took to wearing a white hat of rough-spun cloth. I pulled it off and put it on my head. 'Is it the new fashion?' I asked.

'It's the style Gandhiji wears.'

'Is he the half-naked little bald man who's always talking about salt and spinning?'

He laughed and gave me the strangest look.

'Do you like Mr Gandhi?' I asked.

'Subhas Chandra Bose has a better way to free India. Gandhi believes in non-violence but we're fighting a war, and who's heard of a war without bloodshed?'

I'd never heard of Mr Bose, never mind his strategy, and so I thought I'd change the subject to avoid revealing my ignorance.

'Your friend Charu doesn't like me, does he?'

'He doesn't know you.'

'Doesn't he like British people?'

He laughed. 'You and your mother are not quite British, are you?' He kissed me to stop me arguing, and I lay back on the sofa thinking that one day I might be Mrs Banerjee. And then I imagined Mam and how she would die of anger and disappointment, so I put the idea to the back of my mind, not daring to think of the future and disciplining myself to see only as far as the next lesson. I didn't give a thought to the war engulfing the world, and I knew nothing of the shock every British person was supposed to feel when Singapore fell to the Japanese. I felt no sense of panic as the Japanese marched through Burma, threatening to invade India, and I didn't notice the city was emptying of ordinary people and filling up with troops. Apart from the irritation of the blackout at night and the brown paper stuck to the windows, the cataclysm of the Second World

War didn't seem to have anything to do with me. Sunil was the only thing on my mind.

It seemed unbelievable that no one guessed what we whispered or did in that once-dull room. We were careful to listen for warnings of approaching danger: Pushpa's faint footsteps as she went barefoot about her chores; the swish of the sweeper's soft grass broom; the heels of Mam's shoes tip-tapping on the floor before she put her head around the door and asked, 'How's she doing?'

'Better, much better,' Sunil said, grinning, his *kurta* smoothed down and a large book balanced on his lap.

He was right; I was better, much happier than I had been for years. He wound my hair around his fingers and sighed. 'Can I take a piece?'

'Just one small lock,' I said, and thought how lucky I was to have a man who loved me so completely.

I told him I was pregnant during the rains.

He didn't move, not even an eyelash, and stared unblinking at me.

'Impossible,' he whispered. 'We've only done it three times – those times your mother went out.'

'I know. I know,' I cried. 'But it's true.' My stomach was beginning to swell and Mam kept giving me worried looks and reminding me not to eat so many cakes and fries. 'Pushpa's sure of it. She's seen me being sick and she sorts my washing for the *dhobi*. She noticed my period hasn't come – not for months. Please, Sunil, what are we going to do?'

He put his head in his hands. 'I don't know.'

'We can get married.'

He shuddered as if the thought of marrying me was worse than the news I was pregnant. 'Our families would never allow it. I have to marry someone my parents choose,' he said. 'You can't marry an Indian and I certainly can't marry a white woman. There are things you don't understand.' He began to shake. The man who had loved me and lain with me drenched in sweat on Mam's chintz sofa had become a youth with trembling hands and a dry mouth.

'What am I going to tell Mam? She'll kill me, and you too.'

'You mustn't say it was me.'

'But she'll guess. She's not stupid.'

'I can't do this. I need some time to think. I promise, I'll be back soon.'

He left, forgetting his things in the rush. I packed his books and pen into his case and put it by the door for him to collect. And I gave him time, waiting for him to save me from at least one type of disgrace. Every day the sweeper cleaned round the bag, and Pushpa comforted me, stroking my head while I lay crying on her bed, my belly swelling by the week. Sunil didn't return to claim those things, the books he loved and the pen that was going to write the great literature of the new India. He didn't want them, or me, and he didn't want his child. He'd treated me like a prostitute, as if I were my mother.

'You bloody little tart,' Mam said, slapping me so hard across my face that I spun sideways.

'And to think I was worried you were going to be a fat girl. I hadn't reckoned on you being a pregnant one.' She threw her arms in the air as if imploring the God she usually ignored. 'What will people think of us?'

It was a silly question because no one thought much of us anyway.

'Why have you done this?' she spluttered, taking big slurps from her glass. 'Think of everything I've done for you.'

I was terrified, not because she was shouting at me but because she wasn't raising her voice. Her eyes rolled like a mad woman's, her breathing deep but without rhythm. Pushpa said I had to tell her. She said Mam would find out soon enough and it would be better to let her know rather than waiting until my shame was so big it would be obvious to everyone.

'I'm sorry. I didn't think it could happen like that. It was all over so quickly. It only took a few seconds,' I cried.

'Who was it? Uncle Terry? Uncle Donald? Was it that bloody flight sergeant?' Mam stomped around the room, sloshing drink over the floor.

I shook my head.

'Well, who then? I swear, when I get hold of them they'll have no balls left.'

Even Sunil, the hopeless runaway, deserved to keep his balls and so I said nothing.

At last her voice broke into a shriek. 'Who? Who?'

'Sunil,' I murmured.

For a moment she was shocked into silence, and then her expression softened to pity. 'Oh, my darling girl.' She put her arms around me, rocking me from side to side. When she let go, she wiped the tears from her eyes and took a deep breath. 'We'll get the bastard, Maisy. I'll be on to the police this afternoon – you know I've got connections there. He'll be put away for years for raping a white girl.'

'It wasn't rape, Mam.'

Mam gaped at me, her colour rising. 'You mean you let him? An Indian clerk? That sodding little idiot scribbler?' She was dumbfounded. 'I paid him to teach you English literature so you could be a lady, not some wog's tart.'

'It wasn't like that.'

'Don't tell me what it was like. The thought makes me sick.'

'Please, Mam. Please.'

'What will you do now?' She paced the room. 'Who'll want an unmarried girl with a half-breed child?'

I shook my head and began to shake uncontrollably, a sickness welling up from my stomach and vomit spraying in two curving lines through my fingers.

Mam pushed my hair back from my forehead and cupped my face in her hands. 'I want something better for you than this. I want you to have a better life than I've had.'

'I'm sorry, Mam.'

'I'll not have my beautiful girl throw her chances away. You'll not be like me: you'll not be some man's fancy piece. I came to this country to find a good life and I'll die before I let my daughter end up the same way as me.'

She settled me on the sofa and cuddled me while Pushpa called the sweeper to clean the floor.

'You can still meet a nice man. It's not too late.'

It was good to be in Mam's arms. It was comforting and warm, and I curled into her embrace like a small child. She really did want the best for me – all those things she'd craved for herself, and never actually enjoyed.

I was so terrified standing in the doctor's surgery that the wee ran down my legs and pooled around my sandals. My only thought was to escape from that place with its grimy windows and its bed covered in sheets marked by the fuzzy brown outline of blood stains.

'Don't worry, my dear,' the doctor said. 'This is a simple procedure. We'll soon put you right. There's a little pain involved but the worst is over in a moment or two and then nature will take its course.' He scowled in what was meant to be a smile of compassion and, taking off his worn jacket, he rolled up his sleeves and put on a large apron before beginning to sort through lengths of rubber tubing and a collection of metal instruments on a table. He was supposed to be the best – best at dealing with mothers heavy with unwanted babies – but Pushpa insisted he wasn't a doctor at all; he was a quack, and that I'd end up dead or unable to have another child. She cried, saying she knew what to do: she would take the child herself and raise it as her own.

'Nonsense,' Mam said, and shut her up with an angry look. 'What a crazy idea.'

That was how I ended up in Dr Turner's clinic, lying on sheets with a faded record of the other women who'd been there before me. The doctor lifted my feet into stirrups and as he squinted between my legs the sun shone on his perspiring bald head. Although the certificate on the wall validated him as an important doctor trained in London, I was sure he'd never been outside Calcutta. I could tell from the way he talked; he spoke English like me.

'How long will it take?' Mam asked while sitting on a chair by the doctor's desk, her bag on her lap. She gave me encouraging but unconvincing little smiles.

'It will all come away in a day or two. Everything will be cleaned out and she'll be spick and span.'

Mam blew her nose quietly into a handkerchief and fanned her face with an envelope.

A nurse in a soiled uniform hovered over me, holding a piece of gauze.

'This is something to help keep you calm,' Dr Turner said. 'It'll make you feel sleepy.'

And just then, almost as if it were a miracle, the baby quickened inside me, kicking once, twice, then again and again, as if it were running.

The gauze smothered me and I couldn't breathe, the smell filling my nose and throat. I clamped my mouth shut and pushed the nurse's hand away. And despite my growing belly, I kicked my feet out of the stirrups, swivelled round, knocked over the instrument table, and leaped off the bed. Dr Turner was not going to stick his metal prongs and rubber tubing inside me and my baby wasn't going to die on his tainted sheets or be flushed into a thunderbox.

I pulled on my skirt and ignored Mam's calls to stop. I was off, out of that room, the wee now dried on my legs. I didn't care about the shame of being an unmarried mother. I didn't care if the baby turned out to be as brown as his father. I didn't care about Mam or Sunil. I cared only about my baby, and I walked down that street, almost five months pregnant, watched by the old men smoking their hookahs in the shade of the shops. I held my head high and, when the breeze lifted my skirt, I didn't care either that I wasn't wearing any knickers.

Chapter Four
Pushpa

CHARLIE'S BIRTH WAS even stranger than his mother's had been among the tins of peaches and fruit cocktail. He arrived earlier than I expected, proving I'd not been keeping such a close eye on Miss Maisy as I'd thought. My calculations were wrong by a full month and so, when she complained of pains, I told her to rest in bed. Twenty minutes later she was sitting up panting and saying the child was on its way.

'We've got to get her to the maternity home or the Presidency General,' Mem yelled.

Miss Maisy wasn't going to move from her bed, never mind clamber into a taxi for the ride to the hospital. The local *dai* was summoned by Cook and bustled in to take charge. I don't know who looked in more pain: Miss Maisy in the throes of childbirth or Mem witnessing an Indian midwife delivering her grandchild. She trusted only British doctors and nurses, even though most of the nurses in the maternity homes or PG Hospital were Eurasian, and so not quite white.

We heard the sirens in between Miss Maisy's squeals.

'That's all we need. A ruddy bombing raid,' Mem groaned.

The street's self-appointed air-raid warden, an old British man with a giant curling white moustache, banged on the door and Mem flung it open.

'Take cover. Take cover,' the warden shouted. 'Get to your shelter.'

'My daughter's giving birth. How are we supposed to take cover?' she shrieked.

Mem ran back into the bedroom and was transfixed by the sight of the *dai* cutting the baby's cord. She tied it with string and then stopped, the baby naked on her lap and still streaked with blood. We heard a low pounding in the distance.

'Is that thunder or bombs?' Mem asked. The sound came again, a boom with an echo like no thunder I'd heard before. My stomach tightened. Perhaps it was an omen – the city was being visited by strange occurrences at the very moment the child was born.

'Aeroplanes are bombing the docks,' Cook called.

The *dai* wiped the child and handed him to Miss Maisy. He stared at his mother with a frown on his face, and she gazed at him in surprise.

'Hello, little one.' She brushed his cheek and he turned his head, opening his mouth.

Miss Maisy drew him close and even though he was still coated in the white film of the newborn, the fine down covering his body made him look dark against his mother's pale breast.

'Look how much hair he has,' his grandmother exclaimed. Hesitantly, she reached out and touched his head, her finger gently stroking the jet-black hair that swirled in tiny damp curls.

I called Charlie 'Idiot' because he was such a beautiful baby.

'Why are you calling him a name like that?' Mem glared at me and took him out of my arms. I'd said the word in Bengali but Cook, feeling spiteful, had translated it for her.

'It's to keep him safe from the evil eye,' I said. 'If we call him a bad name no one will envy us and the bad spirits will ignore him. They only take the best children.'

Mem grabbed a cloth and wiped away the big spot of soot I'd put on his forehead. It was a mark to make him ugly and divert the jealous looks of the neighbours, especially those of the old, thin Eurasian woman down the lane, who'd had nothing but daughters. I'd seen her sitting on her veranda, day after day, chewing *paan* with her few remaining teeth and looking at Miss Maisy as her belly grew rounder.

'His name's Charlie,' Mem said. 'And one day he'll be Mr Charles Brooks. It's a proper English name.'

It's a proper English name, I thought, but he's not a proper English colour. Although Memsahib had wiped the black spot from his face she couldn't wipe away the brown in his skin.

I didn't listen to Mem. She didn't understand our ways and she was ignorant of the danger. She was simple like that. So whenever I took Charlie to the roof and massaged him with oil in the sunshine, I smeared soot on his face and I whispered 'Idiot' in his ear. And when he was old enough, when his thin, newborn legs had plumped out and he could kick them with joy, he smiled back at me and laughed.

Mem got the latest news about the war from her customers. Some of the soldiers stationed in the city became clients, and a few of the old regulars still visited too, bringing tales of the latest battles. Donald Sahib, who was a supervisor in a jute mill and wore nothing but jute-wallah whites, had been a fixture in Mem's living room since the end of her romance with Percy Sahib. He hadn't been in her bed, though, for years. Mem said it was because Donald Sahib had a problem with his penis and that he now saved all his energy for talking and playing cards.

With an imperceptible nod of her head Mam ordered me to refill her gimlet and Donald Sahib's whisky and soda.

A faint breeze moved the blinds and the beaded curtains, and Mem leaned back in her chair. 'When's this bleedin' war going to end, Donald?' she asked, stubbing out her cigarette.

Donald Sahib took a deep breath. 'I dinnae ken,' he said in his jungly Scottish accent that was so difficult to understand I had to concentrate hard to make sense of it. 'The Japs are a fair way through Burma.' He swatted a mosquito struggling to find the skin under the tangle of thick grey hair on his arm, and then handed me his glass. 'Give us another wee bevvy, Pushpa,' he said.

Mem thought for a moment. 'They won't get to Calcutta, will they? For Christ's sake, we're safe here, aren't we?'

'I'm no sure, hen. It's tough in the jungle for our lads. The Japanese are used tae it, and they're vicious, canny bastards. I met some of our boys last week. They'd rescued half a dozen POWs. Poor buggers had been marching shackled at the ankles. I'm no' exaggerating, their skin had turned tae raw flesh. It was festering with maggots and reeked. One laddie lost both feet by the time they got him tae a field hospital. The rest were starving and they all had the shits; they'll be good for nothing for months.'

Mem frowned. 'Should we go up to Darjeeling? I couldn't live in Calcutta if it was a Japanese city.'

'What if it was Indian, lass?' Donald Sahib asked. 'One of the independence leaders has set up an Indian government in exile. He's joined the Japs. He's a Bengali – Bose. You've no' heard of him?'

'I haven't, though it doesn't surprise me. Bengal breeds traitors; I wouldn't trust one of them.' She glanced at me as if she'd forgotten I was there. 'Except for Pushpa, of course. She's as faithful as a . . .' She paused. 'She's as faithful as the day is long.'

Donald Sahib adjusted the electric fan on the table between them so that it faced him directly, the breeze filling his shirt through the gaping holes between the buttons. He radiated a smell of perspiration and the musty, mildewed smell of clothes that never dry thoroughly in the monsoon.

Mem put a perfumed handkerchief to her face, although it was clear Donald Sahib's sweat wasn't the only thing troubling her.

'God forbid we end up with an Indian government. We'd be better off in the hands of the Japs,' she said.

'Aye. Well, you'd better be getting yirself ready. India's going tae be run by Indians. People like us won't be welcome here any more.'

'That's years away, Donald. The Indians can't rule themselves. Didn't you hear about last week's right old ding-dong? A Hindu procession went past a mosque, and the Mohammedans got so upset by the music, they tore a Hindu shop apart. They took everything in the place and burned it down. The owner was lucky to escape with his life; half the bones in his body were broken.'

'All the same, Babs, I wouldn't bide my time here. Book the first passage home when the war's over. India won't be the same place. It'll be finished for us.'

For all Donald Sahib's gloomy predictions, and all the talk in the bazaar about Bose and his Indian Army, I couldn't imagine the British leaving. No one would have believed it if they'd seen the number of troops arriving, and the planes parked on Red Road. The wide avenue on which the British paraded up and down from the Maidan to Government House was turned into a runway. Upcountry men and even many city people looked on in surprise as the heart of Calcutta was transformed into an airfield. And if that wasn't enough to prove they were invincible, the grand buildings and mansions were still there to remind us that the British had been in India for so many years that no one could remember a time when they didn't rule. Even so, Donald Sahib's words made me nervous. I didn't want Mem to go back to England because how could I ever bear to be without Miss Maisy and Charlie?

Charlie grew plump and as good-natured as his mother.

'You're getting too heavy for me to do this,' Miss Maisy groaned as she lay on the bed lifting Charlie above her head. She put him down on the sheets and he wriggled and gurgled while she tickled his tummy.

'Mam says he looks like me,' she said, examining his face. 'What do you think, Pushpa? He doesn't look much like Sunil, does he?'

I agreed, though it was a lie: the child was the image of his father.

'People won't guess he's half-caste, will they?'

'Maybe not, Miss Maisy,' I said, trying to sound convincing. 'We can say he's been playing in the sun too long.' It was a foolish idea because no one would believe it: Charlie was as dark as his father and his great-grandmother, the long-forgotten wife of the bacon wallah.

The child fed again and fell into a deep sleep, milk dribbling from the corner of his mouth. His eyelashes fanned out on his cheeks, black and silky. Missy Maisy brushed her fingertips over them and curled her body around him so that they slept contented under the mosquito net.

Charlie was greedy over milk and when he was older he'd toddle around the house after me holding an enamel cup in his hand. 'Milk?' he pleaded.

'You've already had too much,' I said. He'd push the cup against my leg and I didn't have the strength to refuse him.

'Say "thank you",' I told him, as instructed by Mem.

'Tanch foo.' He grinned up at me and I was disarmed every time by his sparkling brown eyes that were flecked with green.

'Good boy, Charlie,' Mem said. 'Always remember your manners.' She turned to me. 'We're raising a gentleman, Pushpa, don't forget.'

As her plans for Miss Maisy hadn't worked out well, Mem was pinning her hopes on Charlie. Miss Maisy was unlikely to marry a rich man and be a lady. She had the good looks, and she'd read a lot of English books, but nothing was going to solve the problem of Charlie. No one could make him white or make him born from a marriage bed. Master Charlie marked Miss Maisy as a spoiled woman just about the time she stopped being a child, and with him in her arms, she lost the privilege of being white.

'We'll have him riding a horse the moment he can sit on a saddle,' Mem said. 'And we'll send him to the best school in the hills. You never know, we might make a fortune and he can go back home to be educated with the toffs.'

I didn't know where they would find the money for such an expense. Mem only just managed to pay the rent. Each year she had fewer customers and although the war had brought more clients to her door, they were poorer men, rarely returning for a second visit. It may have had something to do with Mem's thickening waist or the lines on her forehead; she was no longer the beauty Brooks Sahib had married. She kept her spirits up, though, by revitalising herself with her usual tonics.

'It'll kill you, Mam,' Miss Maisy said as she watched her mother pour another drink.

'Nonsense,' Mem answered, like a mantra. She looked at her daughter's worried face. 'Don't worry, love. My mam's got Scottish blood and my dad's family were Irish. They're hard drinkers and it never did them any harm. We've constitutions like iron.'

'And how do you know they are still alive, Mam? You've haven't had a letter from them in years.'

Mem paused as if the thought hadn't occurred to her, and downed her drink in one gulp.

The flesh trade in Calcutta had never been slow: there were too many men and too few women in the city for the business of selling sex to flag. The war only made a profitable trade more lucrative. Thousands of soldiers arrived in Calcutta, and many of them wanted entertaining. I visited Kamala on the eve of Dipaboli, making my usual detour so that no one in my respectable life should know I was associated with the brothel quarter and the shame with which it marks you.

Kamala, decked in yet more gold bangles, rings, chains and many long earrings, stood with her arms folded, cheerfully scolding two white soldiers.

'How much is the one with the big tits?' one asked in English, swaying and leaning on his friend.

'I like the one with the pretty face,' the other said, breathing whisky over me.

Kamala laughed and turned to me. 'In five minutes these two clowns will be asleep or sick. It's hardly worth me taking money from them.'

She took it all the same, pocketing four times the going rate for girls who'd been in the trade for a few years. She'd always been smart. That's why, though we'd started in this business at the same time, she'd ended up owning the brothel and I was a servant in someone else's house.

The gold glinted in Kamala's teeth. 'We can't get enough girls to cope with the demand,' she said, counting out her cash. 'We've had to bring in old women and it's a good job these Tommies are drunk; they can't tell they're not fresh. We've opened a place in Bowbazar for the white men and there are new houses on Ripon Street and Marquis Street. Sonagachi is for locals. It's out of bounds for the foreigners so I don't know why these fools came here. Maybe their rickshaw wallah is also drunk.'

Half a dozen girls wearing bright saris and heavy make-up sat on a long bench looking bored. One at the far end was rouged so heavily that I glanced a second time; the thick face paint only drew attention to the fact she was well past her prime.

We sat on the floor on a clean sheet and leaned against a

pile of misshapen cushions. A boy from the teashop skipped in with half a dozen cups of tea rattling on a tray.

Three more soldiers staggered through the door and glanced at the line of girls.

'Got any white ones?' They turned to Kamala but she looked at them without understanding.

'White?' they repeated. '*Goree?*'

This time she understood and I translated her reply for them.

'You'll find them on Karaya Road. It's in the white part of town. Ask for Madame Dubois.'

'Are they English girls?'

'A few. Most are Russians and Jews. There are some girls from Hong Kong, too. Lots of women from all over the world. You can take your pick.'

The men grunted. 'Let's go and find some pretty Jews. We'll try the Chinkie and Indian pussy another time.'

Kamala shook her head. 'The idiots will pay five times as much for a white girl. And that Madame Dubois is so stupid. I don't know why I'm sending her business: I'm such a good soul. She won't speak to people like me. She thinks she's better than us because she sells white cunts.'

Kamala glanced up and smiled at Samita, who stalked in followed by a servant weighed down with packages and a pile of new saris.

'The price of silk is up, Ma. They said it's because of the war but I reckon that sister-fucker of a tailor is a thief. He's taken some of the green silk, I'm sure of it. You can't trust anyone.' She pulled a wad of notes from her blouse and handed it to Kamala.

Even though she was middle-aged, Samita was still as striking her mother had been. The baby I'd played with and hidden under my bed while her mother entertained her customers had grown-up sons of her own.

Kamala ordered fried snacks from a stall near the end of the road. They were my favourite: *singaras,* pastry parcels filled with spicy potatoes and peas.

'Here, Pushpa Aunty, have more.' Samita pushed the paper bag soaked with oil in my direction and I took another helping.

I liked those times with Kamala and Samita. I loved being with Miss Maisy and Charlie, and the times I spent with Madan were some of the best in my life, but in Sonagachi I didn't have to pretend to be someone I wasn't. I was Pushparani, who many years before had been the prettiest, but not the wealthiest, girl in the brothel. That honour was Kamala's. And for a moment, while eating the *singaras* and the sweets that Samita unpacked from her pile of shopping, I felt a sharp stab of jealousy. I looked at Kamala's strong but worn features, at her mouth carefully painted in a dark shade of red and for a moment I wanted to be her. It was not her gold I envied, or the treasures she kept in a safety deposit box in the Imperial Bank of India. It was something much more precious; I envied Kamala her daughter. In Sonagachi, a daughter is your fortune. If Samita had been mine, she would have been my joy too.

Muslims eat a lot of meat. Madan said that's why they have so many children; it turns them lustful, like the animals they consume. His clients told him we had to take special care of our girls in the neighbourhood because everyone knew that a Muslim would rape a Hindu girl if he got the chance. I didn't believe a word of it. I'd met enough shameless Hindus raised on rice, dal and vegetables to know it wasn't only eating meat that stiffened a man's penis and made it go wandering where it didn't belong.

Behind New Market, the carcasses of cows and goats hung on big hooks in the shops of the Muslim butchers. Cook brought meat there, but I rarely walked through those lanes. The smell turned my stomach. I couldn't forgive the British for eating cows, even if their religion permitted it, but to my mind, the Muslims were worse because they knew how offensive cow-killing was to us Hindus. Madan said they did it on purpose, just to madden us, and I think he may have been right.

The yellow pye-dogs scavenging in the butchers' lanes were bigger and better fed than those in the rest of the city. They lazed by the open-fronted shops, satiated by the bits of gristle and twisted entrails that were shovelled into the gutter. Only a small portion of the butchered animals was discarded because the customers would eat almost everything else: liver, brains, testicles. It was sickening. I preferred fish every time; fish coated in spices and fried in mustard oil, or made into a curry with coconut milk, the flesh of the fish so tender that the pieces flaked and melted in my mouth.

In the days when food supplies were uninterrupted by war or famine, a food stall used to do good business a short distance from Armenian Street. The owner grew stouter by the year, sitting from mid-morning until late in the evening frying fish steaks and stirring vegetables that simmered in a fragrant sauce. I went there often and Charlie would sit on my lap, his fingers dipping into a bowl of rice and *machher jhol*, a spicy fish stew, as if he was a real Bengali boy and not just half of one.

I shouldn't have eaten so much but I have a weakness for

food, and although it bothered me that the fat around my stomach formed into rings that bulged beneath my blouse, I couldn't help myself. I knew every food stall and teashop in Calcutta and, because I was a regular customer, they always gave me a good deal, the choicest pieces and the most generous helpings. Madan laughed at us when we stood together, and we did indeed look a strange sight; he was so skinny, and I was rounder by the day.

'You're a rare thing in Bengal,' he joked. 'A big fat widow.'

'That's why I can never resist the temptation of food,' I said. 'I had a widow's diet for a year – a year of one meal a day and nothing but broken rice and a few vegetables. And I had to work from dawn to midnight. I was thinner than you.' It was a mean thing to say because, until he met me, Madan had a diet like that almost every day of his life. I made a point of spoiling him with leftovers from Mem's kitchen; I saved him Cook's special mutton curry because Madan had no qualms about eating meat. He said he was too poor to be fussy, and barbers didn't need to worry about keeping the rules of high-caste people because he didn't have much status to lose. He even ate the strange English plum duff pudding that I was horrified to find was made with cow fat. I was sorry I complained about my hungry widowhood to Madan, but the memory of it haunted me. It had remained engraved on my mind and in my behaviour as an irresistible urge: eat now, while you can.

Madan's wife and mother had a problem with their weight too, but for them the problem was the struggle to keep enough flesh on their bodies to prevent them fading to nothing. His mother developed sores where she rested against the floor, her bones pressing against her skin, thinning it as if the sharp edges of her skeleton wanted to break out of its dry casing. By the time she died she was the size of an emaciated child. I went with Madan to the ghats on the Ganga and I watched from a distance as she burned on her funeral pyre. Madan garlanded the old woman with flowers and then stood and looked on intently as the flames devoured her body. One of her hands poked out of the fire, refusing to burn, and the *doms* tending the pyres used long poles to push her limbs under the wood. By the end of the afternoon she was reduced to ash and was brushed into the Ganga, a cloud of grey quickly merging into the brown river. How long would it be, I thought, before Madan's invalid wife would follow her mother-in-law and become dust swept away towards the sea? Not long, I hoped. Not long.

I stopped recounting my year of hungry widowhood in the hot season, a few months after Charlie was born. Hunger had gnawed at my innards, and that was bad enough. It didn't kill me the way it did the wretches piled high on Calcutta's burning ghats in 1943.

The dying began arriving in the city when the weather was still cool. Donald Sahib said the war was responsible; supplies of rice were cut off and wicked merchants were hoarding food in godowns while they waited for the prices to rise. Peasants in the countryside were starving.

'Villagers in the *mofussil* are selling their children,' he exclaimed. 'I read it in the paper. But even if they sell them, there's no food tae buy.'

Mem shivered. 'Poor people. The Government needs to take charge.'

If the Government did take charge, I couldn't see any benefit; the city was descending into a nightmare. When I rode down Bentinck Street in a rickshaw, a big yellow pye-dog strutted by, its tail held high, the victor in some recent battle. I glanced, and then looked again more carefully, not believing what I saw. The headless body of a baby dangled from the dog's mouth.

By the hottest part of the summer, people lay on the streets, shrunken by lack of food and desiccated by the baking sun. Calcutta stank from rotting bodies and municipal carts trawled the streets collecting corpses. Outside the hospitals, crowds fought over the contents of the bins, digging through the dressings to find scabs and diseased tissue to eat, cramming bandages soaked with blood and pus into their mouths.

The city's pye-dogs grew fat. Vultures sat on bloated, bleached corpses floating down the Ganga, pecking first at the eyes and the soft bellies. Near Outram Ghat I walked around a ragged woman sitting against a wall with her naked baby. The woman cradled the child, its face pressed against her flat, empty breast. She gazed down at her daughter, motionless, her skin pulled so tight over her skull she looked as if she was smiling. Flies crawled over the fluids oozing from the cracks in her flesh. She must have died several hours before. I stopped and took the baby, prizing her out of her mother's stiffening embrace. I couldn't have left her to die like that.

Miss Maisy gasped when she saw the shrivelled child, as different from her plump son as it was possible to be. She tried to feed her but the baby was too weak to suckle. I put a few drops of milk into her mouth but she regurgitated them moments later, until even that was too much effort and the milk must have dripped into her lungs. A faint gurgling came from her chest and we gathered around her wondering whether she was dead. She had hovered between life and death for so many hours that one state was almost indistinguishable from the other.

When her body was cold, I gave her to the corpse collectors and they tossed her on to the back of the cart. She disappeared among the jumble of rags and sharp bones, and I couldn't bring myself to cry for her; it was too shocking. The city was like that during the famine; a place of dread and very few tears.

I didn't go hungry and most city people escaped starvation; it was Bengal's villagers who died in their millions. Mem had a wartime ration card that provided enough food for us all. She was generous with her supplies, too. She gave flour and rice to Cook to send to his family and, when she was especially good-tempered after enjoying a lot of gimlets at lunch, she even handed out some of her favourite tinned sausages to a neighbouring family of very poor Eurasians. It was an unusual gesture because she had never spoken to them before nor said a good word about them.

'They're very brown,' she told Miss Maisy when they'd first moved into the street. 'They can't have any white blood in them. They're probably untouchables who've converted to Christianity and think that makes them British.'

She forgot her generosity the day after donating the food and called Cook in to see her.

'You're a thieving bastard. I had four tins of sausages last week and now there are only two.'

Cook shook his head, protesting his innocence. He'd have his revenge for the unjust accusation. He always did. He'd increase his cut from the day's shopping allowance and take a few more annas. Mem guessed he pocketed some of the house-keeping money because all the cooks did it, and there was nothing their memsahibs could do about it.

The Eurasian family was grateful. They called to Mem in the street but she'd forgotten she'd been into their home. She gave them a blank stare and tutted.

'This is bloody awful,' Mem said, putting a handkerchief over her nose as we passed another body that had lain for hours on the corner of the road. 'It's worse than the Black Hole of Calcutta. The bloody Japs will rot in hell for this.'

I'd heard it wasn't just the bloody Japs who'd caused such terrible suffering: it was the British and some of our own leaders who worked with them. They dismissed all the warning signs and no one listened to the horror stories from the villages. The famished peasants flooding into the city were ignored and the Government didn't feed the dying, even when those who were still alive were being eaten by dogs on the streets. They didn't care about the starving while they themselves ate in the city's restaurants and cooks prepared their breakfasts, tiffins and *burra khanas* – their big dinners – troubled only by a shortage of sugar. I hoped those people banqueting in Government House would rot like the piles of dead dumped and decomposing by the building's grand, lion-topped entrances. I detested them more than I detested my daughters-in-law from long ago. I wanted them to share the fate of the tiny girl we tried to save and who ended up, tossed as if she were a piece of rubbish, into the corpse collector's cart.

Chapter Five
Maisy

GIRLS LIKE ME didn't go to the Grand Hotel. I didn't have the right clothes, and I definitely didn't want to go to a dance with Mam after she'd swigged a pint of gin before we even left the house. I worried she'd embarrass me and that my new American uncle would notice she'd been drinking. I was relieved when I saw her balance was sound and that she walked to the taxi with a jaunty kick of her red heels. She didn't often get leglessly drunk in those days. I think she must have built up a tolerance for it, and few people would guess she'd been on the bottle if it wasn't for a trace of it mixing with the smell of mint imperials on her breath. I was harder to fool: I could spot it immediately because her face became slack and she looked her age.

'What if someone asks me to dance?' I asked Mam while we rummaged through her old dresses searching for something suitable for me to wear. My training in feminine skills had been patchy and hadn't included any instruction in dancing. Although Mam whirled me round the living room a few times, the furniture left no room for spinning or any other complicated

Louise Brown

manoeuvres, and Mam ended up tripping on the rug and stumbling awkwardly over the arm of the sofa.

'That's not the way to do it,' she cackled, pulling her dress back down over her knickers.

In the car, an old jalopy driven by a large, bad-tempered Sikh at breakneck speed, Mam told me to be calm and not fuss. 'Just follow the man. Let him lead you across the floor.' She put her arm around me. 'Trust me, Maisy, with a figure like yours no one will be bothered about what your feet are doing.'

We pulled up with a squeal of brakes outside the Grand Hotel's arcade on Chowringhee and Mam laughed far too loudly as we walked into the hotel past the magnificently dressed *durwan* and the porters in starched, white uniforms. Three American GIs watched us and grinned. They said something to Mam and she turned to me, eyebrows raised, and mouthed, 'Queer accents.'

It was the best time of day, the late afternoon sun giving way to a warm, hazy dusk. It was my favourite time of year too, on the cusp of the seasons when the spring weather turns almost overnight into months of scorching heat. The hotel courtyard was crammed with British Tommies and American servicemen, the place filled with cheery voices and laughter. Above us, high on the dusty palm trees, crows cawed and every now and then one swooped over the heads of the guests and landed with an angry flap of black feathers. They strutted on the grass, waiting impatiently to be thrown scraps of food. The more brazen jumped on tables when the guests left and pecked at the plates in the few moments before the bearers arrived to clear the mess.

Chandeliers sparkled as lights were switched on in the bedrooms surrounding the courtyard. I was thrilled by the splendour of it all, and the sheer energy generated by so many jolly people. I counted my blessings, happy to be in white town among the well fed and well heeled.

'You'd never know there was a war on,' Mam said, eyeing the food. 'Though I reckon these soldiers are a dead giveaway.' She winked at me and my heart sank: she was scouting for new business.

We found the American uncle buying a round of drinks in the jam-packed Casanova Bar where the beer flowed freely and tension was brewing between American and British troops. The uncle complained about the quality of the local whisky: he said he liked something smoky and southern, and his companions laughed, slapping him on the back and telling him the war would soon be over. Uncle Donald told Mam you could get good imported stuff on the black market but it cost a fortune and so Mam never bothered. She stuck to the local brews, even for her customers. I hoped she wouldn't buy anything special for the American. I didn't like him, especially the way his nostrils flared when he shouted.

'Drink gimlets,' Mam advised him. 'You can drown the gin with a dollop of sugar and a big twist of lime.'

The uncle wasn't impressed with the gimlet the barman handed him. I don't think he was impressed by Mam either, but there were so few white women around that even the plainest girl had a dozen men at her beck and call. You'd have to be seriously old and as ugly as a pig to be a white wallflower in Calcutta in 1944.

The Eurasian girls were in demand too, and that night the Casanova bar was full of them.

'Look what a spectacle they're making of themselves, trying to trap a decent white boy and go home as a war bride,' Mam said, and glared around the room at the pretty girls with their caramel skins and dark eyes. Her gaze settled on the far corner of the bar and she huffed. 'Filthy old tarts,' she said, motioning to three European women who were drinking with American men. They must have been in their forties but were dressed like twenty-year-old chorus girls. 'Wherever the army goes, the prostitutes follow,' she said to me. The uncle raised his eyebrows, flared his nostrils and laughed in Mam's face as if she'd made the most hilarious joke. I shuddered: he was the most revolting uncle since the plaque-toothed Uncle Jim and the vicious child-molester, Bill, who I no longer dignified with the title 'uncle'.

A group of GIs, boisterous with drink, hollered across the bar to two Eurasian girls who were getting chummy with a couple of British sergeants.

'Yoo-hoo. Come and join us, ladies,' they shouted.

The girls giggled and, picking up their evening bags, they said goodbye to the Tommies. One of the men reddened.

'He thought he had a bed for the night,' Mam said.

'Our guys have more money,' the uncle said. 'And they know how to treat a lady.'

'They're no ladies,' Mam added, and was about to say something else when the red-faced sergeant launched himself across the bar, knocked over a table, and rammed into one of the GIs. The girls screamed, dropping their glasses. In the corner the white prostitutes took their attention away from their drinking companions. The management weighed in to the brawl but not before the sergeant had been punched to the floor and the GIs had kicked him several times in the head.

'Let's get you ladies out of here,' the uncle said, ushering us out, his hand resting on my bottom.

Outside the bar, we heard the fight continue.

'Who'd have thought it could happen in the Grand Hotel?' Mam said.

'There's too much hooch and too few dames,' the uncle said. 'Five hundred Americans are billeted here so the Tommies don't stand a chance.' He grinned. 'You like that tune?' he asked.

A band was playing in the ballroom. 'You wanna dance?' I thought he was speaking to Mam, but he was looking at me. Mam looked surprised, and then her expression changed to confusion. I didn't know why he was asking me to dance when Mam was his guest. Americans, though, were known to lack manners, and so perhaps his rudeness was only to be expected.

'What's this song?' I said.

'It's Glenn Miller,' he said. 'Gee, they said you Brits in India were behind the times. They weren't kidding.' He grasped my hand. 'Come on.'

I looked in panic at Mam but she didn't notice: she'd regained her composure and diverted her attention to a couple of middle-aged British men who'd arrived at the hotel dressed in tweed jackets.

'Jute wallahs,' she whispered to me, breathing cigarette smoke in my face. 'They're Scottish but filthy rich. I could be made.'

I stood frozen with nerves as Mam talked to the men. She said something amusing to them, and they all enjoyed the joke.

'We're going for dinner in the Prince's Room. Would you like to join us?' one of the men said. He was tall and pink-skinned, and he glanced at me several times while talking to Mam, who was taking long drags from her cigarette, the butt thickly coated with crimson lipstick. 'It's quieter in there,' he said. 'No riff-raff permitted.'

'Maisy's just going to dance with this gentleman,' Mam said, chivvying me in the American's direction. 'But I'd love to join you.' She winked at me and walked into the restaurant without looking back. As the GI seemed to have given up on her, she'd set her sights on a bigger prize.

Mam had been right. The American didn't complain when I stepped on his shoes and after an hour in the ballroom I thought I'd got the hang of dancing. It was more difficult to judge the tempo when the scrawny French star appeared. She'd seen better days. One of the guests, an ancient English gent who must have seen better days himself, said she wouldn't be performing at the Grand, or in any decent Calcutta cabaret, if it wasn't for the war. She couldn't go home because her country was full of Germans, and only a few stars were doing what was left of the Far Eastern club circuit. Thanks to Hitler and the Japs' U-boats, no fresh faces were coming out to replace the tired acts.

I escaped from the big American by pretending to go to the ladies' powder room, and instead I hid next to a couple of officers who were looking over a circular balcony into the hotel lounge. A massive chandelier illuminated the guests below. Mam was playing cards with the jute wallahs and being so friendly you'd think they'd known her for years. The pink-faced man glanced up at me and waved. His hair was sandy blond, and from my vantage point thirty feet above their table I could see the bald patch on the top of his head was burned cherry red.

When he joined me a few minutes later, I couldn't see the

sunburn because he towered over me, bigger than the American and fatter too, his shirt taut around his stomach. The officers beat a retreat.

'Your mother plays poker very well. I've left her making light work of my friend. Poor Harris has had too many *burra pegs* to know what he's doing. Do you play, too?' he asked in a Scottish burr. He sounded a bit like Uncle Donald but was much easier to understand.

'I never learned.'

'A wise decision. British women in Calcutta spend too long gossiping and playing bridge.'

Mam did plenty of things in addition to playing cards and gossiping, but I didn't think it polite to list them.

'Do you play tennis?' he asked.

'I've never been on a tennis court.'

'I can introduce you to a very good coach at the Tolly.'

I murmured something about my busy life, omitting to mention the cause of the busyness; Charlie and the making of a gentleman.

'Are you Scottish?' I asked.

'Aye, I'm definitely no Sassenach,' he laughed. 'And with that accent you must be from . . . where? Let me guess; is it Cardiff?'

I was baffled.

'Shall we dance?' He offered me his hand and led me into the ballroom. The French singer warbled, the band played, and Mam's new friend pulled me towards him.

'I'm Gordon MacBrayne,' he said. 'And I'm in jute.'

'I'm Maisy,' I replied while thinking, I'm in trouble.

He radiated heat, his sweat seeping through my dress, and I

imagined how much more he'd perspire in the monsoon. We moved around the floor, his breath heavy on the top of my head. I was sure the style Pushpa had worked so carefully to create would be spoiled and that my hair would lie flat and damp against my scalp. The music stopped and he took a step back, studying me, and I felt even more uncomfortable, as if I were half naked. This man was Mam's new friend, and I wasn't sure I wanted him to be mine too.

'You're a bonnie lassie, but you've the footwork of a heifer,' he said bluntly.

The music restarted and he drew me closer, guiding me, sometimes towing me, up and down the length of the ballroom.

'I'll teach you to dance, Maisy,' he said more gently, 'so you really will be the belle of the ball.'

'I look like a frump,' I said, staring at my reflection in the mirror.

'Don't be ridiculous,' Mam snapped. 'The *darzi*'s done a good job on this frock. You wouldn't know it used to be mine.'

'Everyone can see it's my mam's cast-off. This style was in fashion before I was born.'

Mam rooted through the pile of clothes on the bed.

'God damn those bleeding moths,' she said. Half a dozen big holes had been munched through her favourite winter dress – the blue one she couldn't squeeze into any longer.

I ran my hands over my waist; the last visible sign of my pregnancy had vanished.

'He'll never guess,' Mam said.

Charlie cried in the other room and Pushpa began singing

to him. I moved towards the door, meaning to kiss him good night.

'There's no time,' Mam said, shoving her evening bag into my hand. 'The taxi's here.'

I hesitated.

'You'll be fine. There's no need to be nervous. He'll be good for us: jute wallahs are loaded. He's not an ordinary supervisor like Donald. He runs the whole bloody shebang.'

'Do you think he'll take me to Firpo's?'

Mam scowled. She'd not been to Firpo's, Calcutta's finest restaurant, for years, not since she'd become disgracefully drunk with a client and careered into a table where a *burra sahib* was hosting a luncheon party. After being barred from the restaurant she'd taken against it, damning its crystal chandeliers and brilliant white tablecloths as old-fashioned, and the clientele as stiff and stuck-up. She didn't fool me: I knew she longed to eat prawn mayonnaise and drink French wine on the veranda overlooking Chowringhee as dusk fell and the fairy lights sparkled.

'He won't take you there,' she said. 'Half of Calcutta would see you and what would he tell his wife? He might take you for a chinkie feast at the Nanking Restaurant, although I bet you'll go to a shebeen off Park Street.' She brushed some imaginary dirt from my shoulder. 'Don't go anywhere with him after dinner. Get straight back here. Understand? Don't let him take you for a drive down the Gariahat Road. They all try that one. They say they'd love to go for a romantic drive to the Dakaria Lakes when all they want is to stop in a dark lane and get inside your knickers. Believe me, Maisy, he'll only have one thing on his mind, and you've got to keep him waiting for it.'

I nodded and took some deep breaths to calm my nerves. I wasn't anxious about the jute wallah's designs on my body: I was far more worried about using the right cutlery.

My first date with Gordon was in a smoky, dimly lit club on a road off Park Street where white men were dining with beautiful Eurasian girls. The manager led us across the restaurant. 'Your usual table, sir,' he said.

'You're looking bonnie,' Gordon said as we sat down.

I smoothed the worn cotton of my dress. 'It's the very latest thing. The design is straight from home.'

The cabaret began and Gordon motioned to a buxom singer. 'That Russian lass is a belter. The shows are much better than they used to be. When I first came out to India they wouldn't allow European women on stage. They thought it would send the wrong message to the Indians.'

The bearer filled my glass from a bottle in the middle of the table. I took a sip and grimaced.

'You're not wanting a drink?' Gordon asked.

'I hate the taste.'

'And I suppose you don't smoke either?' He offered me a cigarette from an engraved silver cigarette case that reminded me of Father's.

'Maybe I'll start,' I said, taking one.

Gordon caught the eye of the bearer hovering near the table. 'Pineapple juice for the memsahib.' He glanced at the menu and ordered food for both of us. 'I promise you will like everything,' he said.

He studied my face. 'Are you new to Calcutta? You're not new to India – not with your accent.'

'I was born here in Calcutta.'

'Aye, right. And where did you go to school? La Martiniere, or maybe somewhere in the hills? There are some very good schools, though I'm told they've been spoiled by admitting too many Eurasians.'

'I was taught at home.'

'By a governess and private tutors?'

'Something like that.' I had a sudden vision of Mr Banerjee with his head in his hands, and Sunil and his harsh lessons in love.

Gordon stopped eating. 'But why haven't I seen you before? You're far too pretty to be invisible. Calcutta is swarming with natives but we know almost every British person living here. In some ways it's a small place.'

I had a feeling Gordon was playing games with me. Surely he knew we wouldn't be admitted to the members' enclosure at the racecourse or be invited to receptions at Government House. For God's sake, I thought, couldn't he see I was wearing a poor girl's dress? He'd spent over an hour with Mam, during which time he must have seen her down half a dozen *burra pegs*, so he was certain to know we'd never be welcome at the Tollygunge, or even the Saturday Club, for that matter.

'I don't go out much, and I've been busy lately,' I said.

He cocked his head to one side. 'Busy with a fiancé, perhaps? Though I see you're not wearing a ring.'

'I'm not engaged.' I put my hands under the table.

'There's another man, though, I'm sure of it.'

'Yes, a very small one.' I felt sick; perhaps it was the cigarette. 'I have a son,' I blurted out. 'Charlie.'

'And your husband?'

119

'He died. In Burma.'

'I'm sorry to hear it. The war's taking so many of our best young men.'

We ate in silence and I hoped he wouldn't ask questions about my imaginary husband: I hadn't thought of a name for him. It was bothering me, too, that I should feel ashamed for not being married when Gordon was the one who should be blushing: he had a wife and I was young enough to be his daughter.

'And will Charlie mind if I take you out?'

'He's one year old.'

'I was pulling your leg. Forgive me.'

'Mam told me you had a wife. Does she mind you taking girls to dinner?'

He sighed as if he'd heard the question many times before. 'She won't care, providing she doesn't know. If anyone here asks, I'll say you're my niece. But they won't ask. It's not done, not in a club like this. Calcutta is full of scandal; it reeks of it, but it's all done on the quiet and no one speaks about it publicly. The British pretend to be terrible prudes and to be beyond reproach when in fact they're all having affairs. What's important is the way these matters are handled. That's the rule for us British: things have to look right.'

He's like Mam's regulars, I thought. Soon he'll be telling me his wife doesn't understand him.

'Maude and I lead separate lives. She spends a lot of the year in Dundee so she can see the boys when they're on holiday from school. And when she comes here she bolts to Darjeeling at the first opportunity. She hates India, even in the cold season. She can't tolerate the filth.'

'Why don't you go back home with her?'

'My work's here, and the Dundee jute industry's no friend of Calcutta. We're competitors, and Calcutta is winning hands down. I like to win, Maisy, and when I return I can guarantee I'll have few supporters in my home town. My business went through a bad patch after the Depression but it's doing better now. War's always good for jute: the military needs millions of sandbags and tents. I made a fortune during the last war, and the world's crops are still packed in gunnies and hessian from my mills. I'll be in jute until the day the Germans invent a synthetic replacement. Besides, I like the life here.'

'It's better than Scotland?'

'India's been good to me. I grew up in a Dundee tenement where we had no running water and we shared a lavvie with ten other families. My father worked in a shipbuilding yard and my mother was a jute weaver, and somehow they scraped together enough money to send me on a scholarship to the Technical Institute. I came out to India when I was seventeen and grafted for a year as a clerk in a mill ten miles downstream. After that I came to Calcutta as a broker in a managing agency. I made some good investments, worked my way up the agency and started out on my own. By 1928 I ran three jute mills, a coal mine in Assam and had steamers to transport my jute.'

'You were lucky.'

'It's got nothing to do with luck, Maisy. I'm canny and I work from dawn to dusk, six days a week. I'll even work on the Sabbath when I have to.'

Gordon liked talking about himself and it was much easier to listen to him than to concoct some story about myself.

'Mam says you're very important and that everyone in Calcutta knows you.'

121

'I've an influential position in the Indian Jute Manufacturers' Association, and I work behind the scenes in the Bengal Chamber of Commerce. I pull a lot of strings.'

'Do you know the Governor and Mr Gandhi?'

Gordon stopped eating. He pointed his spoon at me, the chocolate sauce dripping on to the tablecloth.

'I'm not well acquainted with those gentlemen. And I'm thinking you and your mother might have the wrong impression. I don't mix with the Governor and his friends. They look down on men like me. The politicos in London and the pen pushers in the Indian Civil Service despise us because we get our hands dirty in trade and industry. But the eejits forget that if they didn't have taxes from businesses like mine they wouldn't be able to run their bloody Raj and be able to afford to sit round talking politics. Without our money, they couldn't keep their fucking jewel in the crown.'

The people at the next table stopped eating and turned to watch Gordon, his voice loud above the Russian woman's gusty singing.

'Thirty-five years after I arrived in India, I've a mansion in Alipore, a swimming pool, a dozen servants and my sons are being educated in the best private school in Edinburgh. That's why I'm not going home any time soon.' He was sitting upright, staring at me intently, and I'm sure he'd grown six inches as he spoke. The jute wallah was not a man to be trifled with: he knew what he wanted and, at that moment, it was me.

Gordon sweated like a beast when we had sex. Perhaps that was why he was so particular about undressing before he climbed on top of me. He placed his shoes by the bed, draped his shirt carefully over a coat hanger, and hung his hot-weather, washable suit in the wardrobe. It was good we didn't stay long in the room at the Great Eastern Hotel because, if we had, his clothes would've been impregnated with the smell of mothballs, and that would have been a pity because Gordon's one concession to vanity was to wear Caron's *Pour un Homme* cologne and the reek of camphor would have detracted from the expensive fragrance. Gordon may have grunted and perspired like a labourer in that hotel room, but he smelled like a gentleman.

Although he lacked charm and didn't possess a single romantic bone in his body, Gordon was unfailingly, spectacularly generous. Only a week or two after our dinner date in the smoky club, he gave me a string of pearls and a gold bracelet from Hamilton and Co. Mam stroked the silk-lined boxes, inspecting the gifts, turning them over and looking for hallmarks. She approved.

'He's got good taste. It obviously isn't always true what they say about tight-fisted Scots.'

I wondered if many British ladies spent their afternoons in hotels, and whether they arrived in dark sunglasses and large hats, and signed in under false names. I looked at Gordon in the half-light of the shuttered room and studied the pale, squashy belly, and the big droopy penis that was never quite hard enough, and it made me think that even a respectable woman like his wife might have found herself being unfaithful with one of the dashing young officers the war brought to Calcutta. But if Maude were to appear in disguise at the Great Eastern, I knew she would have been motivated by desire rather than the hope that her family would be saved from eviction. Mam hadn't paid the rent for three months, so the pearls had come in handy at the pawnbrokers.

'Thank God we met Gordon when we did,' Mam said with relief. 'We'd be living in a shack if it wasn't for those pearls. Ask him for some gems – emeralds or something. They'll do us nicely.'

I didn't ask: I got my gems without making a hint, and I didn't complain when they were rubies rather than emeralds.

'I'll put them on for you,' Gordon said, opening the shutters so the light shone directly on me. I was sitting at the dressing table in my underwear. He stood behind me, fully dressed again, and placed the chain around my neck, fastening it clumsily so the fine hairs in the nape of my neck caught in the clasp. The ruby and diamond pendant was set in delicate gold filigree and the matching earrings were smaller versions, clusters of stones that caught the sun and glittered in the oval mirror. They were beautiful and expensive, and as I admired my reflection I realised with dismay and resignation that I was turning into my mother. If I ever introduced Gordon to Charlie, I'd have to say he was an 'uncle'.

Gordon interrupted my train of thought. 'Wear them on Saturday. I'm taking you to dinner.'

'Is that a good idea? Isn't your wife back?'

'Maude's still in Darjeeling. She'll be away until October.'

'Thank you for these,' I said, cupping the pendant in my hand. 'They are beautiful and I don't know what I've done to deserve them.'

He shrugged, rarely knowing the right thing to say.

Our routine was to leave the hotel at the same time, though never together. Gordon's car collected him and I watched Jamal, the liveried chauffeur, salute a little too enthusiastically, making an effort to stand so straight that he bent backwards. Most afternoons, I climbed into a rickshaw for the short ride to the

house, the little wiry men who pulled me thankful not to have
a couple of fat matrons to haul around the city. I gave them a
few extra annas because it made me feel better about the way
they panted with the effort, and less guilty about the sight of
their cracked feet on the road. If it was late and the heat was
fading from the day, I walked, sometimes passing the road to
Dharmatala and continuing down Chowringhee. The walk
cleared my mind. I liked jostling through the congested streets
around New Market, hawkers shoving goods into my path and
offering me anything I could have wanted.

'Look, madam, real gold cigarette case.'

'See my shop. Best embroider shawls.'

'Herbal essence for men. Satisfaction for your wife guaranteed.'

'Mem, a moment please. You like Bengal tiger? Look at
the perfect teeth and no mark on him.' I examined the skin, the
glass eyes and the hole where the bullet ended his life. Looking
at him made me shiver, although I knew Mam would have
appreciated a treasure like him on the balcony. I considered it
for a while and decided not to buy: the white ants and mildew
would soon destroy him and we'd be wiser spending the money
on rent. His presence would also be guaranteed to encourage
Uncle Donald's fantastic tales about how he'd heroically slain
man-eating tigers that had stolen little Indian babies from under
their mothers' noses.

In the monsoon my dresses clung to me during those walks
home from the Great Eastern, and I was glad war shortages
meant we weren't obliged to wear stockings. Before the war,
women who went out of their homes without stockings were
called floozies, or Indian. By the time I got back to our lane
in Dharmatala, I was a bright shade of pink, my face shiny, my

hair wet at the roots. The interior of the house was cool and dark, and it was a relief to close the door on the muggy city. I went straight to the tap and, stripping off my clothes, I crouched naked on the flagstone. I turned on the cistern, the tepid water flowing down a rag Pushpa had tied to the tap. It spread over the floor in a succession of shallow, circular waves, and I dipped my fingers in it, spoiling the pattern. I pulled off the rag so the water gushed, splashing over my legs. I stuck my head under the flow and it streamed down my back. Pushpa came in silently and stood beside me, the bottom edges of her sari lifted off the floor. She'd filled half a dozen pitchers with water ready for my bath, and I squatted with shampoo in my hair and my skin lathered with Mam's best lavender soap while she poured them slowly, one by one, over my head.

Our road wasn't safe in the monsoon. Rain filled the potholes, disguising their depth, and although the puddle at the end of the lane looked shallow, the still surface hid an open sewer from which water spurted in a three-foot-high geyser during every storm. The slurry left on the street smelled vile and we walked cautiously, Charlie toddling in his first pair of real leather shoes, and steered by Pushpa around the biggest turds.

Gordon shouldn't have let his chauffeur drive down the lane in August. The Bentley's wheels couldn't find any traction in the mud and poor Jamal became flustered, revving the engine uncontrollably, large beads of sweat sprouting on his forehead.

'Do it slowly,' Gordon instructed.

The wheels spun, sending two lines of muddy spray behind the car and drenching a porter who staggered past, a four-foot-wide bale of material on his head. The tendons in his neck were taut with exertion and though he flinched at the sticky, brown shower he didn't have the strength to lift his eyes and complain, or to stop and wipe the mess from his legs. He had to keep moving to maintain his momentum.

'Try reverse, man,' Gordon shouted at the nervous driver. 'Try some finesse. You have to treat the car like a woman. Do it gently.' I wondered why he never listened to his own advice.

The reprimands worked and the car rose slowly and then, freed from the sewer, it suddenly sped backwards.

'Maisy, it's appalling you live in such a place,' Gordon stated, transferring his annoyance from the driver to the surrounding streets. 'It's squalid and the whole neighbourhood floods if a dog so much as lifts its hind leg.' He pointed in the direction of the flat where Margaret and her family had lived before they packed up and moved south to a better area. 'That place is as bad as the worst tenements in Dundee. It might not be black town but it's not far off. There'll be no decent British families here, just a lot of Eurasians and good-for-nothing Anglo-Indians down on their luck. I bet there are Hindus here as well. And look,' he said, pointing to a man with a big beard who was disappearing into a nearby house, 'Muslims, too.'

'It's not bad,' I replied defensively. 'The street's not pukka, but it's nice inside the house. I'll show you some day. We've a little courtyard in the middle of the building and we can see half of Calcutta from the roof.'

He placed his hand on top of mine and held it tight.

We drove down Chowringhee, past the great ugly pile of masonry that was the Indian Museum, and turned into Park

Street. The showrooms that had been filled with plush cars before the war were empty and although the posh shops were still busy they were filled with soldiers, not prosperous memsahibs. A long line of GIs queued outside the condom distribution point, and a small group of people gathered outside the Oxford Bookshop, probably for the visit of one of the city's many intellectuals who would be reading from his latest work.

'I lived there when I was small,' I said, pointing up a side road to where Queen Alexandra Mansions once stood.

The car turned south into the streets where, a hundred years before, rich Britons used to live before they moved to more fashionable Ballygunge and Alipore. The old British quarter was not as grand as it used to be: some of the big mansions needed a lick of paint; some were in a state of disrepair, great chunks of plaster missing from their walls; others had been knocked down and replaced by smaller, modern houses or blocks of flats. It was still, however, recognisably white town. We continued, crossing Theatre Street, and drove into a lane.

'Slow down,' Gordon called to Jamal.

I looked to see why we were stopping. A red bougainvillaea hung over a white wall and a *durwan* in uniform stood to attention by glossy black gates. Spotting the car approaching, he rushed to open them. As we pulled into the drive bordered by trees and flowers, he saluted.

'This isn't your home, is it?' I asked Gordon.

'No, it's yours. And one day I'll tell you about the fight I had to stop it being requisitioned by the army.'

I got out of the car and looked at the grand old house, at its verandas and the big, newly painted shutters. I walked over the finely cut lawn.

'Do you like it?' he asked in satisfaction, anticipating my answer. 'It has hot water in the bathrooms and the very latest refrigerator.'

'Yes,' I gasped. 'I love it.'

For the first time in my life, I was going to live in a house with a beautiful garden.

Chapter Six

Pushpa

MISS MAISY HAD found herself a big, fat catch. The new sahib was an ugly man, in the way only a red-faced Britisher can be, but he was rich, and he kept her in the luxury of a garden house in Sahib-para, the old neighbourhood of the sahibs. The bathrooms had copper and brass geysers that gave you hot water whenever you needed it, and the toilets were the latest pull-and-let-go style, which meant we no longer had to call the sweeper to empty a thunderbox.

'Can you believe it, Pushpa?' Miss Maisy asked, skipping from room to room like a happy child.

'I always knew my girl would be a lady and live in a grand house,' Mem said, avoiding the truth that Miss Maisy was not a respectable lady. Madan had been right. Mem had passed her trade to her daughter and, thankfully, she was proving more successful at it than her mother.

Mem wiped a tear from her eye, breathed deeply and surveyed the garden from the upstairs veranda. Her gaze lingered on the lawn and flowerbeds, and she marvelled at the monkey and mango trees, and the spectacular red bougainvillaea. She saw the gardener bending down to weed a row of vegetables and she clapped her hands.

'There's so much land it's almost like a park,' she crowed.

'Will we all live here, Miss Maisy?' I asked. 'Or will it just be you and the sahib?'

Mem's expression changed instantly, as if she hadn't considered the prospect of her daughter leaving home. Perhaps the sahib would want Miss Maisy all to himself and we'd be left in the ramshackle house next door to the Eurasians and poor whites.

'I told him I wouldn't come here by myself. How could I be without Charlie and Mam and you? It wouldn't be home.'

I whispered a prayer of thanks. All my years of *puja* hadn't been in vain; I still had somewhere to live.

Life was easier for me in the big house. The sahib wanted everything to be perfect – or perfect to his mind – and he set about recruiting servants. We had a Nepali *durwan*, Lakshman, to guard us, and Ram, the *mali*, came with the house. He was a small, wiry man, grown old with the garden he'd tended since he was a boy. A *dhobi* visited twice a week and wrapped up the dirty linen in a giant bundle that he carried on his head. He'd return a couple of days later but not always with the same things. I'm sure half the clothes used by the British in Calcutta must have belonged to someone else; their things went around in circles.

MacBrayne Sahib gave us a bearer from his home in Alipore to organise the household. He was called Atul, and I didn't like him. He wore a starched white *achkan* – a knee-length jacket – and trousers, and his turban, with a fan at its peak, sat on hair that was shiny with brilliantine. It matched his large, curving

131

moustache that he oiled until it shone. He spent a lot of time in the *bottle khana,* the serving room next to the dining room, watching and listening, a spy in our midst. I'm sure he thought he was a sahib himself and he ordered me around like I was his servant. He was rude to me, using the impolite form of 'you' as if I were a slave or a dog, and when we gathered to receive our wages, he'd edge me to the back of the queue, behind the sweeper, with a couple of sharp jabs of his elbow. I had a feeling he knew me from long ago.

'You need a new cook,' Sahib stated one day as he took tiffin with Miss Maisy. He wiped his mouth carefully on his napkin. 'I don't like the way your man does mulligatawny soup; too much pepper. His food's a wee bit too Indian for my taste.'

Mem stopped the sahib as he was leaving. 'Cook's been with us for years,' she complained. 'He may be a thieving, bad-tempered bastard but his plum cake is better than the ones from the Jewish bakery in Hogg's Market and his coconut macaroons are the best in the city.'

'Aye, all the same,' Sahib said, dismissing her with a wave of his hand, 'I'll ask my cook to recommend someone: he has cousins everywhere. I'll check their chits and if they're decent I'll choose the best and send him here.'

I was sorry to see Cook go; I loved his fish-fry and his peerless curry puffs, and I'd miss his stories and the gossip he picked up from the bazaar. He was sent away with a month's wages. He grumbled as he left, all the while playing with one of Miss Maisy's gold necklaces in his pocket. Wily old Cook always had the last laugh.

The new man was a cut above the old one; he'd worked for pukka British families.

'I've cooked for the Viceroy,' he reminded us frequently, inflating his chest. He meant he'd placed strawberries on top of the fruit tartlets for a banquet at Belvedere House when the Viceroy visited Calcutta. The new cook and Atul, the bearer, did not get on.

'My last sahib had dinner parties every week,' Cook boasted. 'The very best British civil service people would attend.'

Atul smiled, full of scorn. 'I've worked for MacBrayne Sahib for twenty years, and in his Alipore house he has three canteens of silver cutlery and enough crystal to host a party for a hundred.'

The new cook's previous sahib was an important British man who worked for the Governor, and the fool thought some of the *burra sahib*'s prestige had rubbed off on him. He was sure he was better than us because he'd been the servant of an English Brahmin. Although they won't admit it, and sometimes can't even see it themselves, the British have a caste system stricter than our own. In Calcutta the top people were government officials in the Indian Civil Service, and they were like Brahmins. They didn't mix with whites outside their own caste except to give them orders. They looked down on them like a Hindu Brahmin despises a sweeper. Our old cook told me this, and I know it's true. It's why Mem couldn't go to a club, and why MacBrayne Sahib went to the Tolly and not the Bengal Club. That famous place on Chowringhee is for Brahmins, not box-wallahs. It's for men who speak pukka English, not the jungly sort spoken by Scottish men like Donald Sahib and MacBrayne Sahib. Traders and businessmen, and men who've worked in jute mills, can't get into the Bengal Club however rich they might be.

This way of looking at the world was like a religion for the

British, and when they went to their clubs it was as if they were going to pray at a shrine. When, at last, I realised this, I understood why Mem was so desperate to join; she longed to do *puja* too. I wanted to make her feel better about being barred and was going to say she wasn't the only one to feel excluded: many Hindu temples in India didn't let untouchables in either, but I thought better of it because Mem had a way of mixing up many things I said, and I'd learned to be wary of her sharp tongue.

I controlled the urge to laugh at Cook and Atul as they stood in the kitchen, talking about the rank of their sahibs, the money they had, the grandeur of their homes, the way other white men deferred to them. They were two half-wits pumping themselves up because they worked for rich *burra sahibs*. I felt like saying my memsahib had half a china tea set and a dozen plain glasses, frequently replaced when drink made her clumsy and they fell through her fingers. I suppose they wouldn't have cared that they prepared food and served it to a woman who used to entertain men for money, or that their young memsahib was a kept woman. Although they worked in the garden house, they didn't work for Mem and Miss Maisy. They were the sahib's men; servants of one of the richest jute wallahs in the whole of Bengal.

Atul knew the ways of the British and he knew what Miss Maisy was, and because of that he took a spiteful pleasure in humiliating her.

'Will Sahib and Mem have guest this weekend?' Atul asked every Friday morning.

'Perhaps, Atul,' Miss Maisy replied.

'Guest come many times in Sahib's other house, Mem.'

'I'll leave the decision to the sahib.'

We all knew it was a sly game. No visitors dined with Miss Maisy and the sahib: Atul wanted to shame his new memsahib. The only people who came to the house were Harris Sahib, the sahib's good friend, who came to drink whisky with him late into the night, and a long line of hawkers who arrived with enormous bundles of linen and spread hand-stitched and embroidered tablecloths, napkins, and pillowcases all over the veranda. Miss Maisy and Mem sat on the cane chairs pointing to this and that, marvelling at the delicacy of the stitching and the feel of the fabric against their skin. They always bought far more than they needed, just because they could afford it.

It was the same with the Kashmiri rugs that were unfurled from their tight rolls to Miss Maisy's delight.

'The memsahib knows good quality,' the hawker said in the hope Miss Maisy would make another purchase. He wasn't lying. Miss Maisy had never seen expensive carpets or the homes of the rich. She'd grown up with bamboo matting on the veranda and cheap Chinese carpets in the living room, but when she pushed her fingers against the pile, and looked at the weave and the colours of the rugs covering the floors of Sahib's glorious house, she recognised and wanted what was true and beautiful. It was one of her strengths, and her weakness.

I had a bigger room in the new house and a fat mattress stuffed with new cotton. Unlike the other servants' rooms, at the end of the garden, mine was in the main house. Atul shared a room with Cook, which must have been difficult as they barely spoke to one another and each was obsessive about his own few feet of space and the fussiness of his routine. The *mali* shared a room with Lakshman, which was rarely a problem because the *durwan* spent most of his time dozing in his little sentry box by the gate, even when he was supposed to be on duty. I could hear his snores from the veranda. The sweeper had his own hut further away, far beyond the kitchen garden, so that the others wouldn't be troubled by his presence defiling their own living quarters.

Madan visited me occasionally but it was difficult to arrange under Atul's disapproving eye. He only came to see me on Atul's day off when the spying stopped, and when he could escape the constant demands of the wife who refused to die.

'It's safe,' I told Madan as he hesitated by the gate on his first visit. 'Atul and Cook have gone home for a few days. The *mali*, the *durwan* and the sweeper are here, but they're no trouble. Today, I am ayah, cook and bearer. See, I even open the gate myself because the *durwan* is drunk. And Sahib won't be here either; he's gone hunting in the Sunderbans for a week.'

Madan looked in awe at the house. 'Will you still be my heart's true love now your memsahib is rich?'

'Will you still be my true love now I'm old and fat?'

'You've been fat as long as I've known you.'

'I've saved some mutton chops for you.'

'That's why I love you. You understand a man's needs.'

I did, indeed. Madan was in greater need of a meal and a rest than he was in need of the things he used to ask of me. In that beautiful house he lay with me for a few hours on a comfortable bed – in winter under a blanket and in summer under the luxury of an electric ceiling fan.

On nights when Charlie was feverish or troubled by prickly heat rash, I slept on a cot outside his room in case he should wake. I'd bring warm milk for him while Miss Maisy soothed him to sleep. When Sahib visited it was my duty to comfort the boy and to see he never disturbed the sahib's pleasure or the depth of his sleep.

'Please look after him, Pushpa. Tell him I love him,' Miss Maisy asked. 'Tell him I'll see him in the morning.'

In Dharmatala, Charlie had slept in a cot next to his mother's bed. In the garden house he had his own room; Sahib insisted on it. He said Charlie shouldn't be indulged by having his mother on call. He should be left to cry if he woke. He said it would make the child into a fine boy and strong man, exactly like the sahib himself. It was in Charlie's best interest, he said, and he was only strict in enforcing the rule because he cared for him so very much. It was a lie. Sahib didn't care one bit for Charlie. When he first saw him walking with Miss Maisy round the great tank in Dalhousie Square, he stared coldly without speaking, and then turned away as if he'd been shown a two-headed monster and was too civil to show his distaste. Over a year later, he still cringed when he looked at the child.

'We'll send him to boarding school the moment he turns seven,' the sahib declared. 'It'll be the making of him.'

Mem thought Charlie played outside far too often and for far too long.

'Take him in, Pushpa,' she'd shout from the veranda. 'If he's out much longer he'll look like a coolie.'

It was a pity because Charlie's favourite places in the world were the garden and the drive. By the time he was three he'd worn a little path alongside the gates. He put his head through the gaps to watch who passed by: the pedlars taking a short cut with their donkeys or bicycles fixed with baskets of goods; the occasional funeral procession with its flower-strewn corpse on its way to the ghats; the poor children, a long way from home, who gathered to stare at him before the *durwan* moved them on with a shout. Best of all, he loved the entertainers.

'Pushpa,' he said. 'Pushpa, look.' He grabbed my hand and pulled me to the drive. A *bandarwallah* and his monkeys, dressed in yellow waistcoats, were dancing by the gate.

'Your mother likes these, too,' I told him, and called Miss Maisy.

We sat on the wall by the side of the drive and Lakshman opened the gates so the monkeys could perform for us while the *bandarwallah* played his drums and tugged the animals' chain to keep them moving. A monkey came very close to Charlie and screeched, baring its long teeth and beating its chest while it stood upright, its sinewy hind legs covered in bald, red patches. Charlie screamed so loudly and so long in my ear that my hearing wasn't right for weeks.

Mem screamed as loudly when a snake charmer's cobra slithered across the sitting-room floor, over the Kashmiri rugs and out on to the veranda. The snake charmer was as terrified as Mem. He was supposed to entice the creature out of the bag with the playing of his magic flute. Instead, it tried to bolt the moment the sack was on the floor.

'Forgive me, Memsahib. I am new for this business. Snake need better training.'

'You need better training, idiot,' she cried.

The snake escaped across the grass, avoiding Jamal, the sahib's driver, who was praying on the lawn, his head pressed to the ground so that he didn't see the cobra until Sahib bellowed from the house and Atul flung the incompetent charmer and his flute on to the drive.

Mem had to lie down to get over the shock.

'I swear, Pushpa,' she confessed, 'we had rats at home, and even the fanciest places had cockroaches. We had bed bugs that kept us scratching day and night, but I can't get used to the animals in this place even though I've been here for over twenty years. At least back home the cockroaches couldn't fly. If it's not lizards on the walls and silverfish eating the books, it's snakes about to kill us with a single bite. I wish we could go home.'

Mem was a hopeless liar.

I learned all about the sahib's business because he talked about it often, shouting down the telephone while Miss Maisy sat in the drawing room looking bored. One day, when he'd stopped arguing about the price of hessian bags, she suggested an outing. Her timing was bad because the sahib was in a foul mood, his face livid and a big purple vein throbbing on his temple.

'Can we go somewhere nice? I've stayed in every day this week,' Miss Maisy asked.

'I'll tell Jamal to drive you to the Army & Navy Stores this afternoon,' Sahib snapped. 'Get whatever you want and put it on the account.'

'I meant, can't we go out together? We can go to the pictures. There's the first run of a film at the New Empire, and they've fixed the air-conditioning so it's not like sitting in a furnace.'

'Tomorrow, perhaps. I can't promise. Our mill upriver is giving trouble.'

'What kind of trouble?'

'Nothing to worry you,' the sahib said wearily. 'Just a few Bolsheviks and *badmashes* – hooligans – trying to stir up the workers.'

'Why? Has something happened?'

'Aye, the usual pretext: a woman got her sari caught in a calendar machine and when she tried to pull it out, her hands were caught and crushed.'

'Poor woman; how will she live if she can't use her hands? Does she have family to look after her?'

'I've no idea. I'm not responsible for my workers' domestic arrangements.'

'But she'll get compensation, won't she?'

'A little, hopefully not too much. We often get cases like these, most of them caused by people who are blind drunk or not up to the job. Some even inflict the wounds on themselves because they think they'll get a pay-out.'

'I don't believe it.'

'Then you're naïve. My main concern is to make sure we're not tied up in the courts with this case and that production isn't hit by a strike.'

'Sometimes, I wonder how you live with yourself.'

'It's business; I'm not running a bloody charity. My duty is to the banks and to my shareholders. And there's no need for you to be so self-righteous, lassie, when you're living so well on the profits of my business.'

Miss Maisy fumed and watched the sahib make another telephone call.

'Will there be a strike?' she asked when he'd slammed down the receiver and cursed the man on the other end as a 'fucking eejit'.

'If there is, we'll sack the lot of them and they can see if they can find better jobs elsewhere.'

'That's cruel, Gordon. They're paid so little.'

'They earn what they deserve. We pay them the going rate, and most are happy with it. It's only a hard core of trouble-makers who stir things up. Yesterday one of our engineers feared for his life. A mob trapped him in his office and a wooden bobbin was thrown at his head. Luckily he escaped with a few stitches. It could easily have been worse.'

'They strike because they don't earn enough to survive,' Miss Maisy said, her colour rising and forming two little pink patches on her cheeks. She was baiting the sahib and I was worried the argument would escalate into a full-blown battle. 'It makes me ashamed to be British, the way those people are treated.'

The sahib laughed and pulled her down on to his lap. 'Who says you're British?'

Miss Maisy was taken aback. 'Of course we are. Father said we're British through and through.'

'Aye, right you are,' he said. 'And another thing you should know: most of my shareholders are Indian, not British. Does that make you feel any better?'

Miss Maisy mulled this over and Sahib leaned back in his chair.

'Anyhow,' she said. 'I've heard the servants talking. They say jute workers in the coolie lines live in awful conditions; they're crammed together in horrible shacks.'

He slapped her leg, half in anger, half in play. 'Most Indians live crammed together in horrible shacks, sweetheart.' He smiled tolerantly and began massaging her thigh. 'You mustn't listen to servants' tittle-tattle. I pay them to carry out household tasks and they don't understand the first thing about the world of business. And neither do you, Maisy, so stop fretting about it. Leave the thinking to me.'

Miss Maisy got up, flounced over to a chair and flung herself on to it. She stared out of the open window to where the gardener was playing with Charlie. The old man rolled coloured balls to the boy so he could collect them in a bucket before tipping them out on to the perfectly flat lawn and starting the game all over again.

Sahib took a sip from his glass of Dewar's White Label whisky – the expensive one we were all instructed to hide in case Mem should waste it on a binge. Miss Maisy drew her attention away from her son and gazed around the room. The cream and gold Kashmiri rugs looked pretty against the dark red of the stone floor that had been polished that morning to a glossy shine. Miss Maisy frowned and toyed with the edge of a rug, lifting it with the toe of her shoes and kicking it angrily a couple of times.

'Are ants ruining the carpets?' the sahib said without a trace of insincerity. 'They're buggers to deal with in my Alipore house. They've made a mess of the Persian rugs.'

He walked over to her, pulled her up from the chair and led her upstairs.

Sahib spent more time with Miss Maisy during the hot weather because his wife was in Darjeeling enjoying the cool mountain air. It created a lot more work for the *dhobi*; the bed linen had to be changed each day, and sometimes twice a day, because it was sodden with sweat. I felt sorry for those British men who had to stay perspiring on the plains while their wives went off to indulge themselves in the hills. I could hardly blame the sahib for taking a pretty mistress when his wife was stupid enough to leave him on his own for nine months of the year. Some of those rich British women were fools who had no sense, and no idea of a wife's duty.

Miss Maisy was busier when Sahib visited. I'm not sure, though, that she was any happier.

'Let's go to the Botanical Gardens,' she said, spinning the sahib around while he considered his answer. 'Please, Gordon. They say the old banyan tree is dying and I want to see it before it's chopped up for firewood.'

'Aye, we'll go,' he said. Sometimes he kept his word; more often, though, he did not. Sahib was tired from all his boxwallah work. He'd eat, read *The Statesman*, doze on the veranda, have sex with Miss Maisy and then sleep again.

Miss Maisy became the scholar she'd never been when she had a tutor. She read all the books she'd collected as a pupil of old and young Mr Banerjee, but reading still wasn't enough to fill the long days. Since she'd been a tiny girl she'd played in the streets and she'd walked with me down every lane and alley in Calcutta. She was accustomed to being free. In the years after the terrible famine Miss Maisy became a kind of prisoner in her beautiful home. She was trapped and bored, and the only excitement she had was the spectacle of the pedlars spreading their wares on her veranda.

When she thought Sahib was busy at his mills she'd call a taxi and we'd go to Eden Gardens, or we'd walk up the Strand to Esplanade, through Curzon Park or round the great tank in Dalhousie Square. If Memsahib was sober enough they'd take Charlie's hands and swing him between them, making him shriek with laughter so loudly and for so long that the other people taking a walk would look alarmed by the noise.

'I don't like you spending so much time out of the house,' Sahib complained. 'You can go to the teashops and the restaurants, and the big shops on Chowringhee are fine too, but many public places are not safe, especially for young women. The city's overcrowded with troops, the bloody Yanks are everywhere, and political agitators are causing no end of problems. There's a demonstration demanding independence every other day, and with looks like yours you're a sitting duck for anyone wanting trouble.'

'I've never had a moment's difficulty in the city,' she replied.

'Maybe, but times are changing. I forbid you to go anywhere near black town. You need to stay with your own kind.'

Miss Maisy did not obey.

Chapter Seven

Maisy

LARKSPUR AND SWEET peas die in a Calcutta summer. Traditional English flowers are too delicate to withstand a baking in the hot sun, and they bolt in the rains, becoming straggly, their roots rotting in the soggy earth. An English garden can only flourish during the winter, and only when it's tended with care. Ram insisted that the trick was to use Suttons Seeds developed especially for the Indian weather.

'My other memsahibs wanted an English garden, too,' he said. 'It isn't possible all year so we had an English garden in the cool season and an Indian one during the summer and monsoon.'

'It's a good plan, Ram,' I said, and in that way we inherited the native plants, the bougainvillaea, the night-flowering jasmine and the hibiscus, and added hanging baskets and terra-cotta pots filled with creeping geraniums, violets and begonias. In November the garden was transformed by cornflowers and chrysanthemums, and by February sweet peas trailed around the lattices by the garden's west wall and delphiniums stood in fragile pink and blue spikes under the dining-room window.

Ram had spent over half a century tilling the soil surrounding that old house, and while plenty of British people had passed through during their few years of service in India, it was Ram who knew where things would grow and what would thrive in the shady parts beneath the trees and in the open flowerbeds where there was no escaping the sun. If I was mistress of that house, Ram was surely master of the garden.

Mam asked him to add a dozen potted red geraniums to the many already lining the edges of the veranda, and some new lilies so that the scent drifted around us when we sat in the evening listening to the cicadas, and the bullfrogs croaking in our next-door neighbour's water tank. The owner of the tank, Professor Mitra, an eminent scholar at Presidency College, loved his garden as much as I loved mine and he'd greet me each morning with a jolly wave of his walking stick while he inspected his plants and admired the multicoloured parrots roosting in his magnificent blue jacaranda tree.

Mam stretched out on a cane lounger on the veranda, kicking off her shoes and wiggling her toes. She was happy, she said; everything was turning out well. We had a fine house and lots of servants. It could hardly be better. Back home the war was over and Mam was relieved no more young men would be dying in battle. She decorated the drawing room with Union Jack bunting that she and Charlie had made. Gordon approved, saying it was a patriotic thing to do, but that we still had to defeat the little yellow men, and they were much more of a problem for us in India than Hitler and his panzer divisions had been.

The rains seemed heavier and the humidity more intense in 1945 than in previous years, or perhaps it was simply because I slept more often with the perspiring Gordon. It was a slow, oppressive monsoon. The pictures rotted on the walls and larvae devoured great holes in my favourite Rajasthani wall hanging. Mould spread over my shoes and handbags, and a greenish-white fungus crept across the furniture, despite the servants' attempts to polish it away. My clothes never seemed dry and the sheets and towels returned by the *dhobi* were slightly damp. That year the rainy season smelled even more intensely of white flowers and mildew.

When October saw the rains give way to cloudless skies and cooler air, I opened the tin-lined boxes in which I'd stored my best dresses. 'They're all ruined,' I cried. The beautiful clothes Gordon had bought for me were spotted with fuzzy grey and black dots.

'Don't make such a fuss,' Gordon said. 'You can buy new ones, and some better trunks too. Those aren't airtight.'

'I can't buy new dresses because there aren't any to buy. There's hardly anything in the department stores. You'd never believe the war was over.'

'Then we'll have a tailor copy the spoiled ones.'

'He may not be the most handsome or exciting man,' Mam said after he'd left, 'but no one could say he's mean.'

Gordon was as generous at Christmas. He gave me a diamond bracelet, and he left a silk scarf for Mam and a miniature soldier's uniform for Charlie under the tree.

We had a traditional British Christmas dinner with turkey and crackers, and Cook had a hard time fitting the bird into the charcoal oven. It would have fed a dozen people, not the three of us who sat around our dinner table. Gordon couldn't be with us: he had family obligations.

'I have to go to the morning service at St Andrew's,' he explained. Then he and his wife were expected for lunch with friends. I was glad; I had enough to do keeping an eye on Mam and moderating her consumption of sherry.

Mam's paper hat slipped over one eye as she ate her Christmas pudding. Charlie spat out the currants and sultanas on to his new uniform.

'To Gordon,' Mam said, and lifted her glass. 'God bless him.'

'Merry Christmas, Gordon. God bless you,' I added.

Mam laughed, throwing back her head so her hat dropped on to the floor. 'Shall we go out this afternoon?' she asked.

'Yes. Do you fancy a walk round Eden Gardens?'

'Perfect. Give me a moment while I fix a little flask with some Christmas cheer.'

The tailor sat cross-legged on the veranda throughout the whole of January, and the chatter and whirr of his sewing machine became the new accompaniment to our day. By night he worked on my dresses in his shop, arriving each morning with new copies of the damaged clothes for me to try.

'I don't know where that *darzi* gets material as good as this,' I said to Pushpa. 'There's nothing like it in the shops. I thought the army had grabbed all the silk.'

'You can buy anything if you have the money,' Pushpa said.

I tried on a pink silk evening dress, stepping into it and wriggling to pull it over my hips. It was tight and Pushpa struggled with the buttons running down the back.

'Either the tailor's a fool or you've put on weight,' Mam said, eyeing me suspiciously as she lay on the bed. 'You're not pregnant again, are you?'

Pushpa and I shook our heads simultaneously.

'I can't close it,' Pushpa said.

'That's my girl,' Mam sighed with relief. 'You're growing tits the size of melons. It'll do you nothing but good.'

'He's done a remarkable job,' Gordon said, looking with satisfaction at the pink evening dress the *darzi* had let out. 'He was recommended by the wife of Lawrence Jones in the tea trade. It fits like a glove.'

Gordon lit a cigar. 'A *burra peg*,' he barked to Atul, who had anticipated his request and handed him a drink on a silver tray just moments later.

Atul salaamed, smiled at Gordon and left the room without offering me a drink.

'He's a first-rate bearer.'

'I don't like him. He gives me the creeps. He's always lurking around.'

'He's keeping an eye on things, making sure the house runs smoothly. I trust him absolutely; he's been with me for years.'

'He's sly, and he's rude to Pushpa, too.'

'Maybe she's not doing her job properly. In fact, I've been meaning to talk to you about her for some time. I'm thinking you should get a new ayah; someone younger. Pushpa's more of a burden than a help.'

'Is that what Atul says?'

'He said she's very slow.'

'He's talking rubbish; he disliked her from the moment he saw her and never misses an opportunity to take a dig at her. He's poisonous. There's nothing wrong with Pushpa.'

'She limps and she's expensive: she must eat as much as three normal servants.'

'She limps because she's got a bad hip, probably from carrying me when I was little, and she eats a lot because she used to starve. I am never – I mean never – going to get rid of Pushpa simply because she's old.'

'She's past her time, Maisy. It's the law of the jungle.'

'I don't want to be in that jungle, Gordon. Pushpa's like family and if she leaves this house, I go too.'

Gordon balanced his cigar on an ashtray so it smouldered, the coal a dull red in swiftly falling dusk.

'We'll discuss this later,' he said, finishing his peg. 'Come here.' He pulled me on to his lap, the smell of cigars and whisky on his breath mixing with his cologne. 'You look beautiful, absolutely radiant in that dress.'

My stomach tightened and my spirits plummeted. I knew what the rest of the evening would bring and how after it was over he'd fall asleep, his snores echoing round the first floor of the house, and his hairy arse rubbing against my thigh.

Gordon's Bentley turned into an oven in the hot season. Jamal usually parked in the shade of the trees but the temporary driver who replaced him while he was visiting his family in the *mofussil*, the countryside, was new to the job, and clearly without any sense because even a fool would know not to leave a car standing in April's blinding sun. The heat of the leather seats almost seared my skin through my thin linen dress when I got inside. I opened the window, and was thankful for the breeze ruffling my hair as we picked up speed on Chowringhee. I wished I hadn't pestered Gordon to take me with him. He was calling at the Calcutta Stock Exchange on urgent business and I'd asked to join him for the ride, eager to see further than the edges of my garden, to remind myself of the city that had begun to seem so far from my gate.

On Old Court House Street the driver swerved to avoid a policeman standing in the middle of the road directing traffic.

'For fuck's sake, man. Careful what you are doing. You can drive, can't you?' Gordon roared.

We pulled up outside the Stock Exchange, the wheels grinding against the kerb. 'Bloody hell, that's all I need,' Gordon snarled, glancing at two British men talking on the pavement.

'Who are they?' I asked.

'Some eejit in the ICS, and that must be his new assistant, straight out of Cambridge and still wet behind the fucking ears.'

They looked at Gordon as he got out and slammed the door.

'Good afternoon, MacBrayne,' the older man said, stepping towards him. He sounded like an announcer on the radio.

'Afternoon,' Gordon snapped, even brusquer than usual.

'We hear you have a lock-out again in your upstream mill,' the man said.

'Aye, nothing we can't handle,' Gordon replied, and marched into the Stock Exchange.

The driver sauntered across the road for a smoke, leaving me alone in the overheated car. The man with the posh accent hadn't seen me so I sat very still, listening through the open window.

'MacBrayne? Should I know him?' the younger man said.

'You'll get to know him soon enough. He's the damned fellow who runs the Britannia Jute Mill a few miles upriver.

It's been a bloody thorn in our side for months. The mill has a hard core of socialist agitators and MacBrayne deals with them with a heavy hand. The nationalists are involved and the place is like a tinderbox. We try reasoning with him, and ask him to put up at least a show of sympathy for the workers' demands, but he's bull-headed. You'll soon get to understand the type; he's a classic Scottish boxwallah with his mind on profit. That's why he deals with the Marwari jute wallahs so well: they're cut from the same cloth.'

'Will he be at the Bengal Club for tomorrow's dinner?'

'Henry, you have a lot to learn about India,' the older man said with a laugh. 'Let me put it this way: I don't shoot with the fellow.' He patted his assistant on the back and they walked towards Council House Street deep in conversation.

Gordon was in a worse temper when he returned to the car, and his anger made the driver jumpy. The Bentley accelerated past St Andrew's church, moved swiftly down the side of Dalhousie Square, raced round the edge of Curzon Park and turned with screeching tyres on to Chowringhee.

'Slow down, you bloody fool,' Gordon thundered. He turned to me. 'I thought Jamal was bad, but this one's lethal.'

A couple of cows plodded across the road, oblivious to the traffic, chewing slowly, vegetation hanging from their mouths. 'Look out, man. If you harm those animals you'll be lynched by a mob of crazed Hindus.'

The driver swerved across oncoming traffic, hurtling on to another road only to find it cordoned off and a rally in progress. A crowd was cheering a speaker and waving banners, unaware of the car careering towards them.

'Stop, damn you,' Gordon bellowed.

The driver heaved on the wheel and the car hit the kerb, bouncing over the pavement and stopping with a heavy jolt against a low wall. We sat for a moment, shaken by the accident, and then got out and looked at the damage; the front wheels were bent and steam spewed from the radiator.

The demonstrators were silent and then one laughed, and within seconds the whole crowd was hooting and pointing. Gordon put his arm around me and began leading me towards the big shops on Chowringhee.

'Who are they?' I asked.

'Some young firebrands who make more noise than sense.'

I looked over my shoulder and spun around in surprise. The speaker had turned to face us. He was looking directly at me and he lifted his hand as if he was about to wave. It was Sunil, only he looked different, as if he'd aged fifteen years and not the four it had been since he'd abandoned me and his bag in our house in Dharmatala. His face was gaunt and tired.

Gordon gripped my arm. 'Let's get you away from here. These aren't the Gandhi followers and the Quit India crowd. These people supported Bose and his army of traitors. Those men on the platform were in all the newspapers; they've spent the last few years in prison for plotting to assassinate the Governor of Bengal.'

I glanced back again for a moment in disbelief: perhaps Sunil, my son's runaway father, was not such a coward after all.

April and May were dead months in the garden. Ram watered the terracotta pots and the beds but the flowers remained scant, the earth biding its time, waiting for the rains to bring it to life. Yellow and brown patches developed on the sun-scorched lawn, the heat twisted and cracked the wooden seat of the swing under the monkey tree, and beneath the sun's relentless glare, the glossy black paint began peeling off the gates.

Mam ordered Pushpa to cover Charlie in calamine lotion to protect him when he played in the garden. It formed pink crusts on his skin and didn't stop him turning brown. He escaped from the shade of the house whenever he had the chance, helping Ram with the vegetables, playing with the watering cans, hiding among the bushes behind Ram's godown where the old *mali* stored all his seeds and prized tools, most of them made in Sheffield. After the snake charmer's cobra had escaped into the shrubbery, Mam had become obsessive about the danger of Charlie being bitten, and first thing every morning and late each afternoon Ram was obliged to beat the ground around the bushes with a long cane to flush out any snakes or rabid dogs.

Charlie made a den in the bushes and sat in the little green cave with his teddy. Gordon spotted him peeping through the branches and promised he would have a tree house built for him when he was a bit older.

'He probably wants the lad to fall out of it and break his neck,' Mam said.

'Be quiet, Mam. What if Charlie hears?'

'I'm just telling the truth. You know he doesn't like the boy. He thinks Charlie's an embarrassment.'

I pressed my finger against my lips as Charlie ran in, his mouth so full he couldn't chew.

'What are you eating?' Mam asked.

Charlie mumbled when he tried to speak.

'More sweets,' Mam said, peeling back his lips to look at the toffee and bright syrup cementing his teeth.

'I'll have to be firmer with Ram,' I said.

Pushpa had told me indignantly that the gardener had gone out of the house several times in the spring, holding Charlie by the hand. They walked to a tiny shop where Charlie spent a large proportion of Ram's wages on sweets and cheap toys. I'd taken Ram to task for it and he promised not to indulge Charlie again, or to take him as much as a foot outside the gate without my permission. Charlie, though, was both endearing and persuasive, and I knew he pestered Ram to take him shopping or to bring him more treats. The old *mali* must have been too soft to withstand the constant pleading.

I spoke to Ram in the afternoon. 'You promised not to give Charlie any more sweets, and he's had so many today he's been sick on the new rug.'

'I haven't given the little sahib anything, Mem,' Ram said as he stood barefoot on the veranda, his hands clasped in front of him. He smiled and seemed totally plausible.

Charlie skipped into the sitting room two days later with chocolate smeared round his mouth.

'Where did you get the chocolate? Was it from Ram?'

Charlie shook his head.

'Cook?'

'No.'

'Well, it wouldn't be from Atul. Was it from one of the other servants?'

'I found it.'

'Tell me the truth, Charlie.'

'The nice man told me not to tell anyone.'

'What nice man?'

Charlie pressed his lips together.

'Where did you see him? Tell me or I'll be very cross.'

'By the gate,' he mumbled.

'You mustn't take presents from strangers,' I said, wiping the chocolate from his face. 'It's dangerous. Didn't Lakshman see the man, too?'

'He was sleeping.'

I went to Lakshman's sentry box and found him dozing in a fug of cigarette and alcohol fumes.

'Lakshman,' I shouted.

He shot up, astonished. 'Memsahib,' he said, saluting.

'Have you seen anyone by the gate?' I asked in English, not speaking any of his native Nepali.

'No one, Mem. Today road very quiet. Only one or two car and few rickshaw.'

Lakshman's hangover was so severe he wouldn't have known if an army of men had lined up by the gate. 'Don't fall asleep again or I'll speak to the sahib about you,' I said. 'A man has been giving Charlie sweets and I want you to tell him to go away or we'll call the police.'

Next day I sat on the veranda in Mam's cane chair and kept watch. A couple of wretched children clanked tin cups on the gate; servants from the neighbouring houses went about their errands; a boxwallah selling table linen paused to speak to Lakshman; an expensive car roared towards Theatre Street in a cloud of dust; and a British boy with bloody knees pushed his cycle awkwardly up the road, its front wheel bent. No one gave Charlie sweets, and they didn't on any other day that week either. I started thinking I'd imagined a problem that didn't exist. Usually I wouldn't have been so nervy, but in 1946, when I was hounded by Gordon's constant warnings and tirades about staying at home, and India was jolting uncertainly towards Independence, I was strangely anxious. That's why I jumped to my feet a few days later when I spotted Charlie leaping around the lawn, sucking a lollipop.

I ran to the gate. Lakshman wasn't in his sentry box so I went to the side gate we opened when people arrived on foot, and stepped quickly into the road. I looked towards Theatre Street, but the only person I saw was an elderly *dhobi* pulling a cart piled high with bundles of laundry. I turned the other way, and that was deserted too, and then I paused, my attention caught by something hard to pinpoint. Perhaps I was distracted by the wind moving the bougainvillaea hanging over the garden wall, or the parrot that flew into Professor Mitra's jacaranda tree, but I was sure someone had been there only a few moments before. Although they'd vanished, they'd left something of themselves behind; the trace of something undefinable caught on the breeze. It can't be, I thought in exasperation. After four years of absence, four years of complete silence, Sunil can't be back.

I found Ram planting the hot weather vegetables, his fingers digging into the dry, friable soil.

'Please keep watch on the gate,' I said. 'Take a good look at any man who talks to Charlie.'

'Are there *goondas* in the neighbourhood, Mem?'

'Perhaps.'

'These are dangerous times,' Ram said, looking left and right as he made his way slowly across the lawn.

A week later he stood on the veranda, his hat in his hands.

'I have seen a man at the gate, Mem.'

'What did he look like?'

'Not a *goonda*, Memsahib, but not a rich man. His clothes were old.'

'But he was young?'

'Yes.'

'What else?'

'I don't know, Mem. He was just a young Bengali man and he left as soon as he saw me.'

'And his face? Please, Ram, try to remember. Was there anything about him you can recall? Did you hear him speak?'

Ram smiled nervously, embarrassed because he didn't have answers to my questions.

'There was nothing unusual about him, Mem. He was dark. That's all.'

'Thank you, Ram,' I said. 'Keep watch. I need to know more about this man, and Lakshman is no help.'

He pressed his hands together in front of his heart and grinned, seventy years of smiles drawn in the lines on his face. The *mali* stepped off the veranda on to the path, and then he turned and stopped. 'There was only one thing, Mem. He had a little gap, like this.' Ram pushed his soil-encrusted nail between his top teeth.

It took me several days to gather the composure to write a short, indignant note to Sunil. I watched the ink dry, reread it, and scrunched it up in frustration. It was pointless writing a chit when I couldn't find the right words. I took another sheet of paper from Gordon's desk and tried again, writing quickly and furiously, the pen nib bending back as I pressed it down, the ink blotting messily. *Stay away from us*, I wrote. *Don't come back to this house. You are not wanted here.* I sealed the message in an envelope and went to look for Ram.

The open door of his godown let in little light and the corners of the store were dark. Tools leaned against the walls and the shelves were stacked with dusty tins and glass jars full of seeds and roots. Ram jumped in fright and covered a box with a piece of hessian.

'What's the secret, Ram? Special new bulbs? Have you stolen a cutting from Professor Mitra's prize bougainvillaea?' I knew it was no such thing: Ram was hiding the dried ganja, the cannabis he grew in profusion by the compost heap. 'I need you to do something for me. You mustn't tell anyone else.'

Ram looked anxious.

'Give the man this chit if he comes back to the house. Don't ever let Sahib know. Do you understand?'

The old man brightened at the simplicity of the task and I pressed a rupee into his palm.

Ram wasn't so happy when he shuffled into the drawing room a few days later. I thought he was uncomfortable being in the house because we usually talked on the veranda.

'I gave the man your chit, Mem. He said you should meet him on the Howrah Bridge tomorrow at five in the afternoon.'

'Thank you, Ram.'

The old man bent, put my rupee coin on the side table and then saluted, standing straighter than he must have done in forty years.

Sunil had a cheek, I thought, but then he always had a high opinion of himself. He made a show of helping the poor, writing political pamphlets no one ever read, and he talked about freeing India as if he were a man of great principle. It made me laugh because I knew he was a fraud. When he got the chance to show his courage and the truth of his promises, the charlatan ran off and deserted me. He'd assumed I was like Mam, as if I'd inherited her sins as well as the colour of her hair. I raged at the injustice, knowing I really had loved him, and that even though I now lived in Gordon's magnificent house, it wasn't the same as being in Mam's business. I would never allow a procession of uncles to visit our home, and Charlie wouldn't have to cover his ears with his pillow to deaden the sounds of the night.

It was an insult really: Sunil sent me a message through the *mali*, and expected me to come running. He had a nerve. Well, I'll do as he asks, I decided; I'll meet him and look him in the eye, and tell him exactly what I think about him.

Next day, after tea, I bathed and changed into a fresh dress, and while I was brushing my hair I looked into the garden and saw Pushpa and Ram huddled together under the monkey tree, talking fast. No doubt Pushpa was working Ram's news into an alarming story full of ill omens, and so I rushed to leave before she could delay me with a thousand reasons why I shouldn't meet Sunil.

Lakshman was languishing in his sentry box, sober for a change, and I asked him to call a taxi immediately.

'Howrah Bridge, quickly,' I said to the driver, slamming the door in the hurry to escape. I turned my face away from the house as we sped away, pretending I hadn't seen Pushpa, who leaned out of my bedroom window, waving the end of her sari like a flag.

Calcutta had a new bridge. The ungainly pontoon bridge Father and I crossed on the way to Howrah Station had been replaced by a giant structure of steel girders. I pretended to admire its novel architecture and made my way across the river, jostled by porters hauling gigantic loads, and harried mothers towing anxious children. Bemused new arrivals from the *mofussil* were swept along, and the disabled limped, hobbled or crawled among the feet of the crowds. What am I doing here? I thought. Perhaps I should have stayed at home and taken the time to listen to Pushpa.

It was nearer six o'clock than five, the heat fading from the sun and casting a softer light on the water. I stopped to watch a boatman steer a passage under the bridge.

A beggar woman holding a snotty-nosed baby tapped my arm and lifted a bowl toward me. 'Please give milk for baby, Memsahib.'

I tossed a few annas into the bowl and as she moved along the bridge, pleading with everyone, I noticed her heavy silver anklets and the deep cracks in her dry heels.

'She has four babies she uses when she begs, and none of them are her own,' Sunil said, appearing from nowhere. 'The one with the crippled arms and pretty face is the most profitable.'

He took me off guard. Feeling ambushed, I stammered something nonsensical in reply. I'd gone to the bridge ready to denounce him, and I'd practised what I was going to say. I'd speak the bitter truth eloquently and with devastating effect. Sunil would be humbled and I'd feel vindicated. But once he was there I was incapacitated by nerves and couldn't look at him. We stood in silence, staring at the river, and my heart pounded in my chest.

'I wasn't sure you'd come,' he said, barely audible over the clatter and roar of an army convoy.

'I wasn't going to. But I changed my mind.'

'Why?'

'Because . . .' I struggled to salvage my prepared speech and instead I swore, the voice that came out of my mouth sounding like Mam. 'Because I wanted to tell you you're a selfish bastard,' I said, taking a deep breath and glancing at him. 'You left me pregnant, I heard nothing from you, and then, out of the blue, you start hanging around my gate, talking to Charlie and giving him sweets. It's bloody sinister.'

'He's my son, isn't he?'

'That hasn't bothered you before now. The last time I saw you, you said you needed some time to think. Sunil, you've been thinking for four ruddy years. It's incredible, in all honesty. I'll never forgive you.'

'I couldn't come back: I was arrested on my way home. Surely you know that? It was the time of the Quit India movement. Do you remember?'

I didn't remember.

'No, of course you don't,' he said with a laugh. 'You're not aware of things like that because they're not important to you. But the fact is, I was arrested and I didn't come back because I couldn't. I was caught up in a demonstration. The streets were chaotic: there were cars and trucks on fire; the police were shooting; and I ended up being thrown in prison because I was in the wrong place at the wrong time. The irony is, I wasn't even a member of Congress. They kept me in gaol without a trial, and I was only released a few months ago.'

'Gordon said you went to prison for trying to blow up the Governor of Bengal.'

'The jute wallah doesn't know what he's talking about. I wasn't involved with that operation, though I would assassinate him very happily if I got the chance.'

'Don't talk like that.'

'Like what?'

'Saying you'd kill someone.'

'It's a war, Maisy, and people get killed. You see things differently because we're on opposite sides.'

'I'm not on anyone's side.'

On Armenian Ghat, hundreds of people were walking down the steps and into the river. I watched them so I didn't have to look at Sunil.

'I'm sorry I wasn't there to help you, Maisy, but I'm not the only one who needs to apologise. You didn't reply to my letters.'

'You didn't send any.'

'I did: I gave them to Charu.'

'I never got them.'

'I went to Dharmatala when I was released and no one knew where you'd gone. The neighbours said you abandoned the house. You disappeared and didn't even take the furniture with you. And now I know why.' He snorted with derision and amusement.

'What's so funny?'

'That you're Gordon MacBrayne's mistress. I saw you with him after the car accident; it didn't take long to follow him and find you set up in that garden house as a kept woman.'

I hesitated, embarrassed and angry: Sunil made me sound cheap.

'Yes, I am his mistress. I didn't have many alternatives,' I snapped. I wanted to ask what I was expected to do when I was an unmarried mother and Mam was broke. Gordon came along when we were on our uppers: he had money and, unlike Sunil, he offered to help me. 'He looks after us well,' I said bluntly.

'Maisy, he's one of the most loathed jute wallahs in Bengal,' Sunil exclaimed. 'He's hated by the nationalists, the socialists and the communists. I hear most of the British hate him, too.'

'That man you dislike so much pays for the roof over your son's head, the clothes on his back and the food he eats. Which is a hell of a lot more than you've ever done for Charlie; we would have starved for all the help you gave us.'

'How could I help? I was in the damned prison. I was detained without trial by the people you like to call your countrymen.'

A group gathered round to gawp at the argument. We edged along the railings and I snatched the chance to look properly at him. He'd grown dark in the hot season, the skin on the back of his neck burned black, and he seemed so much older than when he'd sat on Mam's sofa. He was bigger, no longer a youth, and if I hadn't been so angry I would have reached out and touched him.

'This is such an odd place to meet,' I said. 'Eden Gardens would have been better.'

'The air's good here, and it's safe: we can get lost in the crowd.'

A south-westerly breeze sprang up in the late afternoons at that time of year. It blew over the bridge, cooling me. Maybe

Sunil saw my face relax and assumed I'd forgiven him, because he moved close and looked straight into my eyes and for a moment we seemed to be the only people on the bridge, and I remembered what it felt like to be seventeen and in love with a boy who wrote poems and trembled when he touched me. If I hadn't wanted to shove him over the railings and into the river, I would have wrapped my arms around him and kissed him right there and then, on the middle of Howrah Bridge. But no one did that kind of thing in 1946, except in films, and even then it was only white people who kissed. It was completely unthinkable for a British woman to kiss an Indian.

A whistle blew as a launch prepared to leave one of the jetties, and a steamer pulled slowly to the centre of the river on its journey upstream to Assam. I'd never seen the Hooghly so busy, or so many cargo ships and liners moored by the embankment along Strand Road.

Sunil's tense expression bothered me: I could almost pity him, and so I searched for some conciliatory words. 'I know I'm biased, but he really is a wonderful boy,' I said. 'Mam says he looks like me, though I know he doesn't.'

'I looked exactly like him when I was a child, and I can see he's clever. He's also inherited that from me,' Sunil said, smiling at his lame joke. 'You have to believe me when I say I'm sorry for what's happened. It must have been hard for you.' He said it so sadly and with so much remorse that I nearly believed his story. 'It's been hard for me, too. I'd no idea he'd been born, or whether either of you was alive. I'll admit I wasn't sure what to do when you told me you were pregnant, but I've had time to think – four years is long enough – and I really would like to meet him. I mean, I want to meet him properly.' He

165

tapped his fingers on the top of the metal rail, and I saw his nails were bitten down to the quick. 'I don't want to hide by the side of the gate like a criminal.'

'It's too late to start playing the loving father. I can't risk Gordon finding out: he has a foul temper at the best of times. At first I told him I was a war widow and my husband was killed in Burma. Then, when he saw Charlie, I couldn't keep up the pretence and so I told him some of the truth: I said you were Charlie's father and that you'd died. I don't know why I said it, but I did, perhaps because you were as good as dead to us. Gordon would be furious if he knew you'd contacted me. He's absurdly jealous; he doesn't even like me going out of the house. He can't know we've met. I only managed to get away today because he's hunting in the Sunderbans. He's a well-known *shikari* – a great hunter. It's all he does: work and hunt.'

'He has you to amuse him, too,' Sunil said indignantly. He stood by my side and I could feel every point at which his body touched mine. 'Do you love him?' he asked abruptly, his voice sharp, rising above the noise of the traffic. I turned to him, pressing my fingers to my lips.

'Do you love MacBrayne?' he said, louder.

'No, of course not. I hardly know what to feel any more. It's an arrangement, that's all. And you've no right to be angry and speak to me like that.'

'I spent four years in Alipore Gaol dreaming about you, and when I'm finally released, I find you've made a life with a man who stands for everything I hate. How can you say I've no right to be angry?'

A lump rose in my throat and I struggled not to cry. I focused my attention on a large mat of weeds floating by.

'What a mess,' he said, his anger fading. 'And the worst thing is, I have no idea how to resolve it. I can't marry you; not at the moment, not until the British have gone. But we can start a new life after Independence.'

I knew Mam would say something about men's empty promises and seeing the colour of his money. And did he seriously think I was going to abandon everything to marry him when I hadn't seen him in years? Prison must have addled his mind.

We moved toward the Howrah end of the bridge to avoid being thrashed by a young man with tiny limbs who scooted along on a trolley, beating people's calves with a stick.

'You have to leave MacBrayne. You can't stay with him,' Sunil stated.

'Where do you expect us to go?'

'Doesn't your mother have any money?'

'Not a single anna.'

He sighed. 'I'll make amends, Maisy. Trust me.'

My trust in Sunil had run dry four years before. 'I have to go,' I said. 'It's late.'

'Can I see Charlie?'

'I'll think about it. I don't know how I'll explain it to him.'

'And can I see you? Can we be friends, like we were before?'

I didn't reply because it was a ridiculous question. In 1942 I'd been a silly girl, thinking only of romance. Now I had to think about filling my son's belly and keeping Mam in booze, and however handsome Sunil was, however much I was drawn to him, he was an indulgence I couldn't afford.

We walked towards Strand Road, his fingers sometimes touching mine. I should have moved away from him, but I didn't, and I cursed myself for my weakness. He stopped by a man selling garlands swinging from a bamboo pole, and bought a thread of jasmine and miniature pink roses.

'I'd give you jewels, but I'm a poor man,' he said, trying to hand them to me.

If they were a peace offering they were too little, too late. I shook my head and brushed them away.

The last rays of the sun silhouetted the girders of the new bridge against a fading blue sky. A fisherman hurled his nets into the water with a splash and Sunil hailed a taxi.

'Meet me tomorrow?' he asked through the open window. 'I know where we can go. It's safe and we can talk.'

'No,' I said, adamantly.

'Does the great *babu* demand all your attention?' he asked, his voice spiky with annoyance. 'You said he was hunting. Please, Maisy, give me a chance. I want to talk to you.'

'The time for talking is long gone. My life's different now, and there's no room in it for you.'

'I'll be at the Royal Palace Hotel on Harrison Road at three o'clock.'

'Go,' I said to the driver, who was struggling to get the car into gear.

Dusk settled over the Hooghly. The azan was called from the Nakhoda mosque and a steamer festooned in lights drew up the river, its passengers crowding on deck to marvel at the city of palaces. Another military convoy thundered by and a group of agitated young men ran past shouting incomprehensible slogans, their voices wild and guttural. One youth's call was louder than the rest, his yell higher pitched, almost inhuman. Sunil looked away from me and, as he listened to the sound, my heart stood still, paralysed by an inexplicable fear. The driver selected first gear with a graunch of metal and as we accelerated towards Harrison Road, my heart jolted back to life.

I thanked God Gordon was in the Sunderbans: I couldn't have endured him that evening. It was difficult enough dealing with Pushpa's indignant face. I ignored her, and took no notice of Mam's drunken babbling about how she'd not seen Uncle Donald, or anyone else for that matter, for months on end. After Charlie went to bed I sat on the veranda in an old planter's chair. I dragged it closer to the lamp, the legs scraping on the blue and white tiles, and leaned back with a *nimbu pani* – a fresh lemonade. Listening to the bullfrogs in Professor Mitra's tank calmed me, and I collected my thoughts, grateful it was Atul's day off and he wasn't there to smirk at my frayed nerves and the way my hands trembled as I relived the day and swung between loving Sunil and hating him.

It's easy to despise men if you're in Mam's line of business. Although I hadn't had the best introduction to men, I didn't dislike them; in fact, some of my uncles were pleasant, and a few were very kind. The trouble was, even the nice ones had wives or girlfriends they called 'sweetheart', and that's not what they ever called Mam. Uncle Donald's wife lived with him in the giant compound of the Howrah Jute Works, and according to him she was a gentle, caring woman who spent her time planning menus and doing charity work for the Church and impoverished native babies. Clearly, however, this gentle nature hadn't stopped him spending two hours a week with Mam for the last fifteen years.

I knew for a fact some men were good – my father, for one – and I was sure things would have been different for our family if Mam's drinking hadn't driven him away. He mightn't have been ensnared by the Indian woman if Mam had been sober and more loving, though I was always comforted by the thought that he didn't desert us after we saw him with her in the shabby flat. He came back to us and, in the end, it wasn't a mistress but typhoid that stole him from me.

Before I had Charlie, Mam planned a decent life for me. I'd marry a British officer, someone white and with a respectable job. I wanted something decent too, but it wasn't what Mam had in mind. I didn't want to marry an Uncle Donald, or a Gordon who had a wife in Darjeeling or Dundee. I didn't want a role in make-believe, and to perform the way Mam did for the uncles. I wanted to trust someone, and to be the centre of their world, the way I was the centre of Father's world until I learned I had to share him with the Indian woman.

Gordon spoiled me and he was usually considerate, but I didn't love him. I only stayed with him in Sahib-para because he gave me and Charlie somewhere to live. Perhaps that makes me a little like Mam, I thought, reluctant to admit I was a bit player in the trade. But with Sunil it was different: I'd loved him since I was seventeen, and the feeling was real, untainted by business. That's why I decided to go to Harrison Road. I'd go because I wanted to, and because I couldn't throw away the chance to find something better than I had in that beautiful, soulless house. I won't interrogate him too much, I resolved. I'll trust him and I'll learn to believe he didn't abandon me. I'll forget I know so little about him, and that I have to share him with his friends, his family and his political fancies without even knowing much about them. I realise he loves many things, not just me. I won't turn into a cynic and check his story to see if he really was imprisoned. I'll tell myself I'm too busy to investigate. I won't dare delve deeply because I don't want to find out he's a liar and I'm a fool. On Gordon's beautiful veranda I closed my mind to alternative truths because it was the only way I could believe the world was good, men were honest, and I was more than I am.

Mr Das, manager of the misnamed Royal Palace Hotel, looked at me over the top of his spectacles whenever I slipped from the street into the lobby and tried to make my way unobserved towards the stairs.

'Such a great heat today, Memsahib,' he said. 'Alas, the monsoon is late this year.'

When I tried to leave the hotel unnoticed during the rains, he'd rush from behind the cramped reception desk. 'Mem, it is most dangerous on the roads today. The heavens have opened and the city is completely and totally flooded. Please, stay until the storm has passed. You can wait in our most comfortable lounge.'

I never stayed. I plunged into the rain, panicking because I was late, detained by a spell that had kept me bound in a room on the second floor.

The rickety hotel was less intimidating than the Great Eastern and I liked it a lot more. Sandalwood incense wafted down narrow, dusty corridors; an old bearer rushed silently to and fro; and the clanking lift sounded like the building's failing heartbeat. Sunil and I fitted in well among the other peculiar guests. Two permanent residents, rumoured to be scions of an illustrious but now impoverished Rajpoot family, lived on the first floor and appeared in full regalia, supported by aged

171

retainers, among the battered armchairs of the guests' lounge, which Mr Das insisted was modelled on a London club. Most of the other guests were Indian businessmen of very modest means, and upcountry families from the heart of the *mofussil* who occasionally tried to economise by cooking on the balconies, lighting fires that an outraged Mr Das claimed would burn down the whole of Burrabazar. Noticing the ornate carved verandas that ran round the building, I decided he had a point, and was relieved when the monsoon broke and torrential rains soaked the tinder-dry wood.

Even on days when the city was deluged and the streets flooded, the hotel frequently ran out of water. Airlocks disturbed the plumbing and a few drops of water spluttered from the taps along with a lot of whistling. I lay next to Sunil in the shade of the shuttered room, listening to the gurgling and groaning of the pipes, and the returning supply trickling and then whooshing back into the antiquated system. Sunil slept through the singing of the plumbing and the sounds from Harrison Road below. From inside my beautiful house, Calcutta sounded like a distant hum; in the Royal Palace Hotel I heard the familiar tempo of street life, the city's unrelenting racket.

Sunil stirred and drew me close, brushing damp curls from my face and kissing my forehead. He rearranged the string of jasmine he always bought for me, threading it gently back through my hair. Although he no longer wrote poems, he whispered the same words of love and, once again, I believed him, completely and without question.

'You didn't sleep?' he asked, stretching out on the bed, his lean body dark against the thin, crumpled sheets.

'I was worried about the time.'

'It's better than worrying whether your mother is about to burst through the door.'

'I have to get back. Gordon's coming for dinner.'

'No doubt Calcutta's greatest *babu* will get a grand feast,' he said bitterly. 'I bet you'll give him roast quail and wine. Perhaps you're going to put on silks and all your jewels like a real courtesan.' He groaned and punched the pillow.

Turning away from him, I lay on my side, feeling him bristle with jealousy. He was silent for a long time and then ran his fingers along my back, the lightness of his touch making me shiver.

'I'll be away from the city for a while,' he said, his anger gone.

'Where are you going?'

'To the countryside.'

'That's a bit vague.'

'My family have land in a village. It's our ancestral home.'

'Can I go?'

He laughed. 'You wouldn't like it.'

'I might. You're always leaving Calcutta and I never know when I'll see you again.'

He curled himself around me, kissing the back of my neck and reaching round to cup my breast in his hand.

'Sunil, you haven't answered my question.'

He rolled me over. 'What question?' He took my nipple into his mouth, and I pushed him away.

'I'm going,' I said, annoyed. 'It's getting late.'

'Please,' he said. 'I don't know when I'll be in the city again.'

I scrambled to the bathroom. We had the only room in the Royal Palace Hotel with its own shower. More accurately, it was a spout placed high on the wall, from which the water dribbled, spluttered or gushed over the floor depending on the whims of the plumbing. Sunil followed me and I watched him turn the rusty tap. The water splashed on his face and he closed his eyes. It flowed over him, the hair on his chest washed into a few dark streams. I ran my fingers over his hard, flat stomach. He pulled me towards him, and I guided him into me, knowing but not caring that I'd be home dangerously late. Loving Sunil did that to me; it made me bold and a little bit mad.

Pushpa wasn't always sweet and no one should have been fooled by her gentle expression. She wasn't a simple, doting ayah: she had a steely, sanctimonious side that turned her into a nagging harridan. I saw her often in intense discussions with Ram, the two old heads bobbing simultaneously, no doubt hatching some plot to put an end to my visits to the Royal Palace Hotel or the occasional walks I took in Eden Gardens with Charlie and Sunil, who rowed us at great speed up and down the lake, disturbing the lotuses and making Charlie yell with excitement. Sunil recruited Ram as a go-between, delivering chits that told me when he was in town and when we could meet, but the *mali* was a reluctant intermediary and though the messages arrived on time, Ram was troubled by his role, dragging his feet when he delivered the notes, his face downcast. Afterwards, he always hurried off to speak with Pushpa and I'd see them in a little agitated huddle by the godown.

'Have more sense, Miss Maisy,' Pushpa ranted when I returned after a long afternoon visit to Harrison Road. 'You are late, there are bel flowers in your hair and your lips look bruised.'

She raised her hands in despair. 'Think of the danger. You were a wild, reckless child and you've grown into a wild, reckless woman.'

She paused, taking a big breath. 'Think of your son.' We both looked out of the window. Charlie was stuffing his mouth full of mangoes and Ram was indulgently checking over the fruit and giving him the best.

Pushpa yelled and scurried into the garden. She knocked the mango from Charlie's hand and spoke so harshly to Ram that he fled into his store.

'The poor child will have diarrhoea again,' she shouted. She came closer to the window, trampling on the flowerbed, her face inches from the mosquito netting. 'He'll suffer a lot worse than diarrhoea if you carry on behaving the way you've been doing.'

'What have I been doing, Pushpa?'

'Meeting Sunil Banerjee. He'll bring us trouble. I see it.'

'You see what, exactly, Pushpa?' I laughed to hide my exasperation. 'All the ideas you have about seeing the future are just mumbo jumbo.'

I turned my back, sat down and picked up a novel. Bitter, jealous old woman, I thought. How dare she speak to me like that?

'My head, the pain: it's my blood pressure. You're trying to kill me,' Mam said, ricocheting around the room, bumping into chairs and knocking over a footstool. She stood still for a moment. 'Pushpa's got it wrong, hasn't she? You've not really taken up with that brainless clerk again?'

My heart sank: Puspha had confided in Mam, so now I'd

have the two of them harping on at me. I stared at Mam, who turned, wild-eyed, to Pushpa. 'She's lost her mind,' she exclaimed.

Mam breathed deeply. 'I need a drink.' She poured whisky from Gordon's favourite bottle and glanced at the label. 'I might as well try it now while I've still got the chance.'

Mam shook with rage, although in hindsight it might have been fear. 'What pathetic excuse did he give for buggering off after he got you up the stick?'

'He was in prison.'

'Bleeding hell; he's a ruddy criminal, too.'

'He was a political prisoner.'

'I bet he says he can't marry you just now.'

'We'll get married later.'

'Let me guess: he says, "Now isn't the right time."'

'He's busy working for independence.'

'Christ, he's trying to get us kicked out of India. I don't know why the wogs want us to leave when we've done so much for this fucking country. Mark my words, he targeted you because you're British and he got you pregnant as some sort of sick revenge.'

Pushpa hovered near the door, keeping watch for the other servants. 'Be careful, Mem; Atul might hear,' she hissed.

Mam lowered her voice for a moment but it soon grew loud. 'What'll happen if Gordon finds out?'

I ignored the question. 'I love him, Mam.'

'You don't know anything about him. He's taking you for a complete fool; what's the betting he's married already? He's probably got a wife and four kids in a shack in the *mofussil*.' She shook her head and gave a hollow, cheerless laugh. 'Love like this won't get you anywhere, Maisy. He's spinning you some bleeding story and he'll be off before you know it.'

Mem rubbed her temples. 'Promise me you won't see him again. If Gordon finds out, we'll be on the streets. I swear, I'll throw myself off the sodding Ochterlony Monument if you don't give him up.'

'Stop shouting, Mam.'

'And don't get pregnant again. Not by either of them,' she raged. 'It'd be bad enough if you produced a baby the same colour as the man who pays for this house. I don't imagine he'd be pleased if you dropped another one the same shade as the sweeper.'

'Shut up, Mam.'

'Let's not pretend you haven't got a track record.' She flicked her head in the direction of Charlie, singing in the hall, his voice muffled by the saucepan he'd put on his head. 'You've been able to salvage something good from disaster, Maisy, but don't try it a second time.'

I didn't reply. I'd no intention of bringing ruin on my family and I was infuriated with Mam and Pushpa for their advice. They'd no right to tell me what to do when they weren't so perfect themselves: Mam loved her friend the bottle every bit as much as she loved me and Charlie, and Pushpa spent as much time as she could with a crippled woman's husband. It was an unspoken secret that she loved the old barber with the misshapen legs. Mam and I knew all about his secret visits, that he came for food and to sleep for a while in her room. The smug Atul knew too, rarely missing an opportunity to sidle up to us, whispering tales about the fat ayah and her low-caste lover. Enraged, I looked at Mam and Pushpa and promised myself I'd ignore everything they said. They wanted to rein me in and keep me under control, and I wasn't going to let them rule me: they'd turned me into their cash cow, the money-spinner saving them from destitution, and I wanted more from life than that.

Chapter Eight

Pushpa

K AMALA CLOSED HER new brothel in Bowbazar after the war and complained her best customers were going home to spend their money on Yankee girls with yellow hair. The troops left gradually on overcrowded ships, rationing eased and Cook no longer had to limit his baking to one day a week because of the shortage of sugar. Calcutta, though, never went back to its old ways and the city felt no safer in peacetime. One war had ended but another was already beginning in India. Only this time we weren't threatened by the Japanese or starved to death by callous rulers; we were slaughtered by our own people. Ma Kali had no answer to the cruelty about to be inflicted on the city. Like the terrible cyclones that sweep through Bengal every few decades, ripping up trees, demolishing houses, flooding the land and killing thousands, the horror of the bloodbath was preceded by warning signs. When a storm approaches, animals become nervous and birds suddenly take to the air, the rooks cawing loudly. The sky grows dark in a few seconds and a powerful wind springs up from nowhere. It was the same with the Great Killing. All the signs and omens were there. They were obvious, if only I'd had the sense to see them.

'I need a wee,' Charlie said, tugging on Miss Maisy's hand.

'I told him to go before he left the house but he just held his willy and said it was empty,' Mem said, pretending to scowl at him.

The open spaces of the Maidan were full of cricketers and sweaty-faced British soldiers, shirtless and sunburned, who charged after a ball and roared triumphantly whenever they kicked it between two poles.

'Come on, Charlie,' Miss Maisy said, leading him to a tree. 'You can do it here.'

'I knew it was a bad idea to come out today,' Mem complained. 'It's too bleeding hot.'

'It's good to get out of the house, Mam. Poor Charlie never goes anywhere. When I was little I played in the street every day.'

'You did not,' Mem said.

'I did. You never realised: you were always asleep.'

We walked slowly: Charlie's legs were too short; my hips were too old; and Mem was a pale shade of yellow.

'We'll get a taxi,' Miss Maisy said, taking off her sunglasses. She couldn't spot a taxi any more easily without them.

We plodded over the Maidan. A line of a dozen goats trotted past us, a white and brown one trailing at a distance with a kid that couldn't have been more than a few days old. The mother stopped every few steps to nibble at fresh green blades of grass and her kid took every chance to suckle. The exasperated herder whacked the mother with a stick to hurry her along but she hardly budged and so he picked up the kid, tucked it under his arm, and marched after the rest of his animals, the nanny goat rushing after him, bleating with temper.

'I'll try that trick,' Miss Maisy said, lifting Charlie and balancing him on her hip.

At the Victoria Memorial, Miss Maisy shifted him on to her other hip. 'You're getting too big for me to carry such a long way,' she said, kissing his cheek. 'You'll be carrying me soon.'

By the time we got to Chowringhee, Charlie had to walk on his own two feet.

'What's that din?' Mem asked.

A crowd began to sweep past us and, within seconds, we were caught in a flood of tightly packed demonstrators. '*Jai Hind, Jai Hind,*' – 'Long Live India,' they chanted.

I was shoved forward and marched with the men. I'd lost Mem, and though I spotted Miss Maisy's blonde hair, she quickly disappeared.

The mob surged up Chowringhee and I weaved my way through the crowd and stood on the pavement. Mem was being jostled by a couple of young men who pushed her into a group of onlookers. She was too far away for me to hear what she said but judging by her hand gestures and angry expression it was one of Mem's favourite English curses. Miss Maisy joined her a few moments later and the look on Mem's face turned instantly from anger to horror.

'Charlie,' she screamed so loudly that the demonstrators halted the march to stare at the shrieking white woman. 'Charlie, where are you?'

The mob thinned and the chants of the excited young men

grew fainter. Miss Maisy ran along the road, and then stopped to pick up something from the gutter. It was Charlie's shoe.

'Oh, my God, he's been kidnapped,' Mem howled, beating her chest. 'My grandson's been snatched by *goondas*.'

'He was with me, and then he was gone,' Miss Maisy wailed. 'He was holding my hand and next thing, he was pulled away. I didn't have time to pick him up.'

'Where's the sodding police when you need them?' Mem ranted, waving the shoe at everyone who walked by.

'Have you seen my son?' Miss Maisy asked, dashing from one person to the next. 'Have you seen a little boy? He's lost. He's about this big.'

Everyone shook their heads and many joined us in the search, looking behind the bushes and trees edging the Maidan.

It took me several minutes to spot him. He was sitting in the arms of a food stall owner and sticking his fingers into a bag of *jhal muri*.

'Where's your mother?' the man asked him in Bengali.

'I don't know,' Charlie replied, and then caught sight of me. 'Pushpa,' he said, pointing. He grinned and held out his arms.

Miss Maisy rushed past me. 'Charlie. Thank God,' she cried.

The stallholder was confused. 'You're his mother?' he asked Miss Maisy.

'Yes, of course I'm his mother,' Miss Maisy said, and took him from the man. 'Thank you, thank you,' she said, choking on tears and covering Charlie in kisses.

'I saw you looking for a child,' he said. 'I didn't think it could be this one.'

The trouble started in the north of the city. No one could agree exactly how it began but everyone was sure it'd been brewing for a long time. Madan swore he'd seen men in the *bustees* sharpening daggers and fashioning park railings into spears. 'Don't go out tomorrow,' he told me. 'It'll be bloody.'

I did go out; I went to Whiteaway's department store with Miss Maisy, and I wished I'd listened to his advice. I knew something was wrong when trams stopped travelling to north Calcutta. Soon after, rising smoke sent messages of disaster before the reports of the killing began to spread. Near Esplanade terminal, passengers poured out of a tram, some running frantically while others stood in shock, unsure where to go. A middle-aged woman stumbled towards me and grabbed my arm. 'You wouldn't believe what I've just seen.'

A nervous crowd gathered round her. 'I saw Muslims looting a Hindu shop and when the shopkeeper complained they gouged out his eyes and set him and his shop on fire.'

Another passenger added his own tales. 'Ten or eleven of them went into a Muslim house. They raped the women and girls; we could hear them begging for mercy. Then they brought a pregnant woman into the street, cut open her belly, ripped out the baby and threw it to the dogs. All of them were killed, hacked to pieces with machetes, even the children.'

'Don't take any notice, Miss Maisy,' I said at the sight of her appalled expression. 'People are spreading rumours to make trouble. Nothing like that could happen here.'

After the horror of the famine, I should have known better: we had come to believe human life was cheap.

'Let's get home quickly,' Miss Maisy said nervously. 'You might be right, Pushpa, but that woman was too upset to be making up tall tales. Did you see her eyes? She was petrified.'

Another demonstration chanting '*Jai Hind*' was making its way up the road and we stood aside to let it pass. A group of youths stepped on to the pavement near us.

'Hey, you,' one of them called to an elderly Muslim man who was carrying a bag of vegetables, a bunch of coriander sticking out of the top. He stood silently and looked at them.

'*Jai Hind. Jai Hind,*' they shouted in his face.

One of the men drew a short knife and, in an instant, plunged it into the man's stomach, pulling it out with a hard yank of the blade. He stabbed again a few inches higher, forcing the knife between his ribs. The old man gasped. His brow furrowed and his mouth opened in surprise. He crumpled and fell to the ground, his shopping bag spilling its contents over the pavement. A few potatoes and an onion rolled towards us, and the coriander lay in a fast-spreading pool of blood, the leaves floating, startlingly green among the bright red. The youths laughed and rejoined the cheering demonstrators. The tales from north Calcutta had been right.

A curfew was declared by nightfall. On the roof of the house the usual sound of croaking bullfrogs was overlain by the distant, eerie baying of the mob.

'What are they yelling, Pushpa?' Mem asked. 'I can't make it out. Are they killing each other?'

'I don't know,' I answered. 'Perhaps they're trying to sound as frightening as possible so no one attacks them.'

Miss Maisy drew a shawl around her shoulders as if she were cold. 'I imagine hell to sound like that,' she said.

Bloodcurdling screams tore the air. 'That's coming from Park Circus,' Miss Maisy said in alarm. 'It's so close.'

'It's a good job we've got Lakshman on duty,' Mem said to comfort us. I didn't add that Lakshman's sentry box smelled of alcohol and he was so deeply asleep he might as well have been unconscious. The *durwan* brought local spirits for Mem and liked to sample them himself, often with as much self-control as the memsahib.

'Lucky old Gordon chose the right time to go to Darjeeling,' Mem said.

'It's not you *feringhees* – foreigners – they want,' I said.

More howls came from further north, from the neighbourhoods around New Market, perhaps even Dharmatala. I closed my eyes and prayed Madan would be safe.

Atul and Cook went home early next morning to protect their families. Atul came back a couple of weeks later but Cook never returned. Ram heard Cook's family was massacred by a mob and he found their naked bodies thrown down a well. The same mob caught him later and hanged him from a tree. Atul said the *mali* was wrong: Cook discovered his mother, wife and children dumped in the well, but he wasn't murdered. He was driven crazy by grief and the desire for revenge and joined a gang of marauders hunting for blood. Atul claimed Cook led a group of men who flushed Muslims from their hiding places and devised ever more sickening ways of killing them. He heard it from several people who'd witnessed it first-hand and the story appalled me. I hoped Cook had been hanged from the tree because it was a better way to end his life.

The army was on the streets a day after the massacres began, and lorries and Red Cross vehicles toured the city collecting the dead. Bodies stacked up on the burning ghats and mass graves were dug. Banks, courts and big offices closed, and food became scarce within a couple of days. I went shopping with Miss Maisy but there was nothing to buy and most shops were shut. Sahib sent a car and driver for us to use and we travelled quickly, keeping the windows firmly closed against the stench of rotting flesh. Outside the bakery, the smell was unbearable and Miss Maisy held a perfume-drenched handkerchief over her nose. Sweepers lifted a manhole cover in the road and staggered backwards, sickened by the smell of the disintegrating corpses blocking the sewers.

'I don't think I fancy any bread today,' Miss Maisy said, barely controlling the impulse to retch.

'That's lucky, Miss Maisy,' I said, looking up at the vultures circling overhead. 'There's no bread left.'

Sunil and Madan didn't contact us during the Killing. It was too dangerous to travel and a curfew kept us inside the gates except for short trips around white town. Miss Maisy sat on the veranda, agitated and unhappy, oblivious to the scene before her. While the people of Calcutta were being mutilated and murdered, Ram's late monsoon garden bloomed, a place of beauty and peace among the horror.

'Where can he be?' she said. 'He hasn't sent a chit for over a month.'

'He'll be a long way from the city,' I said. 'He'll be safe.'

'No, Pushpa, I don't think he is. I have such a horrible feeling,' she cried. 'Something bad has happened to him. I feel it in the pit of my stomach.'

I felt the same dread for Madan and was elated when I saw him standing at the gate three weeks after the madness had begun. The fury unleashed on the city was gradually receding and he had at last dared to make the journey from Dharmatala.

'She's dead,' he said through the bars of the gate, and I was startled to see him crying. His wife had died of natural causes during the height of the terror and had been burned on the ghats surrounded by hundreds of others who had died suddenly and violently at the hands of men. Madan was sad, dropping on to my bed with a sigh, his hands trembling.

'You should feel happy. She is out of her pain and misery,' I counselled, annoyed he felt any grief.

Tears rolled down his cheeks and all of a sudden my glee at his wife's death evaporated, and I was ashamed. The poor woman had been unable to cut her ties to the things she loved, and she'd clung to this world, existing only in the shadowy space between life and death. I was dismayed to realise that during all the time I waited for her to leave me her husband, I'd not spared her a single moment's pity or compassion. I'd thought only of my longing to claim him as my own – an old man with bad legs and very few teeth.

Many people were changed by the Killing: some were made vengeful, and others forever wary of their neighbours. A few survivors were broken, their spirits crushed. By some marvel others searched for something positive after the carnage, a way to repair our wounded city. The upheaval, though, did nothing to change Atul, who came back to us full of his old cunning and mindful only of himself.

Within an hour of his return, I caught him lurking behind the rear wall of the house, leaning round the corner to spy on Miss Maisy as she sat on the swing beneath the monkey tree. His fat back was turned to me so he didn't see me tiptoeing towards him. He jumped, startled by my sudden appearance at his side and, almost as quickly, he relaxed and gave me his familiar, self-satisfied smile.

I've been worried most of my life. When I was a child I was anxious about our next meal and whether the harvest would be good. As a young widow I was unsure I'd live long enough to become a woman. In Sonagachi, I feared for the babies growing inside me and whether they'd survive more than a few days. I was nervous about clients and money and I never felt confident about how long I could keep working when the customers began preferring the younger girls. In the garden house, too, I waited for my world to come crashing down. As 1946 rolled into a new year, I couldn't enjoy the easy work and the good food because I knew it was only a matter of time before they were snatched away. Two months after the Killing ended, Sunil returned to Calcutta.

Mem and I worked together, concocting stories to explain Miss Maisy's absences and the many times she returned late from shopping without having bought a thing. Lies and dread filled our days when Sunil was in the city, sending chits the *mali* delivered with downcast eyes, complicit in a secret he didn't want to share. The sahib paid Ram's wages and the *mali* was far too old to find another garden to tend.

Miss Maisy became melancholy whenever Sunil left, reading though the sahib's newspaper to find any news that could be linked with him. I'm sure she was as addicted to Sunil Banerjee as Mem was to her *burra pegs*.

'Where does he go?' I asked Madan.

He shrugged. 'He's busy fighting everyone.'

'He wants the British to go.'

'We all want the bastard white skins to leave.'

'I don't.'

He looked at me in surprise.

'What will I do if they leave?' I asked.

'Live with me.'

It was a pointless suggestion because Madan's income was drying up along with his trade as a pavement barber. During the summer, he'd developed a trembling in his hands, and throughout the following monsoon and winter, the shake grew more severe, deterring even his regular customers. Lack of money forced him to move from the *bustee* in Dharmatala to a *kutcha* bamboo shack, which he shared with a rickshaw wallah from out of town.

I caught his wrists and held them, and we watched his hands tremble.

'What kind of life will that be?' I asked. 'How can we live in a shack with a rickshaw wallah? And how will we eat?'

He didn't answer.

'Anyway, Mem won't go back,' I said. 'She hates England. And Maisy and Charlie were born here; they don't know anywhere else.'

Madan lit a *bidi* and took a long drag. 'People like them are used to being in charge, and that's going to change when independence comes.'

'Mem isn't in charge of herself, never mind anyone else. And the only thing Miss Maisy has power over is the sahib's penis.'

'Everything will be different when we're free: different for them, and better for us. Everyone will have a pukka house. I've heard it from many people. I went to a rally where Charlie's father said the land is going to be divided and given to the poor. There'll be no more landlords or moneylenders, and all the jute mills, mines and tea gardens are going to be owned by the workers.'

Sunil and Madan must have been feverish when they planned their new world. They hadn't listened to the sahib shouting down the telephone or the way he cursed the Marwari jute wallahs and the British men in the big managing agencies. Sunil and Madan were no match for men like Sahib and his Indian rivals. They were fools, I thought. Fools and dreamers.

I was relieved when Sahib showed no sign of packing up and leaving Calcutta. Mem dug for information constantly, often interrupting the sahib when he was with Miss Maisy and asking questions about the state of the jute trade and the sahib's plans for his business.

'For Christ's sake, will you leave it be?' Sahib said in exasperation. 'How many times do I have to tell you? I am not leaving India just yet.' He stubbed out his cigarette and brushed away a sprinkling of ash that had fallen on to the cuff of his white dinner jacket. He was dressed to go to a party to which Miss Maisy hadn't been invited.

'Won't the Indians take over the industry after independence?' Mem persisted, undeterred by Sahib's scowl.

'I'm here to make money, not save an empire. I don't care who runs the bloody Government as long as my mills operate and we can make a profit.'

Mem seemed satisfied and she took her drink on to the veranda, the bamboo squeaking loudly as she settled into her chair.

'Your mother's panicking too much,' Sahib said. 'Independence won't mean a thing unless the Indians start playing politics with the economy. Communal rioting is my biggest worry. The last curfew hit production badly.'

We all worried about another massacre and I took heart when Madan said Gandhiji was coming to Calcutta to help keep the peace. But despite the news that former enemies were linking arms in the streets and chanting 'Hindus and Muslims are one,' Sahib still wasn't taking any chances. The day before Independence he presented Lakshman with a gun, and they practised firing it across the lawn, terrifying the birds, which took flight, and distressing Mem, who was sure a bullet would ricochet through the open window and strike Charlie dead. Lakshman waved the gun without coordination, pointing it awkwardly and missing the empty whisky bottle placed on a nearby wall as a target.

'Good God,' Sahib exclaimed, snatching the gun from Lakshman. 'You're a Gorkhali, aren't you? You Nepalese are supposed to be fighting men.'

Calming down, he called to Miss Maisy. 'You need to see this,' he said to her. 'I've a revolver for you, too. You'll have to keep it locked in a chest in the bedroom.'

Showing far more patience and care than he did with anything else in his life, Sahib demonstrated how to load the gun. 'That part is easy,' he said. 'Now comes the difficult bit. Watch carefully.' He scanned the garden and the returning wildlife. The great *shikari* narrowed his eyes, took aim and fired. A multi-coloured parrot in Professor Mitra's jacaranda tree plummeted to the ground in a cloud of feathers, and Miss Maisy gasped in horror.

Sahib left in his grand car, which was now flying the flag of the new India. He gave Lakshman some final instructions through the window, then shouted to Miss Maisy, 'Stay in tonight. Ignore any celebrations and don't be tempted to unlock the doors.'

Mem certainly had no intention of joining in the celebrations. When Miss Maisy switched on the wireless and we heard Pandit Nehru's crisp British voice say, 'At the stroke of the midnight hour, when the world sleeps, India will wake to life and freedom,' Mem was fast asleep on the sofa, snoring loudly, her head thrown back and her mouth hanging slack.

Calcutta didn't descend into slaughter, and in the morning Madan arrived at the house, an Indian flag draped round his shoulders and a spring in his usual hobbling step. 'Come to the party,' he called from the gate. 'There are hundreds of thousands of people, and not one angry face. Everyone is happy.'

'Let's go,' Miss Maisy said.

'There'll be a bloodbath,' Mem said, appalled.

'You heard what he said: it's a party. There's no danger.'

'You've no sense when it comes to danger.'

'Mam, this is history in the making.'

'I don't want to be part of this history. I liked things the way they were.'

Madan was right: Independence Day in Calcutta was a carnival. Euphoric men toured the crowded streets in packed trucks, people distributed sweetmeats, and women blew conch shells from the rooftops as if we were at a joyful wedding rather than a change of government.

We stood among the festivities on Chowringhee. '*Jai Hind*,' Madan said to Mem, and spun her round. He began to dance, taking no notice of her stricken expression and forgetting his ruined knees in his ecstasy. Four or five other poor men in scruffy clothes began to dance with her, too.

'*Jai Hind*,' they chanted, bounding around her, waving their arms and thrusting their faces into hers with laughs that swung between delight and menace.

Mem hopped from foot to foot, looking stricken, and cheered a feeble, '*Jai Hind*,' before Miss Maisy rescued her from the revellers.

We made our way home leaving Madan to continue the party, invigorated by an excitement that had kept him awake all night. I looked sadly at the kind-hearted fool, knowing that he was rejoicing at the thought of the pukka house that would soon be his. As we headed back towards Park Street, Madan joined his new friends marching to Government House to watch the flag-raising ceremony, not a trace of a tremor in his limbs.

His trembling returned with a vengeance by nightfall. He sat exhausted on my bed. 'It was the best day of my life,' he said.

'You'll have a bad head tomorrow,' I said.

'I haven't had a drink, or any ganja. I didn't need any today.'

'Did you see the new flag outside Government House?'

'More than that: I saw inside Government House.'

He must be lying about the drugs, I thought. He's probably

been enjoying *bhang* – a milk, sugar and cannabis drink – all day.

'It's true, Pushpa,' he said. 'I didn't see the flag-raising ceremony but these very eyes have seen the Throne Room. We went right inside. There were hundreds of us and no one could stop us. I saw it all: the chandeliers, the pictures, the furniture. It makes this house look like a poor man's *kutcha* hut. I sat on a chair of velvet, and then we took it in turns to sit on the throne. I rubbed my hands on it, thinking: that's where the Viceroy and the Governor used to sit, their white arses on the same cushion as mine.'

He's high on something, I realised. Maybe those new friends took him for an opium pipe in the Chinese quarter.

'You don't believe me, but I'm telling the truth. We walked round the whole of the building. We found food in the kitchens and we took a look at the bedrooms. I was so tired after not sleeping last night that I lay down on the biggest bed. It was soft as air, the pillows like clouds. I would've slept if it hadn't been for the *paan wallahs* who climbed on there with me, getting their dirty feet on the pink cover. They talked and sang, and it kept me awake so that I saw the woman's face when she came out of the bathroom.'

'What woman?'

'The British Governor's wife. You should have seen her eyes almost popping out of her head. The police had to take her away quickly before she fainted. Someone said they saw her and the Governor being smuggled out of the back door.'

Poor Madan; his brain was fermenting after too much excitement.

'I have souvenirs for you,' he said.

He put a bundle on the bed and unwrapped a towel from around a small painting. He handed it to me and although it was surrounded by a pretty frame, the colour of burnished gold, the picture itself was nothing special. It was of a fat ugly white man in a red jacket sitting on a fat cream horse, and the unattractive pair was surrounded by a pack of dogs.

'And now look at this,' Madan said in great excitement. He felt among the rags in his bundle and drew out a glass bowl. The patterns cut into the sides were brilliant in the overhead light and a silver latticework covered the top.

'It's a crystal rose bowl from England,' I said, spellbound. 'There's one in the drawing room.'

'It was in the bedroom of the Governor's wife.'

'You stole it?'

'No. It belongs to us now: our ancestors paid for it with their blood and sweat. It's for you: you deserve it more than the biggest *burra mem*.'

Madan hadn't lied about being in Government House; he'd walked in the footsteps of princes, viceroys and governors. I held the bowl to the light, marvelling at the way it sparkled like a jewel. 'It's beautiful,' I sighed.

'It's like you, Pushparani. It's perfect, like you.'

'I've warned you about traipsing around the city,' Sahib thundered, marching up and down the veranda. 'It's not safe and it's not respectable.'

'What's respectable about our lives?' Miss Maisy retorted, sitting, arms folded, on Mem's favourite chair.

'You put yourself in danger. You went into the streets when the nationalist mobs were running wild. Anything could have happened. You might not care about yourself and your mother, but at least give some thought to the bairn.'

'I don't know why you're suddenly so concerned about Charlie. Usually you can't bear to look at him.' Miss Maisy pulled a face behind the sahib's back.

I told her often about a different kind of danger, too, and with just as much effect as the overbearing Sahib. 'I didn't warn you when you first met Sunil Banerjee and I regret that,' I said. 'If I had you might not have had an illegitimate child and no chance of a decent life.'

'How dare you speak to me like that, Pushpa?' Miss Maisy said, inflating her cheeks with fury. 'You're a servant and you've forgotten your place.'

'I speak to you like that because I've known you since you were a baby,' I said. I was annoyed with the silly girl, and I pitied her, too. 'You think you can be in love, but love is a luxury for someone in your position.'

She shook her head.

'What will happen when the sahib finds out? You've no father, no husband, and no brother to take care of you. You've no job and the only money you have is in the gold and jewellery Sahib has given you. Atul keeps watch, and are you sure the *durwan* won't tell the sahib?'

'Lakshman is dim and usually asleep. And why you should scold me when I know you've had that crippled barber in your bed for years is beyond belief. You are a bitter, old hypocrite.'

I didn't understand the last word; she said it in English. I only discovered what it meant when I asked Mem, but I knew as she spat it out that it wasn't nice.

'I'm old, and I could be very bitter when I think I've spent the last twenty years looking after a foolish, spoiled girl.'

'I'm not spoiled,' Maisy hissed. 'I work hard for all the good things my family have, including the things you have, Pushpa. You live in a nice house, and I know the sahib pays you a decent wage. Who's responsible for that? I have to be a bloody good actress to do what I do.'

It was true, I admit it: we lived in a lovely home that Miss Maisy earned on her back.

'You'll throw this life away, Miss Maisy, and for what? For a man who disappears for weeks on end. A man who says he will marry you someday, long in the future. He gives you excuses for why he can't marry you; first it was freeing India, now it's fighting for the poor. I don't believe him, and I don't think he'll marry you. And even if I'm wrong and you become his wife, you'll be poor. Every day will be a struggle to live.'

'You don't understand, Pushpa.'

'Yes, I do. You don't have many choices, Miss Maisy. You lost them when you had Charlie. You're not like other white women now.'

'Shut up, Pushpa. Get out of this house and go and live with your stupid barber.' Miss Maisy ran from the drawing room sobbing, just as Mem wandered in and stared open-mouthed at her daughter.

'Was it another argument with the sahib?' she asked.

Miss Maisy came to my room when I was packing. I ignored her, though from the corner of my eye I could see she'd been crying and that her face was puffy, her cheeks blotchy and her nose pink.

'I'm sorry, Pushpa. Please, forgive me.' She sat on my bed, her breathing heavy and jagged. 'I didn't mean all those horrible things. I couldn't bear it if you left.'

I held her hands. 'I haven't got a daughter, Miss Maisy, because all my children died. But, if I had one, I would want her to be like you. It's why I said what I did: I want the best for you, and I'm sick with worry.'

'That's what frightens me and why I was so angry. I shouldn't have been so spiteful; you've been like a grandmother to me.'

It was the best thing Miss Maisy had ever said to me. She rested her head on my lap and I stroked her hair the way I did when she was a baby.

'I love him, Pushpa.'

'I know.'

I sang the lullabies she liked as a child and within a few minutes she was asleep on the bed. I unpacked my things, carefully unwrapping my precious rose bowl and the painting of the fat man. Putting the bowl back on the table I breathed a long sigh of relief: its dazzling brilliance would have been lost in Madan's bamboo hut.

Chillies and lemons keep evil away. I believe this even though I'm not very superstitious and nothing like the people who run their lives according to omens and the movement of stars. I know some foolish women who are alarmed by black cats, who refuse to cut their hair and nails on a Saturday, and are terrified when they hear owls hoot, believing them to be heralds of death. I've tied enough ribbons on the barren tree to know magic doesn't always work, and that sometimes it rebounds because it gives hope when there is none. I follow the old ways, though, and I go through the rituals just in case there's some truth in them, and I use magic because I need all the help I can get.

Chillies and lemons are different: I know they work. I've seen it myself many times. When we went to the garden house I tied a string of them next to the front door to guard us, and I changed them every week for fresh, glossy chillies and lemons whose scabby skins turned from green to yellow as they dangled in the sunshine, twirling slowly in the breeze, our protection from disaster until the day the thread snapped and evil was invited in.

Sahib started the year with stomach cramp. At six in the morning on New Year's Day he stepped through the door holding a piece of coal, a cake and some biscuits for luck, and demanded a drink of whisky. Atul, half dressed and without his hat, snaked off into the *bottle khanna* and reappeared looking smart, a glass of Sahib's finest whisky on a tray.

'You didn't let anyone through the door before me?' Sahib asked Atul.

'No, Sahib. You are the first.'

Even British people believe in magic, and Sahib wanted to take the first step into the house each New Year because he thought it would bring him good fortune. He was especially concerned about getting the magic right as business wasn't going well for Calcutta's jute wallahs. On the day Madan danced in the streets to celebrate Independence, a line had been cut through the heart of Bengal. The jute mills were one side of the line in India, and the jute growing lands on the other side, in East Pakistan. In a single stroke, West Bengal's mills were robbed of their golden fibre, and MacBrayne Sahib, the jute wallah, had hardly any jute bags to sell.

Sahib sagged into his chair. 'The haggis was off,' he said to Miss Maisy who came into the room, hastily tying her dressing gown and running her fingers through her hair. 'I shouldn't have gone to Harris's party: the old skinflint served local whisky and his cook's an eejit. It's no way to celebrate Hogmanay.'

'Here's to 1948,' Miss Maisy said, raising a glass of pineapple juice. 'Happy New Year.'

Sahib got to his feet and bolted, bent double, into the bathroom.

He left a few hours later, slumped in the back of the car, his skin a strange shade of khaki. Jamal was at the wheel, high on ganja he'd smoked with Ram in the godown. They pulled out of the drive and as I walked back into the house I stopped in surprise: in the still, windless day the thread of lemons and chillies hanging by the door spun fast and ceaselessly.

Sunil Banerjee had a reputation he didn't deserve. Madan sang his praises, dreaming of his pukka house, and Miss Maisy, blinded by love, spoke of him as if he were a god, to which I merely nodded and clicked my tongue. I remembered the skinny youth with a downy moustache who visited us in Dharmatala. To me, the boy lacked sense, and five months after Independence, five months after the British had left Government House, Sunil was still at war, and still promising that one day soon, when the struggle was won, he would do the right thing and marry Miss Maisy. I have heard men talk like this many times, and I knew he was lying. It was ridiculous to imagine an educated Brahmin would marry a poor white woman whose mother had been a prostitute. Miss Maisy might have been beautiful and fair but she didn't have a single rupee for a dowry.

Soon after New Year, Sunil appeared at the gates of the garden house. He was tense and too thin, and couldn't have eaten well in a long time. He'd conducted his sporadic, secret affair with Miss Maisy for almost two years, during which time he'd blighted my life with anxiety, becoming a harbinger of disaster, and yet as he stood pleading by the gate, Lakshman looking on, dim and baffled, my anger towards him eased. It was the first time I had seen him properly since he left a pregnant Miss Maisy six years before. His soft moustache had been replaced by dark bristles and he didn't seem like the devious serpent I'd imagined.

'You'll have to go,' I said. 'The sahib might arrive any minute.'

'Please, bring your memsahib,' he said.

I sat on the edge of the veranda watching how his nervousness reduced when Miss Maisy rushed to the gate. In the side garden he drew her close and kissed her under the monkey tree. She laughed, caught entirely in the moment. Madan often joked that we were like Radha and Krishna, the divine lovers, but he was surely wrong; Miss Maisy and Sunil were the lovers reborn. Charlie ran across the lawn and Sunil swept him up, whirling him in the air, the boy whooping with delight.

I jumped, hearing a sound behind me. Twisting round, I saw Atul staring at them. He glanced down at me, gave his habitual smile and then he turned slowly, spinning on his heel, and I watched his fat back encased in its tight white *achkan* vanish into the shade of the drawing room.

Sometimes I wonder if I could have changed what happened next. If I hadn't been thinking about Atul, if I'd heard the gates open and Sahib's car pull into the drive I could have warned them, and then Sahib might not have witnessed the spectacle that triggered our downfall.

Sahib stepped on to the veranda. He tensed instantly and became perfectly still, weighing up the scene the way he did before he took aim and shot the parrot in Professor Mitra's tree. Sunil had his arm around Miss Maisy's waist, and Charlie was reaching up, showing his father something. Maisy lifted her eyes from Charlie and shock wiped the smile from her face. Sunil moved away from her, his movements suddenly stiff.

'Are you going to introduce me to your friend, Maisy?' Sahib said, walking on to the lawn.

He didn't need to ask who Sunil was: Charlie, who started practising forward rolls on the grass, was a copy of his father.

I got up too quickly, a pain shooting through my hip. Perhaps the quick-tempered sahib is still carrying his gun, I thought. Miss Maisy stuttered something I couldn't understand as the sahib circled around Sunil, looking as if he was about to throw a punch.

'Lakshman,' the sahib shouted. 'We have an intruder.'

Sahib lunged but Sunil moved fast, side-stepping Sahib and shaking off his grip. He ran to the gates and bolted towards Theatre Street.

Lakshman sauntered into the side garden, beaming.

'You're too late, man,' Sahib raged. 'And why are you letting fucking criminals into my property? You're sacked. Get your bloody things and leave.'

The *durwan*'s jaw dropped. 'Memsahib, she say he come in.'

'You take orders from me, not the Memsahib.'

'It's not Lakshman's fault,' Miss Maisy said.

Sahib looked at her, his face deep red, his lips set in a thin, hard line. The big vein throbbed on his temple. 'Get inside,' he said, and stormed off to find Atul. I saw the two men talking, Atul stroking his glossy moustache while he told tales and crafted misfortune.

'Do you want to explain yourself?' Sahib said, marching into the drawing room to confront Miss Maisy. I hid behind the shutters on the veranda and peeped through a crack in the wood. Where's Mem? I thought. How can she sleep through the shouting? Even the fearsome atmosphere would be enough to revive the dead.

'He's the bairn's father, isn't he?' Sahib barked.

Miss Maisy nodded.

'The tutor you claimed was dead?'

'Yes. I thought he was dead, or something like that.'

'Remind me of his name.'

'Sunil. Sunil Banerjee.'

Sahib sucked furiously on a cigarette. 'Atul warned me but I didn't believe him; I was too blind to see what was going on right under my nose. I suppose I should have expected it – a girl with a half-caste bastard was never going to be trustworthy.'

'I'm sorry . . .' Miss Maisy began to say before Sahib's thundering voice silenced her.

'After all I've done for you; after everything I've given you, you skulk around with an Indian. For Christ's sake, Maisy, he's dirt poor. You're going to end up living in a filthy ghetto, although it shouldn't surprise me; you and your lush of a mother have never been quite pukka. You're no lady: you're a fucking whore.'

'Isn't that why you set me up in this place? Because you knew you didn't have to treat me like a lady.'

'Aye, you're right about that,' Sahib laughed. 'But I thought you were an expensive whore, not a cheap one.' He seethed, pacing the room. 'You know, I think you planned this all along; you just wanted some fool to pay for your bastard and to give you a good life while you carried on with your whoring.'

Miss Maisy was doing a bad job of explaining herself. 'It's not like that, Gordon. I promise.'

'Och, I understand well enough, lassie. You think I'm a mug. But I'll tell you this, I may be a bloody fool, but he's your pimp.'

Something in the corner of my eye caught my attention: Lakshman was collecting his things from the sentry box and tying them up in a blanket. He slung the bundle over his shoulder and then paused, looking back at the house. He walked slowly to the front door and, with a quick movement, he grabbed the thread of chillies and lemons twirling in the still afternoon air. Chucking them on to the drive, he stomped away with more speed and purpose than I'd ever seen him possess.

Sahib's voice rose higher and then broke into a loud croak. 'I want you to leave this house; our arrangement is finished.'

'We've nowhere to go.'

'That's no concern of mine. I'll give you to the end of the week.'

Sahib walked on to the veranda and stood right next to me without seeing me. He regarded Miss Maisy with a cold fury. But there was something else in his expression that filled me with both pity and fear. The great jute wallah was heart-broken, gripped by hatred and jealousy. He'd seen a love he wanted for himself and that he knew he couldn't buy. In that instant, I saw the power and malevolence of envy and I trembled, for the evil eye was looking right at Miss Maisy.

'Are you happy now?' Mem wailed next morning while Miss Maisy packed things into a trunk. 'We're being chucked on to the streets because of that sodding clerk. Where is he now? How's he going to help you? The bastard's done this before: he's buggered off and left us in the bleeding shit.'

'Stop shouting, Mam. He'll be in touch soon.'

'Right, he will,' Mem said, the cigarette in the corner of her mouth wagging up and down as she spoke. 'And what good will that do us? You should beg Gordon to take you back. You'll have to plead for forgiveness, but it'll be worth it. Tell him Atul's a bloody liar. Tell him you were driven crazy by the heat or that a tropical disease warped your mind.'

Miss Maisy carried on packing in silence and Mem rushed away saying she needed a drink. By late afternoon she was unconscious on the veranda. Not even the frantic honking of the Sahib's car horn brought her round. I went to open the gates because although Lakshman had left, none of the other servants thought to do a job that wasn't officially their own. Atul was already snubbing Miss Maisy by not carrying out his own duties: he must have heard the sahib's verdict from his hidey-hole in the *bottle khanna* and knew she would soon be gone.

Jamal blew the horn again and again.

'Be patient,' I said, exasperated.

The car sped in and stopped with a jolt. Jamal would usually get out and open the sahib's door with a flourish, but that day he scrambled from his seat and dashed across the garden, vanishing into Ram's godown without saying a word of thanks to me. I looked into the back of the car in surprise: Sahib wasn't there.

By nightfall Jamal hadn't reappeared and lamplight shone through the cracks in the wood walls of the *mali*'s hut. When I knocked, no one answered, so I pushed the door open. Ram and Jamal sat in a cloud of ganja smoke, Jamal startled and jittery.

'Sit down, sister,' Ram said. 'You need to listen to this.'

MacBrayne Sahib was one of those men you respect but find it difficult to like. He was abrupt and cold and understood nothing of my country even though he'd lived here over half his life. But, in my opinion, he didn't deserve what happened to him, although I know many people who say he escaped lightly and that he should have suffered a harsher fate. Jamal agreed with me and said it was unjust. Sahib didn't warrant the horrors inflicted on him, and I trust Jamal's judgement on this because he saw it all.

I sat Jamal on the veranda and called Miss Maisy. Mem woke up and stared at us, confused and bleary-eyed. They had to hear the story from Jamal's own mouth; they wouldn't believe it from anyone else. The feverishness of his speech and the terror in his face guaranteed he was telling the truth.

'Tell them,' I said. 'Start from the beginning and don't leave anything out.'

Ram placed a hand on Jamal's shoulder as the driver began

to speak. Miss Maisy translated for Mem, who looked as if she wouldn't understand a word, even in English.

'We were going to the Britannia Mill,' Jamal said. 'It's the big one upriver. Sahib sometimes goes by boat but today I took him in the car. He was expecting trouble. Sahib's been worrying about that mill for weeks. There's always some problem there: lockouts, no jute, communists stirring up the workers. Sahib curses them all the time; he shouts and swears in the back of the car. It makes driving hard when he's angry.

'Everything seemed normal when we arrived. The *durwans* opened the gates and we went inside, but then *goondas* surrounded the car and the guards vanished. There was no one to help us. They dragged Sahib out before I could restart the engine, and when I shouted at them to stop they pulled me out too and marched us both into the mill. I knew Sahib had his gun; he always carries it these days, and I hoped he'd use it but they tied his hands behind his back and he couldn't reach it.'

Jamal paused, breathing deeply.

'Then what?' Mem said, shrilly, suddenly wide awake. 'Get on with it.'

'The men were talking to the sahib but I couldn't hear what they were saying. The noise of the machines in the mills is deafening. All the jute wallahs were rounded up by men with knives and herded into another part of the mill. Sahib was furious. I heard him shouting above the sound of the looms. And he went very red; you know the way he looks when he's angry, that big vein pulsing in his neck and the smaller one throbbing on his temple. I thought his heart might burst with temper.'

'What did Jamal say?' Mem asked me. Miss Maisy had stopped translating. I suppose she must have dreaded what she'd hear next.

'I'll never forget the smell of jute dust and sweat, and the clanking of the big machines,' Jamal went on. 'They found the manager and hauled him through the mill with us, and the ringleader ranted in Sahib's ear, shoving him this way and that. We stopped in the part of the mill where they finish the hessian. They push it through big rollers to make it smooth. The leader cut the rope tying Sahib's wrists, and straight away he went for his gun. But the men were too quick. They snatched it from his hand, and in the fight the leader – may the curse of Allah be upon him – shot the manager though the back of the head and his brains exploded over the floor.

'I thought I'd die, there and then. I said a prayer and when I looked up that son of a pig had put Sahib's fingers on the calendar machine's rollers. A *goonda* pulled me to my feet and held a knife to my throat. I heard the leader talking about accidents in the mill and how it was Sahib's turn to know how it felt.'

Jamal dried his eyes and used the sleeve of his uniform to wipe away the trail of snot running over his upper lip.

'What happened? Did they kill him?' Mem asked in a high-pitched voice, and for a moment I was uncertain whether she was horrified by the ordeal the sahib had faced or whether she relished it.

'The man forced Sahib's fingers between the rollers. I've heard men scream like that during the Killing. I heard them in Burrabazar. But I never saw them scream, or saw their faces. His hand . . .' Jamal said in an anguished rasp. 'His hand was gone. It was eaten by the machine. He couldn't pull his arm out and it was sucked in, bit by bit.'

Miss Maisy was stunned, her white skin turning grey. 'Poor, poor Gordon,' she exclaimed.

'Is he dead, then?' Mem asked, a little too eagerly.

Jamal shook his head.

Mem fidgeted while the rest of us sat still. 'Tell us the end of the story,' she said.

'The guards arrived with the police and there was a fight. The *goondas* got away by boat, but some of them must have been injured because there was a trail of blood down to the river ghat.'

'The police have gone to pot since the British left,' Mem said. 'They couldn't catch a criminal if one walked into the sodding station and handed themselves in.'

'Did they rescue Gordon? Is he all right?' Miss Maisy said.

'They stopped the calendar machine.'

'And, is he alive?'

'He's lost a lot of blood but he'll live, *Inshallah*.'

'Thank God.'

'But his arm's gone, Mem.'

I tried to rid myself of the idea of Sahib's contorted face and mangled arm, and the thought of his blood soaking through the hessian that had made his fortune.

Miss Maisy shivered. 'Who would do such a sickening thing?' she said.

'I don't know the men, Memsahib,' Jamal said. 'I've never seen them before. But the sahib did. He knew the ringleader. He told the police before the ambulance took him away.'

'Who was it?'

'You won't know them, Mem. They are revolutionaries; angry, confused men.'

'What names did Sahib give?'

'Only one, Mem. His name was Sunil Banerjee.'

Chapter Nine

Maisy

I DIDN'T BELIEVE Jamal. Sunil was incapable of such evil; it wasn't in his nature. I could see Mam, though, looking at me as if to say 'I told you so,' and Pushpa rocking backwards and forwards, her brow knitted tight.

'There's been a mistake,' I said.

'Tell that to the police,' Mam said. 'He's rotten to the core and he's ruined this family.'

No one knew what else to say, and in the shocked silence I sifted through my memory, discovering things I'd rather have forgotten. I remembered sitting on the chintz sofa in the living room in Dharmatala while Sunil told me Mr Gandhi's non-violence wasn't the best way to achieve your ends. And I recalled standing on Howrah Bridge as Sunil proclaimed we were at war and that he'd happily kill the Governor of Bengal if he had the chance. Sunil loathed Gordon, and I'd lost track of the times he'd damned him in a fit of jealousy as 'the great white *babu*', one of the worst capitalists in Calcutta. I wouldn't admit it to anyone – and especially not to Mam and Pushpa, who both hated

Sunil – but I began to think he might have it in him to inflict a savage revenge.

'Poor little bugger,' Mam said, hugging Charlie, who'd staggered on to the veranda, half asleep. 'Now it turns out his father is a ruddy murderer. It's a cruel world: the lad's already got enough problems to deal with.'

Pushpa whispered a prayer, closed her eyes and opened her hands in supplication.

'Can you drive, Jamal?' I asked.

He nodded and, paying no heed to how he weaved his way to the car, we all squeezed into the back seat, Charlie balancing on my knee, and Mam and Pushpa fighting for space.

The Presidency General was West Bengal's finest hospital. Its very name, though, filled me with dread, because it was where my father died. Everyone I knew who went into PG Hospital came out worse, or dead. I think that's why I was so confused when we arrived. I didn't know how to explain why we were there, or how to find our way around the wards. So many people were milling about waiting for news in the place where Gordon was being treated, that I stood, perplexed, at the head of a ragtag group. Charlie was tired and grubby, Mam was nervous and shrill, and Pushpa still murmured incantations. I spotted Harris, Gordon's friend, who was talking to a policeman and some important-looking white men. He pretended he hadn't seen me, and turned his back to us.

'Can I help you?' a nurse asked.

'We've come to see Mr MacBrayne,' I said, and it suddenly occurred to me that Gordon might not want to see us.

'I'm sorry. Mr MacBrayne is not receiving visitors. Can I pass on a message?'

I hesitated, and saw two middle-aged women look at me in distaste. One of them stepped forward. 'And who are you?' she asked, her voice curt and hard.

'Friends,' I said.

'Is that right, Mrs MacBrayne?' she asked the other woman.

I was taken aback: I'd imagined Gordon's wife to be elegant and refined but in real life she was dumpy and plain and much older than I'd thought.

'I've never seen them before,' Mrs MacBrayne said in an accent coloured by Dundee.

'Never mind who we are, who are you?' Mam asked the posh lady.

'My husband works at the Deputy High Commission. He's standing over there with Mr Harris.'

The two women whispered, Mrs MacBrayne's face twisting into an expression of utter despair.

'I really must ask you to leave,' the diplomat's wife said. 'Your presence here is not helping the situation.'

'How is Gordon?' I asked.

'Go immediately,' she said to me while patting Mrs MacBrayne's arm.

Gordon's wife began to sob. The posh lady called to her husband, 'Richard, please can we have these people escorted from the hospital at once?'

'We're not leaving until we've found out what's happened to Gordon,' Mam said indignantly.

I wished we hadn't come: I should have realised Gordon's family would be there.

'Come on,' I said to Mam, pulling her away.

The diplomat's wife spoke to her husband, her sharp voice carrying down the corridor. 'How on earth can they let themselves go to such a dreadful extent?'

Mam bridled. 'Ruddy stuck-up bitch,' she seethed, preparing to turn back and give the woman a tongue-lashing.

'Let's not make a scene,' I said.

Mam took a deep breath, calming her rage. 'Did you see her?' she asked.

'Who?'

'Gordon's wife; that moon-faced thing. No wonder he took a shine to you, Maisy. She's old and dried up. And she's been stuffing herself with too much haggis and plates of tatties and mince.'

A woman walked down the corridor towards us holding a pile of files, her crisp white uniform starched so heavily it seemed to be made of card. I looked at her face as she came closer and then I stopped. 'Margaret?' I said. 'It is you, isn't it?'

It took a second for her to recognise me, and then she nearly dropped the files in surprise. 'Maisy,' she said. 'I can't believe it.'

In that grim building with its overpowering smell of disinfectant, Margaret somehow managed to glow. She was luminously beautiful, even with her jet-black hair scraped off her face and hidden under a stiff cap. Time had filled out her face a little so even her nose, that one thing that had made her seem less than perfect, appeared smaller, more in proportion.

She steered me into what appeared to be a storage room containing a few old wooden chairs and bits of broken furniture, and she dropped her files on to a metal bed frame. The others trudged in behind us and collapsed on to the chairs.

'You did it, then; you're a doctor,' I said.

'Not quite,' she smiled. 'I'm only a nurse. I couldn't get into medical school.'

She took my hands, squeezing them.

'What are you doing here?' she asked. 'Are any of you ill?' She glanced over at Mam, Charlie and Pushpa, who all slouched in the makeshift waiting room.

'We're fine. Actually, we came to see someone but I can't find any news about them.'

'What's their name?'

'Gordon MacBrayne.'

'He's my patient. Come to the ward now.'

'I can't. We've been there and were asked to leave. Please, just tell me what you know.'

Margaret looked from me to Mam and I thought I saw compassion in her eyes. She thinks I'm like Mam, I realised. She thinks I've followed in her footsteps.

'He still hasn't come round, so you couldn't see him anyway,' she said, as if to make me feel better.

'Will he live?'

'Oh, yes, providing there's no serious infection in the wound.'

'They said his hand was crushed.'

'And part of the arm, too. His elbow is intact and the surgeon managed to save the bone and flesh three or four inches below the joint. The real danger was blood loss, but he seems to have stabilised.'

The relief must have shown on my face.

'Don't worry, Maisy. He's getting the best care: his surgeon is brilliant. If anyone can save him, it's Dr Chatterjee.'

'Dr Chatterjee?' Mam said in surprise. 'Aren't there any British surgeons left?'

We heard voices in the corridor.

'I must go,' Margaret said, and gave me a hug. 'I've thought about you so often and wondered what happened to you after we left Dharmatala.'

'I'm hungry, Mum,' Charlie piped up.

'Is this your little boy?' Margaret exclaimed, smiling at him. Her eyes darted to my hands. Unlike Margaret, who wore a new, shiny, gold wedding ring, my fingers were bare, and I fancied I saw that compassionate look again.

Gathering her files, she stopped at the door. 'It's wonderful to see you, Maisy. It really is.'

We trudged through the hospital, Charlie whining about the pain in his empty tummy.

'So much for being a famous doctor and all those airs and graces her half-half family used to put on,' Mam said. 'She hasn't done very well for herself, has she? Imagine having to wipe shitty arses all day. It's not much better than being a sweeper.'

'It's a damn sight better than what we do, Mam.'

'That's your opinion.'

Outside PG Hospital there was no car and no Jamal.

'A *burra sahib* told him to drive to Alipore, Mem,' a porter said. 'He left a few minutes ago.'

It was late and there were no taxis or rickshaws. 'Let's walk home,' I said.

'What home?' Mam snapped.

'I'm tired,' Charlie wailed.

'It's not far,' I said. He began to cry. 'Come on,' I coaxed, kneeling down. 'I'll give you a piggyback.'

He scrambled on to my back, wrapping his arms around my neck and burying his face in my hair. We began to walk, the night air clearing my mind. Mam rushed ahead, stalking along, full of resentment, and behind me, barely visible in the dark, Pushpa plodded, lost in prayer.

No one came to the house after the attack. I expected a visit from the police and rehearsed what to say, but no detectives arrived, and for that I was grateful. We didn't need a *durwan* because some greater force seemed to keep people away. The hawkers vanished, the beggars stopped clanging their bowls on the gate, and not a single parrot perched in Professor Mitra's jacaranda tree. If I didn't know better, I'd say the place was cursed. Pushpa certainly thought so. I saw her threading more chillies and lemons on to a string and hanging them by the door. She sprinkled Gangajal – water from the Ganges – on the floors from a little copper pitcher, and rushed from room to room, chanting as she went. Mam forgot her dislike of heathen magic and joined Pushpa in improving our luck: they went to see a fortune-teller together, and came back more subdued than when they'd left. Later that day, a loud hammering brought me to the front of the house. Ram was standing on a ladder, fixing a horseshoe above the door, closely supervised by Mam and Pushpa.

No news is supposed to be good news. After those days of limbo I know it's a ridiculous notion. No message came from

Gordon and no chit was passed to Ram. I checked the newspaper, expecting to find something about Sunil: a story that he had been captured, or killed. I held my breath as I scanned the headlines, afraid of what I might see, but the only story the journalists seemed interested in was the assassination of Mr Gandhi. I read and reread every page, poring over un-related stories in the hope of gleaning the tiniest clue as to where Sunil might be, but every day my spirits sank as I folded up the paper, still none the wiser. It was as if he had vanished off the face of the earth.

'I don't know why you're holding a flame for that man. You can't keep denying he had something to do with it,' Mam said in exasperation as she watched me reading.

I wished she'd soften for once, and stop stating uncomfort-able truths. I was doing a good job of convincing myself that Gordon had made a mistake. Sunil had to be innocent; he couldn't be involved in a murder and gruesome torture because that would make him monstrous, and how could I love a monster? All I wanted just then was for Mam to hold me close and tell me everything would be all right. Mam, though, always put practicality before emotion.

'I suppose some good might come of it,' she said thoughtfully.

'Like what?'

'Well, you can't marry a man who'll swing for murder, and Gordon will have fewer choices now he's a cripple. It stands to reason, the women won't be queuing up, will they? Besides, he'll count himself lucky to have you back after he's looked at his wife's ugly mug for a while. You mark my words.'

I gulped, taken aback by her heartlessness. She was talking

about a death sentence for the man I loved as if it were a foregone conclusion.

'Mam, the last time we saw Gordon, he told us to pack our bags and leave. The attack won't make him feel different.'

'You don't understand men, my girl. There's nothing some lipstick and fancy knickers can't fix.'

We would have left the house if we'd had anywhere to go. Instead we stayed, paralysed by poverty and uncertainty, waiting for Sunil to reappear, or for Gordon to return. But although we clung on to our unhappy home, a revolution had occurred in the house and turned it upside down.

Atul no longer salaamed when he saw me and I could have sworn his smile, always faintly supercilious at the best of times, became mocking, only an inch short of rude. He rarely appeared, even in the *bottle khanna*, and seemed to spend most of his time in the kitchen. I used to be woken each morning with bed tea on a tray. After the attack, Pushpa brought me a glass of water and promised to go to the kitchen and make a brew for us all.

One day when lunch didn't appear and none of the servants was around, I went to investigate the delay, walking along the covered path that joined the main house to the kitchen. I stopped outside the door and listened, craning to hear in a way worthy of our crafty bearer. Atul and the new cook were making merry. Atul mumbled and laughed, his mouth full of food. It made it difficult understand him, but with dismay I picked out the words 'worm-eaten woman' and wondered if he was refer-ring to me or Mam, or even Pushpa, whom he despised with a passion.

I stepped into the room. They were sitting on the floor, the giant platters in front of them piled with a mound of bright white rice and surrounded by little bowls of meat, fish and vegetables in the traditional Bengali style. It was a feast fit for a wedding party. Glancing up, Atul crammed another handful of rice into his mouth. I'd intended to ask about lunch but was so surprised at the scene before me that I turned tail and walked slowly back into the house with as much dignity as I could muster, the blood pounding in my head. Atul had heard Gordon tell us to leave and he knew I was no longer mistress of the house. I had no place there; I had no money and was given no respect.

When Charlie's growling stomach and complaints of hunger grew louder, Pushpa and I returned to the kitchen. Cook was asleep outside in the winter sun, satiated and lying on a string bed, the blanket covering him tucked tightly around his neck. The kitchen assistant, a boy of about thirteen who I'd rarely seen before, was washing the dishes, all the plates and bowls arranged in a tower and covered in soap suds. Atul was preparing to leave, cleaning his teeth with a twig and readjusting his clothes.

'It's not your afternoon off,' I said.

'Today is holiday,' he replied with a smile. 'It is custom.'

It was a phrase I heard repeatedly in those days. 'It is custom' became the servants' excuse for every failure to carry out their normal duties.

'Is it custom to forget to bring us lunch?'

Atul grinned, not replying, and the boy doing the dishes scrubbed at a burned pan, avoiding eye contact.

Pushpa took some puffed rice from the store cupboard.

'What's this?' Mam asked, sitting on the veranda and looking in distaste at the handful of dry rice Pushpa gave her. 'Are you joking?'

Later, when night fell and the fireflies danced around the bushes at the far end of the garden, Pushpa and I went to the kitchen. It was in darkness. Cook's string bed was propped against the wall, and the dishes had been rinsed but not put away. I squatted down next to Pushpa and helped her prepare peas *pulao* and *alu dam,* the slow-cooked spicy potatoes I loved so much. She worked fast, slicing the vegetables with a *bonti,* a big curved knife set into a wooden block, which Mam insisted I should never go near for fear I should fall on it and impale myself. My eyes watered as I mashed onion, ginger, garlic and chillies to a paste.

'Where did you learn to cook like this?' I asked Pushpa.

'My mother, of course,' she said, concentrating on her work. Her fingers, which were gnarled at the knuckles and beginning to twist, moved fast, chopping tomatoes, frying potatoes, adding cinnamon and cardamom, stirring in yoghurt and sprinkling coriander, the smell so delicious it turned my hunger to a gnawing pain.

We ate a late dinner on the veranda, Mam sitting on her cane chair and balancing the plate on her knees. The rest of us sat cross-legged on the floor.

'Brother,' Pushpa called to the *mali* in his godown. Ram hovered on the edge of the lawn and Pushpa slid a plate of food towards him. In the soft light of a lantern Ram turned his rheumy-eyes to the meal.

'It's food for the gods, sister,' he sighed, settling himself on the grass. He was the only servant left in the house, apart from Pushpa, who didn't count because she was more like family really.

Even Mam, who said Indian spices upset her digestion, agreed that the meal was tasty. 'We can do without that sodding cook,' she said. 'You're better than him, Pushpa, any day.'

I was glad the food was so mouth-watering and memorable because it was the last meal we ate in the garden house.

Gordon's return was as short as it was dramatic. He strolled in looking better than I could have imagined, though he was thinner in the face. His arm – what was left of it – was hidden in the sleeve of his jacket, which was discreetly stitched so it didn't flap empty and revealing.

He cast an eye around the drawing room. 'I thought you'd have gone long before now,' he said to me.

'How are you, Gordon?' I asked, my voice quavering, amazed by his sudden arrival and the entourage of servants and packers who flooded into the house with him. It seemed like the start of a military campaign. Pushpa took Charlie by the hand and fled from the room.

'I'm as well as can be expected,' Gordon said tersely.

'We came to the hospital but they wouldn't let me see you.'

'Maude was very upset to meet you there.'

Gordon gave some brusque commands and several men rushed in with packing crates.

'You'd better take what's yours quickly otherwise it'll all find its way into these tea chests and be sold at auction or shipped to Scotland.'

Mam arrived in a panic. 'You're going back home?' she said as if reeling from a violent blow.

'Aye, India's finished,' he said, annoyance making him shower tiny droplets of saliva over the sofa as he spoke. 'The jute's on the other side of the border, the Hooghly's silting up, and the Government has its crooked fingers in every aspect of business. It's a bloody farce. I'm selling everything I have here and I've bought a mansion in Dundee. We're leaving tomorrow.'

'What will we do?' Mam asked.

'That's no concern of mine.'

The packers wrapped the ornaments in cloth, pressing them into the crates surrounded by straw and strips of hessian. They pulled the crates over the floor, scratching the red polish and making a hideous screech.

Stripped of all her usual feistiness, Mam looked about, diso-rientated as the house was emptied around us.

'Take everything of value,' Gordon said to a young British man with a clipboard, who began instructing the coolies heaving furniture on to the back of a truck, and telling the men rolling the Kashmiri rugs to do it more carefully and avoid creating damaging folds.

'Where will we go?' Mam asked, a pathetic warble in her voice.

'Probably back to that slum in Dharmatala where I found you.'

Mam ran after Gordon, who was walking out through the front door for the last time. I followed her, worried she was going to embarrass us further, and watched Gordon get into the car. He wound down the window with difficulty, reaching over with his left hand, and paused to stare directly at me. I wished I'd been calmer because perhaps I'd have been able to read his eyes and know what he was thinking. He looked at Mam. 'You could always come to Dundee,' he said, the laugh accompanying his words hollow and brief. 'It's the British Calcutta.'

Jamal reversed out of the drive between the trucks, almost scything the side of the Bentley against the gate in his haste to be away. Gordon, like the British Government before him, was departing India in a hurry and leaving chaos in his wake.

Inside the house, the whirlwind of packing continued and Mam and I struggled to hold on to the contents of our wardrobes, insisting we brought the clothes with us to the house, even though it was a lie.

'Where's Pushpa?' Mam screeched. 'What's the point of having servants if they're not here when you need them?'

Mam scrambled among her things, desperate to save her photographs of handsome Jack and her brother, Freddie.

'I'll have to ask you to go now,' the young man said, fanning himself with his clipboard, his moustache prickly with anxiety. 'I have my instructions.'

Half an hour later the gates were locked and we stood in the road with three trunks at our feet.

'Fat lot of help you were,' Mam said to Pushpa, who reappeared at last carrying two small bundles. 'Where the hell did you go?'

Ram fetched a taxi and as he waved goodbye I heard Pushpa calling to him, crying about the *maya* and how her heart was hurting.

In the back of the Royal Palace Hotel, in a room next to the Rajpoot princes, we sat wearily on saggy beds.

'What a dump,' Mam said flatly.

'There's no water,' Charlie shouted from the shared bathroom down the corridor.

When he ran back in, Pushpa closed the door softly and took a package from the bottom of her bundle. She tipped the contents on to the quilt, and we all gasped as my jewellery tumbled out, sparkling in the light from the small window.

'How did you do it?' Mam said, full of wonder.

Pushpa grinned. 'Magic,' she said proudly.

Chapter Ten

Pushpa

MacBrayne Sahib's glorious house has left a legacy in my bones. I've become spoiled and accustomed to soft beds, and I'm in misery when I sleep in the usual way with nothing but a bamboo mat between me and the ground. Mem told me it was because I'm old and have arthritis in my hips and knees, and she was probably right. Whatever the cause of the pain, the mists and chills of winter make my joints ache, and the rains aggravate them almost as much. In the drab flat Miss Maisy rented in Bowbazar, the hardness of the uneven floor was unbearable under the thin mat I unfurled each evening in the corner of the kitchen. Feeling guilty at the way I grimaced as I hobbled around doing the work of three servants, Miss Maisy bought me a fat mattress stuffed with freshly teased cotton, and since then, wherever I've gone, and whatever misfortunes I've faced, I've taken the mattress with me. Its deep, fluffy padding soothes my nights.

I needed extra special comfort in those days because I was the only sane woman in that flat. Miss Maisy was tormented by demons and Mem's many troubles put her into a bitter mood, relentlessly blaming the 'bastard clerk' for their terrible luck.

'I can't believe it,' she said, sitting on a chair in front of a broken electric fan and banging on the base to restart it. 'Three months ago we were living in a mansion and now we've got two rooms in a tenement in ruddy Bowbazar. We're surrounded by Indians and half-halfs on all sides. I can't stand the smell and there's no bloody toilet.'

Charlie didn't like some things about his new home either. At night he woke crying miserably, his skin irritated by bites. We covered him in lotion and citronella, and stood the feet of his bed in bowls of water to stop insects crawling up from the floor.

'It won't do any good,' Mem complained. 'This place is infested with bugs. They're in every nook and cranny.'

Each afternoon, I examined Mem's scalp in minute detail. She sat in sunlight from the open window and insisted dozens of lice were living in her hair.

'You've missed some big fat runners, Pushpa. I can feel them moving about,' she said, rubbing her head. 'Your eyes must be as jiggered as your legs.'

As spring drew to a close and hot weather began to fry the city, Charlie developed prickly heat rash. Mem sat with him in the stuffy, airless room, constantly reminding him to stop scratching. His condition began to improve only when the rains came and Miss Maisy let him run in the downpours, his clothes soaked as he jumped and splashed in puddles.

Living in the flat was good for Charlie despite its bugs and the damp that made the walls run with water in the monsoon. A whole new life opened up to him when his mother finally let him out of her sight. In Sahib-para, he'd glimpsed the world from between the bars of the gates. In Bowbazar, he played on the doorstep of the building and soon made friends with a boy everyone called Bapu. He was six, a year older than Charlie, and within a few days the two were inseparable. After school, Bapu changed out of his white uniform and put on a patched *dhoti* and a large shirt that looked as if it belonged to one of his older brothers. He paused at the door to the flat, too nervous to come in, and Charlie scrambled after him down the dark stairs.

Bapu's brothers let the two little ones tag along with them, especially when they needed the boys to sabotage the opposing team's batting in the never-ending cricket games played in the square at the end of the road. I watched Charlie and Bapu sharing sherbets and sweets, and racing barefoot to keep up with the gang as they charged upstairs to fly kites over the city's rooftops. Mem insisted the rain had washed the boy's rash away but I think he recovered because he was no longer imprisoned in a sweltering cell with two mad women.

Worry made Miss Maisy thin and miserable. Her pretty, round cheeks vanished along with her breasts and curvy hips. In the spring of 1948 the flowers on the trees stood crimson and scarlet against a blue sky, but Miss Maisy couldn't see their colour, and when the monsoon came and the scent of her favourite jasmine, chameli and gardenia filled the air, she didn't notice their fragrance either. She thought only of Sunil and how she could find him, and it hurt me to see her like that, day after day, obsessing about an unworthy man. You can love too much, I thought, seeing her despair.

'Don't pick at your food,' Mem snapped, looking at Miss Maisy push her meal around the plate.

'I'm not hungry.'

'You look like a ruddy TB patient. Tell her, Pushpa. She needs to eat or she'll fade to nothing.'

I don't know how Mem had the boldness to scold Miss Maisy for not eating when she replaced her own meals with arrack more times than I could count. Mem fixed angry, worried eyes on her daughter. 'We'll need some more money soon enough. Prices are going up every day. Pushpa says even onions cost a ruddy fortune. They'll be charging for air next.'

'There's some jewellery left.'

'It won't last long.' Mem sat back and lit a cigarette. 'What happens when you've nothing left to pawn?'

'I'll get a job.'

'Doing what?' she said, glaring at Miss Maisy. 'I've got an idea: why don't you go to the Grand or the Great Eastern and see if there are any men around who'll buy a girl a drink?' She paused, thinking. 'I know,' she said brightly, sitting up straight, 'we can go to Darjeeling.' She was excited by the idea, enthusiasm relaxing her strained face. 'We can stay in a nice place for a few days and you can meet the owners of some tea gardens. They're always lonely and bored silly after being stuck in their bungalows in the hills for months on end with only natives for company. I can imagine you as the wife of an estate owner, Maisy. You'll have acres and acres of land and so many servants you'll not have to lift a finger. I can see it now; it'll be perfect.' Stubbing out her cigarette, she turned to me. 'Look sharp, Pushpa; go and buy some plum cake. Maisy needs to put on weight quickly. We've no time to lose.'

Miss Maisy closed her eyes and sighed. 'Mam, the country

is in turmoil. Refugees are everywhere and law and order is breaking down. It's too dangerous to travel.'

'Your problem, my girl,' Mem shrieked, 'is you have no ambition.' Her eyebrows knitted together tightly, months of worry carving two deep creases that ran from her forehead to the bridge of her nose. She poured herself another drink and swallowed it in a giant gulp. 'You could have wed an officer if you hadn't let that bastard clerk get you up the stick. The bugger stole your future – and mine. You could be with a rich feller now if you made an effort to cheer up and take care of yourself; men can't abide scrawny lasses. But, instead, you throw away your looks like they're of no value, and all because you're pining over some insane killer who's left you – twice. Use your nous, Maisy. Do we have to starve before you see sense?'

Miss Maisy stood up, her chair falling backwards with a clatter, and she dashed out of the room. We heard her heels on the stairs and the door bang as she ran out into the street.

'She's doolally; she'll end up in a bloody asylum,' Mem said to me.

They both would, I thought. Standards had slipped since the simple, disciplined days in Queen Alexandra Mansions. I remember Brooks Sahib sitting at his desk on payday and lecturing us servants on the importance of routine and the way the British liked to keep good order. I wondered what he would think of the flat in Bowbazar: the way the soiled clothes were dropped and left on the floor; the dirty dishes piled up in the sink; the bewildered expression on Miss Maisy's face as she stared at the food I brought from the market. Without servants, the hygiene standards demanded by Brooks Sahib were abandoned. There was no cook to soak vegetables and salad in pinki-pani

– a solution of potassium permanganate – to kill the germs, and nobody thought to boil drinking water unless I reminded them, pointing out that cholera was stalking the city again and we all had to be vigilant. An old woman like me could only do so much to keep the neglect from turning to squalor, and those two, sunk in depression or a drunken haze, were as good as useless. Brooks Sahib often said, perhaps as a warning to himself, that it's easy for a man to sink in India. Looking at the shabbiness, and Mem and Miss Maisy's jaded faces, I thought how much easier and quicker it is for a woman to sink.

No good will come of this, I thought, treading wearily after Miss Maisy in her hunt through the city. I was helping her search for a man who would bring her grief and I was relieved we never found him. Sunil Banerjee was tainted by the horror of those terrible minutes in the Britannia Mill and, though he evaded the police, I knew the blood he'd shed would stick to him like glue. Madan told me about the jute wallah Sunil shot: he was British, like MacBrayne Sahib from the land of the Scots, and he left this world in the fullness of life. He wasn't old, and his body hadn't grown cold, preparing for death. He was young and full of vigour, with a wife and three small children. He was not ready to cut the *maya* binding him to all he loved. Wherever Sunil is, I thought, the mill manager will be with him, too; though he can run from the police, he cannot hide from a ghost.

The city seemed full enough to burst and every day more Hindu refugees arrived from East Pakistan, the new country made for the Muslims. They set up camp in the streets in makeshift homes strung together with sheets and bits of wood. They built shacks on waste ground and erected huts in the spaces between pukka buildings, so no place was left untouched by their desperate flight. The flow wasn't just one way because many left Calcutta too, the city emptying of Muslims. I saw those who remained, standing in huddles outside their mosques, wary and talking in whispers. They were like hunted animals preparing for flight, and when I passed them I could smell their fear.

Thousands of wretched Hindu families lived their entire lives on the platforms of Sealdah Station; eating, sleeping, washing, waiting in vain for someone to help them.

'He won't be here,' I said to Miss Maisy.

'It's easier to hide in a crowd. He told me that.'

'Please help me, Memsahib,' a woman of about fifty said, catching hold of the hem of Miss Maisy's dress. Judging by her plump body, and her face filled out by a lifetime of good food, the woman was prosperous. 'I have lost everything.'

Miss Maisy stopped, startled by the woman's desperation.

'My husband was killed. And they burned my son and daughter-in-law to ash. There is nothing left. Nothing,' she wailed. 'I have to look after my grandchildren and I am alone.' She tugged again at Miss Maisy's dress and pointed to three dazed children. The girl, who was nine or ten, cuddled her brothers, squeezing them tightly as the mass of people closed around them.

'I have no money and no food for them,' the woman pleaded. 'Our home is gone. Our crops are gone. We left with only these clothes we are wearing.'

Miss Maisy was shocked. The woman was a well-off,

unworldly, upcountry grandmother who had no idea how to survive in the city, even in the best of times. She had no skills she could sell: she couldn't be a servant because she'd never cleaned a house in her life; she'd struggle to hold her own among Calcutta's scavengers, and she was too old to sell her body. She'll be a beggar, I thought, and her grandsons too, but not the girl. My heart bled for the pretty little thing with her large, almond eyes because she would soon be caught by the pimps.

Miss Maisy searched her pocket for coins. The movement of her hand alerted a dozen homeless paupers who began clamouring for help. She recoiled, stepping away, and for a second I thought the woman was going to throw her arms around Miss Maisy's legs and be dragged out of the station.

'Please, Memsahib, take pity,' the woman said. 'I am from a good family and we cannot live like this.'

We backed out of the station. The woman hadn't lunged for Miss Maisy as I expected, and I looked back at her, sitting immobile, watching us, tears running down her cheeks. I picked my way through the confusion and she drew the children to her as I approached.

'Here, sister,' I said, giving her a few annas.

The woman and her granddaughter looked up at me in thanks, and I was disarmed by their bright amber eyes.

'It's too much, isn't it, Pushpa?' Miss Maisy said, threading her way through the crowd. 'I mean, I couldn't do anything for that poor woman. There are too many people to help.'

We walked in silence. Calcutta hardens your spirit, I thought. A tender heart can't survive this city.

Louise Brown

Miss Maisy's search for Sunil was thorough and so strange it must have been the product of madness. We went to the Oxford Bookshop regularly, though it mystified me why a fugitive from the law would be so stupid as to spend his time in a shop on one of the busiest roads in the city. After a lot of detective work we found the address of the Banerjees' home, but the neighbours said the family had left years ago after old Mr Banerjee died from heart trouble. They hadn't seen Sunil since he was a youth and the last they knew, Mrs Banerjee had withdrawn from the world and was living in a widows' ashram in Kashi. It's a blessing, I thought; his parents would be spared the knowledge of what their only son had done.

We toured the streets in a rickshaw and on foot; we tagged along at rallies, scanned faces at demonstrations, and joined striking tram workers in the hope he'd be there, too. I was dragged into political meetings, heard endless impassioned, nonsensical speeches, and spent long afternoons pacing Howrah Bridge and walking around the lake in Eden Gardens. At least once a week, we called at the Royal Palace Hotel on Harrison Road.

'Have you seen him?' Miss Maisy asked the manager.

He looked at her over the top of his spectacles. 'I haven't seen the gentleman for months, Mem.' He said the same thing every time.

'But have you heard any news about him?'

'I'm afraid not, Mem. I know only what I told you before: I understand the gentleman in question has left the city.'

Mr Das's information seemed as reliable as anyone's. We had bits of news, never anything definite, and although Miss Maisy

234

sometimes believed she had a lead, her hopes were soon dashed. She clung to crumbs of gossip and tried to make sense of the tales. Some whispered that he was in the countryside organising a campaign to help the landless, others said he had gone to Delhi and was plotting new atrocities. A few insisted he'd died, bleeding to death during the escape from the mill.

'I'd know if he was dead, Pushpa. I'd feel it,' Miss Maisy said with a confidence I didn't share.

So much rumour surrounded Sunil that we had no idea of the truth. Miss Maisy swiftly built him into a legend, and a god, a divine Lord Krishna. But to my mind, if he was a god he'd have been nothing more than a puny, malicious spirit who danced with Ma Kali in the dark corners of the cremation grounds.

It was dangerous to be different in the city in those terrible times. The days when Hindus and Muslims celebrated independence together, walking arm in arm as brothers, were gone. Calcutta was being cleansed of anyone who was Muslim, Bihari or Sikh. The white skins had to go, too. Five months after we were thrown out of the garden house and MacBrayne Sahib left for home, another attack chilled the British who'd stayed on in free Calcutta. In the Turner's factory in Howrah, two British engineers were thrown into the blast furnace and another was stabbed.

'It was him; I know it,' Mem said fiercely.

'You don't know it at all, Mam,' Miss Maisy said in a huff.

'He's done it once, and I told you he'd do it again.'

The gruesomeness of the deaths gave even Miss Maisy reason to pause and think. She said nothing but I saw doubt enter her mind, her suspicions revealed in the shadow that sometimes crossed her face. Our searching of the city began to slacken, and my aching hips gave thanks.

It's uncanny how we find missing things when we are not obsessed by the hunt for them. That's how it was in our search for news of Sunil.

Charu was the last person we expected to see in New Market. Miss Maisy was buying fabric to repair a large burn in the sofa caused when Mem had fallen asleep and dropped her cigarette. We turned a corner and Miss Maisy almost crashed into him. She jumped in astonishment, and Charu walked off in a hurry.

'Charu,' Miss Maisy said, overjoyed. She followed him up the aisle and he looked back at her with cold eyes. 'I'm Maisy, Sunil's friend.'

He muttered something and carried on.

'Have you heard from him?' Miss Maisy said, ignoring the rebuff. 'Some people told me he's dead but I don't believe it.'

'They're right: he died months ago,' Charu said abruptly.

Miss Maisy recoiled as if she'd been punched. Charu walked away, and Miss Maisy took a deep breath, taking in the shock of the news. Then, remembering something, she rushed after him and stopped him among the bustle of customers and coolies outside the market hall.

'Did he do it?' she asked.

'Do what?'

Shoppers paused to watch the curious scene: a frantic white woman gripping the arm of an angry Indian man.

'Did he kill the jute wallah? Did he attack the Britannia Mill?' Her voice cracked with emotion.

He paused for a second, shrugged her off, and moved on.

'I need to know,' she insisted. 'I deserve to know. I was going to be his wife.'

She tugged his arm again and he pushed her aside so she stumbled and fell, the contents of her bag scattering over the ground.

'Wife?' he said in disbelief, and laughed. The coolies gawked at the show, looking from a stricken Miss Maisy to Charu, his face full of contempt. He began to stride away but stopped and turned with a sneer. 'You're right about him being in the mill, but you're wrong about being his wife: you were nothing but his whore.'

True Britishers passed through India and all the *burra sahibs* and pukka white people went home eventually. Only the *chota sahibs* stayed on from one generation to the next, their real British blood cooked by the Indian sun, boiling it so it no longer counted as genuinely white. Lost in grief, Miss Maisy forgot this truth and instead remembered her father's stories of Britain, Brooks Sahib's beacon of light in a dark world.

'Go back? Go back?' Mem said, choking on her own saliva in fury. 'For Christ's sake, Maisy, you didn't believe all that bollocks your father told you about England?'

'It's got to be better than here.'

'Don't bet on it. He was dreaming. Dear old Blighty was all in his flippin' head.'

They argued night and day. Miss Maisy was convinced they could sail to a better life, to a place where they could start afresh. Mem bawled back at her, angry and exhausted, certain no such place existed.

'Where will we live?' she shrieked. 'Don't think we can go to your nan's; the house is poky and Leeds is a dump.'

I heard them quarrelling over every point: the weather; their lack of money in India; the help you got from the Government in England; the houses, and the schools for Charlie; the peaceful streets. Yet among the many things they argued about with such passion, my name was never mentioned, not even once. Mem said that poor people didn't have servants in England and that Miss Maisy would have to do all the housework herself, but she didn't suggest I go with them, and she didn't wonder how I would live in Calcutta after they'd gone.

Many years ago, when the British men I worked for returned home to England and Scotland, they'd pass me on to new arrivals. But in 1948 I was too old to be passed on to anyone; too old for a new family to employ me as an ayah. I'd always believed I'd live out my days with Miss Maisy and Mem, and that I'd spend my free time with Madan. I realised, with shock, that they'd been such foolish plans.

'My family is leaving,' I wailed to Madan.

'They're not your family. They don't treat you like you're part of their family. Would they leave their own grandmother behind if they went to England?'

I didn't want to listen to his words because I knew they were true, so I changed the subject and focused on the trembling of his hands. His mind and his tongue were as sharp as ever but his body was deteriorating month by month. He was earning next to nothing and his *kutcha* shack in Howrah had been swallowed by a tide of refugees. Madan couldn't help me in my distress because he couldn't even care for himself.

What's going to happen to me? I thought, suddenly over-whelmed by fear. Am I going to be a *paan walli*, selling betel leaf on the street? Am I going to be so desperate I'll beg for a few paise? My future was bleaker than it had been since I was newly widowed. Perhaps it was the beginning of the end, I thought. Maybe I'm being separated from my children because I'm preparing to leave this life. All my fondest attachments are unravelling to make it easier for me to die.

Mem didn't sleep on the night before they left. She said it was impossible to get up at dawn so she might as well stay awake and repack the trunks.

'Careful,' she said to the taxi driver who strapped them to the back of the open-topped car and jammed a trunk on top of Madan, who was sitting in the front seat. He gasped at the weight on his legs. 'The fruit of my whole bloody life's in there,' she said to me, bitterly. 'And judging by the state of this old crate my life's going to end before we even make it to the docks.'

No one came to see them leave. Despite all the men Mem had known in Calcutta, not one came to say goodbye. Those who stayed on after the British Government left hadn't visited her for years, and others had gone back home with the *burra sahibs*. Even Donald Sahib had abandoned her, as well as India. He came only once to the flat in Bowbazar, and was shocked by the state of the place. Mem looked dishevelled and Miss Maisy stared blankly out of the window like an imbecile.

'I'm away home, Babs,' he said. 'I've got a job at the Imperial Works in Dundee and the wife's had enough of Calcutta. Looks like you should be heading home, too, hen.' He had one last *burra peg*, shuddering at the quality of the whisky, and left.

Only the *dudh wallah* and the street sweepers saw the car bump and shake through the lanes of Bowbazar, one of the back wheels screeching. The driver accelerated as we skirted Eden Gardens and Mem tied a headscarf tightly under her chin to stop the wind whipping her hair into a bushy tangle. We rattled along Strand Road as morning light spread over the river.

'Is that the boat, Mum?' Charlie asked, pointing to a liner moored alongside one of the jetties.

'Our boat won't be as posh as that, Charlie,' Miss Maisy said.

'You're not kidding,' Mem grumbled. 'We're going home in a ruddy old tub.'

In the Kidderpore Docks, Mem sniffled into a handkerchief. I thought she was crying because she might not see me again.

'This is a crackpot idea,' she croaked. 'The stupid girl hasn't got a clue what life's going to be like at home. She thinks there'll be a red carpet and brass band waiting for us in Blighty, and she'll fall into some cushy job and live in a castle.'

Mem was so distressed I did something usually unthinkable: I put my arm around her shoulder. It felt odd; like comforting a stone. 'It might not be as bad as you remember,' I said.

'Oh, it will. And there'll be no one like you in London, Pushpa.'

A lump rose in my throat: Mem was going to miss me. In over twenty years she'd said no more than a handful of kind things to me and at last she was softening and revealing her true feelings.

'We'll have no one to do the cleaning and look after Charlie,' she said in despair.

She rummaged in her handbag, searching for something, and I thought she was going to give me a parting gift, some little memento, a 'thank you' for all my years of service. She pulled out a wrinkled cigarette, tobacco sprouting from the tip. 'Christ,' she muttered, continuing to scratch among the rubbish at the bottom of the bag. 'No bleeding matches.'

'Have you got any?' she asked, turning to Madan, who was leaning against a tea chest, giving her hostile, sideways glances. He'd told me it was going to be his final chance to tell Mem what he thought about her, and for a moment I dreaded there'd be a nasty scene and the last thing they'd remember about me was Madan's resentful words about bad blood. I gave him a warning look and clicked my tongue, and when he looked directly at Mem he just shook his head and turned quickly away. Mem sighed and trudged down the quay to find someone with a light.

The dock was jammed with ships, and dockworkers were arriving for the dayshift, gang masters shouting to the carriers and assembling them into lines. Mem disappeared into a crowd of sinewy men, so thin and wiry they made Madan look fleshy. The doors to the shed next to us opened and the shed supervisor asked us to move on; we were blocking the gangway and they were about to load a cargo of jute.

'Take this,' Miss Maisy said, dipping into her pocket and taking out a little box. I recognised it immediately. It was from Hamilton's and I knew it contained a broach from the sahib. It was the only thing Miss Maisy hadn't pawned. Miss Maisy pressed her finger to her lips as Mem returned, puffing violently on her cigarette. I wrapped the box in the end of my sari and fastened it with a tight knot.

Miss Maisy was distracted, rifling through her papers. 'I don't know which ship it is,' she said. She was so anxious it was hard to imagine the journey was her idea, and for a moment I hoped she'd change her mind. We'd all go back to the flat, and I'd be saved. She spoke to the supervisor, who pointed along the quayside, and then she gathered their trunks into a pile while Mem gave confusing directions to a perspiring coolie, cursing him for his doziness.

'What a stink,' she said, wrinkling her nose at his stained clothes. 'That's one thing I won't miss about India: I'll be glad to see the back of the pongs.'

We walked along the dock, Miss Maisy moving briskly between the lines of coolies who ran up the gangways carrying bulging sacks. Charlie held her hand, skipping and turning round to look at me as I walked slowly with Mem, who was moving like an old woman, taking tiny steps and dragging her feet.

'I've got a fucking awful headache, Pushpa,' she said. 'It's too early and I'm parched. I could do with a peg or two. The hair of the dog would set me up for the day.'

Miss Maisy and Charlie moved further ahead, and I kept losing them among the coolies and the sailors returning from a night in the bars and brothels. I wanted to call out to them, to ask them to slow; in fact I wanted to beg them to stop, to stay where they belonged, but I couldn't shout the words. I couldn't even speak.

When we caught up with them, we stood by their ship's gangway in silence. Even Mem stopped complaining.

'Don't cry, Pushpa,' Miss Maisy said at last. 'We'll come back one day. And we'll write, I promise.'

'You've got the address?' I asked.

'Show her, Mam,' Miss Maisy said.

Mem dug into the bowels of her bag, found her purse and

opened it. Inside was a folded piece of paper. I'd asked one of the *babus* by the General Post Office to write Kamala's address on it.

Miss Maisy hugged me and I held her tightly, smelling the scent of her freshly washed hair. I thought my heart would break and even when she pulled away saying it was time to board the ship, I couldn't let go.

'That's enough,' Madan spoke sharply. He prised my fingers from round Miss Maisy's arms and sat me down on a broken bale of jute by the wall of the cargo shed. Unable to watch them walk up the gangway, I buried my face in my hands.

'Do we have to stay here all day?' Madan asked after we'd waited for hours and the sun was high.

Mem and Miss Maisy had vanished inside the old cargo ship, its paint flaking and blistered, every part of it streaked with bright orange rust. Charlie ran out now and again, hurtled up and down the decks, before waving to us and then disappearing inside once more.

I watched a couple of upcountry women clearing grass from the quay and wondered if my bad hip would allow me to do a job like that. By midday they had cleared the area in front of the shed and Madan and I were both falling asleep on the jute pile.

'Move on,' a harsh voice shouted. The shed supervisor was silhouetted against the sun. 'You can't sleep here; it's a dock not a refugee camp.'

The man thought I was homeless, and he was right.

'We are waiting for this ship to sail, sir,' Madan said. 'And we don't know why it's taking such a long time.'

'A shortage of river pilots,' the supervisor said and paused, looking sharply at us. 'And why are you waiting to see a ship like this leave?'

'Special cargo,' I said.

They sailed in the late afternoon. We missed the moment the ship drew away from the quay because we were on the far side of the dock, kept on the move by a dock inspector who thought we were decoys being used to smuggle goods from the sheds. I hope Mem and Miss Maisy saw me as they left. Madan said they waved, but I couldn't be sure of it myself. I waved back and watched the ship pull out of the dock into the river.

'Goodbye, *haramzadi*,' Madan shouted, at last able to say what he thought, even though Mem wouldn't be able to hear across the water, and probably wouldn't understand if she could.

'Never say that,' I said in shock. Mem was a lot of things but she wasn't a bastard born from a prostitute.

We took a rickshaw from outside the brothels next to the docks and travelled as far as the racecourse before the rickshaw wallah came to a halt with a lot of panting, his skin shiny with sweat. We sat without speaking on the tram up Chowringhee and walked the rest of the way to Bowbazar.

The flat was a shambles, the drawers turned out, things scattered on the floor.

'Nothing here's worth much,' Madan said, but he still collected the clothes and the crockery to take to the market. You can sell anything in Calcutta if the price is right. Mem used to have a few valuable things, including Brooks Sahib's teak writing desk and the long mirror, but she left them when they moved from Dharmatala to the garden house. What remained was the rubbish from their final year in India. I picked up Charlie's broken kite from the floor, and Miss Maisy's compact, the powder rubbed to an oily shine. The place felt as if it had been abandoned long ago, and perhaps it had. In all the months we lived there it never felt like home. I'm sure it didn't to Miss Maisy, and it certainly didn't to me.

Madan filled three jute bags and bumped them down the stairs and I thought the plates wouldn't survive the journey. He helped carry my fat mattress down the dark, narrow stairwell and heaved it on to a rickshaw. I balanced two bundles of possessions on my knee and held the mattress firmly.

'Where are you going?' the rickshaw wallah asked with a deep sigh, looking from me to the mattress.

'Masjid Bari Street,' I said, and for the second time in my life I headed for Sonagachi.

Chapter Eleven

Maisy

'DO YOU THINK they eat this chewy beef in the first-class dining room?' Mam said, hacking at the meat on her plate. 'It must have been a ruddy stringy old cow. The gravy's horrible as well; it's too bleeding watery.'

Nothing was good enough for Mam on that voyage. She was disappointed to be sailing tourist class from Bombay to Tilbury and she'd been even more upset about the voyage from Calcutta to pick up the liner. We had to take a cargo boat because she refused to travel to Bombay by train, saying the Indians had made a speciality of railway massacres and we were likely to be butchered. She found a cargo boat only slightly more acceptable than the train.

'I came out here on a cargo boat and I won't go back on one,' she said. 'If I have to go to Blighty, I want to do it in style.' She was adamant she wouldn't return to Britain looking like the dregs of the Empire. In the end we compromised: we'd go on a cargo boat round India and then take a tourist-class cabin on one of P&O's 'White Sisters' sailing out of Bombay. Mam looked at the brochure in the shipping agent's office and admired the drawing of the majestic white ships with their buff-coloured funnels.

'This looks more like it. We want a cabin with its own bathroom,' she told the polite young clerk.

I kicked her shins under the desk and she let me arrange the rest of the booking while she scowled at the sample menu cards.

Leaving Calcutta made Mam cry. On the dockside, she snivelled into a hanky and Pushpa was almost as upset. She clung to me and I had to leave her quickly and shut myself in our cabin because I knew I'd get too emotional if we said a long goodbye. When the moorings were loosened we hurried on deck and saw two little figures on the far side of the dock. Puzzlingly, Pushpa was waving at the wrong ship.

Charlie swung on the railings and poked his head through.

'Will Pushpa come to see us?' he asked.

'Perhaps,' I said. I'd given her a broach, the only piece of jewellery I had left after we'd flogged the rest to pay for the journey. She said she was going to sell it so she and Madan could set up a business making *singaras*. Although her *singaras* were even more delicious than the ones from the best stalls and teashops, I couldn't imagine her affording a passage to Britain if she fried snacks for a thousand years.

'We'll send her some money as soon as I've saved enough, and then she can visit us,' I said. 'And when we're rich, we'll come back to Calcutta for a long holiday.'

In the open sea the ship began to roll and the cargo shifted in the hold. The ancient boat creaked and groaned its way across the Bay of Bengal and into the Indian Ocean. Mam spent most of her time in the cabin or heaving her guts out over the side of the ship. It was a dismal start to the voyage.

'I told you we should have stayed at home,' Mam said. 'I'm too old to be put through this kind of ordeal.'

'Mam, you're fifty.'

'But I've been through a lot. It knocks the stuffing out of you.'

Although she perked up once we were on board the liner in Bombay, her good mood didn't last; not only was the beef chewy at dinner, our tiny windowless cabin made her feel claustrophobic, entombed while still alive. Worse, she failed repeatedly to be allowed on to 'B' and 'C' decks where she wanted to drink cocktails in the first-class Veranda Bar and where she said she would like the chance to take a dip in the swimming pool. The bell boys working the lifts got to know her very well as she tried to sidle past them.

Mam didn't like much about our deck except the tourist-class bar and the visits she made to the steward's cabin. He had a supply of spirits he'd lifted from the stores and instantly became Mam's close friend. I was disappointed. She'd promised me she was going to behave on the voyage; she was going to turn over a new leaf and start afresh in England. I had to wring the pledge out of her. When I found the empty bottle stuffed down the side of her bunk on the cargo boat, I knew why her voice had lacked conviction.

'Mam, you promised,' I said.

'It's medicinal. I need it to settle my stomach. It's churning. I haven't got my sea legs yet.' Mam said her privations would start when we docked in Tilbury and until then a little tipple was a necessity.

She'd disappear for an hour or two at a time and I'd find her snoozing peacefully in a deck chair, her face reddening in the sun. Shortly before we got to Gibraltar I lost her for most of the afternoon. The steward helped spot her. At last she'd managed to sneak herself into the first-class lounge and was talking in her best English accent, a cocktail in her hand. An elderly gentleman with a large white moustache and a very florid complexion was giving her his undivided attention.

'Do have another one, dear,' he said. 'A drink for the lady, my man,' he called to the waiter.

'Oh, George, you are so naughty. I feel a bit squaffy.'

'Do you mean squiffy, my dear?'

'That as well. I'm not used to drinking like this in the day. In India we always kept the golden rule: no drinks before sunset. And to top it off, this seasickness is paying havoc with my digestion.'

She saw me and jumped. While George was busy polishing his monocle she winked and motioned me to leave.

'I'm a navy man, of course,' George said. 'I'm an admiral – retired. I never suffer from seasickness. One becomes accustomed to it.'

'How impressive. I suppose you've been everywhere in the world,' Mam gushed.

'I sailed the seven seas and commanded some of our finest warships in the naval battles of the Great War.'

'By Jove, George. I bet you have some tales to tell.'

'Indeed, I do. What do you say to us repairing to my state-room? I can tell you all about it over a bottle of champagne. We can start with the Battle of Jutland.'

Louise Brown

Mam stubbed out her cigarette and adjusted her hat. I didn't know whether to cringe or laugh: the old girl still had it in her.

I began to feel better on the voyage and my sadness started to lift. Fleeing Calcutta was a relief because I could almost pretend the nightmare hadn't happened. I'd spent too long mourning Sunil, and mourning the death of my idea of him, and I didn't know which loss hurt me most. My great love had been built on a lie, and I had to run away to free myself from the voices in my head that chattered, shrill and insistent: 'You're exactly like Mam; Sunil thought you were a prostitute, and he paid you in bel flowers.'

For the first time in months I noticed the night sky; it was crystal clear, full of the brightest stars, and the days were hot, the light dazzling on the ocean. Charlie and I woke early and watched the porpoises and flying fish swimming alongside the ship, leaping from the water, flashes of silver in the deep, dark blue sea. In Aden, Charlie was transfixed by the *gili gili* man's magic tricks and, as we passed through the Suez Canal, we watched the women doing their laundry on the banks only a few feet from us.

The deck games were lots of fun and Charlie found a friend to play with. The little girl was never without a doll that she kept wrapped in a lace blanket.

'Are you an Indian prince?' she asked him.

'Don't be an ass, Elizabeth,' her big brother scoffed. 'Look at his clothes. And he's got a tourist-class ticket. That's why you don't see him in the first-class nursery.'

Elizabeth ignored her brother and she and Charlie ran off

to make a bed for the doll under the cover of one of the lifeboats.

It was hard to pinpoint exactly when the weather changed. It was sometime after we'd sailed through the Straits of Gibraltar. Mam rooted a cardy out of her suitcase.

'Get used to this, Maisy. It's going to be a lot worse in England.' She shivered her way towards the dining room, grumbling again about the unnecessary voyage and why we couldn't have stayed in Calcutta. I didn't know whether it was the chill in the air or our closeness to Britain that affected her. All her moods were heightened, her complaints turning to morose depression and her tipsy good humour into euphoria. She was up or down and nothing in between.

'Are you sad, Nan?' Charlie asked as Mam banged the cabin door and fiddled with the lock.

She sighed. 'A bit, Charlie.'

'Why?'

'It's nothing for you to worry about, love. I'll be right as rain.'

While we sailed through the Bay of Biscay, I was called to the first-class lounge. Mam was singing and draping herself over Admiral George, who had forgotten he knew her.

'Will you get her off me?' he said in exasperation.

The ladies in their fine clothes watched as I led her away. 'Beastly,' I heard one say.

The next day, Mam couldn't remember a thing and that evening happily set about repeating the performance. She hadn't returned by the time I went to sleep at midnight and I guessed she must have made up with George. When she didn't appear for breakfast I began to worry. Maybe she was comatose in

George's suite. The steward – such a kind man – helped in the search. The admiral had seen nothing of her.

'You mean that coarse old tart?' he said aghast to the steward. 'I haven't seen her since she sang her dreadful music-hall tunes and embarrassed herself by fawning over me the other night.'

The rest of passengers confirmed his story. George had spent all of the previous day with them and had played billiards with the men until the early hours.

The captain ordered a search of the ship. They checked everywhere: in the lifeboats, the engine room, the kitchen stores, among the dirty linen in the laundry. She had vanished into thin air.

The captain spoke in a calm and measured voice. 'Miss Brooks, we have to face the possibility that your mother has fallen overboard.'

'That's impossible. She would've had to throw herself off the ship. She couldn't have slipped; the rails are too high.'

'I am sorry, Miss Brooks; one could come to that conclusion. A crew member saw her shortly after dawn making her way along the games deck, clearly the worse for wear. We will search the ship again because there remains a slim possibility that she is still on board. Be assured that we've gone through our usual, and very thorough, procedures, and we've sent out a message to all shipping in the area informing them we may have a passenger overboard.'

'She isn't a good swimmer.'

'To be brutally honest, even a strong swimmer couldn't last more than a few hours in the English Channel. The police will have to be involved when we dock, and I think you need to prepare yourself for the worst.'

George, the pompous old twit, came to see me. 'I heard it was suicide,' he said. 'My condolences; she was a grand girl. A bit boisterous but lots of fun. A good head for naval strategy, too.'

I couldn't believe it. She wouldn't do it; she wouldn't choose to leave me and Charlie. She was mad with the drink and fell. That was the only explanation.

Charlie ran frantically up and down the decks, searching behind every door he could open, and scrambling under the lifeboats howling, 'Nan, Nan.'

I stood towards the bow of the ship as it parted the grey waters of the Thames and held Charlie so close he said I was hurting him. His tears and snot were wiped in sticky lines over my cardigan and soaked the ends of my hair. Mam had got at least part of her wish: she wasn't going to return to Britain after all. She was lost somewhere between the home of her impoverished childhood and the country of her unfulfilled dreams.

Chapter Twelve
Pushpa

F OR THE SECOND time in my life, I had an iron bangle on my wrist and vermilion in my hair. I rubbed the powder into my parting at the start of each day. It was like a wound, red among the hair that had turned completely white in the months after Mem and Miss Maisy left. It was strange to see the mark of a married woman on my skin, just as it did when I was twelve years old. Madan gave me a new red sari and a blouse for the wedding. He must have begged the money from Kamala. She was so generous it embarrassed me, but her kindness was also my good fortune. No other old woman had such an influential friend in Sonagachi. It was a blessing to be given shelter and food when my husband was ailing, when I had no sons or daughters to take care of me, and when my memsahib had left with the children I loved as my own.

From the door of Kamala's brothel, I could see Madan – my god and my life's true love – sitting where Masjid Bari Street twists to the left, a short way before the brothels begin to thin out and the road joins another more respectable one that's full of shops and the homes of ordinary people. The tools of his

254

trade lay by his side: a new mirror, the blade of his knife freshly sharpened, the soap already worked into a lather. Business was slow. The *babus* and the clients who were too drunk to go home the previous night were all still asleep, and when they woke they'd be sure to keep their distance from Madan's razor. He'd had few clients since the day his shaking hand slipped and he carved a groove in the face of the meanest pimp in Sonagachi.

'You sister fucker,' the pimp shouted, and knocked out the last of Madan's teeth. He would have knocked the life out of him too if Samita, Kamala's daughter, hadn't marched down the street, her gold bangles and the bunch of keys tied to the end of her sari clinking in time to her step.

'Leave him,' she said to the pimp. Samita's two sons, who were tall, well-fed young men living in the shadow of the lanes, appeared from nowhere at the shake of her keys and stood beside her. 'It was an accident,' she said to the injured pimp. 'You shouldn't have moved under the razor.'

The habit of a lifetime kept Madan there, day after day, trying to earn his living. Whenever he saw me he waved and grinned as if he hadn't seen me for weeks when really we'd spent all night squeezed together on my luxurious mattress in the corner of the room we shared with the servants.

We weren't servants ourselves, of course. When I returned to Masjid Bari Street, the mattress threatening to topple off the rickshaw, Kamala came out of the brothel, put her hands on her hips and laughed. 'The fortune-teller said you would come back, little sister. I didn't think it would take forty years.'

She could have asked me to sweep the floors or wash the clothes in return for my keep, but Kamala wouldn't let me do such demeaning work. Instead, I slipped back into the rhythm of Sonagachi as if I hadn't been away. I fell asleep at dawn, woke in the afternoon and spent the rest of my time sitting with Kamala. While Samita managed the business, we fat matrons reminisced about the old days, had night-long feasts and discussed plans for the holidays. Kamala was enjoying the fruits of her long life and in the months after I returned to Sonagachi she was engrossed in preparations for a special Kartik Puja.

'I'll have the biggest, best *pandal* in the whole of Sonagachi,' she declared.

She clapped her hands in delight when she saw the seven-foot-tall Lord Kartikeya the potters had made for her at enormous expense. The painted clay god was covered in flowers and dressed in silk as fine as Kamala's own, and he stood in a replica of a temple in the road outside the brothel.

'He'll bring us rich customers,' Kamala said, certain her investment was wise.

'Not as much as she will,' Samita laughed, pointing to a girl who sat silently in the corner, her eyes on the floor. Navneeta was a new, rare beauty, prettier than any of the Nepali or Bhutanese girls.

Kamala slid a parcel towards me over the carpet. 'Open it,' she said eagerly.

A deep green silk sari bordered with gold embroidery spilled on to the carpet. I ran the soft fabric through my fingers, and thought with pleasure where it was made. I, Pushparani, was going to wear a sari of Benares silk.

Kamala's procession was breathtaking. We followed Lord Kartikeya as he was carried to the Ganga, Kamala loaded with her finest gold. We were a colourful, dazzling party. The drummers beat a hypnotising rhythm, and the women of the brothel quarter danced in the street.

'See how they envy us,' Kamala said proudly, cocking her head at the crowds. Kamala's eyes must have been fading because there was no admiration on the onlookers' faces. The men mocked, saying crude things to their friends, and the women, peeping from their windows, were scandalised as the broken women of Sonagachi passed by. Near the river the police hurried us along, wielding bamboo canes and striking a young woman on the thighs. We moved faster, the dancing more energetic, and on the banks of the Ganga, Kamala watched, sobbing with joy, while Lord Kartikeya was submerged in the water.

Kamala's Kartik Puja was a triumph and everyone agreed her *pandal* was the best in the whole of Sonagachi. She'd paid a fortune for the *pandal* and she gave a handsome donation to the local temples, but I wasn't sure it was money well spent. To the rest of Calcutta, she would always be a filthy whore.

The thrills of Kartik Puja warmed Kamala's heart too much. The flesh she'd piled on over the years pressed against her lungs and made her breathing laboured and gradually shorter until the day she complained of a crushing pain in her chest and she began to sweat, her skin growing cold to the touch.

Samita wailed and knocked her head on her mother's feet.

'Gangajal,' Kamala gasped.

I don't know whether the water the pimp fetched was really holy water from the Ganga, but it soothed Kamala as we poured it between her blue lips.

A few hours later her grandsons and two pimps from the next lane carried her flower-strewn bier to the cremation ghats.

Samita let me stay on in the brothel, and for this I will be forever grateful. I was her aunty Pushpa and she treated me with respect. Without Kamala for company I no longer sat around talking and eating, and Samita said I should keep myself busy. I spent my time oiling the girls' hair, threading their eyebrows, showing them how to do their make-up, and giving them advice. They called me 'Aunty', although, really, I was more like a grandmother to them.

Samita was as ambitious as her mother. She wanted her girls to have richer clients who would visit more often and spend more of their money. With this in mind she bought the house next door, knocking the two brothels together and decorating the building inside and out so everyone who walked down Masjid Bari Street noticed the freshly painted walls and the shiny green shutters. She dressed her girls in fine clothes and told fantastic stories about their families, whom she claimed were courtesans in the courts of maharajas in the days before the British ruined the old Indian culture. She drew me into these games too, making me talk in English when some of the better-off clients visited. They were astonished that an elderly woman in a brothel could speak the King's English. I was part of the entertainment, like the dancers who performed in front of the customers before the men went to enjoy the plump, firm flesh in the back rooms. In truth, I spoke better English than many of the clients. Some of them had poor accents and the things they said sounded odd. They'd learned their English from bad Indian schools, not, as I had, from the mouths of real British people.

'Pushpa was carried in a palanquin when she was a girl,' Samita told the customers as I brought a tray of glasses filled with whisky into the room, the powerful smell jogging a memory of Mem's breath.

'Men were bewitched at the sight of her,' she went on. 'She was the favourite of a maharaja and she met a *burra sahib* at a *nautch* – a dance party. She won the heart of the Viceroy and lived in the *Andar-Mahal* – the very inside – of Government House. That's where she learned English. She was the sun and the moon in his sky. He never slept a night with his thin, aged wife when Pushpa was in his palace.'

The customers lay on the mattresses and smoked.

'She danced for the King of England,' Samita said, weaving a story of my life I couldn't have imagined. 'Show them the gifts, Pushpa,' she said.

I put my rose bowl in front of the men.

'The Viceroy gave her this.' Samita turned the bowl, the glass sparkling in the light. 'It's from England. And he gave her this likeness of himself to remember him by.'

She passed around the painting of the fat man on a fat horse. The men glanced at it and were unimpressed, far more interested in Navneeta, who sat cross-legged on the floor, her hands folded in her lap.

Navneeta no longer cried when she met the customers; she'd listened to Samita's warnings about how ugly she'd look if tears made her make-up run, and how she needed to look pretty and attract the customers because she had to earn her keep. I pushed a plate of *luchis* towards the girl, the flatbreads still hot and puffy from frying. She was too nervous to eat and I had to remind myself that this life wouldn't be so bad for her; she'd get used to it in time. We all did, although some adjusted quicker and better than others. Even Memsahib, a woman from a different race, had taken to the business as if she'd been born to it. I paused for a moment before wrapping up my rose bowl, wondering whether Miss Maisy was following her mother's trade. I prayed she wasn't, and put the thought right out of my mind. It was common sense: Miss Maisy was in England where she'd be the fine lady Mem had always wanted her daughter to be.

I'm sure Navneeta's mother never dreamed her daughter would find herself in a place like Sonagachi, not even in her most terrifying nightmare. No one wants or chooses to come to Sonagachi.

'What happened?' I asked Navneeta the day after she arrived, her clothes soiled and her long hair so matted it took me the whole afternoon to tease out the tangles. 'Are you pregnant?'

She shook her head, refusing to speak. The agent who sold her to Samita insisted the girl wasn't mute, but he'd also sworn she was a virgin, and that had proved false. The *dai* checked the girl, and said the agent was a liar, and her value immediately plummeted.

'She could have been raped a dozen times on her way here,' Samita said, and then gave vent to a string of lewd curses. Calming down, she appraised the girl with shrewd eyes. 'I should have asked the *dai* to examine her before I handed over the money,' she sighed.

It was rare for Samita to make such a basic mistake, but even in her scruffy state the girl had so much promise that Samita was in a hurry to buy her, anxious she shouldn't go to another madam. Navneeta was well bred and exquisitely beautiful, and the customers might really believe she was descended from the noble courtesans Samita described so often. Although she had been swindled over the girl's virginity, Samita was guaranteed to recoup her investment very quickly.

'Did you run away from home?' I asked Navneeta, brushing her hair gently, the knots almost gone.

She shook her head again, and looked at me, her eyes pleading.

Navneeta talked to me with her eyes for several weeks, and then one afternoon as we sat drinking tea on the rooftop, she began whispering, her words so faint and hoarse I could hardly hear them. I leaned forward to listen, and began to understand why she'd lost her voice.

'I don't know what I've done to deserve this fate,' she cried. 'I was going to be married. All the arrangements were made.'

Navneeta put her tea on the floor and watched it grow cold. A few minutes later, she began whispering again.

'I don't understand why everything changed. My village used to be happy before the trouble came. My brothers said it started because the country was divided. One day our lives were peaceful and the next day we were told our home was in the wrong place, and the people who were our neighbours and tenants suddenly became our enemies. Why was that, Pushpa Aunty? Why did it happen? How can people be so cruel?'

I didn't know the answer.

'Ma and I saw the men take the cows. I'd seen them many times before. One of them worked our fields by the kadam trees, but he looked different that day. They were all angry; their faces tight, like this.' She pulled her skin taut over her skull. 'And their eyes weren't human, not even like an animal's. They stared without seeing.'

The girl sobbed. 'Ma tried to stop them but they threw her

on the floor, and they did it there, in the house. All of them; the men I knew and the ones I didn't. They took my honour.'

Navneeta wiped her nose, tears and snot soaking the end of her sari.

'My little brother tried to stop them but they killed him. I saw him lying on the veranda when we ran away. They'd smashed his head into pieces with rocks; there was nothing left of his face.'

'Where's your family now?' I asked, trying to steady the tremble in my voice.

'I don't know.'

'Did you get lost?'

'They lost me,' she said with another sob. 'We escaped with some other families from the village, and everyone knew what had happened to me. They all talked and stared, not looking into my eyes but lower, at the blood stains on my sari. Ma tried to wash them out in the river but the marks wouldn't fade; they were always there, signs of my shame. We walked and walked all day and slept by the road at night. And then after three days we came to a crossroads where the track joined a big road, and a convoy of trucks stopped to offer us a ride. Only Baba said there was no space for me. They all got on to the back of a truck, Baba and Ma, and my brother and his wife, and all the other families. Baba said I should wait at the crossroads for the next truck and they would meet me in Calcutta. I saw Ma crying and I knew it was a lie. I knew I was spoiled and Baba couldn't stand the disgrace. I watched them drive away. Baba looked forward up the road, but Ma looked back, her arms stretched out to me. I ran after them, shouting for them to stop, for Baba to turn round and see me, for his heart to soften and for him to remember me. But he didn't hear me and they didn't stop.'

Navneeta rested her head in my lap. 'My life is finished, Pushpa Aunty.'

'No, child. You're starting a new life. You can't go back in time, and who knows where your family is. How would you ever find them in this big city? And even if you do meet them, you can't repair the damage.'

'I'm spoiled.'

'Only a little. Many years ago, I was a girl like you and I promise that you can make a life here. It isn't always a good life but, if you work hard, one day you might have a rich *babu* and servants and more gold than Samita Aunty.'

Navneeta wasn't comforted by the prospect of wealth. She'll need a long time to adjust to the business, I thought, and resolved to persuade Samita to treat the girl with special care. I also needed to make sure she didn't run away. She'd only end up in another brothel where she might be treated more harshly, because not all madams can afford to let a girl eat when she isn't working. Every afternoon I sat with her under the shade of a little awning set up on the roof at Samita's insistence. She didn't want Navneeta's fair skin cheapened by the sun. Bit by bit, the girl talked more, and as I listened to her stories, and her hopes and fears, her whispers grew louder. By Durga Puja she spoke quickly and with a lovely accent that had nothing jungly about it. Navneeta had regained her voice because someone was listening.

Bengalis are very jealous people, and I am Bengali through and through. I had a new home, a husband, and my body wasn't cooling – not yet. But I still grieved for the children I'd lost and resented the country that took them. I was jealous of Mem's family because it must surely have replaced me in their hearts. I was sad and sometimes bitter: they had forgotten me. I'd given Mem Kamala's address; I saw it in her purse and I waited eagerly for the postman to deliver a message, but every day he walked past our house on Masjid Bari Street. I wanted to ask one of the *babus* by the General Post Office to write a letter for me, but I didn't know where to send it.

I thought about them every day. On the banks of the Ganga, I watched the river move towards the sea and imagined them on their long journey. I wondered if they were missing their old home and I couldn't understand how Miss Maisy could bear to cut the *maya* to all she'd known in India. She loved that time of year; spring had almost begun, the skies were clearing and the nights were warmer.

Sometimes I worried their boat might have disappeared in a storm. I'd heard that the sea is very deep and cold, and I knew placid waters can turn greedy and careless with life. Madan said I was foolish: wouldn't everyone have heard if such a mighty ship had been sucked into the ocean? He's right, I thought. It's just my imagination casting dark shadows.

I prayed they would be safe, and that Miss Maisy's heart would be healed. I wanted her to be well again, joyful, the way she was as a child. At Kalighat I tied a thread to the wishing tree and did *puja* to ask blessings for my children who were half a world away. A month later, a huge summer wind ripped the thread from the tree, and I knew, across the oceans, another great storm was brewing.

Chapter Thirteen
Maisy

THE NEWSPAPERS SAID it was a miracle. According to the headlines, a lady fell from an ocean liner in the middle of the English Channel while returning home after serving the colonies for almost thirty years. Displaying the best of British bravery and pluck, she battled for life for three hours until she was dragged, exhausted, from a watery grave by the crew of a tiny French fishing boat. Charlie and I collected her from Calais two days later. She sat in the ferry terminal, wrapped in a blanket and shaking with cold until a sympathetic gentleman on a motoring holiday gave her a slug of cognac from his hip flask.

'I'm chilled to the bone,' she said to me. 'And look at the ugly things they've given me to wear. I thought French women were supposed to be classy dressers.'

Mam's sodden clothes had been thrown away; only her knickers were her own. Her bag, containing her purse and almost all the money we had left, had joined the fish at the bottom of the Channel.

Charlie stood in front of her and she glanced at him, instantly dropping her gaze. He burst into tears. 'They said you were dead, Nan.'

'Well, I didn't die, did I? They should make ships safer. The rails were loose; they could have been the death of me.'

I stared her in the eye and she turned away.

On the ferry, we all sat together and watched the White Cliffs of Dover draw nearer. I held Mam's hand and fought the desire to ask her what had really happened when the ship had come within sight of the British coast. I didn't dare question her: I didn't want to hear the answer. Her blonde hair seemed grey and her skin was puffy. She had left England a beautiful, determined young woman and was returning old and beaten.

England made me feel like a foreigner. I thought I was going to a place where I'd belong, where my feet would stand on the same blessed ground as those of my ancestors. But Mam was right: Father's dreams of home were fairy tales and London wasn't any grander than Calcutta. Worst of all, the heart of Empire turned me overnight into a drudge. I was run ragged being my own sweeper, *dhobi*, cook, ayah and bearer. I'm sure Mam took grim satisfaction in watching me graft. She rarely lifted a finger to help, blaming her sluggishness on the after-effects of her trauma at sea and a lasting coldness that had penetrated her bones.

'See what a skivvy you've become, Maisy,' she said. 'In Calcutta you were someone.'

Mam lay on the bed, staring at a naked light bulb dangling from the ceiling of our room on the second floor of a house in Notting Hill. 'It's as bad as Bowbazar, only colder,' she said in a morose, monotone voice.

The landlord had promised us a nice bedsit in a posh house. Instead, we got walls stained by rain that trickled down the chimney; a wooden crate; an ugly, dark wardrobe; a table for one, and a chair with three and a half legs. It was impossible to sit on it unless you jammed the broken leg against the crate. We didn't have a kitchen, only a gas stove on the landing that we shared with Maurice, a man from the Caribbean island of Grenada, who lived in the next room. Our water was lugged from the ground floor and twenty of us used a toilet at the end of the long, narrow strip of garden that functioned as a dumping ground for rubbish, old lino and discarded furniture.

I missed Calcutta's colour: the azure summer skies; the dazzling flowers; the intensity of the sun that even in winter illuminated the world in bright, vibrant light. Britain was gloomy, the sky heavy as if covered in monsoon clouds threatening a storm that never broke. My mood was as low as the depressing weather. Unlike Father's favourite Christmas cards of English villages covered in blankets of pristine white snow, the snow I encountered was a dirty slush that seeped into my shoes. The bits of London I saw in the winter of 1948–9 were drab, filled out in shades of grey, beige and brown. Smog hung over the houses and factories, coating them in a layer of soot, and even the important government offices and royal palaces were black and caked in pigeon dung. The pasty people, still on wartime rations, wore worn-out clothes, and bombed-out London seemed on its knees. No one would think Britain had just won a war.

I found a job as a domestic in the local hospital, sluicing out the bedpans and polishing the floors. The smell of the hospital

– the whiff of boiled potatoes, cabbage and disinfectant – followed me home from work, clinging to my hair and reminding me of the wards and the sluice room even when I wasn't there. Is it any wonder, I thought, that I long for the fragrance of the small, white flowers of the Bengali rains?

I examined myself in the mirror when I got home from work. The bitter wind and sleet had turned my nose red and my eyes a watery pink. Dry patches had appeared around my mouth and the skin on my cheeks was taut and shiny, covered in a web of fine lines. I wasn't beautiful any more; I was a shadow of the young woman who'd worn bel flowers in her hair.

Mam found it hard holding on to a job. Her stint at the bar in the British Oak ended after three days because she drank more spirits than she sold, and she lasted even less time as an usherette in the Electric Cinema because she slept through the films, her torch rolling under the seats and her tray of ice creams melting over the carpet in sticky puddles.

'You can't expect to have money for drink and fags when you don't even try to earn a penny,' I said.

'I did my best; it's not my fault I'm sick.'

'You're not sick: you're drunk.'

'I only drink to ease the pain.'

She claimed she had agonising arthritis, the result of her immersion in the Channel and her years in disease-ridden India. The doctor believed her and so Mam received National Assistance. She said the Government was acknowledging all the time she'd spent helping to run the Empire. The payments were welcome but they barely covered her supply of grog, and we never had enough money, no matter how much we scrimped and how much overtime I did.

Paying the rent and the tallyman were constant worries. Mam had bought a wireless and a new paraffin heater on hire-purchase in a gin-induced spending spree. It committed us to a repayment of five shillings a week and a knock on the door from the collector, a chirpy, balding man with a bad leg he'd acquired during the war.

'We can't afford it,' I said to Mam after handing over the second instalment. She sat warming herself in front of the new fire.

'I need heat,' she said, adopting an expression of martyrdom. 'You forced me to come here. The least you can do is make sure I don't die of cold.'

There's no remedy for homesickness. I tried lifting my spirits with futile cures: I went to the cinema but thought how shabby it was compared to Chowringhee's plush picture houses; I borrowed books from the library and read in the few moments between getting into bed and falling asleep; I took Charlie for long walks round Kensington Gardens and Hyde Park, remembering as I did so our walks around Eden Gardens. In a rush of triumph and expectation, I found a shop run by a Sikh man who sold Indian spices and I tried adding them to my cooking. It only made the sadness worse because the taste was nothing like the taste of home. My potato mush bore no resemblance to Pushpa's *alu dam*, and the other tenants complained about the disgusting foreign pong, which was rich considering the whole house was filled with sour smells and the reek from the pails they kept under their beds to save a night-time visit to the privy.

'What's this?' Mam said, stirring the awful *alu dam*. Even Charlie, who was usually starving and scoffed everything in sight, ate slowly.

'It's what Pushpa taught me to make.'

'You're having me on.'

Sitting on the edge of the bed, I bent over the bowl balanced on my knee, suddenly engulfed by sorrow. Only this time I wasn't thinking of Sunil; I was thinking of Pushpa – loving, faithful Pushpa, whom I missed more than India itself. She'd been with me ever since I could remember, more caring, more of a mother than Mam had ever been, and yet I'd hardly given her a thought when we left Calcutta. I wondered where she was staying and if she was making a good living selling snacks. My selfishness struck me for the first time and I wondered why I'd been so blind. She had only the crippled barber to look after her, and he was worse than useless. I remembered her hobbling after Charlie, her plaited hair, smelling as always of coconut oil, growing whiter each year. She must have thought we'd abandoned her; and she'd have been right. I couldn't even write to say I was sorry because we lost the address she gave us: it was in Mam's handbag when it sank to the bottom of the Channel. Poor Pushpa. She'd devoted herself to me and Charlie and I'd repaid her love with indifference: I had been so lost in my own tragedy that I hadn't seen hers.

Mam said the two women in the flat above us were prostitutes; they didn't get up until the afternoon, and the thin, less attractive one with mousy hair had green stains on the back of her coat.

'She's giving them knee tremblers up against the trees in the park,' Mam said in disgust. 'How bloody low can you get?'

All the same, she turned our wireless down in the mornings so they could get some decent sleep.

They mustn't have noticed the kindness because they knocked loudly on our door one evening when Mam had gone to get a new supply of booze. They stood on the landing, arms folded. The red-haired woman spoke using only half her mouth, a cigarette clamped in the other corner between bright red lips.

'Where's your ponce?' she said.

I was puzzled. 'You've got me mixed up with someone else.'

'Is the old lady your maid?'

'What old lady?'

'The one what lives with you; the old brass with the dyed blonde hair.'

'That's my mam, and it isn't dyed.'

They eased their way into the room. The thin one leaned against the doorframe while the red-haired woman carried on talking.

'Look, darlin',' she said. 'No one's going to get me and Nance in trouble with the law. We don't want the bleeding bogeys saying we run a disorderly house.'

Nance nodded.

'Make sure you keep your beat well away from here and never bring any punters back. Understand?'

'I don't have any punters. I'm a cleaner in the hospital.'

'Pull the other one, darlin'. You expect us to believe that? A pretty white girl with a nig-nog kid?'

I pulled Charlie towards me. 'He isn't a nig-nog.'

271

They stared at Charlie, who had a rip in the seat of his shorts and old scabs on his knees.

'She might be telling the truth, Gladys. I haven't seen him without his hat before.'

'Let's have a dekko.' Gladys touched Charlie's hair. 'He's not got a nappy head,' she said in surprise. 'So where's his dad?'

'He's dead,' I said. 'He was killed in the war.'

'Foreign, was he?'

'Italian.'

They turned to go, their high-heeled, platform shoes leaving indents in the lino. No one else in the house wore shoes like Gladys and Nance. Most of the women slopped around in slippers even when they were in the street. They chatted all the way up the dark staircase, their heels clonking against the bare wood.

'It's the children I feel sorry for. Poor little blighters didn't ask for it, did they?' Gladys said.

'She said his dad was foreign.'

Gladys cackled. 'Italian, my arse.'

Gladys and Nance softened once they spotted me returning from work in my overall and worsted stockings, and realised I wasn't likely to steal their business. They were friendly and shouted from their flat, inviting me for a cup of char. Sometimes I took them up on the offer and sat watching Gladys pluck her eyebrows and Nance stitch the holes in her stockings or rub at the lichen stains on her coat.

'I don't know why you bother with them, Maisy,' Mam said one day when we heard them outside the door to their flat. 'Tell them to sling their hook.' Mam lay on her bed, the eiderdown pulled up to her chin. 'They're cheap tarts.'

'Are you mental?' Gladys roared, high on Benzedrine, which she said was for her bad chest but which she really took to keep awake and buzzing all night. Mam hadn't heard her come down the stairs. She was standing at the open door with a packet of biscuits in her hand. 'There's nothing cheap about me and Nance. We've got a reputation to think about.'

'That's right,' Nance said, clattering downstairs after her.

'You can't slag us off as cheap when your own daughter's been having it off with a coloured feller.'

Nance nodded. 'It's our rule,' she said. 'We never go with chocolate.'

Mam turned over in bed and faced the wall.

'Here,' Gladys said, giving me the biscuits. 'They're for the nipper. I didn't get them on the ration; a feller gave them to me.'

Charlie's eyes opened wide; he was so hungry you'd think I never fed him.

'Poor little mite could do with some decent clothes as well as something to eat,' Gladys said, looking at Charlie as if he were a pitiful, abandoned orphan.

'What's it to you?' Mam muttered from the bed.

'I'm only saying you'll have the social on your backs if you don't look after him properly.'

'Shut your bleeding trap,' Mam snapped.

'He needs a decent coat,' Gladys continued. 'And some shoes. His toes are going to be sticking out of that pair soon enough; he'll get frostbite.'

Gladys paused by the door watching Charlie shovel the biscuits into his mouth. 'You should come out with us sometime, Maisy. You can't live on charlady's wages. The city's full of geezers looking for a good time. I fell in with a foreigner last night and you can charge them anything. They don't know the value of money, the daft buggers.'

They headed off for their Saturday evening shift, dolled up in scarlet lipstick, Gladys's hair just out of rollers and stiff with setting lotion.

'She's got a ruddy cheek,' Mam seethed. 'Fancy suggesting you become a cheap brass like them.'

I hated the idea too; the thought of joining Gladys and Nance on the game filled me with such absolute horror I'd rather have died.

'As if a cracker like you would be standing with them on the Bayswater Road turning tricks for a pittance,' Mam laughed. 'Oh, no, my girl; you're too good for that. You should work in Mayfair.'

'It's not changed much.' Mam said, walking down the street, her gaze fixed on the house where she grew up. 'But my mam would never leave the doorstep in a state like that. She scrubbed it twice a week.'

Some of the kids playing hopscotch stopped to watch us gather outside the door, Charlie scuffing the toes of his shoes against the kerb and avoiding making eye contact with the children.

'Shall I knock, Mam, or shall we leave it and go back to the station?'

Mam hesitated. She'd insisted we make the journey to Leeds yet once we were there she didn't seem to know why. She'd not heard from her mam and dad since I was little, and the letter she sent from Notting Hill received no reply.

'Go on,' she said, taking a deep breath and steadying her nerves.

A young woman in a hairnet and dressing gown answered the door.

'The O'Neills moved out years ago,' she said. 'Half a dozen tenants have lived here since they left.'

'Do you know where they went?' I asked.

'Not a clue, duck. Try Bert O'Neill at number twenty-five. He might be able to help.'

'He's me ruddy brother,' Mam said in a strangled voice as we made our way to number twenty-five.

The net curtains in the front window parted a few inches before the door was opened by a middle-aged woman in a headscarf and apron.

'Does Albert O'Neill live here?' I asked.

'Bert,' the woman shouted. 'Someone to see you.'

A bald man appeared behind her, his stomach stretching the fabric of his vest. 'Babs?' he said. 'Flippin' 'eck. What the bloody hell are you doing here? We haven't heard from you in twenty fucking years.'

'There's no room to swing a cat in here,' Bert said, squeezing past the sofa in the musty parlour that contained far more people than the chilly, rarely used room could comfortably accommodate. Half a dozen more sat in the back room, several stood in the kitchen, three others lurked on the stairs, and a load of noisy neighbours hung around the front door; twenty or more people arriving in the space of half an hour to witness the return of the prodigal daughter.

Mam's younger sister, Dolly, rushed from a nearby street,

collecting her daughter and grandchildren on the way. She looked bad-tempered and a lot older than Mam, and sat on the sofa next to her daughter, Jean, sipping tea out of Bert's wife's best china and casting angry sideways glances at Mam, who was in full flow about the success of her life in India.

'And it was so hard leaving the servants,' Mam explained to her long-lost brother. Bert nodded and took another slurp from his bottle of beer. 'You see, they become so devoted and loyal. It broke their hearts when we said goodbye. You can't get good staff like that in England these days.'

'What's she blethering on about?' Dolly hissed at her daughter.

Mam continued, undeterred, 'You really need to have at least half a dozen servants, and more for parties, though of course we spent so much time at the Tollygunge Club we were hardly ever at home.'

Charlie sat on a hard chair, his legs swinging and his socks drooping round his ankles. He munched on a sausage roll, not saying a word or looking at anyone.

'Sup up, lad,' Bert's wife said, pushing a bottle of pop and a pork pie into his hands.

'It's strange coming back to England,' Mam said in a voice she'd last used with Admiral George. 'The tiny houses look odd when you've been used to living among so much space.'

'Shurrup, will you, Babs?' Dolly butted in. 'Listen to yourself putting on airs and graces and going on about bleeding India. You haven't asked about our mam and dad. While you were off gallivanting, happy as a pig in muck, we buried them both within a few months of each other. That was five years ago.'

Bert's wife handed Dolly another cup of tea. 'Ta, love,' Dolly said, taking a sip and starting on Mam again. 'The cancer got both of them. Terrible, it was. You should've been here to help out. Me and our Jean were run off our feet.'

'Well, they're here now, and better late than never,' Bert's wife said.

Dolly sniffed. 'Who would've believed it? You were too busy with yer big house and yer husband to think of us. It would've been nice if you'd written to us once in a while. You'd think with all those servants you'd have plenty of time to send us a few lines and ask how yer mam and dad were doing. And with all that money you could've sent them something to help them out in their old age, but, oh no, you sent them nowt. Mardy and selfish, that's what you are.'

'Running a big house takes a lot of time, even when you've got servants, Dolly. You should remember that from our days in service,' Bert's wife said, acting the peacemaker again.

'Are you going back to India soon?' Bert asked.

'I think we'll be staying here for a while,' I said.

'It's better to stick with yer own kind,' he said. 'What does yer dad think about living in England?'

'He died some time ago, Mr O'Neill.'

'Mr O'Neill? Don't be daft, girl. I'm yer Uncle Bert. And you've got to call that woman with the monk on, Aunty Dolly.' Dolly scowled. 'Don't worry about her, lass,' he said to me in a whisper. 'She never got over yer mam doing so well. While she's been living the life in India, yer Aunty Dolly's been working in a factory and raising her kids alone since her husband took off with another woman. She's skint and bloody knackered.' He looked at me closely. 'You know, you're the image of Babs when she was young. Yer eyes are a different colour and yer mouth's not quite the same but apart from that you're the spit of her. Yer a stunner and no mistake.'

'And who's this little lad with you?' Bert's wife asked. 'Did you get him from India?' Charlie looked up from eating a portion of chips and a cheese roll.

'He's my son,' I said.

'Yer kiddin' me,' Bert said.

They all turned to stare at Charlie and a couple of people poked their heads round the door to take a look at him.

'Oh, aye? You adopted him, right?' Bert said.

'No.'

'Then who's his dad?'

'He was a British man. He was killed fighting in Burma during the war,' Mam said a little too loudly.

'You're pulling my leg.' Uncle Bert laughed. 'He's the blackest little piccaninny I've seen round here.'

'His father was a gentleman,' Mam said. 'He played polo and was decorated for bravery. He left Maisy very well provided for.'

Aunt Dolly smiled for the first time. Later, I heard her in the next room explaining the situation to a distant cousin.

'Caps it all, don't it?' she said with a tremor of excitement in her voice. 'She had him to a nigger.'

We left after Charlie had finished all the sausage rolls and drunk every bottle of pop that came his way. You'd think I never fed the boy.

'Tarra now. Don't forget us this time,' Dolly said at the door. 'Try to keep in touch. We know how busy you'll be moving from yer big house in India to another big one in London, but spare a thought for yer poor relations up north.' She smiled again, kissed my cheek and ruffled Charlie's hair.

'Poor little lad,' I heard Bert say to her even before the door started to close behind us.

'Poor us, you mean,' she replied. 'They're a stain on a decent family and I'm having nowt to do with them. The girl's a slut, just like Babs was. They should've stayed in sodding India.'

Soon after Christmas, Mam had a new lease of life. She made up with Gladys, gave her some Woodbines and spent a whole afternoon in her flat. The next day Mam gave me a fox stole and red, peep-toe shoes with Cuban heels and inch-high platforms.

'You'll look a picture in these, Maisy,' she said in glee.

I lifted the fur and looked at the creature's dried black nose, like a large, hard currant, and his blank glass eyes, and in an instant, I was ten years old again and standing, shrieking with Lali, in the taxidermist's shop on Dharmatala Street. 'He's seen better days,' I said with a shudder. The stole was moth-eaten and smelled stale; Mam must have got it from a jumble sale. The shoes were better; they were new and shiny, and almost as high as Gladys's three-tier platforms.

'They're nice, Mam, but we can't afford them. It's Charlie who needs new shoes.'

'They're an investment.'

'What do you mean?'

'Play your cards right and Charlie will get his clothes from Jermyn Street.'

I felt a rising panic, a queasiness that turned my stomach.

'There's a fortune to be made in this city,' Mam said, shaking the stole vigorously, hairs shedding over the room.

'Do you want to put me on the game, Mam?'

'No, of course not.'

'What then?'

'I've seen those Fifis in Mayfair and Shepherd Market prancing about with their poodles and fancy clothes, stinking of perfume. French girls shouldn't get all the money: you're twice as pretty as they are.'

She paused, her enthusiasm dented by my horrified expression, and then carried on, her voice falsely jolly. 'Gladys is right,' she said. 'We can't live on charlady's wages. And it's not like you'd be a tart on the street. You can find a nice room in Soho or Mayfair and go for drinks at the Ritz.'

'Go to hell, Mam. I'd rather sleep with Gordon again than have a beat in Soho.'

Mam stopped talking. She cocked her head to one side and fixed me with a bright-eyed look.

Mam's fox stole soon found a new purpose. I stuffed it along the bottom of the door to keep out the draughts as we huddled round the paraffin heater and were made woozy by the fumes. The fur was always getting jammed under the door and sometimes I could only open it an inch to hand over the rent money or the next instalment on the wireless and heater.

'The tallyman's not been round this week,' I said, counting my change. 'It's lucky because I can't afford to pay him.'

'Don't worry about him,' Mam said. 'He called this afternoon.'

'What excuse did you give?'

'I didn't; I took him in for half an hour.'

I gasped. 'You were supposed to be looking after Charlie.'

'I was. I sent him to play with the other lads in the road.'

'You gave up the business years ago, Mam. You're too old.'

'He was in here like greased lightning and left with a smile on his face. Fellers with a gammy leg can't be choosy.'

I knew it was spring when visitors to the hospital began bringing bunches of daffodils for the patients. Nance no longer looked as perished as she sat on a bench waiting for customers in Kensington Gardens, and Charlie's winter cold finally dried up. By Easter he'd grown out of his shoes and was wearing plimsolls and looking like one of the ragamuffins on the streets. I winced at his stick-thin, brown ankles, his feet slopping around in the baggy pumps, and I thought I'd have to get him some proper shoes before he started school in the autumn. I wanted him to fit in, not to stand out because of his threadbare clothes, though there was nothing I could do about the colour of him or the fact he was starting school almost two years behind the other children.

'He'll be fine,' Mam said. 'He's as bright as a button and he'll be top of the class before you know it. Coleville Primary is lucky to have him. He'll be one of the boys in no time. You shouldn't fret; he's just an ordinary white lad in the wrong skin.'

Mam didn't really want Charlie to go to school in Notting Hill; she had other plans, which almost came to fruition in the summer. I heard her from the street when I returned from work, the sound of her voice growing louder as I trudged up the stairs. She was belting out a song, drunk as a lord, and Gladys, Mam's new best friend, was laughing and lighting another Woodbine as they danced around the room, Gladys high on Benzedrine again.

'"Oh, you'll take the high road, and I'll take the low road,

And I'll get to Scotland before ye,'" Mam sang. She spun between the bed and the wardrobe in a bad imitation of a Highland jig. "'But me and my true love will never meet again,'" she caught sight of me and stood still, giving her all to the final line, "'On the bonnie, bonnie banks o' Loch Lomond.'"

'She's gone mental,' Gladys said. 'She invited me down here for a party.'

'I'm celebrating, and I've never been saner.' Mam waved a sheet of paper in the air and looked at me in delight. 'We're finished with this place, Maisy.' Euphoric, she rushed towards me. 'It's a letter from Gordon. He wants you back.'

Mam's frenzy flummoxed me and I took a moment to recover from the jolt of her news. 'What makes you think I want him?'

'Don't be daft, Maisy. If he got you that mansion in Calcutta he'll probably set us up in a bleeding castle in Scotland.' She turned to Gladys and hooted. 'She'll have a butler who wears a kilt and I'll get me hands on some of the best Scotch in the world.'

'How did he know where we were?' I asked.

'I wrote to Donald. You remember the jute wallah at the Imperial Works?' She turned to Gladys. 'He was always round ours when we lived in Dharmatala; I couldn't get rid of the bugger. Anyhow, listening to him talk has turned out to be time well spent. He went back home to be a supervisor at the Dundee mill and I wrote to him there. He found Gordon's address and sent it to me. There can't be that many millionaires called MacBrayne in Dundee. All I did was send Gordon a little note saying we were in London and that it'd be good to see him.'

'I'm not going,' I said, adamant. The thought turned my stomach.

'He's not angry any more. He's been stuck with a plain lump of a wife, and that'd be enough to soften any man's heart.' She waved the letter in front of my face. 'See what he wrote.'

'I don't want to read it.'

'Listen to this,' Mam said, clearing her throat. 'He says, "You're sure to like Dundee. It's a British Calcutta; a famous city on the banks of a great river."'

I stared, stony-faced.

'That's got to be worth something, Maisy,' Mam said, exasperated.

'What do you lose by going?' Gladys said, adding her voice to Mam's cajoling. 'It's only the price of a train ticket. He sounds an all right geezer, by that letter. I like it when he says "a famous city on the banks of a great river". It's like poetry.'

'He's the least poetic man in the whole world,' I said, furious with the two of them. 'The last time I saw him he chucked us out on to the streets. Who knows, he might want us to go to Dundee so he can get his jewellery back.'

'Bollocks,' Mam said, opening a case and chucking in some clothes. 'We'd better pack every gansey we've got. It's freezing up north.'

Charlie scrambled up the stairs and into the room, his socks sagging and the sole of his right plimsoll flapping loose.

'I'm starving. What's for tea?' he said.

Gladys and Mam looked at me, their eyebrows raised, and I knew I was beaten. I pulled my case from under the bed. Kneeling on the floor, I fiddled with the lock that had grown stiff with rust. I lifted the lid and, for a moment, a trace of the damp, flower-laden smell of the Calcutta monsoon enveloped me. I closed my eyes, remembering a young man with blue-black hair, and I breathed in the fragrance of another life.

Mam cadged the train fare off the tallyman. She must have been taking him in for more than the odd half-hour to get so much credit. And Gladys lent us twenty quid because she was flush and going up in the world after landing a new job as a living statue at Soho's Windmill Theatre where she stood stark naked on stage and had fans wafted around her by sequined assistants.

Mam's euphoria faded not long after we pulled out of Edinburgh Station. She'd been on a high in the two days since she'd received Gordon's letter, which on closer inspection looked more like a hastily typed memo than a love letter promising reconciliation. She hadn't slept and kept humming tunes and repacking the cases until I began to think Gladys had given her Benzedrine as well as cash. As we travelled through Fife, she sat opposite me refusing to glance once at the beautiful country-side, her eyes vacant and her skin covered with an alcoholic sheen.

'Maybe we shouldn't have come,' she said hesitantly.

'It's a bit late to decide that; we're almost there.'

Charlie sat next to me, riveted by the conversation of an elderly couple on the other side of the aisle. The woman did up the buttons of her coat, suddenly chilled although it was summer, as the man told her about a disaster that had befallen a train like ours, describing how it had plunged off the flimsy bridge over the River Tay, all the passengers drowning in the icy water and half the bodies never found.

'It was years ago, laddie,' the man said, catching sight of

Charlie's mouth hanging open in horror. 'Dinnae worry; there's a new bridge now.'

I squeezed Charlie's hand and gave him a jolly, reassuring smile. My lips stayed fixed in that smile as I looked out of the window, feeling anything but heartened. The train was over the water, travelling slowly and my fear wasn't that we would plummet eighty feet into the Tay but that some other disaster would befall us, a growing realisation that I didn't know why we were going to Dundee and what we would find when we got there. The bridge curved over the river and I saw the city on the far bank dotted with dozens of jute mill stacks belching out smoke, smog shrouding the buildings, spilling down over the harbour and on to the Tay, silver in the sunlight. I wished I had some of Pushpa's chillies and lemons to keep us safe, an insurance to keep my mind clear, a talisman to stop me plummeting like travellers in the doomed train, into an abyss.

'You'd think he'd have the manners to show up after inviting us here,' Mam fumed. She'd regained her zest for life and fiery temper, revitalising herself in the bar of the Queen's Hotel with special Highland malts recommended by Donald who, unlike Gordon, had arrived to welcome us. I wouldn't have recognised him if it wasn't for his voice: despite twenty years in Calcutta he still had a broad Scottish accent. That was the only thing about him that remained the same. He'd lost his ruddy complexion and was sallow, his skin leathery and lined in the way of most old India hands. And he wore ill-fitting khaki trousers and a grey cardigan, which was peculiar when I'd only ever seen him in jute wallah whites.

'Babs, you're as bonnie as ever,' he said, convincing me I

couldn't trust a word he said. 'Mr MacBrayne's yer special friend, no?' he asked Mam with a wink.

'He's a friend of our Maisy,' she said.

He raised a bushy eyebrow. 'He dizzna come in tae town much.'

'Why's that?' Mam said.

'There's no love lost round here for men like MacBrayne. People think the Calcutta jute wallahs are traitors; they're destroying the Scottish trade. He'll likely move to the Home Counties soon and be more English than the English.'

'No one gives you any trouble, do they?'

'Some of the mill workers hae a great chip on their shoulder. They tell me I can't lord it over them like I did the darkies in India. To be honest, I'm done with it, Babs. I put a tidy sum away when I was in India, and I'm retiring next month. Jute's finished in Dundee: the future's out East.'

'You remember the old days?'

'Aye. I'd go back if I could.'

'Me too, Donald. Me too.'

I waited for them to recount stories of Calcutta, the kind of fanciful tales Father told about England. Instead they talked about whisky and the weather. They were stiff and anxious despite the drink, two people who had known each other well but whose friendship was born in India and couldn't travel.

They ordered another peg. 'Here's tae us,' Donald said.

'To us,' Mam repeated, their glasses clinking so loudly the other customers turned round.

Donald sank a little in his seat. He swirled the whisky in his glass and breathed in the aroma.

'Fancy more?' Mam asked, with a grin that suggested she

wondered if Donald still had a problem with his penis, and whether he'd fancy visiting our room.

'I cannae. I'm away home; the wife's expecting me.'

Mam gave him one of her special smiles so I knew what she was going to ask next. 'Could you lend us a bit of cash, just for a few days until we've seen Gordon?'

Donald must have realised he'd never get it back. 'For old times' sake, Babs,' he said, handing her some notes under the table. He downed his drink, in a rush to leave.

We watched from the window as he got into a brand-new Morris Minor. Whatever link Mam and Donald had enjoyed in Calcutta was broken in Dundee; Mam had lost the only real friend she'd had among her many customers.

'He doesn't talk as much as he used to,' Mam said with a sigh. She looked sad for a moment before pulling herself upright and smoothing her skirt. 'It's a blessing really,' she said briskly. 'He talked such rubbish.' She patted the money in her pocket. 'I won't be a minute,' she said. 'I'm going to ring Gordon, the bleeding time waster.'

I watched her walk into the hotel lobby: my mam, my pimp.

Dundee's summer is like November in Calcutta. I'm sure the sun in Scotland radiates a different kind of heat and, even in the middle of a July day, it didn't warm me the same way as India's sun. Each morning a breeze blew down from the hills to the north, clearing the smoggy mist as sirens signalled the start of the mill shift and thousands of workers made their way from their tall, dilapidated tenements to a day among the clanking looms. Gordon was right about Dundee being the British Calcutta; the city was built on Bengali jute. Yet in other ways he was quite wrong. Dundee was shrinking while Calcutta was growing, and though the river is powerful and wide, just like the Hooghly, it is a different colour. The Hooghly is brown while the Tay is grey and silver, and it smells of the sea, of salt and seaweed.

In the docks, pukka bales of jute were unloaded from ships registered in Calcutta, and I watched the lascars coming ashore, shouting to one another in Bengali. I listened to them, thinking of home, captivated by the sound of familiar words until the men became conscious of me and commented on the peculiar white woman staring at them. 'Crazy,' I heard them say, and I turned and walked away, realising they were probably right.

Like Calcutta, Dundee has a park near the river. Magdalen Green is a beautiful place near the Tay Railway Bridge where you can see right across the estuary to Fife. The bandstand isn't as big as the one in Eden Gardens but, to my mind, it's more beautiful with its delicate wrought ironwork. And the tunes the bands played were much the same in Dundee and Calcutta, or at least they were that summer's day as Mam and I lay in the sun, the grass making my coat damp. Charlie, at last off the leash and no longer cooped up in the hotel room, ran barefoot from the swings to the bandstand and back again. I was half asleep, lulled by the sound of children playing. Charlie scrambled up, panting, said something to Mam about tigers and then charged off again, his shouts mingling with those of the other boys. He rushed past us a few moments later, and I opened my eyes a fraction to see three much older boys in pursuit.

'Where's yer bow and arrow?' they shouted, whooping as if they were Apaches in a Western.

I sat up in alarm and tried to spot Charlie among the crowds; half of Dundee must have been sunbathing or playing on Magdalen Green. And then I saw him careering round the bandstand, almost losing his footing. He headed back to us, the effort making him grimace. I stood up and he collapsed at my feet. The boys chasing him slackened their pace and stopped, looking at me, cocky and excited until they saw Mam, who was furious and bristling with indignation, ready for action. The lads turned tail and retreated, the biggest one turning to look at us over his shoulder. 'Yer no' in India now,' he called.

That night Charlie worked up the lather from the Lifebuoy soap until he was covered in foam and his bath water looked like thick, syrupy milk. He rubbed his arms vigorously.

'Are you trying to wash yourself away?' I asked, worried so much soap would dry his skin.

'They said I'm a darkie so I'm making myself whiter,' he said, scrubbing harder. 'Tomorrow when we go to the park I want to be one of the cowboys and not the Indian.'

It was too expensive to eat in the hotel and so we made a habit of going to the chippie or buying pies, which we ate by the docks, or sitting on the steps of the huge, ugly Caird Hall until we were moved on by a policeman. Mam had taken Charlie for a special chippie tea on the day the bellboy arrived with a note from Gordon telling me to meet him at the museum in fifteen minutes. In hindsight, I wished I hadn't rushed along Nethergate and through the bustle of the High Street, responding like an anxious servant summoned by her master. I asked directions from a woman pushing a pram, and she spoke to me in such a broad accent I couldn't understand a word she said, but

I followed where her finger pointed and dashed up Reform Street. I arrived flustered at the museum to see Gordon standing by a statue of Robert Burns and seeming no different from when I'd last seen him striding round the garden house like an irate general moving his army under heavy fire. Now, though, he'd acquired a false arm and his artificial hand was covered in a grey leather glove, which I tried not to look at because it made me feel more nervous and a little bit squeamish. Unlike Donald, Gordon wasn't pale; in fact, he appeared to be hearty, the Calcutta sun having burned his skin to a permanent pink.

'I'd have met you sooner,' he said in greeting, 'but we've been away salmon fishing.'

I wondered how he managed to fish with only one hand, though anxiety and courtesy stopped me asking.

He looked me up and down and I felt self-conscious in my worn dress and scruffy shoes. I tried to catch my breath and pushed my unruly hair back into shape.

'Let's go this way,' he said. 'I've no interest in paintings and relics, and I like being in the sun. It's one of the things I miss most about India.'

We walked a short distance and through a gate into an old cemetery, which I thought was appropriate, seeing we were about to try raising something from the dead.

'You're liking England?' he said, glancing at me and then quickly focusing on a gravestone as if seeing me had scorched his eyes. He studied the engravings on the headstones, many of the names smoothed away by the centuries, and I remembered walking, stalked by pye-dogs, through another cemetery, looking in vain for Father's grave. This time, as I walked slowly along the paths, I didn't have the comfort of holding Pushpa's hand.

'England's not what I thought, and it's nothing like my father described.'

'Places always seem better from a distance,' he said, walking further into the graveyard. 'What made you leave Calcutta? Your mother was dead against it.'

'Things changed.'

'And is life more . . .?' He searched for the word. 'Is it more comfortable in London?'

'It's different.'

'Forgive me for being blunt, but you seem a little lost to me,' he said, forcing a smile. He took his cigarette case out of the breast pocket of his jacket and I looked away, not wanting to embarrass him as he struggled to open it. He put a cigarette between his lips.

'Here, let me help you,' I said, taking his lighter.

'For fuck's sake, Maisy,' he said furiously, snatching the cigarette out of his mouth and throwing it on to the grass in a sudden foul temper. 'I'm not a bloody invalid. I'm not finished yet.'

It took him several minutes to calm down and for the big vein on his temple to cease throbbing. We continued to walk round the graves, Gordon stopping to point out famous dead people, to tell me the history of that cemetery called the Howff, the ancient meeting place of the city, and to tell me stories about old Dundee families. It made me feel less on edge, calm gradually replacing my deep discomfort.

'Now, tell me why you came here,' he said abruptly, the gentle talk of history and the city swiftly forgotten.

'Mam wrote to you. It was her idea.'

'But you chose to come to Dundee. She didn't force you.

And I think you came because you thought I'd take care of you.' He paused. 'I can do that, Maisy, if you'd like me to.'

'The last time you saw me you threw us on to the streets. You hated me.'

'Aye, you're right about that. I did. I hated most things then: my business was in trouble; *goondas* crushed my hand and killed my best manager, and you were seeing another man even though I'd given you everything you could have dreamed of.'

Not everything, I thought. He hadn't given me the most important things.

The big vein pulsed again on his temple and I expected him to raise his voice but he kept it under control.

'I won't be humiliated like that. No one makes a fool of me; not the bloody eejits in the ICS, not the Indians with their thieving hands in my business, not you, Maisy, and especially not that bloody communist Banerjee.'

His hair bristled and his colour rose until his already ruddy face was bright red, and purple and white patches appeared on his cheeks. Rage radiated from him, and I was struck by fear. My instinct was to run, to escape the cemetery and flee back to the hotel because I really thought he might kill me there and then; he might crush my head against one of the eroded headstones or strangle the life out of me with his one good hand. He had the strength to do it, and at that moment he seethed with enough anger to be capable of anything, but I didn't run, and it wasn't only fright that kept me there, standing stock-still, staring at his livid face. I knew he loved me as much as hated me and that in that cemetery, surrounded by the city's fine buildings, there would be no hiding his crime.

'I can find you somewhere to stay,' he said, wiping his eyes with a large monogrammed handkerchief, his rage easing and turning to tears. 'I'll even put up with your harridan of a mother and the whinging bairn. I'm guessing you didn't bring the old servant woman with you, too?'

I shook my head.

'It won't be an impressive place like the house in Calcutta. We're back in the real world now, and we all have to tighten our belts and live less lavishly when we return home, but I've recently bought a grouse moor in Angus and there are a couple of cottages on the estate. I could have one done up for you. We can install electricity and running water.'

The vein on his temple throbbed a little less violently, and he gazed at me, waiting impatiently for an answer.

I wavered, unsure what was holding me back when I didn't have any better alternatives. 'I can't,' I stuttered, the impossibility of the idea suddenly clear. I'd hated being trapped with Gordon in a gilded cage, so if he wanted vengeance, putting me in a stone cottage in the middle of a Scottish moor would be a good way to achieve it.

He sucked in air rapidly through pursed lips as if he'd been stung. 'What the hell do you mean? Didn't you come here to ask me to forgive you, to beg me to take you back? That's why you came, isn't it?'

He was right. I had relented under Mam's pressure, packing my case, infused with the smell of Bengal, and taken the long train journey to Dundee because I wanted to be rescued; rescued from my misery, from the damp, crumbling room in Notting Hill, from the hospital's sluice room, from too many bad memories that played repeatedly in my mind. But Gordon, I knew as I looked at him, would provide no refuge.

'I shouldn't have come,' I said. 'I'm sorry I've given you the wrong impression, and I'm sorry too about what happened in the mill and your arm, and whatever part I played in that terrible thing, though believe me when I say I had no idea there was going to be an attack. Sunil told me nothing, and if I'd known I would have stopped him, I promise you. You do believe me, don't you?'

Any sorrow in Gordon's face was gone, washed away by tears and then by shock. Instead, something new was there, something that made me look away because it frightened me far more than his anger, scaring me even more than the thought he might crush my skull or strangle me among the gravestones. The glint in his eye was malevolent and cruel, and it jolted me because I'd never seen him like that: Gordon was often angry and bad tempered with the bluster and force of a tantruming child, but he wasn't cruel or vindictive.

I stepped back from him and turned round, meaning to leave the cemetery.

'Wait,' he said, seizing my left arm and twisting it behind my back. 'You can't walk away from me and think there are no consequences. I won't free you so easily,' he hissed in my ear, slowly increasing the twist on my arm.

'There's nothing you can do, Gordon. You can't punish me,' I said through gritted teeth, stifling a whimper as the pain shot up to my shoulder.

'But I've already done it, Maisy.' I couldn't see his expression but I heard the delight in his voice. 'I've made sure you'll never be with Charlie's father.'

'How did you do that?'

Gordon released his grip on my arm and pushed me away.

'What did you do?' I repeated.

He adjusted the leather glove on his artificial hand. 'I gave him a death sentence,' he said with a smile. 'He was never in the Britannia Mill. Did you realise that? He was nowhere near it. I'd not seen the bastard who killed the manager before that day, but Banerjee will pay the price for his murder. He'll be a fugitive for ever more or he'll be caught and executed. How fitting is that? You're denied your great love and he is robbed of his life.'

'I'll tell everyone. I'll say you lied,' I said, choking on outrage.

'I won't withdraw the accusation. You can shout about the injustice as loudly as you like but no one is going to listen. No one will believe you. Who's going to doubt the word of *burra sahib* and a jute baron? You think the police here or in Calcutta will give a moment's attention to the hysteria of a down-at-heel whore? Face it, lassie, in this world you have no credibility, and you'll be given no respect.'

I ran from the cemetery, turning the wrong way and then rushing blindly uphill and away from the river. I found myself on a cobbled street as the gates of a mill opened and the workers streamed out, jute fibres sticking to their hair and clothes. I joined the flow of people, not noticing where I was going, engrossed in thoughts that took me to the other side of the world. Slowing my pace, I turned and walked downhill to the Tay.

I wondered how I'd ever doubted Sunil. I'd listened to the judgement of others and not to my intuition. If he hadn't been part of that terrible attack on the Britannia Mill, how could he have been injured and died? Trust your gut feeling for once, I told myself; Sunil's alive and he's in Calcutta, and I'm going to find him.

The next morning, we put on every piece of clothing we'd brought to Dundee. Despite the sunny day, Charlie was swaddled in three jumpers and two pairs of shorts, and, underneath her coat, Mam wore two dresses and all her cardies. We slunk out of the Queen's Hotel looking fat and claiming we were off for a day trip to the beach when really we were on our way to the train station, leaving our empty cases in the room and our bill unpaid. We had only one pound seven shillings to our name. As we crossed the Tay, I looked back at the city, this time clear of its smog, its mill stacks standing tall, a flock of geese flying low over the water near the docks, and I wondered how long it would be before I saw the other great jute city on the banks of a wide river. A long time, I thought, and began to brood over all our options. Paying for a voyage to Calcutta was impossible on hospital wages.

'Did you get a refund on those red platform shoes?' I asked Mam.

She shook her head and grinned. 'I sold them to Gladys, but I'm sure she'll let you borrow them.'

Chapter Fourteen

Pushpa

SAMITA KEPT A small bowl of cloves by the door in addition to the usual string of chillies and lemons, and every day she asked me to wash down the doorstep with water from the Ganga. I sprinkled it inside the brothel too, just to be safe. Next, Samita set a piece of paper on fire on the step that was still damp from the Gangajal, and we stood, watching it burn. She was convinced these rituals brought her good fortune, and perhaps they did, but I was more realistic. The money pouring into Samita's treasure chest wasn't only the result of magic; it came from the lustre in Navneeta's kohl-rimmed eyes.

The girl was unrecognisable from the ragged refugee who arrived in Sonagachi: she smiled and talked, and she danced like a courtesan from a nawab's court. Her performance wasn't wild and rough like the low-born women in cheap brothels. It was controlled and elegant, her stamping feet jingling tiny bells fastened to her ankles, her hands making precise, fluid movements. Samita paid a fortune to have a dance master train Navneeta so well, and to dress her in silk, golden shoes and rich ornaments, and it was an investment she was sure to recoup many times if she was half as clever as her mother.

Navneeta had a *babu*, a rich, regular client who was a manufacturer of soaps and detergents. He kept her on a retainer of several hundred rupees a month for his private enjoyment.

'She is a pearl, isn't she?' Samita said to the *babu*. 'We spare no expense: she bathes in rosewater four times a day and has the finest attar we can buy. She deserves nothing less; she's the most beautiful girl in the whole of Bengal.'

Navneeta finished dancing and fell to the ground in front of the *babu*, her hands outstretched, her forehead pressed against the floor and her glossy hair pooling around her. She lifted her face to look at him, her jewelled nose ring catching the light from the lamps, and then she lowered her gaze. Samita had taught her well and the fat *babu* clapped and called, '*Vah, Vah,* well done,' his large stomach jiggling as he chuckled and wheezed, his laugh sounding like liquid bubbling in his chest. He was thrilled to have such a desirable young mistress. He would be envied by every man in the city.

Navneeta, anointed with jasmine perfume, sat with me in the corner of the room while I waited for the call to bring more food and drinks. Samita reclined on the bolsters with the *babu*, sharing a joke, flattering the old man and parting him from more of his cash.

The *babu* struggled to his feet and Samita motioned to Navneeta to join them: it was time to go upstairs with the *babu* to the room that Samita had recently decorated and stuffed with ornate furniture and opulent fabrics worthy of a gracious courtesan. My rose bowl was placed on a teak table and the picture of the man on a horse hung above the bed. Navneeta looked at the *babu*, who was still laughing with Samita, his chin wobbling and his face perspiring with anticipation.

'I can't, Pushpa Aunty,' she whispered behind her hand. 'He's so fat, I can't breathe, and he takes so long.'

'Navneeta,' Samita said sharply, irritated by the delay.

The girl smiled, dropped her eyes to the floor and padded barefoot out of the room and up the stairs, her ankle bells tinkling as she moved. The fleshy *babu* followed slowly, his breathing laboured.

Growing up in a brothel teaches you the tricks of the trade, and Samita put them all to good use. Navneeta's *babu* didn't visit often on account of his age, weight and unpredictable heart, and so the girl wasn't really kept exclusively for him. Samita lied to the *babu* when she said no one else touched Navneeta and that she spent all day and night in her luxurious room, pining for her first love, the great soap wallah. Her other customers were occasional visitors who could afford the expense of a sixteen-year-old beauty who, Samita insisted, had entertained only one previous client. She was as near to a virgin as it was possible to be, certainly fresher than almost any other girl in Sonagachi. I heard Samita list the girl's appeal several times a day: she was more divine and luscious, her breasts fuller, her hips rounder and firmer, her waist slimmer and tauter than the heavenly dancing girls carved on the sacred sun temple at Konark.

I watched this theatre from the corner of the room, lost in shadows, the kind of old woman no one notices, especially in a brothel where all eyes are on youth and beauty. Perhaps the new customer who arrived one evening didn't recognise me because of the darkness, or maybe he'd never noticed me in the first place. I was an unremarkable elderly ayah in a house in Dharmatala, and a plump old maidservant accompanying her memsahib to New Market. But I knew him immediately: he was Sunil Banerjee's friend Charu, the agitated youth who waited so impatiently in the street for lessons to finish, smoking furiously through monsoon rains and scorching heat. The man who'd damned Miss Maisy outside New Market as Sunil's whore had come to buy his own.

He arrived with a group of friends, and they lay, rolling around on the cushions talking animatedly and laughing, already drunk, the smell of the alcohol on their breath enough to make me dizzy. They were well off, educated young men from respectable families; one seemed to be a college professor, another recited verse from his latest book of poems to roars of appreciation, and the other said he would like to bring a camera crew inside the brothel for his next film. They're fine fools, I thought. I fetched *paan* in a silver box, placed it before them, and then disappeared back into the shadows.

'Would you like *paan*, gentlemen?' Samita said, smiling at them, her lips and teeth stained red with betel juice, a drop of it escaping from the corner of her mouth and running down her chin. She wiped it hurriedly away.

'Very good, Aunty,' Charu said, giggling. 'And something a little stronger, too. We need whisky and *bhang*.'

'It's his birthday,' the professor said between hiccups. 'We are celebrating. He can have whatever he likes: all the *bhang* in the world and the prettiest tart in the whorehouse.'

Samita clapped her hands and two seasoned girls began to dance. The men watched entranced, the poet murmuring verses about heart-breaking beauty, struggling to concentrate on the performance, his head lolling to one side until he snapped it back upright.

Navneeta skirted the edge of room, trying to avoid being seen, but the space was too cramped and the men still sober enough to spot her.

'Wait, wait,' the professor shouted so loudly the harmonium player jumped and the music stopped. 'Aunty, why have you been hiding this goddess from us?'

'She is our jewel,' Samita said proudly. 'She was deflowered only last week.'

'Come, girl, don't be afraid,' the poet said, beckoning her. He sat up straight, focusing on her face. 'She's almost too exquisite to be a whore.'

'She's so fair,' the film director sighed. 'Is she Eurasian?'

'No,' Samita exclaimed, offended. 'She's pure Indian.'

'She's almost as white as a European,' the poet said, patting the cushion between him and Charu, and telling Navneeta to sit.

'Pah,' Charu yelled. 'She's more beautiful than a white woman. And you can't compare Indian women with Europeans. Whites are very dirty people. They don't even wash their arses after they shit.'

'But you have to admit, some of them look attractive even if they stink,' the film director said. 'I knew a whore in Ripon Street, an English rose with blonde hair and pink cheeks.'

'I know the one you mean: I saw her too and she was old enough to be your mother. The white prostitutes only came out to India when they were too old to find any business at home,' the poet said.

'All white women are wanton,' Charu stated, and fell back on to a mound of cushions. 'Loose and filthy.'

The music started again: an old man played a haunting tune on a sarangi and then the harmonium player pumped air into his instrument, closing his eyes as his fingers pressed the keys.

When they'd finished playing, the film director looked at Charu. 'Which girl are you having?' he asked.

'It has to be the goddess for the birthday boy,' the poet stated. 'No one else will do.'

'Tonight, gentlemen,' the professor said, standing up and speaking in English, 'let us raise a glass to our friend, our comrade, our beloved brother, Charu.' He wobbled and regained his balance. 'Twenty-eight today and an incredible record of achievement behind him: top of his class at school, and at the forefront of the struggle to kick the unwashed foreigners out of our Motherland. Charu, we salute you.'

'Charu,' they all cheered, and agreed it was the best birthday celebration they could remember for many years.

'But someone is missing,' Charu said, sad for a moment. 'A fellow's birthday party isn't complete without his best friend.'

The men became suddenly quiet and looked into their glasses. I sat perfectly still, sure Charu was mourning Sunil.

The poet took a long drag of ganja. 'Our poor brother,' he said. 'He's missing out on all the fun. We should get him now and bring him here.'

What's that? I thought, astonished. Who brings a dead man to a brothel?

'It's too dangerous. He might be spotted,' Charu said.

'He could wear a burqua.'

'He's too tall to be a woman and he doesn't walk like a girl.'

'We could take the goddess to him,' the professor suggested. He turned to Samita. 'We can take her out for a couple of hours, can't we? We have a friend who hasn't been near a woman for years.'

Before Samita had time to say no, Charu spoke sharply. 'We're not taking him a girl. He hates whores; he hates that kind of—'

'What about the white girl and the bastard child?' the film director butted in.

'That was a mistake,' Charu said, infuriated.

'I say we take him a whore,' the poet stated.

'We'll take him ganja,' Charu said.

'You know where to find him?' the professor slurred.

'Yes, in a place you'd never expect,' Charu said. 'Let's go now.'

The men howled.

'Not so fast,' the film director said. 'We've business here first.'

The friends haggled over Navneeta's price and handed a wad of notes to Samita. 'Happy Birthday, brother,' they said.

Navneeta went silently upstairs and Charu followed her, turning at the door and saluting the men. They roared approval and stamped their feet before they, too, chose girls and went with them into the tiny rooms at the back of the house.

At two in the morning, the brothel quarter was busy; the lights were on, customers were leaving, and a few stragglers were still arriving. Mistresses said goodbye to their *babus* before the men returned to their wives. Boys ran back and forth to the restaurants and stalls delivering food. In the more expensive houses the musicians were packing up their instruments, and pimps hung around on street corners in the hope of making a late deal. Further away from Sonagachi the streets were darker, quieter, and I was grateful for the shadows and for all the alcohol the men had drunk because it made them slow and stupid. Staggering through the city, their arms around each other's shoulders, they tripped occasionally, and often went the wrong way and had to retrace their steps. I'd melt back into the blackness of an alleyway and watch them pass, glad my bad hips were getting a rest before I began following them again.

They headed south, taking a confusing, meandering route that saw us walk down the same lane three times. And then they paused in a square where the lights were still on in many of the windows. Charu slipped through a blue door into a large, dilapidated tenement. The others followed, the poet missing his footing and falling on the step. The door closed quietly behind them and they were gone. I looked round the square in surprise. Who would have thought the best place for Sunil Banerjee to hide was under the noses of the people searching for him: the murderer's refuge was right next to a police station.

In the brothel, Navneeta was removing her thick make-up and I thought how much prettier she was without all the paint.

'Was he good to you?' Samita asked. 'It must have been better than having the fat *babu* squash the life out of you.'

The girl shook her head, unhappy about something.

'What? Did he fall asleep?' Samita laughed. 'Did they pay good money for an expensive snooze?'

'No, Samita Aunty. It wasn't that.'

Samita became instantly alarmed. 'The snake! He didn't hurt you, did he? He didn't put his dick in your mouth?'

Navneeta shook her head.

'Did he put it in your arse? The disgusting pig! I'm going to find him and wring his neck like an old hen. And I'll charge him double.'

'No,' Navneeta said aghast. 'Don't do that, Samita Aunty. It's just that he didn't like me.'

'Didn't like you?' Samita bellowed. 'Don't be a fool, Navneeta. You are a goddess among women.'

'He said I wasn't pretty, and he lay on my bed and smoked. He didn't even try to touch me and when I went near him and did the things you told me to do, he pushed me away and cursed me.'

Samita stared at the girl and clicked her tongue. 'It must have been the drink,' she said. 'Sometimes it makes their dicks soft.'

In the corner of the back room, Madan slept curled up on my comfy mattress and, although it was late, I was unable to sleep when I lay down beside him. Drink does strange things to people, I thought, remembering the disasters that had befallen Mem when she was high on spirits. It loosens their tongues, and turns them into fools; and, like Charu, it makes them betray secrets they wanted to hide.

Chapter Fifteen

Maisy

W<small>E RETURNED TO</small> Calcutta's cool winter nights and morning mists. As dawn broke, a group of men wrapped in tattered shawls huddled around a fire at the end of our lane, hawking phlegm on to the pavement. The smoke from their fire drifted in banks, adding another layer of haze to the soft pink, early morning light. The men ignored me when I passed on my way home from work, and despite the tiredness that made me ache to my bones, and the big glob of green mucus that flew towards me and landed with a wet slap on my shoe, I was glad to be back in India. Father claimed Calcutta was cut from the jungle by Englishmen and he was adamant the place would fall apart if we left. He said abandoning the city to the Bengalis would be its death knell. But four years after the British fled India, four years of food shortages, corruption, and the arrival of countless refugees who strained the very seams of the city, Calcutta was muddling through.

We stayed in a boarding house that must have been a magnificent place in its day. Its owner told me it was built for a British merchant and adventurer over a hundred years ago, only a few years before another trader built Gordon's mansion, two streets away. I passed the old garden house sometimes, on my way to and from the club where I worked on Park Street, though I tended to avoid it if I could. It didn't stir up troubling memories for me: it was just that I didn't like the fact it was turning into a mess. Whoever owned it wasn't bothering with its upkeep, and in India you need to be meticulous about maintaining buildings because everything falls apart incredibly quickly in the heat and rain. Gordon had packed up and left only three years before, and yet weeds were already beginning to grow through windows, over the verandas and into the very walls, jungle fast reclaiming what the British merchant-adventurer stole.

Ram had gone, and perhaps it was just as well: he would be horrified to see his treasured garden. It'd been turned into a squatter camp and a dozen families had moved into the house, their belongings cluttering the verandas, their washing draped over the bushes. People had set up home under the trees, building shanties all over the lawn from sheets and old packaging material. Ram's godown no longer stored seeds and tools but housed ten or more men who slept in shifts. The gates were always open but no cars parked in the drive, and Lakshman's sentry box was appropriated by an elderly man who said his family were lost in Pakistan. A couple of pots of stunted geraniums sat on the veranda, barely clinging to life, but everything else in my English winter garden had vanished. The lupins, the delphiniums and the larkspur had been drawn back into the earth. Only the red bougainvillaea remained growing in profusion over the once-white wall.

I stopped occasionally to witness the next stage in the house's disintegration. The lawn between the huts became sun-scorched and baked hard in summer, and a sapling sprouted through the veranda, forcing its way through a crack in the west wall and growing a foot a week in the hothouse of the monsoon. Yet despite this chaos, the old place still breathed and buzzed with life, and I noticed with satisfaction that parrots once again roosted in Professor Mitra's blue jacaranda tree.

Our new home was in a better state of repair, though the harbingers of ruin were all around us in the crumbling bricks, peeling paint and the bald patches on the grass. The house was owned by Miss Smith, an elderly lady alleged to have a scandalous past. She sat in a little office every morning planning the evening menu, perfectly groomed, her silver hair dressed in an elaborate Edwardian style, and her fair, transparent skin, touched with the faintest suggestion of rouge.

Miss Smith had an odd collection of residents. Two elderly and gallant former British army officers, said to have received dishonourable discharges, shared a room on the first floor; a woman who had nerve trouble, and who we never saw, lived in the largest room and had meals taken to her on a tray. A pretty Eurasian woman who ran a dance studio on Park Street and who, it was whispered, sold more than tuition, had a room overlooking the tank and the waterless fountain; and a young man who was a writer, and who had come to India for inspiration, lived on the ground floor in the room next to ours. He'd been working on a novel for years without ever finishing it, and the sound of his typewriter caused Mam to complain often to Miss Smith.

'They're mental cases,' Mam said the day we arrived. 'We'd better move quickly before people think we're crazy, too.'

Four weeks later Mam was still moaning about the tip-tapping of the typewriter and the oddballs we were obliged to eat with in the evenings, but I knew she was content sitting on the veranda, ordering the house's one slow, aged bearer to bring her another peg from the bottles she kept in our room.

'I think I'll get a taxi down to the Tolly tomorrow and apply for membership,' she said to me almost every night before I set off for work.

She didn't go, but the idea of going, the possibility of sitting on the manicured lawns, delighted her. One day, she would be let into the inner circle of privilege: one day, she would become a *burra mem*.

The sweeper sprinkled the veranda with water in the afternoons, cooling the air around Mam so she woke on her cane lounger feeling refreshed and perky enough to play snakes and ladders with Charlie when I brought him home from school. The sweeper manoeuvred around her chair, the twigs of his brush scratching against the tiles in the permanent struggle to keep litter and garden debris from encroaching on the order of Miss Smith's house. He started work early, with the first light, and many times after a long shift I fell asleep listening to the rhythmic sound of his brush.

On other mornings, during our first weeks in Calcutta, I didn't return home after leaving the club. I changed my high heels for comfy sandals and walked north, looking for Sunil and Pushpa. At dawn a mist lay over the great water tank in Dalhousie Square, and the brilliant white dome of the General Post Office stood proud in the winter sun. The river was still busy; it hadn't silted up, and even at that early hour traffic was beginning to build on Howrah Bridge. On Zenana Ghat, women bathers were venturing into the Hooghly. I took off my shoes and went gingerly down the steps, and though I visited the ghat a dozen times or more, I couldn't see Pushpa among the old ladies drenching themselves in holy water.

I walked briskly to Harrison Road, wondering how I was supposed to find anyone in the frenetic city when no one would help me.

Mr Das in the Royal Palace Hotel smiled fulsomely and provided not a scrap of useful information.

'Have you seen the lady who used to come here with me?' I asked him. 'She's old and she limps.'

'Alas, I see a lot of crippled old women,' he said. 'I cannot bring the face of this particular one to mind.'

'And Sunil?'

For a fraction of a second he faltered. 'Sunil?' he asked.

'Sunil Banerjee.'

He shook his head slowly. 'You would like a cup of tea, Mem?' he said, signalling to a bearer. 'You look tired, and it is an exceedingly chilly morning.'

I drank quickly and left, walking with a new urgency through Burrabazar, along Zakaria Street crammed with Muslim families, their men eyeing strangers warily, watchful of a danger I thought had passed.

Near the synagogue in Bowbazar I was stopped by a beggar woman, pitiful in a collection of rags that barely covered her bony body.

'Mem, do you remember me?' she said.

I didn't recognise her. I can't remember every beggar I see; there are thousands in the city and many look similarly wretched.

I gave her a couple of annas and she followed me down the street trailed by two small boys, bothering me with her unrelenting call.

'Remember me, Mem. Remember me.'

'Get away,' I said, annoyed.

She scurried after me and looked me right in the face and for a moment I was disarmed by her eyes. They were dull and red-rimmed but her irises were rich amber. I brushed her aside, frightened by her persistence, and walked on. I don't know why she was so insistent; I'd never seen her before.

The beggar woman had rattled me and I needed to concentrate, to focus on the task of searching for Sunil and Pushpa. I'll never find them, I thought in despair: I've returned to Calcutta to search for ghosts.

'Give up,' Mam said when I trod wearily into the boarding house and sank on to a chair. At the far end of the veranda, the young writer sitting at a table by his open door, stopped typing and watched us.

'You need to forget about them and start again,' she said. 'Plenty of Englishmen have stayed on; you should set your sights on one of those. And let's face it, Maisy, Pushpa's probably popped her clogs. I mean, she was getting on.'

'I have to find them, Mam. Think what it cost me to come back here.'

'It was cheap at the price, love. You'll never have to wash your own knickers again,' she said with a laugh.

I wanted to cry, and Mam leaned over and put her arm around my shoulder.

'You've tried your best, Maisy, but you're not ruddy Sherlock

311

Holmes. It's time to stop: you're knackered and you've searched everywhere.'

I closed my eyes, replaying scenes from my childhood, times so distant I'd almost forgotten them. I remembered tram rides with Pushpa up the Chitpur Road, and smiling ladies with painted faces.

'Not everywhere, Mam,' I said. 'I haven't been everywhere.'

Part of Sovabazar is a nice, quiet residential area, full of traditional Bengali houses, some of them with carved wooden shutters and doorways that give intriguing glimpses of charming court-yards filled with plants. And yet when Masjid Bari Street crosses Central Avenue, the road changes character and Sovabazar turns in a matter of a few yards into a very different world. I slowed my step, sure I'd been there before. The neighbourhood was busy; pimps hung around the alleyways; pedlars touted their wares – lipstick, snacks, herbal remedies – and women in vivid clothes and bright make-up came to their doors to look at me. Some laughed and called to me, surprised when I answered in Bengali. They beckoned, inviting me in, and I stopped for a while, drinking their sweet milky tea, made just the way I like it. They were really very ordinary women in an extraordinary place. What on earth brought them into a life like this? I thought. What tragedy, or betrayal, or dreadful poverty leads a girl to Sonagachi?

I said goodbye and promised to return another day and bring my son.

'You have only one?' a woman said with pity as I left.

Further along the road, where it bends a little, I looked up at a big, freshly painted building with green shutters. A young girl was framed in one of the first-floor windows and I paused, startled by her beautiful face. She took a step back into the darkness but I knew she was still watching me because I saw the glint of her gold earrings. I waited a few moments, hoping she would come back into the light and when she didn't I carried on, walking past the onion and potato seller and the elderly barber who sat in the sun without any customers, bent over and concentrating hard as he sharpened his razor on a stone, his hands trembling so much I thought he might do himself an injury.

And then, just as the brothels began to thin out, I heard a shout behind me. Turning, I saw an old woman with snow-white hair step out from a doorway and walk slowly towards me, squinting to see me better.

'Missy Baba,' Pushpa cried, calling me a name I hadn't heard since I was a small child.

Mam was almost as pleased to see Pushpa. When she arrived at the boarding house, Mam clapped her hands in delight and told her to fetch a gimlet immediately.

'She's not your servant any longer, Mam,' I reminded her.

Pushpa hurried to get the drink anyway, accustomed to a lifetime of service.

Charlie was thrilled to see her, too, and jiggled with excitement.

'Look at you,' Pushpa said in wonder, bending down and sitting on her haunches to examine him. 'You've grown so much. What did they feed you on in England? You're a real sahib now.'

Charlie touched the vermilion in her parting and looked at

the red powder on his fingers. He wiped it in two lines across his cheeks and ran into the garden with an Apache war cry that made the writer flinch and stop typing.

In London I'd thought about all the things I wanted to say to Pushpa, how I'd tell her I was sorry, that I was selfish and hadn't considered her when we left, but that I'd missed her more than she could know. Yet when she was sitting next to me on our little bit of Miss Smith's veranda, watching Mam and Charlie play croquet with ancient, crooked mallets on the bumpy, badly patched lawn, I couldn't find the words, and I wasn't sure I needed to. There was comfort in being near her, in smelling the coconut oil in her hair.

'I knew you'd return,' she said.

'You did?'

'The *maya* brought you.'

'I came back to find you and Sunil.'

'That's what I mean.'

'And now I've found you, I've got to find Sunil, too.'

Pushpa clicked her tongue and looked away.

'I know what you're thinking,' I said. 'You think we'll search the whole city and never find him. But listen, Pushpa, I know he's not dead.'

'Even if you are right, he's still a murderer and that's worse than being dead. You can't waste your life on a worthless man.'

'He's innocent. He wasn't in the Britannia Mill and so he couldn't have killed the manager. Gordon made it up. I saw him in Scotland and he said he lied to punish me.'

Pushpa sat in silence for a long time. 'Miss Maisy,' she said slowly, 'I don't know what to believe. I don't know if he's a murderer, a madman, a *badmash* or a fool. But I do know Sunil

Banerjee treats you badly. He doesn't cherish you and he doesn't take care of you. His whole life is a series of risks and gambles, and he'll put you in danger. If he dies, or is imprisoned, you'll suffer, too. He'll drain you of life.'

'He is my life.'

'He'll be your ruin.'

'Pushpa, you're talking as if you know he's alive.' I caught my breath, my heart hammering in my chest. 'You know where he is, don't you?' I said, grabbing her wrists.

'Yes.'

'Will you take me?'

'I will, and I hope you forgive me.'

Wearing a sari is an art and I hadn't mastered the way to fold the material so it fell neatly and elegantly. Mam looked on, mystified, while Pushpa took charge and dressed me as if I were a three-year-old child again. She tucked the fabric round my waist and draped the end of the sari over my head.

'It doesn't look right,' Mam said.

The young writer thought the same. When we left late that evening he was smoking on the veranda, 'I say, are you going to a fancy dress party?' he asked, enthusiastically.

'No, she's turning Indian,' Mam said wildly.

Many of the residents of Burrabazar were equally startled by the sight of the white woman stealing through the streets. Pushpa told me to cover my hair and face, and to avoid attracting attention, and though I followed her instruction and peeped out through my disguise, my white feet poking from under the sari gave me away.

At a busy intersection Pushpa stopped and pulled me into

the shadows. We stood in darkness observing a tenement that was so rundown it looked on the verge of collapse.

'What are we waiting for?' I asked.

'Ssh,' Pushpa hissed, and then scurried silently behind two men who walked across the square and struggled with the lock before opening a big blue door. She beckoned to me and we slipped after them into the blackness of an unlit stairwell. The men climbed the stairs, their step sure. Their voices echoed and grew fainter.

'How do you know where to go?' I said.

'I don't.'

We crept along a corridor and Pushpa stopped outside a door. A chink of light showed beneath it. Gently, she pushed against it. It didn't open and she put her eye to the lock and backed away immediately. We continued tiptoeing down the corridor, my eyes becoming more accustomed to the dark. My foot caught on something and I stumbled, stepping forward blindly. Unable to keep my balance, I fell on to a pile of rags.

The rags shifted beneath me. 'Be careful,' an old man's sleepy voice croaked. He sat up and lit a match, and for a few seconds the corridor and stairs were illuminated.

'Watch where you're going,' he grumbled.

'Sorry, brother,' Pushpa said soothingly.

He looked at her. 'Who are you?'

'We're family of one of the tenants. Who are you?'

'Their servant,' he said, pointing to the locked door.

The match began to flicker.

'We're looking for our kinsman. He's a young man.'

'Plenty of young men live here,' he said, blasting us with the odour of festering gums. 'But not on this floor. Up there.' He pointed to the stairs. The last glimmer from the flame guttered and died.

'Can you spare us a few matches, brother?' Pushpa asked the grumpy servant.

'Take them,' he said, throwing them at her, and then fell back on to his rags.

The wooden stairs were bowed and worn by decades of use. A few were rotten at the edges and crumbled under my feet. We climbed slowly, Pushpa holding the banister with one hand and a match in the other. On the first floor a door was flung open and light flooded the landing. A man walked out saying something vicious to a woman, who stood behind him holding a baby. He left without closing the door.

Pushpa paused. 'We're looking for a man. A young man,' she said.

The woman stared at us as if we were insane and kicked the door shut.

Two girls shrieked abuse at each other on the floor above us, and someone else played a wireless too loudly. A man cursed, yelling at them in filthy language to keep the noise down; it was late and people had to go to work early the next day.

Pushpa bent down and shook the shoulder of an old lady who was lying on a bamboo mat on the landing.

'Who lives upstairs?' she asked.

The woman described the occupants, counting them on her fingers. None of them sounded like Sunil.

'Isn't there anyone else?' Pushpa said.

'Not here.'

My spirits sank.

'But the Brahmins and scholars are that way.' She pointed to a door cut roughly into the wall.

'Brahmins?'

'They're always reading and arguing. One of them is a strange man: he hardly ever goes out and he burns papers on the roof. I think he does black magic so I keep away.'

The doorway led to a passage linking the dilapidated tenement with the building immediately behind. In parts, the ceiling was so low even Pushpa had to bend to walk through. We stopped at the end of the passage. A door was ajar and a pale light shone through the gap. I pushed it gently, the hinges squeaking, and then pressed harder, swinging it wide open. Two men sitting on a string bed jumped in surprise and another, reading at a table in the glow of a lamp, looked up from his book.

Cigarette smoke and the sharp, oily smell of kerosene filled the room. The lamp cast grotesque shadows and I was startled by one of the men, who lunged forward from the bed and stood between me and the table.

'Out,' he ordered. Although the light was behind him and his face was in shade, I knew the voice.

'Charu?' I said.

'You're not allowed in here.'

He hustled me through the door and I staggered back, banging into Pushpa. Charu shut the door behind him and we were in darkness.

'How did you find this place?' he said, his voice amplified and reverberating down the passage. 'If you've betrayed us, I'll . . .'

'You'll what, Charu?' I hissed.

'I swear by Ma Kali, we haven't told anyone,' Pushpa whispered.

'He doesn't want to see you,' Charu said.

'He's here?' I gasped, and tried to elbow past Charu, who stood immobile in the doorway. 'Let me through,' I said, furious. 'I've come halfway round the world to find him.' I pushed him in the chest and we scuffled. Charu hit out in the dark and bashed his head on the ceiling. Squeaking with fright, Pushpa grabbed my blouse.

'Let them in, brother,' Sunil said, opening the door.

It was little wonder I hadn't recognised him: his face was much older and he had a short beard. He couldn't have shaved for two or three weeks.

I slipped into the room and Pushpa followed, her eyes wide.

I'd imagined that moment countless times. From the day I'd stood beside the Tay and resolved to return to Calcutta, I'd rehearsed every second. It was the dream driving me back to India, the hope helping me survive bleak months and a beat in the heart of Mayfair. I'd pictured the warmth of our meeting, the relief I'd feel, the overwhelming joy, but in that tiny room reeking of kerosene and tobacco, we stared at each other in an agony of uncertainty. Charu was next to me, jumpy and enraged, his breathing ragged, and Sunil looked perplexed and unfamiliar, like a man I hardly knew.

'I thought you said you didn't want to see the slut again,' Charu said.

'Enough, Charu,' Sunil snapped.

'Chhee, chhee,' Pushpa said.

'Don't call me a slut,' I added angrily. I wasn't a slut. And how dare the hypocrite criticise me? Pushpa told me about his visit to Sonagachi, so he couldn't call me filthy names while he pretended to be virtuous.

'Give us some time,' Sunil said to Charu and the other man. Charu hesitated, as if he was about to argue, and then shrugged and stormed out, his friend in pursuit.

'I'll wait near the sweeper woman,' Pushpa said, and shut the door as she left.

The tension was worse when we were alone. Sunil gazed uneasily at me. I've been deluded, I thought. I've built my whole life around this man, and I don't know him. Perhaps he's changed, or perhaps I never knew him. He even looks different; the Sunil I knew didn't have lines on his forehead and shadows under his eyes.

He reached forward and pulled the end of the sari from my head. 'Has your *babu* found a new mistress?' he asked.

I was puzzled.

'You left Calcutta with MacBrayne,' he said. 'You went to Scotland with him, and you took my son. They told me.'

'Who told you?'

'Charu.'

'Charu's a liar.'

'Why would he make up something like that?' Sunil said.

'He's hated me since the moment I met him.' I paused, thinking back. 'Actually, he hated me even before he set eyes on me. Do you remember him standing in the road fuming while you were supposed to be teaching me?'

'We had work to do and he resented me taking time off.'

'Sunil, I left Calcutta with Mam and Charlie because that spiteful, malicious friend of yours told me you'd died in the mill attack. I didn't leave with Gordon, and I've not been living with him in Scotland. I've been in London, and it's been one of the worst times of my life.'

'Did he lie? Charu's my best friend, my brother, and he does what he does to protect me.'

'From what, Sunil?'

'From myself.'

'You're making me feel like I've done something wrong,' I said, conscious of Charu's poison still lingering in the room.

'Haven't you?' He leaned against the edge of table. Pushing aside the books and the empty leaf plates, he placed his hands on the wood and I looked at his long fingers and his nails that were still bitten. 'You left Calcutta. Why wouldn't I think you were with MacBrayne?'

'How can I convince you?'

'Why did you come back?'

'I discovered the truth. Gordon told me you weren't at the mill. I met him briefly – just for a few minutes – and he said he lied to incriminate you. It was his revenge, and it worked, didn't it? He's got exactly what he wanted.'

Sunil was unreadable and unreachable.

'I was furious when he told me, but it also meant Charu was wrong and you might be alive.' I stepped towards him. 'I came back because I needed to come home, and because I love you,' I said, not caring that I sounded desperate. I'd given everything to be there and I might as well lose the last shred of my dignity before I conceded I'd lost him.

'Come,' he said, smoothing the thin blanket on the bed and motioning me to sit with him.

He bent forward, his elbows on his knees, his head resting in his hands. 'I've thought about you every day,' he sighed, sounding like the old Sunil. 'And I've loved you, and hated you.'

'You hated me?'

'Passionately,' he said, turning quickly and looking at me, his dark eyes brilliant even in the dim room. 'I hated you when I thought you were with the jute wallah. I don't want to share you.'

'You say you love me but your best friend just called me a slut. Is that what you think, too?'

'Of course not.'

'You think I'm like Mam, don't you? Pushpa says that's why you wouldn't marry me.'

'Pushpa is an old woman, with old ways of thinking. She doesn't know me.'

'Do I, Sunil? Do I *really* know you? When you add up the time we've spent together, it's not actually very long. You were always vanishing and reappearing and I didn't know if I'd see you again. Mam said you were married and had a wife in the *mofussil*, and I think that might be true. I never knew if you were alive or dead: it was like being in love with a ghost.'

'Look at me,' he said, lifting my chin and cupping my face in his hands. 'I haven't got a wife, and I'm not sure how I'll do it, but I promise I'll change. You won't always have to love a ghost.'

'Will you stop fighting your battles?'

He laughed and it made me uneasy because it was a melancholy laugh. 'You know me better than that, Maisy. But I'll find time to spend with you and Charlie. Trust me.'

He lay me on the bed, and my doubts disappeared. I closed

my eyes, listening to Sunil's whispers; I was his beloved, his life.

I didn't notice how narrow the bed was until I woke and found myself jammed against the wall while Sunil clung to the very edge, almost toppling on to the floor. I pulled him close and lay with my face pressed against his skin. He looked older but he smelled the same. He was intoxicating.

'I'll visit every day,' I said.

'That's a terrible idea: it's far too dangerous. Didn't you see the police station next door? The police are bungling and corrupt but even those dim-wits in the *thana* will start asking why a white woman is coming to such a poor part of town. Thanks to the jute wallah I have to skulk around or I'll be captured and tried for murder.' He paused. 'I don't suppose MacBrayne could be persuaded to withdraw his claims?'

'Not a chance. He's so full of envy and malice he'd do anything to destroy you.'

Sunil stroked his beard. 'It doesn't matter; I'd still be in trouble even if he remembered things differently. The Congress Government is as bad as the British: they've imprisoned half my comrades. You know, it's astonishing you tracked me down. How did you manage it when the police haven't done it for years?'

'Pushpa discovered you.'

'We should recruit her for the revolution; we need women like her. She has more brains than Charu and half a dozen of the others put together.'

His hair was longer than it had ever been, the ends turning

into black silky curls, and I twisted a piece around my fingers. 'Maybe I should take a lock,' I said.

He laughed and kissed me, and I drew back to study his face.

'You still haven't explained why Charu dislikes me so much,' I said. 'It takes real hatred to make up lies the way he did.'

'He thinks I should commit myself entirely to politics. Women are a distraction.'

'Charu doesn't stick to those rules himself. Pushpa said he visited a brothel in Sonagachi.'

'Ha,' Sunil exclaimed. 'Maybe Charu is relaxing a little. That must be the first time he's indulged himself.'

He stared at a lizard sitting on the wall and at the holes where the plaster had perished.

'I know a little village on the coast,' he said, suddenly animated. 'It's near a big town but it's completely safe. We can go for a few days. And another time we can take Charlie.'

'And Mam?'

'Please, no. I can't bear your mother. I want time alone with you and I know you'll love the place. Imagine mile after mile of beaches and sunsets like you've never seen before.'

'How will we get there?'

'The best way is on the train, although I'd be insane to go near Howrah Station.'

Sunil sat up, making plans. 'I know someone with a car. Perhaps we can drive south. I'll be memsahib's dutiful driver.'

I couldn't wait to go; I'd not seen the Indian countryside before. In fact, apart from my journey to England, I'd not been outside Calcutta in my whole life. Going to Ballygunge and the Botanical Gardens didn't count.

'Is it like the Sunderbans? Will there be tigers and elephants?' I asked.

Sunil thought this was funny. 'There's no jungle, only fields, a few goats, and the sea.' He ran his fingers through my hair. 'I want to show you something,' he said, reaching under the pillow and pulling out a book. It was in Bengali script.

'Is it your novel?' I asked. 'The one about the orphan?'

'No.'

'Did you ever finish the story? In the last chapter you read to me, the poor boy was going to sleep on the steps of the High Court.'

'I left him sleeping,' Sunil said, 'although one day I'm going to wake him up and write a happy ending for him.' He opened the book. Pressed between the pages was a lock of golden hair tied with a red ribbon. 'Do you remember this?'

'Yes. Pushpa was horrified to find such a big chunk missing.'

'It goes everywhere with me. Even in gaol I had a piece of you.' He closed the book and tucked it back under the pillow.

'Where are you living?' he asked.

'In a boarding house near Theatre Street.'

'So, you went back to Sahib-para.'

'The house is old and grand but we've only one room, and we share it with black cockroaches and hundreds of silverfish. And, when I think about it, the neighbourhood's not been Sahib-para for a long time. Most people living there are Indian, and almost all the houses are owned by Indians.'

'I guarantee it'll be more luxurious than where we're going.'

'I'm sure I'll have stayed in worse places,' I said, recalling the bug-house in Notting Hill.

A scrambling in the passageway spooked Sunil and he leaped to his feet.

'Quick,' Charu said, wild eyed and breathless as he burst into the room. 'Police are searching the building. You have to leave now.'

Sunil pulled on some clothes and stuffed a few things into a bag. He grabbed his book from under the pillow.

I panicked: I've only just found him, I thought, and now I'm going to lose him all over again. 'Where are you going?' I cried. Realising I was naked, I snatched my creased sari from the bed and held it in front of me.

'I'm going to another safe house. Don't worry.'

'Hurry. Forget the fucking woman,' Charu shouted in panic. 'They're coming up the stairs. Let's go.'

Charu opened a door leading on to the roof.

'When will I see you again?' I pleaded, on the verge of hysteria.

'Tomorrow. Meet me at noon in the Royal Palace Hotel.' He kissed me quickly, his lips brushing my cheek, and then he was gone. I watched them scramble over the wall that ran around the edge of the building and glimpsed their shadows flitting over the higgledy-piggledy rooftops of Calcutta, the escape route rehearsed well in advance.

I dressed, fastening the sari clumsily so it dragged on the floor and I tripped over the fabric when I bent to walk along the passage. Everything was quiet. The girls had stopped arguing and the radio was switched off. In the pitch-black corridor I found Pushpa sitting next to the sleeping sweeper woman.

'It's all right,' I whispered. 'He got away; he's safe.'

'Got away from what?'

'The police.'

'What police?'

I listened to the creaking of the old building. Rats scurried across the first-floor landing and a man's snoring reverberated throughout the second floor. When a truck drove past the shutters rattled, and below, in the square, a lunatic caterwauled, baiting the officers in the *thana* to arrest him. No policemen, though, charged up the stairs, smashing down the doors of unsuspecting tenants.

Pushpa took me by the hand and led me though the dark. 'I'm going to take you home, Miss Maisy,' she said.

'I'm already home, Pushpa.'

Chapter Sixteen
Pushpa

PEOPLE TELL ME I've grown wise in my old age, but I'm sorry to say it hasn't stopped me doing foolish things I wish I could undo. I shouldn't have taken Miss Maisy to Sunil: I led her into danger and sometimes the guilt weighs heavily on me. I excuse myself with the knowledge that she wouldn't have rested until she found him and I only hastened what was inevitable. The *maya* had brought her back to Calcutta because while England is a glorious, rich country, it isn't her home. She couldn't cut the roots her heart had sunk in India, nor break the tie binding her to Sunil Banerjee. I knew, though, that some of the things Charu said outside New Market and in the gloomy hideout were true. I was certain Sunil loved her, and just as certain she'd never be more than his mistress. Miss Maisy was beautiful but she was too poor to be fully white, and too white to be a good Indian. Worst of all, she was the daughter of a prostitute, and that stigma lingers over the child as much as the mother.

The day after we found Sunil I struggled to get up from my bed, unable to stand straight, my joints fused and my mind fuddled.

'Why are you getting up so early?' Madan groaned.

'It's not early. It's nine o'clock and I'm going to Sahib-para.'

'You're not going to be their ayah again, are you? They couldn't be bothered with you when they sailed off to England and now they're back they expect to you come running at first light. They snap their fingers and you become their slave.'

'Is it any different here?' I whispered. 'I'm going to check Miss Maisy is all right.'

'Well, be careful, and don't go across the river. There'll be trouble in Howrah.'

In the bedroom of the boarding house, Miss Maisy was putting on a new cream dress and pretty sandals. She must have bought them in England. Her hair was still in pins and she fussed over her make-up.

'Am I still pretty?' she asked. 'I used to look old in England.'

'You're prettier than when you were sixteen,' I said, truthfully. She was vivacious and bright, like a teenager. It's the kind of beauty that's hard to sustain when you work in one of those shameful clubs off Park Street where they call you a waitress to your face and something else behind your back.

'I'm meeting him in Harrison Road. Do you want to come with me?' she asked. 'We can go in a taxi and it'll be easier for you to get back to Sovabazar from there.'

'Don't be surprised if he doesn't arrive, Miss Maisy,' I said. 'Think how many times you've waited for him and how many times you've been disappointed.'

He's not changed, I thought. We sat on lumpy armchairs in the dark, wood-panelled lounge of the Royal Palace Hotel, and

Miss Maisy checked her watch every five minutes. He was almost an hour and a half late.

'He'll be here soon,' she said. 'It's difficult for him to move around the city.'

Miss Maisy looked out of the window at the unseasonal rain. The street was choked with traffic and two men were arguing. I guessed there must have been an accident on the rain-slicked road.

A bearer came in with tea and the usually composed Mr Das followed, distressed and shaky. 'Such a bad business,' he said. 'The bridge is closed, and they are running riot in Howrah. You can see smoke from the fires: not even this rain can dampen them. Oh my God, it is beyond belief. What is the world coming to? It is happening again.'

Miss Maisy moved towards the door.

'Stay inside, Mem,' Mr Das said in a sharp, anxious voice. 'The last time this happened people were dying outside my hotel, their bodies were lying in the street. Such madness you would not believe.'

She ignored him and stood outside under the covered walkway. The traffic began moving but didn't get very far. Cars and trucks reversed and became jammed. Men who were hanging on to a stationary bus suddenly jumped off and ran south along the lanes towards Dalhousie Square. A man thrashed the bullocks drawing his cart, the beasts tossing their heads, too scared to move.

Shopkeepers closed their shutters with a loud clatter. A group of men raced from a passageway and scattered, and then an unnatural quiet settled on Harrison Road. Above us, a door on to a veranda opened and girls' lively laughter broke the silence until the doors banged shut. A car weaved along the road from the direction of Howrah Bridge, its horn blaring. It came to a halt, its way blocked, and the driver got out and fled.

The sound of conch shells floated eerily over the city. Miss Maisy stared at me, and as she did we heard a cry, a howl that was so inhuman it could have been from a rabid animal. It came again, longer and louder.

The colour drained from her face. 'I've heard that sound before,' she said. Her eyes grew wide and terrified. 'Sunil,' she gasped and, turning, she ran down the road by the side of the hotel and into the heart of Burrabazar.

'Come back. It's not safe,' I called after her. She couldn't have heard, or she didn't want to hear, and by the time I got a short way along the road, she'd disappeared. I followed, unable to move quickly. The stupid, stupid girl, I thought, angry with her for making my heart beat fast and for making my breathing so laboured I feared I might die. This was foolish even for Miss Maisy, who made a habit of placing herself in danger. She could be such a selfish, silly girl.

'Did you see an Englishwoman?' I asked a middle-aged man peering out of the door of his shop.

'She went that way,' he said, pointing left. I'd gathered just enough breath to thank him when he slammed the door and drew a heavy bolt across it.

The narrow lane was deep in thick brown mud where a burst water pipe had remained unrepaired for weeks. Miss Maisy wouldn't have gone that way, I thought, not in her new cream sandals. I edged along, struggling to keep my balance as my feet almost slipped from under me. Two yellow pye-dogs watched from a dark doorway. One snarled and hunkered down.

Deciding to retrace my steps, I shuffled backwards and sank, ankle-deep, in a stinking gutter. It was better to go on, I realised, and jumped from one dry patch of earth to another, the dogs baying behind me.

The drizzle had stopped and the skies were clearing. I paused in a shaft of sunlight and then leaped into the shade in fright as I heard a cry, then another. It was that human voice again, and more menacing than the dogs behind me. A short distance ahead, the lane divided, and I would have turned round but the pye-dogs still barred my way. I hesitated. To the left the lane twisted into blackness; to the right it was brighter, the buildings lower. The cry came again, and I hurried on, moving down the right-hand path, kicking off my shoes. I balanced better without them, feeling the ground against the soles of my feet.

I knew that lane well; usually it bustled with people. Where it opened out into a wider road, manufacturers of bamboo furniture normally stacked chairs and tables in front of their shops, and further along traders sold spare parts for every type of machine ever made; little engines, rubber belts, cogs of various sizes all cluttered on shelves and hung precariously on hooks. You wouldn't have known it on that day. It was silent and empty, the shutters closed. Half-way down the road, three or four buildings were smouldering, the last of the flames extinguished by the rain. Their roofs had vanished and the remaining timbers were blackened. The walls were coated with thick soot from the smoke that had poured up from the ground floor of the buildings, and someone had left a string of fresh white flowers to wilt in the charred remains.

The road divided and I couldn't decide which alley to take.

One way, I knew, led towards the Nakhoda Mosque. A child peeped through the tatty blinds of a rickety house and then disappeared. A loud argument echoed from another and was hushed by people who spoke just as loudly. An old woman staggered on to a veranda and shouted something to me, her words indistinct, her mouth all gums. Someone grabbed her and pulled her back inside. The shutters closed and the street was quiet and still again.

At the crossroads a band of youths ran by me, crowing and whooping, the hands of the first two covered in blood. They slowed, and one shrieked and thrust his face into mine, his saliva blinding me for a second. He waved a machete and I braced myself for the blade to crash down on my head, cleaving my skull in two.

'Get off the streets, old woman,' he yelled. He ran down the alley after the others and skidded into a narrow passage. I looked in the direction they'd come and walked slowly to where the alley opened into a small sunlit square.

A few sparrows hopped around a shrine and smoke from incense sticks curled out of the niche where a little figure of Ma Kali stood garlanded by marigolds. A boy hurried past, bent double. He picked up a bicycle lying on the road, jumped on it, and sped away.

The pye-dogs had followed me into the square, their step quick, and I expected them to bite. In surprise I watched them trot past me.

The sun shone directly along the whole length of a lane and the residents were beginning to come out of their houses. The men looked both left and right, and urged their children to stay indoors.

The streets were drying fast, the rainwater running into drains alongside the buildings.

'Who are they?' a man asked.

'Muslims, I think,' another answered.

A fat man wearing only a *dhoti*, his belly a perfect circle, ushered me in the direction I'd come. 'Don't go that way, sister. Go home quickly.'

I pushed past him. A young man lay in a puddle, his blood turning the rainwater red. A machete was embedded in his stomach. Another man, older than the first, was slumped against a cart, his head severed almost completely from his body, twisting it so his open eyes stared down in surprise at his own back. The biggest pye-dog sniffed at the arm hacked from his body. The fat man kicked the dog and it scuttled away momentarily before darting back to lick the severed limb.

A woman wept as she looked from a window and a boy retched violently into a drain.

'Get inside. It's still dangerous,' the round-bellied man told the onlookers.

A police van drove leisurely up the lane and stopped where it narrowed, unable to go any further. A young officer got out and surveyed the scene coolly. He looked at the bodies and waved a pistol half-heartedly. 'Go back into your homes,' he said, unruffled by the bloodletting.

The fat man called to him. 'The *goondas* are still in the neighbourhood, sir. They went that way.'

The officer climbed back into the van and it reversed as slowly as it had arrived. In the sunlit square it stopped and then turned left, ignoring the fat man's pointing finger.

Further up the lane a group gathered around another body.

'This one's still alive,' someone called.

The fat man ran towards them, puffing, and I followed, puffing just as much.

'Stand back,' he shouted.

A man was pinned to the ground by a four-foot long park railing that had been driven through his left shoulder. Blood welled up from the wound, forming a bright red circle on his white *kurta*. I moved around him and shuddered; the side of his head had been caved in, his brain bursting through the wound. I wouldn't have believed he was alive if it wasn't for the flicker of his eyes and the slight movement of the spear as he struggled to breathe. I looked away in distress, and then turned back, seeing through the tension contorting his face and altering his features.

'You know him?' the fat man asked.

'Sunil,' I said, kneeling beside him.

His eyes flickered.

'It's me, Pushpa.'

The spear trembled and he opened his eyes very slightly. He tried to speak but the words wouldn't form themselves. His lips were taut and immobile from the effort of living. The railing quivered again and his shallow breath grew fainter. The tension left his body and he lay as if he were sleeping, his expression peaceful.

I'm glad Miss Maisy saw him that way. I'm glad she wasn't there when he died. That way she could remember the face he had in life and death, and not one disfigured by the terror of the moments in between.

The first things I saw were her cream sandals: she'd come through the mud after all. She kneeled beside Sunil and made no sound. She stroked his face and clasped his hand. Leaning forward, she lay her forehead against his chest, the railing pressing against her head, her hair lying in the blood pooling around the wound.

'Move,' a man said. He stood over us and was joined by another, and then another, their silhouettes large against the sun. 'Leave him,' one said.

Miss Maisy didn't move: she didn't hear or see them. A man grabbed her and lifted her up. She stood limply and began to weep.

Another man pulled the spear but it was embedded in the earth and wouldn't move. His friend joined him, and together they pulled slowly until Sunil's body was freed. I looked closely at them for the first time and recognised Charu and the college professor who'd visited Samita's brothel. They bent down and prepared to lift him.

'No,' Miss Maisy shrieked, her hair swinging around her face and smearing her cheeks with blood. 'Where are you taking him? He's got to be with me.'

'He wouldn't have been here if it hadn't been for you,' Charu spat. 'We told him not to go out. We said there was trouble, but he insisted. He said he had to meet you. He risked everything for a dirty whore.' His voice cracked, and he sobbed, the sound anguished and desolate, his face contorted with grief. Charu's heart is breaking, I thought as I watched him touch his friend's cheek, like a man touching his beloved for the first time.

The men raised Sunil on to their shoulders and Miss Maisy grabbed his lifeless arm. Pushing her aside, they carried the body down the lane.

'He loves me,' she screamed after them. 'I'm going to be his wife.'

Overhead, vultures soared in a clear blue sky.

I think I've been brave most of my life; it's been a useful trait because I haven't always been lucky. My parents didn't tell me if any of this bad luck was written in my horoscope, and perhaps it's best I didn't know what my future held. I remember the frightened child in my first husband's bed, the thin widow at the mercy of her in-laws, the pretty girl in Auntie's brothel, the many men who passed so quickly through my life, and I'm surprised to find I'm proud of what I've done. There's one thing, though, I'm very clear about: I don't want my family to know my story. They wouldn't understand, and I wouldn't want to blacken their name. They would think I'm a spoiled, broken woman, and I'm neither of these things.

I often relive my childhood, the beauty of Bengal, the smell of flowers on the breeze, my mother teaching me to fry fish, to weave baskets, to prepare the floor of the house – all the skills she thought I would need. And I think of my parents promising they would find a fine husband for me, someone who would treat me well. Madan is the husband I was promised, even if he's been late in arriving and his teeth and legs are not what I'd hoped for in a husband when I was a young woman. I'm sad only that our lives together will be short. It's that sense of time slipping away that made me brave again and made me do something I've rehearsed, over and over in my mind since I've been twelve-years-old; my long journey home for Durga Puja.

It was exactly as I remembered it, the way we used to see it from the river in the years before the cyclone tore off the thatched roof. The coconut palms were just as tall, the mango trees as dark, the sky the same aquamarine. And this time as I neared the riverbank, there was no mirage and my eyes didn't trick me: a woman sat on the veranda and a small girl was running from the house to the bamboo grove.

I clambered out of the skiff, aware of my age; my legs and arms so rigid I thought I'd tumble into the river. The boatman passed me my plump mattress and small case, and I looked around in wonder. Some things had indeed changed. The khas grasses were thicker and the bamboo grove wasn't as big. I'm sure the river had moved in the fifty years since I last stood on its banks; the house used to be much closer to the water.

The girl skipped towards me.

I smiled and bent down to greet her. 'Hello. What's your name?'

She was breathless. 'I'm Anjali.'

An old man waved from the veranda. A youth lifted him down the step and the old man shuffled towards me. When we were closer, I saw his smile. Under the lines and wrinkles he was as handsome as he'd been when he was seventeen years old.

'Welcome home, little sister,' he said. 'We've been waiting for you.'

He hugged me and I was shocked by how thin he'd become; my big brother had shrunk into a tiny old man.

They made me a feast; a special fish-fry in mustard oil and chilli.

'Jiban caught it this morning,' Hari said. 'He's an excellent fisherman.'

Hari grinned at the boy, his youngest grandson, and Jiban hid his embarrassment by calling to his sister.

'Anjali, come and talk to Aunty Pushpa.'

'I haven't forgotten a thing,' Hari said to me. 'I think of our other Anjali every day.'

'Baba and Ma would be proud,' I said. 'You've made the old house better than it ever was.'

'It's not me they'd be proud of,' Hari said. 'They'd have been proud of you, Pushpa. It was you who sent the money to pay the rent and hire a man to work the land. I was able to marry because of you. I just wish you could have met my wife. You'd have liked her a lot.'

I was sure Ma and Baba would be ashamed of me if they knew the truth, but I said nothing and watched Hari pick bones from his fish. When he spoke again emotion made his voice shake. 'If it wasn't for you I'd have died a crippled servant in Uncle's house. You sweated in that terrible jute mill for so many years to send me money, and I don't know how I can ever thank you. You gave me a life.'

I looked at Hari's son and daughter-in-law sharing a joke by the door, and Jiban and Anjali playing a game on the veranda. The scene was like I always imagined; like it always is in my memory.

'You're coming home to stay, aren't you?' my brother asked. 'You can't wait over fifty years to return and then disappear again. How will I cut this *maya* if you leave?'

'I have to go, Hari. My home is in the city and I have to look after my husband, and my memsahib and her daughter, too.'

'Pushpa, you should be resting and enjoying your old age,

not slaving for the *feringhees*.' He sighed and shook his head. 'You are the best of women, Pushparani. You're the same as you were when you were a girl, although I hadn't imagined you could get so fat. You must eat well in Calcutta.'

When Durga Puja ended, I left Baba's house for the last time. Jiban carried Hari to the river and they watched me clamber aboard the skiff. The boatman steered us away and Hari's face grew blurry. His daughter-in-law returned to the house, her blue sari bright on the veranda, and Anjali skipped along the riverbank, keeping pace with the boat. I watched them intently, the image growing fainter.

I called goodbye, although it wasn't a genuine farewell because I've never really left that place of my childhood. I've too much *maya* to say goodbye. I return often in my dreams, and sometimes Hari will be old, as he is now, and other times he's young, standing strong and handsome on his boat, or he's bringing in the harvest, bundles of paddy balanced on a pole over his shoulder. Sometimes, it's my own sister who plays by the bamboo grove and sometimes it's the second Anjali. They are fused in my mind: a little girl busy with chores and running in the fields, her plait flying behind her. The thought makes me glad I've no jewellery apart from Kamala's bracelet and my bride's iron bangle. In truth, when the sun shines on Baba's house by the river, and on my brother's family living in it, the image is more precious than gold.

When I was young, Calcutta's finest courtesans travelled in palanquins. These days Navneeta, Sonagachi's most stunning courtesan, rides in a taxi, visiting the Great Eastern and the big hotels on Chowringhee. When the car stops at road junctions men look in and marvel at the girl in the silk sari, her kohl-rimmed eyes glittering as she looks at them briefly before pulling a veil over her face. Samita worries she won't come back, that one day she'll run off with a client who'll set her up as his mistress, and Samita will see her investment ruined. I don't think she'll desert us; we're her family and though she's wary of Samita's sharp tongue, I know she loves me. So, for now, the big brothel with the green-painted shutters on Masjid Bari Street continues to be a cut above the rest. Samita is so prosperous we eat better than maharajas, and in a fit of generosity inspired by a *babu*'s drunken spending spree, Samita has bought Madan his own mattress so he doesn't wake me with his bony body. Now he lies next to me rather than on me, and although he's still skinny and can do damage with his sharp elbows, he's putting on weight for the first time in his life. His trembling is lessening since Miss Maisy paid for him to see a doctor who gave him medicine to control the shakes. If he carries on this way he'll live to be the oldest man in Bengal, though we can't prove it because Madan has no idea when or where he was born. I've married a simple fool and it's fortunate for him that I love him as much as I do.

They don't eat so well in the boarding house in Sahib-para. I've seen the dinners: dry, tasteless dishes, the worst kind of English cooking even if it's put on china plates, set out on white linen tablecloths and eaten with polished silver cutlery. Miss Maisy and Charlie long for proper meals and so sometimes I'll cook them *alu dam* or another of their favourites, and if there's too much to do in the brothel and I don't have time, I'll buy food in the bazaar and take it in a tiffin tin for them to eat on the veranda.

Louise Brown

I visit them in the late afternoons. Miss Maisy has a rickshaw wallah collect me and, later, take me home. I sit next to Mem on a big cane chair, and it's lucky there's a bearer to run errands because it would be difficult for me to help Mem the way I used to. It takes a big effort for me to get out of one of those chairs. They are not designed for old, infirm people and once I sit down it's very hard to stand up.

Mem sleeps a lot and when she's awake she tends to talk about the same things.

'We'll be moving from here soon,' she says. She's been saying the same thing for two years and I no longer believe it. 'This place is full of cranks.'

I think she means the guests are unusual, and perhaps a little bit mad. They are people out of place, some of the wreckage left behind at the end of the British time in India. Some of them might once have been *burra sahibs* and *burra mems*, but now none of them is really pukka, and if this is what Mem means when she calls the other guests 'cranky', then she's found the right place to stay.

Either the afternoon light plays tricks or Mem's sight is about to fail. There's a deep yellow tinge to the whites of her eyes. I've noticed, too, that she's sunburned, and she agrees, saying she won't sleep outside any more because the sun's glare can penetrate the shade of the veranda even when the fresh green bamboo blinds are lowered. She doesn't go inside despite the tan she's developing, and instead she stretches out her legs on the wicker foot rest, looking at her toenails, which Miss Maisy has painted a vivid crimson.

'I'm clapped out, Pushpa,' she says, and falls asleep again. Soon she'll be as brown as a Bengali.

342

She wakes when Miss Maisy brings Charlie back from school. It would usually be time for her sundowner drink, although recently she's been asking for tea instead. Mem has been drinking strong spirits for over twenty-five years, and it makes a surprising change to see her sober; she's politer when she's not drunk.

'Tomorrow let's go to Tollygunge and join the Tolly,' she says to me, so I know her eyes must be truly terrible.

Miss Maisy smiles at her: she's heard it all before.

Charlie does his homework on the veranda in the hour before the mosquitoes begin to bite. He's a clever boy but a lazy student and it's a miracle he comes top of his class. Miss Maisy says he must have inherited his father's genius. When they first came home he'd forgotten a lot of his Bengali and it took him a few months to become completely fluent again. Now he talks like a native, though he still walks like a little sahib. Miss Maisy has promised him they're going on holiday, just as soon as Mem is feeling better and it's safe to leave her.

'We're going to Puri,' he tells me. 'Mam says the beach goes on for miles and miles, and the sunset is the most beautiful in India.'

The rickshaw wallah pulls me past the plot of land where MacBrayne Sahib's house used to stand. They're building an enormous block of flats that'll occupy almost every scrap of the garden. The monkey tree has been uprooted, there's no trace of the white wall and the gates lie rusting at the side of the lane. The huts and shanties were flattened several months ago and the families living inside the old palace were evicted by men with long bamboo canes. It's part of the Government's effort to deal with the squatter problem, although we all know the homeless haven't disappeared but have been shifted to some other overcrowded part of the city.

I don't believe the sahib would care about the destruction of the old house. He didn't have much *maya* for this place and he lived in India without truly liking it. He loved the life of the sahib, and he loved the privileges and prizes that came with being a *burra sahib*. Miss Maisy was one of his prizes until the day on the veranda when envy turned love to loathing and he set about destroying what he realised he couldn't have.

I used to think it strange that a man like Sunil Banerjee could provoke so much emotion and the attention of the evil eye. He'd been nothing more than a youth, a poor clerk with down on his face, who'd grown up to be a dreamer, a revolutionary caught in the momentous tide of change sweeping our country. He was full of passion and fire and I wasn't sure what he achieved except to burn the lives of those around him. But, as time passes, I think more fondly of him. It's hard to remain unmoved by his story, and although I'm not sure exactly why people were drawn to him, I recognise their feelings were deep and enduring. Madan believed Sunil's promises of pukka houses for the poor and Miss Maisy adored him from when she was a girl. She continues to love him now, though he's been dead for two years. And then there is Charu – angry, jealous Charu. I doubt Sunil knew the depth of his friend's affection, or suspected it was anything more than the love of comrades and brothers, but I know few men can resist Navneeta, and I saw Charu's fingers on Sunil's cheek as he lay in a corpse-strewn lane. I heard the cry of the broken-hearted and, although I may be wrong, I've a feeling he loved Sunil every bit as much as Miss Maisy did.

I wonder how Charu mourns his treasured friend. It's unlikely to be the same way Miss Maisy grieves. I remember the months in Bowbazar when she suffered a depression close to madness, and I dread a return of the same kind of sorrow. Against all common sense, she refuses to believe Sunil is dead. She denies it, even though I tell her I saw the last breath leave his body.

'Your eyes are bad,' she says. 'You know you need spectacles. He was alive when they took him away.'

I try to persuade her, to make her see sense, but she's adamant. And so, when she isn't working in the club, she often searches Calcutta for him, and many times I've wished I hadn't taught her to navigate the back alleys and bylanes of the city so well. I follow to keep an eye on her, like a mother does a troubled daughter. Someone has to look after her, to keep her safe, and Mem isn't capable. It worries me that I'm old and my time is almost at an end, because who will care for Miss Maisy, Charlie and Navneeta when I die? I'm not sure I'll be able to cut my ties with this world when I'm bound so tightly to it and my children.

At the very least, I want my health to improve and my hips to stop giving me so much trouble. I need to keep up with Miss Maisy and find out where she goes. It's not good for someone my age to hurry, and I pause to catch my breath, losing her in the packed streets. Although I usually give up the chase, occasionally I manage to spot her again, her golden hair making her easy to pick out among a sea of dark heads.

Everyone tells me my sight is worsening. It's true my eyes are blurry at times and it's hard for me to see things when they're very close. Only last week, I didn't notice a diamond was missing from Navneeta's most costly nose ring. I've promised that one day soon I'll do as I'm told and get some spectacles. But I swear by Ma Kali that my sight is nowhere near as poor as they claim and I can distinguish things in the distance almost as clearly as I did when I was young. Even in summer, when the heat haze rises, distorting the view of those with the most perfect vision, I can stand on the middle of Howrah Bridge and see the railway station on one side of the river and Armenian Ghat on the other. Providing I've kept pace with her, I can make out Miss Maisy's blonde head as she moves among the crowds. I squint because there often seems to be someone with her, a dark-skinned man who appears by her side and then melts away into the congested streets. Actually, it's not my eyes but my judgement people should question, because no matter how hard I look and how hard I try to understand the images I see, I can't decide whether it's a ghost or a fugitive who stands with Miss Maisy on Howrah Bridge and who walks with her as dusk falls around the lake in Eden Gardens.

Bonus Material

The Inspiration Behind *Eden Gardens*

Reading Group Questions

Bonus Material

The Inspiration Behind Eden Gardens

Reading Group Questions

The Inspiration Behind
Eden Gardens

I've loved South Asia ever since I had the good fortune to live there twenty-five years ago. My husband, of the time, was working for the British aid programme to Nepal, and, for two years, we lived in the Kathmandu Valley, towered over by the snow-capped peaks of the high Himalayas. It was the first time I'd lived in a developing country, and I experienced a profound culture shock. The country was stunning, its mountains breathtaking, its temples more beautiful than anything I'd imagined, but it was also terribly poor, and the unfailingly friendly people often acted in ways I didn't understand. My disorientation wasn't helped by the fact that we arrived at the start of a popular revolution which overthrew the absolute monarchy of Birendra Shah. Since those confusing, heady days, I've never stopped travelling in the north of the subcontinent and, over the years, it's lost none of its charm and fascination.

Like me, generations of Westerners have been captivated by this part of the world, and we tend to repeat old clichés: the colours are brighter; the smells more intense; food tastes better; the countryside appears untouched by time; the mountains are majestic; the jungles lush and wild, and the cities buzz with life. I promise these clichés are often absolutely true.

From the 1990s, I worked as an academic at The University of Birmingham. I researched the trafficking of women and children, and visited many of the big red light districts in India, Pakistan and Bangladesh, including Kolkata's Sonagachi, reputedly the largest brothel in Asia. Most of these places have been brothel quarters for decades, sometimes centuries. Hundreds, and often thousands, of women live in their maze of streets, in old subdivided buildings, plying their trade in little rooms. For some girls and women, together with a few boys and transgendered and transsexual people, working in the brothel is the only way they can make a living and survive. Others are sold into the business by traffickers, and, over and over again, I heard the story of a poor village girl who was offered a job as a domestic servant or a factory worker, only to find, at the end of her long journey to the city, that the job was actually in a brothel from which she could not escape.

Many of the women support impoverished families back in their villages. The earnings of others are pocketed by pimps and madams, and despite the many clients they serve, the women remain trapped in a cycle of poverty and exploitation. All women of the red light district, however successful they might be, share the stigma of being a prostitute, and they are vilified by wider society. It's been a never ending source of surprise to me that people in such difficult circumstances live their lives with dignity and often with a great deal of humour. Women like this have inspired the portrait of Pushpa in *Eden Gardens*. Amazingly, they are courageous, compassionate and generous despite a lifetime of social exclusion and personal tragedy.

For several years, I made frequent visits to Heera Mandi, Lahore's brothel quarter, where I stayed with a family of traditional courtesans. The neighbourhood is tucked into the corner of the Old City, bound by its ancient walls, and situated right next to the superb Badshahi Mosque and the Lahore Fort, which still retains some architectural gems, such as the Palace of Mirrors in the harem of the Mughal Emperors. In Heera Mandi, I watched the daily life of the brothel quarter, noting the arrival of new women and their clients into nearby brothels, and documenting how, among the traditional families, girls enter the business at around fourteen years of age, usually at the time mothers retire to manage their daughters' careers. All this was set against the backdrop of a busy Shia Muslim religious calendar and the subcontinent's changing seasons, which are much more complex than our own. A winter of chills and mists was followed by a brilliant, beautiful spring that was always too short. In the summer, everywhere was choked with dust until the parched city became afflicted by the stickiness and torrential downpours of the monsoon. Then, at last, there was relief as an exquisite autumn unfolded, bringing perfect temperatures, and clear, bright light.

Often, I find it difficult to be a British traveller in South Asia: I feel a frequent compulsion to apologise for my forebears. In Britain we tend to have a nostalgic view of the Raj, imagining we took lots of good things like railways and an efficient civil service to a chaotic and backward land, and that we exported stiff upper lipped gentlemen, and posh ladies who enjoyed tea parties and wore elegant frocks. However, there is a much darker side to our colonial past. Today, we ignore our record of exploitation and racism, or perhaps it is simply that we have forgotten about it, if, indeed, some people ever cared. Although many in the subcontinent seem to have no idea that the British used to rule India, a sizeable number do, and their memories of this period are not kind. Nowhere is this more acute than in Kolkata – the new name for Calcutta – once the second city of the British Empire, and which could lay claim to being the centre of the world jute trade, and home to India's most highly developed intellectual culture.

For many years, Kolkata has had a terrible and undeserved reputation, and people love it or loathe it. I definitely love it. It is commonly described as a city in ruins; a giant, insanitary slum populated by the wretched poor. Comparing Kolkata today with photographs of the neat main streets of the early twentieth century city reveals much has changed, but a lot of this change was unavoidable. After Partition in 1947, and then after the Bangladesh War of Independence in 1971, the city was inundated by wave after wave of people fleeing conflict. Millions of refugees placed an enormous strain on Kolkata's infrastructure and its social fabric. Few cities have ever had to face such challenges.

Today, the best way to see the city is to walk around it. I've done this many times, in all seasons, sometimes with a guide, but mostly alone. Large parts of Kolkata's past can been seen this way: the grand, official building of the British Raj; the crumbling mansions of the burra sahibs; the eerie tombs of long-dead Britons in the South Park Street Cemetery; the magnificent homes of the Bengali elite; the narrow, crowded roads in the poor parts of town; the temples, churches, mosques, gurdwaras and synagogues – evidence of the many religious and ethnic groups who've lived in Kolkata. And on the pavements we continue to see the homeless, entire families who spend their whole lives under shabby blankets and plastic sheets.

On foot, the shape of the city is clear. Kolkata changes, from what was once 'white town' with its imposing buildings and wide streets, to the poorer, more congested, Bengali 'black town', though it's debatable whether this often repeated distinction was anything more than superficial. 'White town' was always run with Indian labour, and lots of wealthy Indians lived among the white burra sahibs or owned the homes they rented in Alipore and Ballygunge, or, during an earlier period, in the area off Chowringhee. In between these two Calcuttas are the neighbourhoods of people who belonged in neither 'white' or 'black' town: the Jews; the Chinese; the Armenians; the Muslims; the Anglo-Indians – people referred to in *Eden Gardens* as 'Eurasian,' the term used at the time, and whom we would now call mixed-race.

The kind of house in which Gordon kept Maisy is fast disappearing, and it's easy to miss the crumbling mansions dotted around the city. Frequently, they are hemmed in by giant new developments. Their gates are missing, their gardens have become dumping grounds for old cars, and the lawns have vanished to be replaced by worn cricket pitches. Looking at these dilapidated remnants of another era would be enough to evoke nostalgia for the Raj, if I actually believed it was something to be proud of.

The Calcutta that Maisy, Mam and Pushpa knew has gone, but there are many things they would recognise if they were to visit today and walk with me around the city. The Great Eastern Hotel has been refurbished after a long period of dereliction, and the Grand Hotel is probably fancier than it was in the 1940s. The Hooghly still slides by, murky and brown, though no big ships dock along the Strand. Every day, thousands of people cross the Hooghly Bridge and, while it is no longer new, it still looks impressive against the setting sun. Eden Gardens has been truncated, its land eaten up by the giant cricket stadium, but the lake and Burmese Pagoda survive, and the Victoria Memorial attracts an enormous number of tourists and local day trippers, though I don't understand why because, to my mind, it remains a very odd place. The Maidan is unchanged, and has stayed surprisingly free from the clutches of developers. The city fizzes with vitality, and those clichéd 'colours of the East' are just as bright. I've been to Sonagachi again recently and I'm sure Pushpa would be happy, and perhaps astonished, to know the women there run a collective that campaigns for sex workers' rights, helps them with loans and provides education for their children. Almost as important, she'd be glad to taste the food at the busiest street stalls and the sweets in the teashops, and find they are as delicious as ever.

Kolkata isn't beautiful or charming, but it's certainly up there among the great cities of the world. Rich in character, culture and history, it's full of intense human stories, some sad, and others uplifting. If any nervous traveller asks whether they should visit the 'City of Palaces,' I will tell them to ignore the city's critics and see this exceptional place for themselves. Maisy went home to Calcutta after a brief spell in London and Dundee, and she didn't return solely because of Sunil: for me and Maisy, and countless other people, the Indian subcontinent gets under your skin and never lets you go.

Reading Group Questions

1. How did the novel expand your understanding of the female experience in colonial India?
2. Maisy's mam is perhaps not an idealised maternal figure, but she still fiercely protects her child at points. What do you feel the novel has to say about motherhood?
3. How did you relate to Maisy's choices in the novel, especially those concerning Sunil and Gordon? Did you sympathise with or disapprove of her decision making?
4. Pushpa's past experiences are only ever revealed to us and not Maisy or her mother. Why do you think this is?
5. Did you find Sunil Banerjee a reliable or an unreliable figure in the novel? Did you find the reasons for his absences plausible?
6. What did you think of the comparison between London and Calcutta?
7. The line is often blurred in *Eden Gardens* between abuse, prostitution and consensual relationships. Discuss the various examples and manifestations of this.
8. What did you think of the comparison between Sunil and

Gordon? Did you feel any sympathy with either of them?

9. The novel has a rather enigmatic ending. What personal conclusions did you draw about the fate of Maisy and Sunil?

The Sunrise
Victoria Hislop

In the summer of 1972, Famagusta in Cyprus is the most
desirable resort in the Mediterranean, a city bathed in the glow
of good fortune. An ambitious couple open the island's most
spectacular hotel, where Greek and Turkish Cypriots work in
harmony.

Two neighbouring families, the Georgiou and the Özkan,
are among many who have moved to Famagusta to escape the years
of unrest and ethnic violence elsewhere on the island. But
beneath the city's façade of glamour and success, tension
is building.

When a Greek coup plunges the island into chaos, Cyprus
faces a disastrous conflict. Turkey invades to protect the Turkish
Cypriot minority, and Famagusta is shelled. Forty thousand
people flee their homes, taking possessions and fleeing from the
advancing soldiers. In the deserted city just two families remain.

'Enlightened and humane . . . Hislop's fiercest narrative weaves
a vast story to tell, through a poignant, compelling family saga'
The Sunday Times

'Adroitly plotted and deftly characterised, Hislop's gripping
novel tells the stories of ordinary Greek and Turkish families,
trying to preserve their lifestyle in a maelstrom of the epoch,
betrayal and ethnic hatred. Not to be missed.'

review

978 0 7553 7780 0

The Sunrise
Victoria Hislop

In the summer of 1972, Famagusta in Cyprus is the most desirable resort in the Mediterranean, a city bathed in the glow of good fortune. An ambitious couple open the island's most spectacular hotel, where Greek and Turkish Cypriots work in harmony.

Two neighbouring families, the Georgious and the Özkans, are among many who moved to Famagusta to escape the years of unrest and ethnic violence elsewhere on the island. But beneath the city's façade of glamour and success, tension is building.

When a Greek coup plunges the island into chaos, Cyprus faces a disastrous conflict. Turkey invades to protect the Turkish Cypriot minority, and Famagusta is shelled. Forty thousand people seize their most precious possessions and flee from the advancing soldiers. In the deserted city, just two families remain. This is their story.

'Intelligent and immersive. . . Hislop's incisive narrative weaves a vast array of fact through a poignant, compelling family saga' *The Sunday Times*

'Adroitly plotted and deftly characterised, Hislop's gripping novel tells the stories of ordinary Greek and Turkish families trying to preserve their humanity in a maelstrom of deception, betrayal and ethnic hatred' *Mail on Sunday*

headline
review

978 0 7553 7780 0

The Silvered Heart
Katherine Clements

1648. Orphaned heiress Lady Katherine Ferrers is forced into marriage for the sake of family honour . . . but with Cromwell's army bringing England to its knees, her fortune is the real prize her husband desires. As her marriage becomes a prison and her privileged world crumbles, Katherine meets her match in Rafe – a lover who will lead her into a dangerous new way of life where the threat of death lurks at every turn. . .

Enter Kate Ferrers, highwaywoman, the Wicked Lady of legend – brought gloriously to life in this tale of infatuation, betrayal and survival.

'There are echoes here of Daphne du Maurier. . . an enjoyable romp' *The Times*

'Eloquent storytelling and superb characterisation breathe life into this historical tale of adventure, passion and betrayal' *Sun*

headline
review

978 1 4722 0426 4

The Fortune Hunter
Daisy Goodwin

In 1875, Sisi, the Empress of Austria, is the woman that every man desires and every woman envies.

Beautiful, athletic and intelligent, Sisi has everything – except happiness. Bored with the stultifying etiquette of the Hapsburg Court, Sisi comes to England to hunt and to find excitement. There, she discovers the dashing Captain Bay Middleton, the only man in Europe who can outride her. Ten years younger than her and engaged to the spirited Charlotte, Bay has everything to lose. But Bay and the Empress are as reckless as each other. . .

'Timeless, tantalising and ultimately, hugely satisfying. A terrific novel' Richard and Judy, Richard and Judy Book Club

'Sparkling and thoroughly engaging. . . highly enjoyable' *The Times*

'A hugely enjoyable historical romp and a major new talent' *Sunday Express*

headline
review

978 0 7553 4811 4